TASTES LIKE CANDY

JESSICA LACY

sourcebooks
fire

Published by Sourcebooks Fire, an imprint of Sourcebooks
1935 Brookdale RD, Naperville, IL 60563-2773
(630) 961-3900
sourcebooks.com

Originally self-published as *Tastes Like Candy* in 2020 by Ivy Tholen.

Cataloging-in-Publication Data is on file with the Library of Congress.

Printed and bound in the United States of America.
VP 10 9 8 7 6 5 4 3 2 1

For Paul,
Obviously.

PROLOGUE

Meg's first memory of Belldam, Texas, was the Senior Scavenge. Or rather, the girls who attended.

Her mom had gotten a job as the Vice President of Some Random Very Important Thing at an *obviously* evil company called the Eaton Group.

"Why is it obviously evil?" her mother asked.

"It sounds like 'eating.' Sharp. Rawr." Meg made monster claws.

Meg's mom gave an impassioned speech about what the Eaton Group did for the world. To Meg, it sounded like all they did was lobby politicians so they could legally dump toxic waste on puppies without a fine.

Meg was willing to look the other way—her mom made a ton of money and her new job kept her busy enough that she didn't have time to micromanage Meg's life—until she found out the new job meant a big move, and Meg's entire world turned upside down.

"You're going to be a freshman," her dad told her when she begged him to make her mother reconsider. "You're starting at a new school anyway. Your mom worked hard for this promotion, and it's a done deal."

"I don't want to live in some tiny town in the middle of nowhere where everyone knows each other and they all share a cow!"

"It's not a tiny town, it's a midsize city. We're moving four hours away, within the same state. Nothing about your culture will change. There is no cow; however, there are *two* H.E.B.s, which is one more than we have here, so if anything, Belldam is a bit *faster* paced."

"What about my friends?" Meg cried. She'd had the same four best friends since their toddler playdate days. Besides, Meg became friends with the girls because their mothers introduced them. No one ever forced her to make friends from scratch; she didn't know how.

Her dad didn't care. "Y'all all have phones. And Belldam isn't too far away from Baytown. Maybe we can arrange visits."

This was wishful thinking on her dad's part. His back trouble prevented him from driving long distances, and her mom would *never* spend eight hours round-trip in a car so Meg could gossip with her friends in person when they had a perfectly serviceable group chat.

On moving day, Meg didn't remember her parents loading her into the backseat. She got carsick, which made her anxious, so her mom gave her two Valium before the drive and she didn't fully wake up for three days. Her bedroom was unpacked, but she didn't remember doing it. She knew the last two weeks of summer were filled with dread, but the memory was a feeling in her stomach, not pictures in her mind. Her family went to orientation before school started, but she couldn't recall a single thing that was said.

But on the first day of school? Things that happened that day imprinted on her *soul*.

The memory blurred around the edges. Pritchett High's commons—an area outside the cafeteria designated for loitering—was much larger when she looked back on it in her mind, and most of the students didn't even have faces, but she'd memorized every detail of the senior girls.

There were nine girls sitting on and around a huge rock fountain, all dressed in various shades of Pritchett peacock blue, smiling and laughing like they didn't know every eye in the vicinity was fixed on them. One girl—a tall Latina in a Pritchett ROTC T-shirt and camo pants—sat on a bronze dedication sign. Her shiny combat boot dangled above the ominous words IN LOVING MEMORY, CLASS OF 1999. A girl with iridescent star stickers on her cheekbones blew bubbles. Her friend popped them with her fingers, then wiped the bubble solution on her Pritchett High basketball jersey. A warm, glowing light shone on them from the skylight above. They were a pack of real-life Jennifer Checks, and she was feeling a bit Needy.

"They're *beautiful*," Meg whispered to herself. She crouched behind a pillar like a constipated gargoyle to watch them, hoping no one would see her, because spying crossed a line, and she was giving herself the creeps.

One girl wore a cheerleader's uniform with a C embroidered over her heart. Her midsection sparkled in the sun. Later, Meg would learn that the entire squad contoured their abs with shimmery bronzer. Another wore a T-shirt with PRITCHETT HIGH FFA on the front and PRESIDENT on the back. Several had letterman's jackets with various varsity patches on the shoulders. They were happy, glowing, and not at all nauseous or sweaty like Meg. As people walked past, they nodded, or stopped to chat with the girls. The first warning bell rang, and as they trickled off to their various classes, they hugged and wished each other luck. One girl in a teal hoodie and jeans sniffed.

"It's our last first day of school!" Hoodie Girl cried breathlessly. FFA Girl hugged her, whispered in her ear, and pointed her toward the stairs. She walked past Meg, who squeezed her eyes shut and clung to the pillar, praying Hoodie Girl wouldn't see her gawking. She opened her eyes just in time for a quick peek at the graphic on the girl's back: a circle with an upside down, roller-skating peacock. The words I SURVIVED THE PRITCHETT HIGH SENIOR SCAVENGE 2017 curled around the circle.

"She'll be okay."

Meg jumped. A girl in a shiny spandex cowgirl dress had appeared out of nowhere and was also staring as Hoodie Girl disappeared from view.

"What?" Meg asked. She tried to pretend she hadn't been staring. "Who?"

She didn't sound very convincing.

"That's Dina," the cowgirl said. "Those are happy tears. More or less."

Meg had never cried happy tears in her life.

"I'm Meg," she told the girl, who made a sour face in response.

"I didn't ask," the cowgirl said flatly. A group of kids walked past, and the cowgirl allowed herself to be swept into the crowd.

Meg turned into an ice-cold lump of goo and intended to sink into the cracks between the tiles, but the senior cheerleader whistled and she shot back to attention. A gaggle of younger girls in less-revealing uniforms descended upon her like kittens nipping at their mother.

"Everybody, let me see your schedules!" she said. "If you're not sure where you're going, ask another cheerleader. That's why we're all in uniform today. If any dance team bitch wearing one of those ugly fringey-spandex western dresses tries to give you directions, ignore her. They have a tradition where they mess with our JV squad. *They are not to be trusted.* That goes double if they tell you to go to the STEM building. If someone does that, *run.*"

Meg made a mental note not to talk to anyone on the dance team, and prayed someone else would ask what was wrong with the STEM building, but no one did.

The mama cat senior shuffled through the schedules. "Hartley!" She pointed to a girl with tight blond curls, then gestured past the cafeteria. "You're on the first floor; turn left at the trash cans. Go. Kentleigh, you're with her, and so is Gertie. Go. Mila, you're in five-oh-three, which is on the second floor, on the left. Take the back stairs, and it's right there on the corner."

An alarm blared inside Meg's head. Room 503 was on her schedule as well. She'd already had an anxiety attack about it. Usually she'd expect room 503 to be on the fifth floor, but Pritchett High was only two stories, and she didn't know how to read a map. This was her chance to find her class, make a new friend, and possibly assimilate into the clique that included the senior girls from the commons.

"Can I walk with you?" Meg blurted out before she could second-guess herself. Ten sleek ponytails flipped as the girls snapped their necks to check out the interloper. She braced herself for bitchiness, but the older girl smiled and nodded at Mila.

"Girls supporting girls," she said. "Mila, you two go find your seats before the bell. If you get caught between classes, they'll give you detention, and that's an automatic demerit. *Go.*"

"What does a demerit mean?" Meg asked Mila when they were out of earshot.

"Three strikes and I'm out," she said. "Off the squad. I've wanted to cheer at Pritchett my whole life. I'd die. Walk faster."

Meg scurried as fast as her little legs would allow, but she still huffed and puffed next to Mila, who walked with a bouncy spring in her step. Mila climbed the stairs two at a time, while Meg nearly got pushed back to the first floor by some defensive linemen who were too tall to see the tiny girl under their feet. Thankfully, Mila waited for her at the top of the stairs.

They entered the room, and a girl in a baggy green jacket jumped on her chair and waved at Mila, who squealed and did a little dance, then bolted for a seat next to her friend.

Meg's heart sank. Of course, the pretty cheerleader didn't need her.

But then Mila remembered "girls supporting girls," and she called for Meg to join them.

"Hi," she said hesitantly. "I'm Meg."

"James Parker," the girl said, extending a hand. Meg took it. James had a *very* firm shake and spoke like a comedian portraying a politician on a sitcom. "Good to see ya! We've been waiting here for twenty minutes because this one here was scared we'd get stuck in traffic."

James's friend, a quiet girl with mousy brown hair, smiled. "I'm Violet Warren."

"Where's the teacher?" Mila asked James.

"Mrs. Montemayor just ran outta here in a panic 'cause someone called in a bomb threat at her son's elementary school."

"That's terrifying," Meg said. What kind of midsize city had her parents moved her to?

James waved her off. "Oh, it's fine. She didn't run out because she was worried about her son. She ran out because her daughter is the one who called in the bomb threat, and now she has to bail her outta jail. The office is sending a sub, but it's *Lord of the Flies* in here until one arrives."

Meg had never read *Lord of the Flies*, but she didn't want James to know that, so she smiled and nodded.

Mila rested her chin on her hand. "Wait," she said, her eyes lighting up. "Have we met before? Did you go to Bluebonnet? Are you friends with Lindi Thatcher?"

"I don't know who that is," Meg said. "I'm new in town."

James wiggled her eyebrows. "Really? New in town? What are three other things about you?" Her inflection implied there was an inside joke Meg wasn't privy to, which made her shrink in her seat.

Violet smacked James's knee with the back of her hand. "Don't act like that," she scolded. "She's gonna think you're an asshole."

Meg wanted to groan. She saw right through Violet. She might as well have worn a T-shirt that read "My Friend Thinks She's Funny, Please Don't Hate Us." Back home she'd have been comfortable enough to tell someone how desperate they sounded, but at Pritchett she was the lowest rung on the ladder, and she had to be stepped on a few times to prove her worth before she could shut that shit down.

"I *am* an asshole," James said, laughing.

"You're a *fun* asshole." Violet flashed Meg a tight-lipped smile. "She's going to think you're an *insufferable* asshole."

"I am an insufferable asshole. 'Fun' and 'insufferable' are not mutually exclusive, dude."

Violet chuckled. James flipped around in her seat and rested her cheek on Violet's desk. Violet patted her hair. Meg couldn't tell if

James and Violet were best friends or a couple. As she watched Violet pet James like an emotional support animal, she thought, *Is this it? Am I going to be stuck with these assholes for the next four years?* After the display in the commons earlier, she'd expected more from the girls at Pritchett High.

"What are y'all's schedules?" Mila asked.

"We've got six classes together," James said, nodding toward Violet. "Everything except fifth period, when I have BCP and she has orchestra. What you got?"

Mila produced her schedule. The girls did the math and found that Mila would be in their geometry class.

"Where are you third period?" Mila asked Meg.

Meg fumbled for her card. "Mrs. Jannise, room one-fourteen."

"Same as us!" James whooped. She twisted her neck to read Meg's schedule card. "Megan McClendon. How alliterate."

"James!" gasped Mila. "I'm so sorry, Meg. Our district has pretty high literacy standards compared to the rest of the state. You shouldn't be shamed for being in remedial classes."

James, Violet, and Meg stared at Mila, open-mouthed, trying to parse what she'd said.

"The fuck you talking about?" James said, finally.

"You called her illiterate. It's not her fault her old school sucks. Plus, she might have dyslexia. Are you dyslexic, Meg?"

"I don't know what's happening," Meg replied.

"She meant *alliterate* with an A, not *illiterate* with an I," said Violet. "Both her names start with an M."

"But what's the value of Y?" James asked.

Mila blushed. "Maybe I would've known what you said if you didn't talk like your tongue is too big for your face!"

"Hey!" James said, grinning and raising her voice. "I didn't have teeth for *years*! I had to take speech therapy lessons! You're over here defending a complete stranger while I, your friend since kindergarten, sit with my self-worth at an all-time low because of your words. Thanks a lot."

"I misunderstood you!" Mila yelled in frustration. "I know definitions! I know...*words*!"

"Not escaping that dumb cheerleader stereotype, are we there, Meels?"

"Fuck you, James!"

James winked at her and returned her attention to Meg's schedule.

"Hey Meg, why do they have you as an office assistant instead of in an elective?"

Meg groaned. Freshmen at Pritchett took the same few classes. English, geometry, biology, all the usuals, plus one elective. Meg spent a full five minutes pouring over Pritchett High's offerings before she gave up and chose the "I would rather staple papers than make a proper decision" option.

"It was impossible to pick," she told them. "Half of the programs require a pre-requisite. I hate sports. I'm not artistic, and I don't want to take shop class with a bunch of dudes."

"Stop talking about what you don't want," Mila said, smiling. "What's your 'thing?' What do you do after school?"

Meg thought for a moment. "Doomscroll on social media, mostly."

"*Bleak*," said James. She glanced at their unamused faces and explained herself. "I'm not joking this time. That's super sad. How are you not bored out of your skull?"

Meg wanted to slam her head on her desk. No one ever told her she needed a "thing." None of her old friends had a "thing," and they certainly never pitied her for not having a "thing" either.

"I thought you found your 'thing' in high school. Maybe I could be a cheerleader like you, Mila. Is there a way to try out?"

Mila laughed, then realized Meg was serious and stopped herself. "The Pritchett squad is elite. You have to decide you want to join when you're little or you won't make the cut. I took Mommy and Me tumbling classes at *two*," she said gently. "That was late. The captain of our varsity team could do a split before most kids could walk."

Meg felt mildly disappointed—she didn't actually want to be a cheerleader, she just wanted an easy out—but she latched on to Mila's mention of the captain and used it to turn the conversation in a more interesting direction.

"Was that the girl in the commons?" Meg asked.

"Yeah. Paisley. I saw you ogling her from your hiding place. I figured you didn't want me to say anything, so I didn't. Until now, I guess."

"I was watching all of them!" Meg exclaimed, as if that made it better.

Mila grinned. "Don't get upset. Everybody thinks they're the cat's meow."

"Who are they?" Meg asked.

"They're *the* seniors," said James with a hard emphasis on the word "the."

Meg didn't understand. "There are only nine girls in the senior class?"

"They're like, the cool ones," Mila explained. "They're the leaders of all the clubs, have the highest GPAs, they're grotesquely attractive, you know the drill."

Meg had never dealt with a social hierarchy like this before. Girls in Baytown were either hot or ugly, and grouped themselves accordingly.

"So they're like, nine best friends who rule the school?" she asked.

"That's not a thing that happens in real life," James said. "Our lovely principal, Ms. Holden-Jones, rules the school. They're just girls everyone thinks are fun, so they get lots of perks. They throw the best parties, win all the awards, and have cool after-school jobs at the funky shops over on Belldam Boulevard."

Meg remembered Hoodie Girl and her roller-skating peacock.

"What's the Senior Scavenge?" she asked. "I saw it written on someone's shirt."

"That's one of the perks James was talking about," Mila said.

James leaned in close and motioned for the others to do the same. "It's like a secret mission," she said. "The senior girls who just graduated ask the incoming senior girls to break into the school at midnight for a scavenger hunt; then they stuff their faces with pecan pancakes the next morning while they share all the secrets of being awesome. I wanna get invited so I can rappel from the balcony and stake my claim on the rock memorial. That thing is so fucking cool. We have a little waterfall in our school! How fun is that?"

James made it sound like a spy thriller. Meg wasn't particularly interested in stalking the halls at night, or swinging around on ropes, but the stuff after, the pancakes and sharing secrets, she could get behind that.

"How do you get invited?" Meg asked.

"We've come full circle," Mila told her. "Find your 'thing,' be better at it than everyone else, and they'll pick you."

"Game recognize game," a guy behind them barked.

James cocked her head. "No one asked your opinion, Alberto."

Alberto cleared his throat and became very invested in his phone.

"So if I understand correctly," said Meg. "I need to have a 'thing' so all the other girls with 'things' will like me and ask me to hang out with them?"

Mila nodded. "Exactly!"

"What are y'all's things?" Meg asked James and Violet.

"I play violin," Violet said, offering no further explanation.

"It's her entire personality," James said, giving Violet a double thumbs-up. "I'm not in anything yet, but I want to master C++, and colleges love when you lead shit, so I'm starting a coding club." James paused to consider her words, lest someone expect her to follow through with her own plans. "*Eventually*."

Meg had never seriously thought about college. It was way too mature for her; she could barely handle high school, and college was the real world. People in college could vote. Meg knew they rarely did, but they could if they wanted to, and that was enough.

"Pritchett has a million clubs and extracurriculars," Mila said. "You don't play any instruments, no sports... Are you political? Do you like journalism?"

"There's always FFA," James said. "If you don't mind stinking like cow shit."

"I knew there was a cow here!" Meg exclaimed.

Violet snorted and shook her head. Meg couldn't tell if she was laughing at James's joke, or if she enjoyed the idea of Meg covered in manure. Meg couldn't stand the quiet types. It was impossible to tell whether they were laughing *with* her or *at* her, and if she asked, they'd slink away in embarrassment without answering the question.

"Oh!" Mila said, her eyes bright. "You can be a Peacockette!"

Meg's gut reaction was to scream *Absolutely not!* She didn't know what a Peacockette was or what being a Peacockette entailed, but she knew better than to join an organization with "cock" in the name, even if peacocks were the school mascot. No way, no thank you.

But she held back, and simply asked, "What is a Peacockette?"

"The dance team," Violet said nonchalantly as she shuffled through her backpack.

The lights dimmed, and Paisley's words ran through her head: *If any dance team bitch wearing one of those ugly fringey-spandex western dresses tries to give you directions, ignore her.*

"Paisley acted like the dance team girls were monsters." Meg told Mila. "I think you're right about me joining a club, but is aligning with a bunch of fringe-covered assholes the right choice?"

"It's a playful rivalry," Mila assured her. "Paisley's best friend is their colonel. They have fun and don't require you to be as…*athletic* as the cheer squad."

With the tone Mila used, Meg took her words to mean *Fatties welcome.*

"Jesus, dude," James sneered. "Just because they can't fly through the air with the greatest of ease like you, it doesn't mean they're bed-rotting blob monsters."

"I didn't say that!" Mila squealed.

"You don't have to be as *athletic* as the cheerleaders," James said, mocking her. "Think before you speak!" James turned to Meg. "You aren't fat. At all. Don't listen to her; she hasn't consumed anything except Cherry Coke Zero and protein shakes for like, five years, and she likes to take out her hangriness on those of us who chew food."

"I chew food!" Mila yelled loud enough to silence the buzzing class around them. She turned pink, then smiled and waved like a pageant queen at the other students. They rolled their eyes and returned to their own conversations.

Violet tapped Meg's desk with a finger. "The Peacockettes have freshman tryouts in a couple of weeks, and you don't have to have any special skills except for the ability to count to eight."

"You also have to know your right from your left, little lady," Mila added.

"The Peacockettes won't even care if you're alliterate!" James paused for a reaction from Mila. When she didn't get one, she continued. "Dance team girls don't have to take gym. Made me think about joining for a hot second, but they have a rule that requires them to smile politely whenever they're in uniform, and they have to wear that shit to school on game days. I'm not walking around here like—" James pulled a Joker face. Mila smiled. Violet snorted. Meg was exhausted, and it wasn't even nine a.m.

"I thought about joining too," Violet said. "I would do anything to miss running the mile, but you can't be in dance and in orchestra at the same time, so I joined the marching band for the required credits. I'm carrying the Texas flag."

"It's a sweet gig," James said. "She doesn't even have to go to practices because any idiot can maneuver a pole."

Violet chucked a banana-shaped eraser at James's face. James ducked, and the eraser bounced off Alberto's head. He flicked his eyes upward, glared at James, and went back to his phone.

James apologized to Alberto over her shoulder. "Didn't mean for you to catch a stray. Sorry."

He gave her the finger without looking up.

James's jaw dropped. "Nice, Alberto. Real nice." She sighed.

"Maybe you have other options. They have such a stupid name. Pritchett Peacockettes. There's an actual word for female peafowl, and it's *not* peacockette."

"Peacockette is cuter than Peahen," Mila countered.

James narrowed her eyes and stared at Mila. "Agree," she said after a moment.

Then Violet—who until that point was in danger of becoming Meg's sworn enemy—said something that changed the course of Meg's life forever.

"It's an easy way to get into the Scavenge. The Peacockettes' colonel is *always* invited."

Meg's eyes lit up.

"What's your phone number?" James asked. Meg told her. James immediately sent her a text with a link to the school's website. "That's the signup form for Peacockette tryouts. You looked like you might need it."

Meg tapped the link, scanned the form, and filled it out. She'd walked into Pritchett High a basic boring bitch, but come hell or high water, she was going to leave reborn as one of the golden goddesses.

For the next three years, Meg didn't worry about her classes beyond the bare minimum grades she needed to pass. She kissed all the right asses and ignored all the wrong ones. Her focus was clear: become colonel, get invited to the Scavenge, have the best senior year ever, and figure out the rest of her life later.

She did everything right.

And it worked.

Or so she thought.

Three years later, an older, more cynical version of Meg McClendon lay splayed out on a lounger in her friend Kylie Dunn's backyard.

Kylie was a year older, and she was thirteenth on Meg's "People Who Don't Make Me Sick" list, but everyone else had blown her off since school ended, and she needed answers.

The honest-to-God truth was that Meg had done nothing wrong. Not any one thing, not like Sadie Chase, who everybody hated because she rapped along with "Hot Girl Summer" *uncensored* on Blythe's stream. What crime could she have committed to make people dislike her as much as a girl who was stupid enough to scream "I can shake my ass like Tina Snow!" while she poorly twerked for six million of Blythe's closest friends?

Everything was fine—more or less—until school ended. Then one day, after Peacockettes summer practice, River Ellis drove past the practice field, did a U-turn, and stopped so Willa Berkley could climb into the back seat.

"Since when do *they* hang out?" Meg asked the random freshman next to her.

The freshman stared at her with wide eyes and stammered, "I…I don't know…people? I'm sorry. Ma'am. Can I leave?"

Meg grimaced. She'd become colonel for the clout, not to babysit freshmen. "Yeah? I released y'all ten minutes ago."

The girl stared blankly at Meg, who rolled her eyes and shooed the idiot toward the parking lot.

River was never in Meg's top five on the "People Who Don't Make Me Sick" list, but they had fun together. Willa was joined at the hip with the other Peacockettes. They stayed in their little dance team bubble and ignored the rest of the school. Meg didn't even know how River and Willa knew each other. It wasn't from class, because River was with Meg in AP classes, and Willa was still trying to grasp Algebra. Someone must've introduced them, but why? And where were they going? If River was there, Mila was probably there too.

Meg had texted Mila weeks earlier to ask if the cheerleaders would be in uniform on the last day of school. It was a simple question—if the cheerleaders wore their normal clothes, so would the Peacockettes—but Mila left her on read.

And now River, Mila, and Willa were hanging out without her. It wasn't good. The last summer before the Scavenge is when you really had to work to earn your spot, and if no one saw her for months, well…

Her best shot at an invitation was Julia Leigh. Julia was her predecessor, and an invite to the Scavenge was always handed down to the new colonel along with the cute hat and baton. It was a done deal.

But if that were true, why did Meg's stomach still hurt so much?

It all came to a head one day in Kylie's swimming pool. Kylie was back from spending the summer with her dad in Florida, and Meg jumped at the opportunity to hang out when she texted. Kylie was on the inside. She had an invitation to give out and everything, but it was earmarked for River. They'd been friends since Girl Scouts. Meg had no hard feelings.

At Kylie's, Meg played along and listened to Kylie's crazy Florida Man-filled adventures. When Kylie shrugged off her swim cover-up, Meg realized she could use Kylie's ugly bathing suit as a segue.

It was a retro thing, red-and-white striped with a little skirt. Kylie thought she was channeling Katy Perry back when Katy Perry was cute and relevant. Meg was feeling strong circus tent vibes.

"I saw a rumor online. Is it true the Scavenge is at the carnival this year?" Meg asked, hating herself. She'd only been able to wait seven minutes before mentioning her great obsession. Kylie wasn't even done recapping her trip to Disney World.

"Of course," Kylie said pointedly. "The Scavenge."

Kylie slid off her lounger, silently descended the pool steps, and dipped below the water to wet her hair. She swam back to Meg and rested her chin on the edge of the pool, rubbed her shoulder on her ear to drain some water, and squinted in the sun. "I guess this means we're done talking about how Cesar vomited churros all over my boobs on the Tower of Terror? It was kinda traumatic for me. A group of Mormon missionaries called me a trashy slut who ruined their ride photo with her puke tits."

"*They did?*" Meg forgot about the Scavenge for a moment. Public freakouts fascinated her.

"They *almost* did. I could tell they were thinking it."

"Oh. Well, if you opened with 'puke tits,' I would've listened to the entire story."

Kylie sighed. "Noted." She sucked in her cheeks. "To answer your question, yes. The Scavenge is at the carnival. Weird choice since the whole thing is supposed to be about tradition and school spirit and all that other rah-rah bullshit, but I don't care. I'm just in it for the pancakes."

Meg's stomach dropped. Moving the Scavenge was an enormous deal. It had always been at the school, so a change of venue would be a big surprise for the attendees. If Kylie wasn't playing coy—and she definitely wasn't—Meg was in trouble.

"Why do you have a tone?" Meg asked.

"I don't have a tone. God, my ear itches. I hope I don't have an infection." Kylie violently shook her head to knock the water out. "Look, I know what you want to ask me. I'm not supposed to talk about it, but you're gonna find out in a few days when the invitations show up in people's mailboxes."

Meg blacked out for a split second.

First day of school, freshman year. She'd just met James, Mila, and Violet. It was Violet's words all those years ago that kept Meg dragging along through the summer, even if Violet herself wouldn't answer Meg's messages.

It's an easy way to get into the Scavenge. The Peacockettes' colonel is always *invited.*

Fucking lying bitch.

"I'm not invited," she whispered.

Kylie couldn't look her in the eye.

"Why?" Meg asked. "Julia swore she was gonna pick me! Even after Claire and I got into it and all the other juniors acted like I was radioactive to pacify her, Julia promised! It was supposed to be my way back in! I haven't hung out with anyone else but you all summer!"

"Gee, thanks!"

Meg banged her head into the lounge chair. "I didn't mean it like that, loser. You're leaving for school soon, and I'm not gonna have anybody."

"You still have all the other Peacockettes. I know they're lame, but you're still *their* Queen Bee."

Meg had a dark thought, something that never occurred to her, despite it being her worst nightmare.

"Oh God, please tell me they didn't invite Willa!" she screeched. "If they invited the lieutenant colonel and not the colonel, why did I even run for office? Colonel wears a white uniform! I look like a corpse in white!"

"No one invited Willa. No one from the Peacockettes at all. Julia showed no solidarity. But for real, Meg. The Scavenge is dumb. Literally only thirty-five people—*many of whom already graduated*—care. It's the seniors who get to invite their friends," Kylie counted off on her fingers. "The juniors who get picked, and a handful of losers who cry over not getting an invitation."

"*Thanks* Kylie."

"I was specific in my wording. I did not include you as part of the thirty-five. You can be unbothered and forget about it. Do you intend to be a loser who cries about this, or are you going to walk into school on the first day of your senior year like everything is peachy fucking keen?"

Meg stared directly at the sun until black splotches clouded her vision, and she had to look away. Her eyes hurt too much to cry.

"So who got invited?" she finally asked.

"Do you really want to do this?" Kylie's voice oozed with pity.

Meg could handle missing the Scavenge, but the "poor baby" looks she'd get when school started would kill her.

"Yes, I want to fucking do this," she said through gritted teeth.

"I invited River."

"Obviously. No hard feelings."

"Thanks. Next there's Mila."

Meg sighed. Mila was the head cheerleader, a totally uninspired choice. This was going to be the usuals, the basic seven plus a new wildcard taking her spot.

"Mila," Meg repeated. "If you have Mila, you gotta have Claire."

Queen Bee Cheerleader and Queen Bee Jock.

Kylie nodded. "And Blythe."

Influencer trash.

"She has such a massive following online," Kylie continued, "we were scared not to include her. None of us wanted to be hunted down by a deranged fan as revenge for snubbing their favorite parasocial bestie."

Meg figured that was fair, plus Delilah Cortez would've picked Blythe, and Delilah hated Meg, so she wasn't jealous.

"James," Kylie continued.

Of course James. Everybody loves James. I don't even like *James, but I still love her.*

"Violet."

"They had to invite her," Meg sneered. "Rat-faced bitch permanently wedged in James's ass."

Kylie grinned. "Now, now," she sang. "As we found out at my birthday party, sometimes she's wedged in Blythe's ass instead."

"True. Your bathtub will never be the same!"

"*Ugh.*" Kylie smacked her mouth like she'd tasted something sour. "Okay. Gracie."

"Can't have River without Gracie. I genuinely don't know if Violet is worse or if she is. Go on, hide behind your fun best friend and give me *nothing*." She stuck her index finger in her mouth and gagged.

"Gracie for sure," Kylie said. "Violet is stuck in her own head. She almost never talks to me. Gracie, like, proselytizes about conspiracy theories. You ever see the meme about birds being fake? She believes it. Talked *at* me for twenty minutes about it."

"It's all the weed. She and River think they need to be high to make their comic. Joke's on them. It's equally unfunny either way."

Kylie sighed. The pair sat in silence. Meg could count, and Kylie could see her putting two and two together: There was one last spot, the one that should've been hers.

"Julia's mom made her pick Sadie Chase, didn't she?" Meg asked, chucking an unopened seltzer into the pool. She would rather guess her replacement than wait for Kylie to tell her. "That's way worse than my general bitchiness, by the way. *She used a hard R!*" Meg nervously shook her head "no" and readjusted her legs, but no matter how she crossed them, she couldn't shake off the anger...or the shame. She now had cold, hard proof that she was a loser and everyone hated her.

"Jesus," Kylie said, fishing in the water for the can. "Sadie sucks in twelve different ways, but that doesn't mean you can throw shit into my pool." She caught the can, cracked it open, and took a sip. "Ew. It's flat. *How?*"

"Jesus effing Christ, can we please just finish? Who took my spot? *Who?*" Meg kicked her legs and threw a toddler-style tantrum.

Kylie had done nothing wrong, but Meg didn't have anyone else who would voluntarily serve as her emotional punching bag. The months of paranoia, anxiety, and unanswered texts had caught up with her, and the snub wasn't something she could shrug off.

But she still felt like a bitch.

"I'm sorry," she told Kylie, truly meaning it. Her behavior embarrassed her, both the tantrum and her years-long quest to suck up to every important girl in school. How embarrassing to want something so desperately, so *publicly*, and then not get it.

Kylie's face softened. "You sound like you mean it. I'm sorry too, for what it's worth. This meant something to you, and it didn't work out. That sucks."

Meg didn't hear a single word. She couldn't hear Kylie over the neon sign in her head flashing the word *who?* over and over.

When it was her turn to speak, she asked aloud.

"Who?"

"Julia's mom forced her. She didn't have a choice if she wanted to keep her car. It wasn't about this girl over you."

Meg wanted to dig her nails into Kylie's forehead and peel off the thin skin like a Korean face mask.

"It's Lolly."

Lolly's face—with her goofy, over-plucked eyebrows—flashed in Meg's head. Those eyebrows used to be thick to the point of bushiness, but someone wrote "Sasquatch" on her locker in permanent marker, so she removed every inch of body hair and reduced her brows to pencil-thin streaks. Someone kinder than Meg taught her how to fill them in properly, but she often skipped the brow pencil, and they never fully grew back.

Meg's brain cracked. "Lolly Bishop," she mumbled, then slipped into a never-ending loop. "Lolly Bishop? Lolly Bishop? Lolly Bishop! Are you for real right now? Lolly Bishop? Lolly Bishop!"

"Lolly Bishop." Kylie kicked off the wall and swam away, desperate to put a little distance between herself and Meg before the incoming nervous breakdown.

"That's who Julia's mom forced her to pick?" Meg laughed. She couldn't handle the absurdity. "You're sitting here letting me shit-talk Violet and Gracie when *Lolly Bishop* got invited? They're at least tangentially cool. Lolly's some weirdo who always sits in the desk closest to the teacher and says things like, 'Have you read Plath?'"

Kylie snorted. "Lolly's not a nobody. She's friendly with most of the other girls, and she's a super genius. She's gonna be valedictorian, go to college, become a doctor, and cure cancer on the moon."

"Friendly with the other girls? They only hang out with her when they need a responsible adult around."

"Now you're just being mean. Lolly Bishop wouldn't hurt a fly. Don't be mad at her, be mad at the grads. They could've made an exception and let someone send out two invitations. It happened last year when they couldn't choose between Maddy and Chloe."

Meg's first reaction was to shout *those bitches!* but…one of those bitches was right there in front of her, splashing around in the water without a care in the world.

"Why didn't *you* ask to invite a second person, Kylie?" she asked, her voice low.

Kylie treaded water and glanced around, looking for the nearest exit.

"I didn't think about it until just now. Meg, I'm sorry."

Meg's skin caught fire. She leapt from the lounger and hovered over Kylie.

"Did y'all discuss the Scavenge attendees when you planned everything?"

The sun had begun to set. It glowed a mean orange behind Meg's head, like a halo made of fire. Kylie never found Meg to be a threat, but suddenly she was scanning the yard, hunting for an exit.

"We had a Zoom call," Kylie replied carefully.

Meg squatted. "Did my name *ever* come up during that call?"

"Please don't do this."

But it was already done.

"I'm going to ask you a question, and you're going to answer with a simple yes or no," Meg told her. "Did. Anyone. Say. My. Name."

Kylie shook her head.

Meg nodded.

Kylie opened her mouth to talk Meg down.

Meg slapped her hand on the top of Kylie's head and shoved her underwater. Kylie splashed wildly, swiping and clawing at any part of Meg she could reach. Her face popped above the surface long enough for her to gulp air, but she also caught a mouthful of water. It rushed down her throat, but she couldn't cough it up without inhaling more. Her vision blurred, and she felt herself slip away from her body. If she couldn't muster enough energy to beat Meg's ass, she was going to die.

Kylie kicked off the wall, which caught Meg off guard, and allowed Kylie to pull her into the water.

Meg flailed as Kylie shot across the pool, pulled herself up the steps, and flung herself onto the deck to vomit up the pool water sloshing around in her lungs.

When she could speak, she wheezed, "What is wrong with you?"

"I just wanted to be special," Meg whined. She'd regained her senses and swam toward Kylie to help her recover.

Kylie raised her arm to protect herself. "You are special! You're a special lunatic! Get out of my house! Leave!"

"Should I call someone?" Meg asked meekly.

"No! Get away from me, you fucking freak! Nobody cares about the stupid scavenger hunt! It's two hours, then it's over! I was so wasted I don't even remember mine! It's a non-event, and you just tried to drown me over it! This is why no one chose you! The stink of desperation is radiating off your weird, crusty skin!"

"Does it smell like pool water?" Meg joked, hoping Kylie would calm down.

Kylie twitched, then took a breath and spoke calmly. "I'm going to make your life easy, because whatever you've got stewing inside your nutbag brain is way more of a punishment than anything I could dole out. I won't tell anyone about this. You're going to leave my house, delete my number, and I'm going to block you on *everything*. I never want to see or speak to you again. Are we clear?"

Meg dog-paddled toward her, but only because Kylie was near the steps. Kylie recoiled.

"Do you think I'm gonna hurt you?" Meg asked, stunned. "I didn't mean it. I'm all worked up—"

"Stop!" Kylie got to her feet and jogged toward the house. "You're a psycho, and I'm not dying over some dumb scavenger hunt! Pack your shit and leave through the side gate right now, or I'm calling the cops!"

Kylie ran into the house, locked the back door, and stared at Meg through the glass with her arms crossed as Meg pulled herself out of the pool. Her cheeks burned from embarrassment, white-hot rage, and a mild sunburn because she'd forgotten to put on sunscreen.

Kylie hadn't left a towel for her, so she squeezed the water from her hair as best she could and slipped an old Peacockettes T-shirt over her head while still soaking wet. It felt like sandpaper against her face, and the damp fabric suctioned itself to her stomach, highlighting her small potbelly.

Meg wanted to yell at Kylie, throw out a few final words as proof that she was unbothered, but she couldn't think of anything clever, so she scooped up her things, stomped across the yard barefoot, and kicked through the wooden gate, only to be rewarded with a splinter in the sole of her foot.

She slopped to her car and drove to the nearest Taco Bell, where she pulled up to the window and ordered James Parker's go-to meal.

"I have twenty bucks," she told the speaker. "Fuck me up."

"Drive around."

The lady at the window gave her a heavy paper bag and a small drink. Meg tossed the bag aside and sipped the soda.

Diet Pepsi.

There was an insult in there somewhere.

Meg exited the drive-thru and turned left across four lanes. Several cars slammed on their brakes to avoid hitting her, but she didn't care. She wasn't invited to the Scavenge, and Kylie would tell everyone she'd *kind of* tried to drown her.

Her life was over.

Taco Bell was only a few streets over from her house, but Meg wanted to drive and drive forever. So instead of turning right on Barclay Road to go home, she turned left toward the highway. It wasn't her intention to drive all the way to the outskirts of town, but when she was high above the city, she saw the Ferris wheel in the distance and knew she was headed straight for the carnival.

Meg pulled into the empty lot, parked as far away from the main entrance as humanly possible, and cut the engine. She rifled through the paper bag, giving each item a squeeze. Everything felt oddly uniform. She upended the bag and dumped out the contents.

Six bean-and-cheese burritos and four packets of mild sauce fell into her passenger seat.

"Are you kidding me?" Meg said aloud, peeling back each tortilla to examine them and confirm that yes, the cashier had just pressed the "bean burrito" button on repeat until she hit the limit. "James always gets a variety."

Meg tore into a burrito with her teeth and chewed with her mouth open as a tear rolled down her cheek.

"It's a shitty carnival anyway," she said, eyeballing the gate as she sucked down warm beans and cheese. "Wouldn't be caught dead at that place after dark."

———

Meg snorted awake a few hours later, covered in crumpled Taco Bell wrappers and disoriented by the darkness. She dropped the burrito stump in her hand and scrambled for her phone.

It was after ten. No texts, no calls, not even her parents.

Meg jammed her phone into the cup holder, gripped the wheel, and screamed, stomping her feet like a small child. She sobbed until she gagged, then threw open her door to air out the rotten egg stench before the burritos made a second appearance.

When she was positive she wasn't going to puke all over the fake leather seats in her brand-new used car, she closed the door and fiddled with the keys.

Bluish light glowed next to her thigh.

"Too little, too late," she told her phone, refusing to check it.

She waited a beat, then snapped up the phone so quickly she hit herself in the face with the screen.

UNKNOWN

Heard you're not invited to the Scavenge.

Meg stared at the message. It was *clearly* a trap. Kylie told the others that she shoved her under water for one teeny, *tiny* second, and now they were punishing her.

MEG

I'm blocking you.

Before she tapped away, another text popped up.

UNKNOWN

I'm on your side. Those bitches hurt me, too.

Come on, Meg. What about a little revenge?

Meg should've been smart enough to put down her phone and ignore the texts, but between the wrestling with rejection and fighting back regurgitation, she was exhausted and would've done anything to feel better.

MEG

Define revenge.

UNKNOWN

They refused to give you what you earned, and now they're giggling about it in their group chats. Everyone is buzzing about you. Everyone knows.

Everyone knows.

Blood rushed to Meg's cheeks and reignited her fire.

MEG

Great. So when you say revenge...

UNKNOWN

I've planned a big surprise for the Scavenge, but I need a little help to set everything up.

> **MEG**
>
> What kind of surprise?

UNKNOWN

Why don't you come to the gate and I'll show you.

Meg laughed out loud. She was no Lolly Bishop, but she also wasn't stupid. Whoever it was, they should've led her on a little longer.

> **MEG**
>
> This is a trap

UNKNOWN

Omg, it is not. Listen, we both know you're gonna do it, so just get over yourself and get out of the car and come here.

Meg read the text repeatedly until the words no longer had meaning. It was moronic to meet a faceless stranger at an abandoned carnival in the middle of the night. That's how girls ended up dead.

But what kind of psycho killer says, Omg?

Meg typed the word *Fine*, then paused. It would be fun for the girls to feel guilty if she died, but she didn't actually want to put herself in an unsafe situation, so she added a little threat.

> **MEG**
>
> Fine.
>
> But I'm bringing a gun.

Meg did not own a gun. Meg had never *touched* a gun, but they didn't need to know that.

It's the threat that counts.

———

The parking lot was dark, still, and silent. Maybe this was the whole prank. Lure her to the middle of nowhere and show her how alone she really was.

Meg clicked her headlights. She expected to see a shrouded figure standing before her, knife at the ready.

There was no one there.

She rolled halfway to the entrance, chickened out, and hit the brakes. Her phone buzzed in the passenger seat.

UNKNOWN
All the way.

Someone was watching.

"Go ahead idiot," she scolded herself. "Fall right into their trap. You're probably being filmed so they can post it online later."

UNKNOWN
It's not a trap. Not for you, anyway.

Meg whirled around in her seat, expecting to find an eavesdropping killer hunched behind her seat, but only found the sauce packets she'd tossed over her shoulder during her binge.

"Did someone bug my car?" she asked loudly. "Can you hear me?"

She held her breath and stared at her phone. When her new friend didn't reply, Meg continued.

> **MEG**
> Who is the trap for?

> **UNKNOWN**
> The seniors.

> **MEG**
> Class of 2020 or class of 2021?

> **UNKNOWN**
> Why not both?

"Unknown" understood. Going after the grads wasn't enough. All the girls needed to suffer. Meg switched on her brights, got out of the car, and walked toward the gates with her eyes glued to her phone.

> **UNKNOWN**
> Wtf are you wearing?

Meg was still in her swimsuit. The oversized T-shirt was dry and crinkly-stiff. Her hair was the same texture as her shirt, and her sweaty feet squeaked against her flip-flops, making farty sounds as she walked.

> **MEG**
> I came straight from the pool.

> **UNKNOWN**
> Is that a Taco Bell hot sauce packet stuck to your leg?

Meg swatted at her calf. The packet flew into the darkness.

> **UNKNOWN**
> You sure you're up for this? I was expecting more fiery rage, less...Fire Sauce.

"I can go back to my car!" Meg yelled at the carnival. "We can call this whole thing off now!"

The "Fire Sauce" joke sounded like James, but she didn't have a vengeful bone in her body. Kylie was still her prime suspect, but she clung to the possibility that another girl felt snubbed too and wanted to commiserate.

> **UNKNOWN**
> Sorry.
> I left the gate open for you. You can call me a bitch to my face.

Indeed, the double doors were unlocked. A dusty breeze blew across the parking lot and gently opened them toward her.

They're luring me in for a hug. A murder *hug.*

She stopped just short of the entrance.

"Hello?" Meg shouted into the darkness. Her voice bounced around the empty park. "I'm not walking in there alone! Come on out!"

When no one appeared, Meg checked her phone. No new texts.

> **MEG**
> Where are you?

No response.

Meg inched closer to the gate. A shape lurked in the distance, behind the carousel. It could've been a tall trash can, but she held her breath, waiting for it to move.

It never did.

"This isn't funny!" She yelled.

Behind her, someone beeped a car horn.

Meg whirled around and stared into the dark parking lot. Her headlights clicked on; two dim circles stared at her, daring her to run. The driver revved the engine. Her phone vibrated in her hand.

UNKNOWN

It's not a joke.

The driver simultaneously slammed on the gas and flashed the high-beams. Meg dodged left. The car veered to follow. She ran down the sidewalk with the car at her heels, its wheels grinding against the curb.

You can't outrun a car, dumbass.

Meg turned on a dime and ran in the opposite direction. The driver threw the car into reverse and chased her backward toward the gate. It zipped past. Meg caught a quick glimpse inside, but couldn't see anything except a dark, vaguely person-shaped figure in the driver's seat.

The car did a half-U-turn and jumped the curb. Meg zig-zagged across the entrance and bolted through the gates in a last-ditch attempt to put a physical barrier between herself and the lunatic driving her car.

Run straight ahead, don't look back. Go into the carnival, slam the gates. Hide. Call the cops.

The wind whipped through her hair, and Meg flew into the carnival feeling like she was gliding on air. But before she crossed over to safety, the carnival sprang to life. Bright, blinding lights stunned her and knocked her to her knees. The carousel turned, smoke billowed from the House of Horrors, and the Ferris wheel spun high in the sky, the lights blinking erratically, hypnotizing her long enough for her stalker to catch up.

Behind her, Meg's car clanged against the iron gate. It screeched to a stop, and the driver flung the car door open without cutting the engine. Fast feet crunched in the gravel.

An arm slithered around Meg's neck.

"Hey, sweets." A familiar voice hissed in her ear as a hot hand clamped over her mouth. "Look at the pretty lights."

———

The next morning, John, the security guard, spent most of his drive to work with his eyes glued to his cell.

His co-worker Ted got him into true crime, but he didn't have the attention span to read books like Ted, so he'd found a goth YouTuber who recapped various cases while preening in a mirror. That morning, she'd released an episode about Vickie Dawn Jackson, an "angel of death" who murdered at least ten patients under her care.

John pulled into the lot and stopped pretending to pay attention to the road so he could devote all his attention to the goth girl. A mile of empty parking lot surrounded him on all sides. There was nothing for him to hit, except for the statue out front: a ten-foot tall, gold-plated skull-faced candy apple. Gloopy caramel dripped down the forehead, narrowly missing the eyes and nose. A stick was stabbed in the temple; the left eye winced in pain.

The statue loomed large in his peripheral vision. He parked and got out, his nose shoved in his phone screen. He walked past the apple, keys in hand, ready to unlock the gate.

But it was already open.

John looked up from his phone and scanned the area. Empty midway to the left, test-your-strength on the right, carousel dead ahead, everything in its proper place. Not a soul in sight. He pushed through the gate, assuming Ted had forgotten the lock when he left the night before.

He turned around to lock it behind him and noticed a pair of legs flopped over the apple statue.

"Oh, this better be a prank!" he yelled angrily, not truly expecting it to be anything else. He stomped through the gate, flew around the statue, and was greeted with a sight so horrific he bolted across the parking lot and turned his back so he wouldn't have to see it again.

A girl was impaled on the candy apple stick like an olive on a toothpick. She hung upside down and sunny-side up with her neck twisted to the side and her hair hanging in her face. An inch of tongue peeked through the greasy strands.

He turned back and stared at her from a safe distance, gripping the carnival keys in one hand and his phone in the other. Ted trained him on how to fix security cameras, and when to eject drunk guests, but he never prepared him for this, except for one single piece of advice: *If anything weird happens, call this number.*

Ted wouldn't elaborate. He just told John, "You'll know."

John had saved the number in his contacts. It rang three times before an angry man yelled, "Hello?"

"Captain Bell?" John's voice squeaked.

"Yes?" Captain Bell sounded like he had food in his mouth. "Who is this?"

"Sir, it's John, the security guard at the carnival. I'd normally call nine-one-one, but the other guard, Ted, gave me your number in case anything *weird* happened that might reflect poorly on the company. Something weird has happened. There's a dead body on the apple. Someone cut her open and hung her upside down on the stick. Her intestines are falling out."

Captain Bell slurped water. "Don't move her, don't touch her, don't call anyone else. Do you recognize her?"

"I ran away," he admitted. "I can't tell from here. Her hair's in her face."

"Get closer. Move the hair if you need to, but be careful. If she's got a beak on her, she might be an Eaton. Whole family is turtle-faced. The protocol for a dead girl at the carnival is different from a dead *Eaton* girl at the carnival."

"You have a protocol for this?"

"Just go."

John slowly turned around and walked toward the statue, praying the wind would blow the girl's hair away from her nose, but he was out of luck. As he moved closer, he realized that what he thought he'd seen—a girl with her innards on display—was an optical illusion. There were no organs at all. Her belly was hollowed-out, and someone had shoved a messy wad of red entry tickets into her stomach.

His eyes dropped to the girl's protruding tongue.

It was the same shade of red as the tickets.

John brushed the girl's hair aside. Her eyelids were open, with the irises rolled back in her head. Her nose was a button—*definitely* not an Eaton girl—and her "tongue" was not a tongue at all.

Whoever stuffed her guts with tickets had pulled the roll up her esophagus, into her throat, and past her teeth.

Without her hair anchoring it down, the damp red rectangle reading ADMIT ONE popped from her lips and stood stiffly at attention, as if it was ready to be ripped off and placed into the hand of an unsuspecting carnival-goer, some poor person blissfully unaware they'd just gained entry into hell.

1

Mrs. Murphy, my neighbor, perched in the big bay window next to her front door every afternoon to wait for the mail. She'd done it for as long as I could remember. Even when I was little, it struck me as odd.

"Why does she stare at her mailbox every day?" I asked my mother one day after kindergarten. "Is she waiting for something?"

"Probably," she said, then immediately changed the subject by asking what I wanted for my after-school snack.

"Peaches and walnuts," I said.

Peaches and walnuts it was.

A few years later, I asked again.

"Mom, Mrs. Murphy is in the window. Has she been waiting for the same letter for *seven years*?"

"Please leave that old woman alone, Violet. Worry about yourself." Her voice wavered slightly, just enough for me to drop the subject.

I found out the truth my senior year of high school.

Mrs. Murphy waited around for her mail because she had nothing else to do.

Mr. Murphy died before we moved in. They had a son, but he walked away from their family and didn't visit often. She never left her house, so her only regular human contact was from our mail carrier.

"She doesn't have anyone, does she?" I asked my mom.

"No."

"Is that going to be you someday?" I asked. I planned to go away for college. She raised me alone; my father didn't want to be a dad, and she never had other kids.

"I've got your grandparents, I've got friends, and even if you're gone, you're not abandoning me, are you?"

I shook my head. "I'll come to visit, and you'll come to visit."

"I don't know if I can handle that horrible Arizona heat," she said, smiling.

I played violin—first chair since sixth grade—and I wanted nothing more than to write music for movies. My ultimate destination was Desert Springs University in Phoenix, a small school with the one of the best music composition programs in the country. Annie Wood—a genius composer with seventy-two major motion pictures under her belt—led the department. It was my dream to play for Annie, for her to fall at my feet weeping over my talent, and for her to beg me to join her orchestra.

"I haven't gotten accepted at DSU yet," I reminded her.

"My only concern about DSU is how I'm going to pay for it," she assured me.

"Is that an actual problem or a joke?" I asked, trying to hide my panic.

"A joke. Calm down."

Calm down.

It's impossible to *calm down* after someone says, *Calm down*, and I was already so anxious that her simple *calm down* had the exact opposite effect. *Calm down.* She was lucky I didn't collapse into a blubbering mess.

Every winter, Annie Wood hosted a workshop for potential new students. You had to record an audition tape, write an essay, and send them into the void with a prayer Annie herself might see them. If she felt you had potential, she sent you a handwritten note, asking you to spend your Christmas in Phoenix. It was the opportunity of a life-time, and it came with a big, fat, silent promise: If you got accepted into Annie Wood's workshop, you were practically guaranteed a spot in the next freshman class.

It took weeks for me to submit my audition. The essay was easy. I can talk about music for days, but actually playing that music for a respected professional? My high school orchestra director thought I was a prodigy, but Annie would see through my shit in a second. I was a hack, and my hero was about to judge me.

I spent the summer before my last year of high school trying to take my mother's advice and remain calm. June was easy. I didn't expect a response right away. July dragged on until I had to question if I'd gotten trapped in a really humid time loop, because it felt much longer than thirty-one days.

By the time August rolled around, I was a full-blown basket case.

Time slipped away, and if I didn't hear from DSU by September, I wouldn't be getting a response at all.

That's when I started sitting in my window to wait for the mail.

That's when I became Mrs. Murphy.

A friendly lady with curly black hair and gold-rimmed glasses delivered our mail. Day after day, she smiled and waved at me as she dropped our mail inside the mailbox mounted next to our front door.

I didn't want to appear crazy, so I would wave back and wait until she turned her little white mail truck onto the main road. When she disappeared from my sight, I would run to the mailbox, sift through the bills, H-E-B coupons, and other random junk, praying I would find a hand-addressed envelope from DSU in the pile.

One afternoon, I received a loving text from my best friend, James.

JAMES

Any news, or are you still a smelly loser who thinks Nepmoon is a planet?

I'd fumbled with the word one time years ago, and she never let me forget it.

VIOLET

I'm tired

JAMES

Pick up

A picture of the two of us at Founder's Park filled my screen. We'd gotten matching face paint. Glittery red, white, and blue fireworks exploded on our cheeks.

"Tell me it came!" she yelled without bothering with an introduction.

I groaned. "Of course not. I'm not good enough for the workshop, I'm not good enough for the school, and I'm not good enough to play in any orchestra bigger than the Belldam symphony. There are thirteen members, and they do one scheduled Christmas performance every year. That's it. One Christmas show."

"They also play weddings and funerals."

She wasn't wrong, but I didn't want to talk about it anymore.

"I told you, *I'm tired.*"

"Yeah, I know. But you aren't listening to me. I'm not talking about Annie Wood. My invite to the Senior Scavenge came today. Did yours?"

I sighed. The Senior Scavenge. Of course.

"Mail isn't here yet," I said.

"Ooh, maybe you'll get your invite *and* your acceptance letter!"

"Your optimism is appreciated," I sneered. "Can we please take this back to text?"

"Fine."

She hung up without saying goodbye. She always did.

Three little dots appeared on my screen as James typed her reply. They blinked for a full minute before my phone buzzed.

JAMES

> Here's the rundown. You've won national awards. You toured with the all-state orchestra. Violet, you got picked to play with the children's orchestra at the rodeo while Beyonce performed.

VIOLET

> It's not the flex you think it is. There were 44 other violinists there.

JAMES

> BEYONCE, Violet. You played with BEYONCE. Your resume is fantastic, your essay was heartwarming, and your audition tape was perfect. PER-FECT.

I smiled down at my phone. I loved having my own personal cheerleader.

Then, as if I summoned her, an actual cheerleader appeared.

MILA

> Did it come?!!!!!!!!!

A selfie of Mila Kelley followed the text. She pressed a postcard to her dimpled cheek and grinned from ear to ear.

Mila was one of the prettiest girls I'd ever met. Her huge green eyes always sparkled with mischief, and her friendly demeanor radiated from deep inside. When people spoke to her, she focused all her attention on their words, and she asked lots of questions. Sometimes it was too intense for me, and I often averted my eyes, lest my awkward self turn to stone from her gaze. She gently mocked me for it. Her teasing made me blush tomato red, which amused her.

The cheer squad at Pritchett wasn't your stereotypical rah-rah-pom-pom basic cartwheel types. They were the cheerleaders who competed on ESPN; she was as much an athlete as our jock friend Claire.

VIOLET

Mail hasn't come. James got hers.

MILA

I know. Claire, Gracie, and River have too. Blythe is far too busy to text me back, but she posted a pic of hers online.

Mila's text came with a gif of Amanda Seyfried doing an epic eye roll in *Mean Girls*.

VIOLET

We're far less important than her followers, don't you know?

MILA

You have no idea

Whenever Mila said that, good gossip always followed.

MILA

Wait. Do you want the Blythe story, or do you want the insane tea behind door number two?

I asked my phone to flip a coin. Heads, Blythe. Tails, whatever other mess Mila wanted to share.

Blythe. Tell me about Blythe.

Mila responded by spamming me with multiple texts in such rapid succession that it was obvious she'd written them out in her notes app and copy/pasted them into texts to send to multiple people.

MILA

I know for a fact Blythe almost didn't get an invite. Hannah Tyson had to beg Delilah to send it. Blythe & Delilah went to lunch at El Toro last week. Blythe spent twenty minutes getting a picture of her taco salad, then she had to craft the perfect self-deprecating caption to make her minions double-tap. Anyway, remember, Delilah is Miss Manners. She waited until Blythe finished so they could eat together. Hannah said Delilah said she was so hungry she nearly ripped Blythe's tongue out.

You didn't hear this from me, but Delilah told Hannah she would only give Blythe her invite if Blythe did a bunch of chores for her. She like, picked up her dry cleaning and walked her dog. She handwrote the cards for them too. How lazy are those bitches if they make us do our own Scavenge invites?

VIOLET

The laziest.

MILA

Indeed.

———

Blythe Lennon was not an A student. She didn't bother to do SAT prep, and she wasn't in any clubs. She hated school, and *constantly* whined about her classes and teachers to ensure everyone was well aware. Her mom barely parented her, but she drew a line in the sand and insisted Blythe graduate. If she hadn't, Blythe would've dropped out after ninth grade.

In Blythe's mind, she didn't need an education.

She was *famous.*

Blythe's descent into internet depravity started after her dad left her mom when he found out she was having an affair with the general manager of the Belldam Tower Resort and Spa. My mom was director of events, and she watched the whole thing play out in real time. Blythe's dad chased her mom through the lobby, calling her every name in the book. Blythe sobbed to me on the phone that night.

"She was in a black lace bustier!" Blythe howled. "She's forty-two! No forty-two-year-old should wear lingerie in public! *Or at all!*"

Blythe's mom was in fantastic shape, and I was pretty sure she didn't *intend* to run through a hotel in her underwear, but I didn't dare say that to Blythe.

Her dad left her mom, and for a while, he left her too, but their relationship changed the day Blythe discovered YouTube.

She was always a girly girl. When we had sleepovers in junior high, she would bring an overflowing makeup crate and give us all terrible makeovers.

During one such sleepover, she turned on her favorite movie, *The Princess Diaries*, for the millionth time. As Anne Hathaway got her princess makeover, Blythe sat on the carpet in the middle of her den, drawing and redrawing jagged black lines on her right eye. Her great shame in life was her embarrassing inability to draw a straight wing with liquid eyeliner.

"Why don't you try a makeup tutorial?" I asked.

She froze with her fingers still stretching her eyelid straight to apply the liner. "What?"

"On YouTube. I wanted to curl my hair when my mom took me to see *The Nutcracker*. I watched a girl do it on YouTube. It helped me a lot."

She released her lid. Her eye was red and watery. "You can watch someone put on eyeliner?"

"You can watch *a lot* of people put on eyeliner."

She paused the movie and opened YouTube. "What do I search?"

"Liquid eyeliner tutorial?"

"Oh. *Duh.*"

The first hit was a pretty blond girl with alien eyes. She held up six liquid eyeliner tubes, and the caption promised she would pick the best product and teach you how to use it. We learned Urban Decay made the blackest liner, while MAC had the most innovative applicator. I didn't know why either of these things would make it easier to draw a wing, but Blythe was hooked.

The next Monday, she ran at me and slammed me into a locker.

"Guess what!" she yelled.

"What?" I asked, struggling to free myself from her death grip.

She closed her eyes, then opened them and batted her lashes. She'd finally done it: two picture-perfect wings, and no broken capillaries.

"Tape!" she screeched. "A girl said to use Scotch tape to make a stencil. It worked! Next, I'm going to learn how to contour."

When her dad came around for their quarterly dinner, her new skills surprised him. She gushed about beauty gurus on YouTube, and he suggested she start her own channel. He bought her a fancy DSLR, a professional-quality mic, and a lighting setup. He even consulted with an interior designer to help her decorate her bedroom to use as a backdrop.

At first, being on camera terrified her. She stammered a lot and couldn't clearly explain her makeup techniques. She tried to mimic other beauty gurus, and she came off as a wannabe. Her dad watched a video where she clumsily compared red lipsticks and told her they might need to return her camera.

His words crushed her soul. She cried to James and me, begging for advice on what she'd done wrong.

"It's so easy for other girls. I don't get it. I'm so *fake*."

"Yeah," James said. "You are."

Blythe wailed.

"You're not fake," I said, hugging her and stroking her hair.

"She *is*. Look at her in the nail polish haul. She sounds like a robot. Blythe, you watch videos like this, right?"

"Yeah," Blythe said between hiccups.

"Are there certain channels you like more than others?"

"Yeah."

"Why? Are they the best makeup artists?"

Blythe stopped crying. "No. I watch the girls I'd want to be friends with."

James pulled up a video of Blythe on her phone. It had seventeen views.

"Do you want to be friends with this girl?" James asked, pointing to her screen.

Then it clicked. Blythe didn't need to develop her skills as a makeup artist, she needed to develop a personality.

Her first big hit was a video titled "How To Fake Being A Beauty Guru." In it, she took the clichés all the other girls used and flipped them around to make fun of them. When she really got going, she dropped her Texan accent and spoke with intense vocal fry. James said she sounded like someone put Kim Kardashian and Britney Spears in a blender. The voice made my back teeth itch. She drew ten identical red lipstick swatches on her forearm and made jokes about how they were *so* different.

My favorite video of Blythe's was titled, "Watching Sad Movies To See Which Depresses Me Most While Testing Waterproof Eyeliner." She spent a month filming commentary videos while wearing dozens of eyeliners. None of the movies made her cry—not even *The Notebook*—so while she watched, she waved various noxious items under her nose to induce tears. Onions, vinegar, things like that. Ultimately, she determined that the best waterproof eyeliner was by NARS, and the best way to make yourself cry was to dip your pinkies in pickle juice and use them to gently pat your tear ducts.

It was also a great way to get an eye infection.

At the end of the video, she dropped the creepy influencer voice and spoke as herself. "My name is Blythe. I have no idea what I'm doing. If you want to watch me make an ass of myself, like and subscribe."

Her video went viral. People love to see a pretty girl with a sense of humor screw stuff up.

When Blythe went full goofball, she was an instant sensation.

A million people watched her accidentally turn her skin green when she added some food coloring to her foundation for Halloween. Three million people watched her go to the worst salon in Belldam to dye her hair blond, and four million people watched her take a trip to a high-end salon New York to get it fixed. Five million people watched her bake a cake covered in craft store glitter instead of edible glitter. Ten million people watched a crossover video where she gave a guy from a prank channel a tattoo of Olaf from Frozen. Poor Olaf looked more like a dick than a snowman.

"Do you want to build a penis?" she sang in tune while she added a snow flurry around Olaf.

Her high view count lured in a slew of sponsors. When you have a million subscribers, companies hurl tons of junk at you in hopes you'll promote their garbage products. PR reps sent her everything from weight-loss tea that made her shit her pants to weird "toilet mints" you dropped in before you used the bathroom to cover the poop smell.

"She's going to need those mints if she keeps drinking that nasty tea," Claire once joked. "I went into the bathroom after her. *Big mistake*. It was like a dead animal rotting on a gas station sidewalk in early September."

Eventually, she didn't need her dad's money anymore because she made a killing on YouTube. She still sent him links when new videos went live; the only time they spoke was when she asked him to critique her work.

As Blythe grew more famous, it became harder to be her friend.

Stuff we bought, movies we liked, mundane conversations about teachers at school—all of it was potential content for her channel. Eating out with her became a nightmare when she developed a satire series on her blog where she took mediocre food pics and wrote about them as though she were describing a beautiful gourmet meal. She pissed Mila off when she tried out for cheerleading as a joke for her channel. We got into a huge fight when she ditched my sixteenth birthday party to fly to LA for a content creators' convention.

Spending a night with Blythe at the Senior Scavenge would be a nightmare.

———

VIOLET

She's not going to film the whole scavenger hunt, is she? She won't right? Pritchett is pretty boring at night in the dark. Unless you believe Gracie.

MILA

NOT re-litigating the ghost thing again. Believe what you want. I cannot wait another second

VIOLET

?

MILA

MEG WASN'T INVITED!

I gasped. Since the first day of freshman year, our classmate Meg McClendon cultivated a bizarre obsession with the Scavenge. She was a new kid among new kids, and like the rest of us, it gave her something to aspire to. Most of us grew up a little and recognized it for what it was: a fun event no different from prom or the senior bonfire on Sandpiper Beach. Meg even joined the dance team and became an officer to boost her chances because—for some unknown reason—she believed their colonel always received an invite. It was *a lot* of work for a little party.

VIOLET

Is she okay?

MILA

Idk. I asked Hannah who all was gonna be there and she told me. You're not gonna believe who got invited instead.

VIOLET

Please not Sadie.

MILA

Omg no, could you imagine. It's Lolly.

I was pleasantly surprised. Lolly was my orchestra buddy; she started out on viola, then moved to the harp in eighth grade. We sat on opposite ends of the orchestra room and made faces behind our director's back when he ranted about his one-sided rivalry with the band director. He claimed she was underqualified, but I think he just was jealous she got free football tickets and he only got a ten percent discount.

We didn't hang out outside of orchestra activities too often, but when we did, I always enjoyed it. Partially because Lolly was sweet as pie, and partially because she was sheltered, and I felt worldly and wild next to her.

> **VIOLET**
>
> Good for her.

It was good for us too. Meg was intense in a bad way that wore everyone out, not in a fun way like James or Blythe. Lolly would be chill and wouldn't try too hard to compete for attention.

> **MILA**
>
> Her name wasn't in the chatter, but it makes sense. If you're picking your popularity predecessors, you've got jocks, talented artists and musicians, however you wanna classify Blythe, it makes sense you would want the smartest girl in school.

> **VIOLET**
>
> Right.

> **MILA**
>
> You wanna hear the OTHER thing I found out?

> **VIOLET**
>
> ?

> **MILA**
>
> It's not at Pritchett this year.

> **VIOLET**
>
> No way.

I wasn't our class historian or anything, but I was pretty sure the Scavenge had been at the school since it began in the 1980s. Things had taken a turn, and the new direction had my attention.

MILA

> Yup. I guess the girls wanted to mix things up.
> Check my photo.

I scrolled back to examine the pic of Mila's invite. The front image showed a row of demonic clown heads, their gaping mouths waiting for someone to fill their gullets with water to inflate the orange balloons on their pointy black hats.

VIOLET

> The Carnival?!

MILA

> Guess so. How cool is that?

In theory, it was awesome. The Poison Apple Carnival was Belldam's premier Halloween-themed year-round tourist attraction for families. When we were younger, we practically lived there, but as time passed, and the carnival got shittier, we dropped down to once or twice a year, and only for special occasions.

In theory, it was awesome. Spooky scary skeletons, a Disney teacup rip-off ride called the Crazy Cauldrons, a kiddie coaster with rotting worm cars, and a midway where you could throw a beanbag in a bucket and win little stuffed werewolves and mummies. Once upon a time there were special events and performances too; Mila performed in a zombie gymnastics show freshman year.

VIOLET

> I'm not a fan of tetanus.

MILA

STOP. IT'S NOT THAT BAD.

The last straw for me was when a grown man squatted next to a trash can instead of going into the men's room. James reported him to security, but they shrugged and said they were short-staffed.

VIOLET

Can't we get in trouble?

MILA

We could get in trouble at the school too

Not the same kind of trouble. If we got caught breaking into the school, Ms. Holden-Jones would suspend us for a day or two at worst. The Eatons—the family whose company owned the carnival—would've had us arrested...*at best.*

MILA

Dude, that's why it's so fun.

I pulled the sheer curtain back from my window and looked out to see our mail carrier walking toward my house. I tossed my phone on my couch and ran to greet her.

"Hi, Misty!" I said. "How's it going?"

"Hot!" she chuckled as she handed me a fat stack of papers with a FedEx bubble mailer on top.

"Good luck keeping cool! And thank you!"

Misty nodded. "Hope you got what you're waiting for, sweetie."

Inside, I dumped the pile on our kitchen counter. The package was some random thing my mom ordered online. Ten different envelopes advertised how she'd been approved for various credit cards. She told me that if you got those, your credit was good. I mumbled "Yay for you, Mom" as I put the envelopes aside for recycling. A state senate candidate smiled awkwardly up at me from a massive red, white, and blue mailer. He promised he would improve the lives of all Texans by exterminating all the weasels in Austin. He did not identify the weasels, nor did he elaborate on how he would banish them from the capitol.

His mailer went straight into the garbage.

At the bottom was a teal envelope addressed to me. I turned it over, and a cartoony doodle of a peacock waved at me from the sealed flap. I ripped the peacock in two and pulled out my scavenger hunt invitation. It was a cute postcard with a poem on the back. I set it aside to sort through the other mail a second time.

No matter how many times I shuffled through the mail, no letter from Annie Wood appeared.

I took my scavenger hunt invite to the couch and belly-flopped dramatically onto the cushions. A Beistle-style jack-o'-lantern grinned at me from the center of the Ferris wheel. Each black gondola had a similar character painted on the side: ghosts, black cats, spooky owls. Orange lights lining the wheel glowed against an inky indigo sky. It was the ultimate Halloween ride, as spooky-cute in real life as it was on the card in my hand—at least before half of the bulbs on the Ferris wheel burned out.

For years, every single time we went to Poison Apple, my friends tried to drag me onto the Ferris wheel, but I refused. Heights scared me to death, and I wasn't one of those people who enjoys being frightened on purpose. James thought I was nuts.

"The gondolas are enclosed!" she laughed. "You're locked in a cage. You can't fall out!"

It didn't matter. Cracked, rusty hinges could allow gondolas to break free. I could be locked in with a venomous spider. The whole thing could be struck by lightning. It was, after all, the second-tallest Ferris wheel in Texas, a perfect lightning rod.

I turned my card over and read Blythe's pretty orange handwriting on the back.

THE POISON APPLE CARNIVAL
AUGUST 29

One Minute Past Midnight
Congratulations, chosen girl
Jump up and down, do a twirl
Walk the grounds and follow the grass
From the ride entrance
Steal a pass.
Meet your makers at the Crave Inn Diner at sunrise.
Hope you like pecan pancakes!!!

Beneath the printed message, Maddy drew eight bubbly hearts and signed her name in black ink. I snapped a picture of both the Ferris wheel and the poem and sent it to James.

VIOLET

Thoughts?

She replied with her own poem. It read:

JAMES

Wet and wild, darling child

A fish tank with no fish

Bring us a sphere stitched with red

Be warned

You may need to hold your breath.

Whatever that meant, it made my heart race a bit for her. Water *petrified* James. She didn't even like to take baths. If her challenge required her to swim, it would likely be me diving in to retrieve it.

JAMES

Ferris wheel fast-pass for you. Baseball from dunk tank for me.

She sent me a pic, and sure enough, the flip side was an artsy dunk tank shot.

VIOLET

Weren't these clues supposed to be mind-bending puzzles?

JAMES

Guess the hard part is breaking into the carnival without getting caught.

VIOLET

What if we do?

JAMES

> Don't be paranoid. We're seventeen-year-old girls. They're gonna shake a finger to scold us and let us walk free.

I wasn't so sure, but I didn't want to argue about it, so I lied and said I needed to practice. James didn't respond.

My mother got home from work early that night. I'd barely seen her since May, but no one wanted to have a wedding in Texas in late August, so she "only" had to work sixty-hour weeks by then.

She knew better than to ask out loud if I'd checked the mail.

At first, right after I applied, she would come home with wide, hopeful eyes, waiting for good news. The longer I waited, the more she pretended to ignore my anxiety. Eventually, it seemed like she gave up altogether.

She dropped her laptop bag on the kitchen counter next to the spot where I'd left my invitation to the Scavenge. She lifted it and read both sides.

"What's this?" she asked.

"Senior Scavenge."

"Oh, fun!" She meant it with genuine happiness, but I was in a mood and took it as sarcasm.

"It's whatever. I have to steal a fast-pass from the carnival. It'll take ten minutes. I might not go."

She placed the postcard on the counter, reached into her bag, and pulled out a single-serve bag of Chili Cheese Fritos.

"Why not?" she asked, crunching into a chip.

"If we're caught, I could go to jail, and you could lose your job."

"Why would I lose my job?"

She ate the chips one by one, chewing so intensely that her jaw remained flexed even when she wasn't grinding Fritos into paste. She was way more into her snack than my drama. It was like she wanted me to stab her.

"You work for the company that owns the Carnival. If I'm arrested for trespassing, it doesn't reflect well on you."

"I'm not concerned. Can we please go sit? I had to give nine tours today. Only three of them booked space."

Guilt hit me like Poison Apple's Whirling Witch Coaster, another ride I refused to go on because of the height. She worked hard with zero help from my father, and I was a whiny, spoiled brat. There were girls who would kill to go to the Senior Scavenge—granted, most of them were freshman—and I couldn't enjoy the gift because I couldn't stop whining about DSU for a few hours.

"You deserve a better daughter," I said.

She stopped eating mid-crunch. "Are you on drugs?"

"No, I'm not on drugs! I'm just upset!" I screamed.

She dropped the Fritos and flicked the seasoning off her fingers. "I was kidding, but you sound a little defensive. River and Gracie are gonna be at this thing, aren't they? You know I prefer for them to be school-only friends. This is Texas. Those girls are playing with fire. You wanna hear what happened to me when I was seventeen?"

"Can we please not?" I groaned. "Every time you try to relate your childhood to mine, you traumatize me. Can you please trust your own parenting and focus on the meltdown at hand?"

"Traumatize you? I've never done anything to traumatize you."

"Dun-un, dun-un," I sang, mimicking the *Jaws* theme.

"Oh, that was one time, Violet!"

I threw back an imaginary shower curtain and stabbed at her with my fist. "Ree! Ree! Ree!"

She threw her hands above her head in surrender. "Fine! Fine!" She scooped up the Fritos and examined the bag. "These used to have more in them." She stared into the empty bag and sighed. "What do you know about the carnival?"

"It's smelly and I always get sweaty there."

"Let me give you a brief history lesson. Ol' Abigail Eaton's husband built it for her for their twenty-fifth anniversary. That's why it's Halloween-themed. She loves all that spooky shit."

"Gracie says she's a witch," I said without thinking. When Gracie's name didn't reignite the earlier discussion, I continued. "The satanic kind, not the Harry Potter kind."

"That would explain a lot. But no, she's just greedy. If it doesn't involve making or losing money, it's not on her radar. The carnival is a wash financially, so she thanked him and moved on."

I had no clue why she was telling me this story. "How romantic," I said sarcastically. "I'm still scared you're going to lose your job. That's what I would like to talk about."

"I'm not, because you're not going to get caught."

I was touched.

"You have more faith in me than I have in myself," I said. "You really think I could pull it off?"

"*Eh.*"

My mother could play me like a fiddle. Build me up, then undercut me with humor. It's no wonder I'd become so attached to James; they were two sides of the same coin. She grinned at me, daring me to say something bratty, but I refused to let her win. I relaxed and let her continue.

"I have faith in *you*, but I have more faith in my knowledge of the Eatons. Abigail herself probably doesn't remember it exists. The carnival is under the management of the hotel. Abigail's son is my boss. Aleister doesn't care, and he spends all of his time at work fucking Gwen Lennon—*don't repeat that*—so it falls on the AGM, Rynn Waters. Rynn is overworked, and spread so paper-thin you can practically see her skull through her skin. She delegated management of the carnival to aquatics because they have a fun and games coordinator. Reesey-Piecey—that's what she asks children to call her—dresses and acts like she's auditioning to be a Disney princess. Reese tried to hire an on-site manager for the carnival, but it didn't work out, so she gave up and left the carnies to their own devices. No one's talked to anyone over there since. Let me ask you this: When was the last time you visited Poison Apple?"

It had been nearly a year ago, on Halloween. A creep got weird with Blythe, and it soured me on the place.

"Last October," I said.

"Was it a little skankier than usual?"

Yes.

"Maybe."

"Well, last I heard, I think there are about fifteen employees left. They probably won't be doing the full seasonal overlay, and I wouldn't be surprised if it dies a slow, quiet death until Abigail notices it's losing her money and torches it for the insurance payout. But that's not happening by next Saturday, so you're safe. You have my permission to have worry-free fun with your friends. Just don't do anything stupid."

I didn't take the bait. I remained silent and rubbed two fingers together. I'd built calluses so thick I hardly had any feeling in my fingertips.

"I haven't started tonight's practice yet," I said, invoking my favorite excuse. "Gonna go knock it out."

"All right," she said, then paused. "You're an amazing musician, Violet. I don't care what some woman in the desert thinks. I always pictured you in New England somewhere, anyway. You've got your big sweater collection. You wouldn't have a use for them in Phoenix. No matter what, you're still wildly talented, no matter what."

I told her thanks and disappeared into my room. The phrase *no matter what* bounced around in my brain. It felt like a consolation prize, like she was resigned to my eventual DSU rejection. I sprawled out on my bed, and instead of picking up my violin, I gripped my pillow.

At some point, I fell asleep and dreamed of Meg and Lolly dressed as clowns, riding the carousel at Poison Apple. They got caught in a violent downpour, the kind where you feel like freezing water is beating down so hard it might tear open your skin. Flood water three feet deep threatened to engulf the carousel. Wind whipped Meg's rainbow wig off. It skimmed the water before a wave rushed past, sucking it into the depths.

I stood at the entrance, where it was still sunny, begging Lolly to come back. She waved for me to come in and join them. She didn't notice the pair of huge, gloved hands rise from the water to pull her beneath the surface. I screamed for Meg to save Lolly.

She swam to the entrance, shook herself dry like a dog, and walked past me with a shrug as if to say, "Not my circus. Not my clowns."

3

On the morning of the Scavenge, my phone ripped me from a
deep sleep at five thirty.

I was trapped in a looping dream where River and Gracie's
comic characters tied me down and forced me to drink Hawaiian
Punch until my teeth turned to dust. I'd break free, my teeth would
grow back, and they'd catch me again, cackling as they restrained me.

It was the latest in a weeklong string of anxiety-induced nightmares that began with my bizarre flooded carnival dream, and it was
bad enough that I googled "How do I stop dreaming?" Because I
was willing to do anything short of a lobotomy to make them stop.

I was deep into an Amazon review for herbal dream suppressants
when a second alarm screamed at me. A warning flashed on my
screen.

> IT IS 5:33.
>
> WAKE UP AND GO TO THE ATTIC.

I had six alarms set, one every three minutes, for a full fifteen minutes. Each alarm came with a progressively meaner message, and I could tell how bad a day was going to be based on how many alarms I snoozed.

> BITCH. ARE YOU KIDDING ME? ARE YOU KIDDING! IT'S 5:36. IT'S ALMOST 5:40, WHICH IS ALMOST 6!!!!!!!!!

I dismissed it, opened Instagram, and checked my DMs. Gracie and I sent videos of birds wearing fancy hats to each other a few times a day. It was usually chickens, but sometimes we got extra lucky and found a pigeon. James sent me political commentary from a guy dressed like Sonic the Hedgehog. She'd added, "Makes you think, huh?"

I watched half of it.

It didn't.

Several alarms later, the meanest message of all popped up to remind me it was 5:45, which was the latest I could sleep and still squeeze in a full practice session.

> IF YOU DON'T WAKE UP, I'M TELLING EVERYONE YOU GOT DRUNK AND LET BLYTHE TOUCH YOUR BOOBS

It was my deepest, darkest secret. James didn't even know. I wasn't ashamed because it had been a girl, but because it had been *Blythe*, and it had actually happened *twice*. Just the idea of people finding out was enough to jolt me fully awake, drag me from bed, and shove me into my practice space upstairs.

This was my routine every single morning without fail.

This is what I loved to do.

———

I started playing the violin because my mother was a terrible parent.

For some reason she'd never been able to sufficiently explain, she thought it would be a good idea to let me watch *Jaws* when I was eight. Or rather, she sat me down on the first day of summer break, said, "This was one of my favorite movies at your age," and hit play. I tucked myself into her side, and she wrapped me in a side hug. Sinister music played over the credits.

"Mama?" I asked meekly.

"It's not that scary." Her eyes remained fixed on the TV. "Don't worry. It's fine."

As if on cue, the shark pulled a swimmer under the water to her death. The scene was at night, and water obscured most of the attack. Still, there was plenty of thrashing and screaming. I squeezed my eyes tight and burrowed my face into my mom's armpit, but she was too engrossed in the movie to notice. The action died down, and there were just a bunch of boring adults talking, so I relaxed a bit.

Fifteen minutes later, a shark ate a kid, in broad daylight, in full, eye-popping detail.

I screamed bloody murder, shoved my elbow into her ribs, and flipped myself over the back of the couch. I landed on my head, and it hurt like hell, but I didn't care.

Nor did I stop screaming.

My mom scooped me up and cradled me like an overgrown baby. "Shh, shh, shh, shh," she said, patting my head. "I didn't think. I'm sorry." She winced the wince of a woman who knew she would be sharing her bed with her child for the foreseeable future.

Later that night, I lay horizontally across her bed because if I lay the normal way, it felt too much like being on a boat. I made her leave the lights and TV on, and while she got the worst sleep of her life, I lay awake watching *Game of Thrones*, which she'd also suggested. Every time I closed my eyes to block out the dragons, I saw the little boy in *Jaws*, his legs kicking wildly underwater, and heard that haunting song.

Dun-un. Dun-un. *Dunundunundunun.*

"Mama!" I screamed. "Mama!"

She scrambled awake, petted my head, rolled over, and screamed into her pillow.

The next morning, we sat on her bed, dazed from lack of sleep and adrenaline overload. "It's just a movie, I promise."

"Sharks don't eat people?" I said, sniffling.

"Well, no. They do." Her face went white. "I mean, they have. They *can*, but... Baby, the shark in the movie isn't even real. It's a puppet."

From then on, anytime anyone mentioned Elmo, I broke out in a cold sweat.

Exhausted, she pressed further. "What was the second-scariest thing?"

"The music."

"*Ohh.* It is a scary song, isn't it? It's kinda famous for being scary. So is the movie. What the fuck is wrong with me?"

"Dun-un," I said, ignoring her swear, and wiggling my hand above my head like a shark fin.

She grabbed my hand and placed it in my lap. "Music can't hurt you. It's intangible."

"What?"

"You can't touch music, and it can't touch you." She picked up her phone. "A bunch of people with instruments sat in a room with microphones and played the song. All the songs, the background music in a movie is called the score." She showed me a picture of an upright bass. It was imposing, and at least four inches taller than the woman holding it. "I'm fairly sure they played the scary parts on a bass. It's a piece of wood with strings. It can't hurt you."

The next day at work, she printed a bunch of bass photos, laminated them, and hung them on my bedroom wall with Velcro. Whenever I got scared, I'd rip one down and stare at it while humming the *Jaws* theme. My mom was convinced she needed to act fast, or I'd end up a serial killer, or worse, a grown adult who still slept in her bed.

"Guess what!" she said brightly one evening. She handed me a brochure for Belldam Community College. "You're gonna go to college!"

"I'm had a lot of trouble with fractions last year," I replied.

She snorted. "Violet. Not literally. They have a program called Kids at College. There's a bunch of different classes. I signed you up for music! You can learn to play bass!"

I glanced at the picture in my hand. A barely transparent watermark reading COPYRIGHT TAKESTOCK PHOTO was slashed across the faded print. I crumpled the laminated paper as best I could and chucked it over my shoulder. I didn't need that garbage anymore.

I was getting the real thing.

Unless it killed me, which still seemed like a possibility.

The next Monday, my mom dropped me off at Belldam Community with strict instructions to go through a red door, turn left, and walk into room 1428. I did as I was told, but when I got to room 1428, it was locked, and the only person in sight was a girl my age. She sat on the floor cross-legged, hunched over a phone, draped in an ugly green blanket. When she heard my footsteps approaching, her head snapped up, and she smiled. Eight front teeth were missing; four on the top, four on the bottom.

I gasped.

Her fingers flew to her lips. "I had a bike accident and landed on my mouth," she mumbled. "My dentist said my adult teeth will come in any day now. I know it's freaky looking. I don't care, but we don't have to talk if you don't want."

A door slammed, and a trio of boys walked toward us. I recognized Troy Edison from my class at school. I'd never spoken to him, but he famously made three substitutes cry, and I didn't want to be alone on the receiving end of any potential torment.

"Can we be friends?" I asked the girl.

She lifted an arm. Her blanket was actually a men's army jacket.

"James Parker," she said, introducing herself like an adult at a business meeting. "Good to meet you." She raised onto her knees and flopped her sleeve around in my face until her little fingers peeked out. The nails were flecked with chipped black polish. My mother wouldn't let me wear anything except clear.

"My name is Violet." I squinted at her fingertips. "Do third graders shake hands?"

James jerked her hand back. It disappeared deep into her sleeve. "We don't have to."

I smiled. I slid my fingers up the sleeve, found hers, and pulled her hand out to shake it.

"*Gay*," said Troy.

James slid her eyes in his direction. "Is that a problem?" she asked, one eyebrow raised. "My dad is gay. Is there something wrong with my dad?"

Troy's friends *ooh*ed, and Troy stammered out an apology, then whispered something about the water fountains and wandered off.

James smirked at me.

"Is your dad really gay?" I asked.

"Nope." She grinned, flashing me her creepy gums. "So, Violet, what are you 'in' for?"

I had no clue what she meant. "In?"

"Do you want to be here?" She asked, surprised.

"My mom showed me *Jaws*," I said. "I'm going to learn to play the theme song so I can sleep in my own bed again."

James's eyes widened. "*Jaws*? My dad let me see that too!"

What were the odds that two girls would be traumatized into music lessons after watching the same old movie? It was kismet. I'd made a new friend, and she was just like me!

"My mom thought if I learned to play the theme song, I would be less scared." I told her. "Is that why you're here too?"

She shook her head. "Nope. *Jaws* is why I quit swim lessons last summer. I'm here because my mom can't handle me all day without a break, and her friend Martina works in the front office. They dumped me here so they can go to Snowflake Donuts for coffee."

"*Oh.*"

I was disappointed, but only for about five seconds. Mrs. Benchley limped into view, and James gasped.

"What?" I whispered.

"*Dun-nun, dun-nun,*" she whispered back, pressing her chin into her shoulder and leaning close. "She lives down the street. My mom makes me be nice to her. She's been *really* crabby since her husband died last month."

"Four?" Mrs. Benchley yelled when she got close enough for a head count. She had a thick East Texas accent and thicker ankles. "I had to come in here for *four* kids?"

"*Dun-nun,*" James mouthed.

"Troy is in the bathroom!" said one of his friends.

Mrs. Benchley swung her cane and made gentle contact with the boy's chin. She used the handle—a sharp, iron bird—to lift his face toward hers. The boy shivered.

"Troy should've been here at eleven sharp," Mrs. Benchley said. "Everybody get in the room! I'm locking the door behind us." Her bony fingers shook as she unlocked the door. She grumbled to herself under her breath as she fiddled with the knob. I wasn't sure, but I thought I heard her wish that someone would kidnap Troy as punishment for running off.

My blood ran cold. My mother terrorized me with *Harry Potter and the Order of the Phoenix* to me when I was far too young, and visions of Dolores Umbridge danced in my head. My nightmares were colliding.

I snapped my spine straight and walked into the room. It was larger than your average classroom, with dusty walls and even dustier posters taped to them with yellowing Scotch tape. I put my hands behind my back and stared at a giant diagram of the anatomy of a cello while Mrs. Benchley spat venom at everyone else.

"Boy in the striped shirt!" She snapped her fingers at him. "Stack these chairs. Boy in the blue shirt, line the stands along that wall! But leave four out!" She narrowed her eyes and glared at James. "What are you wearing?"

James opened her arms wide, like she might ask Mrs. Benchley for a hug. The jacket dangled an inch above the floor. "It's my dad's."

"You can't play an instrument dressed like that. Give me the jacket and I'll hang it on the coatrack."

"I can put it on the back of my ch—"

"No!" Mrs. Benchley interrupted her. "It's sloppy. Give me the jacket!"

James practically teleported out of the green fabric. Without it, she was half the size she'd been before and was twice as mad.

"He gave me that to wear in case I get scared," James whispered, eyeing Mrs. Benchley as she berated Troy for coming to class late. "I'm gonna get her."

I didn't know whether or not to take her seriously, but I was afraid I'd made a new friend, only to discover that she was a psychopath.

"Get her how?" I whispered back.

Before James could answer, Mrs. Benchley pointed at the boys and yelled for them to retrieve five violins from the storage closet. I stopped breathing. I was bad at fractions, but I could count to five. Five violins, five kids.

I raised my hand.

"Yes ma'am," Mrs. Benchley said sharply. She wasn't yelling at me yet, but if I pushed her too far…

"I'm so sorry, but I wanted to learn to play bass." My voice was barely above a whisper. Mrs. Benchley took a deep breath and squished her hands into knobby fists. I continued speaking, because I knew when I was done, she was going to beat me with her cane. "I'm sorry to ask, but—"

James cut me off. "The course brochure said all stringed instruments. If she gets a bass, I want a banjo."

"Banjo!" Mrs. Benchley yelped.

"It's like a guitar, but round. Taylor Swift can play one."

"Is that someone at your school?" Mrs. Benchley asked, bewildered. I'd gotten the distinct impression that kids didn't talk back to her very often, and we were venturing into uncharted waters.

"She's a country singer," James said matter-of-factly.

Mrs. Benchley sighed. "I don't listen to modern music," she said, relaxing her jaw. "Only classical and talk radio."

James cracked the code. If you confused Mrs. Benchley, it disarmed her enough to make her stop yelling.

"Yeah," James continued. "So she plays the banjo, which, like I said, is round."

Mrs. Benchley's face hardened. "I know what a goddamn banjo is! I don't know how to play one, so we won't be messing with any. And you," she pointed at me. "You're too little for bass. I wouldn't let you have one, even if I had one available. You'd keel right over. Everyone learns violin, and that's *final*."

She instructed us to form a line next to the four music stands she'd told Blue Shirt to set aside.

"Don't we get chairs?" Troy asked.

"You're lucky I let you through the door!" she yelled, slamming her cane into the ground. "Y'all need to learn proper posture, and it's easier for me to teach you if you're standing."

We spent the next half hour standing perfectly still, with Mrs. Benchley tapping us with her cane to point out our weak spots. She didn't allow anyone to touch an instrument, and when class ended, she dismissed us with a grunt.

James and I remained silent until we were out of earshot.

"What was that?" she hollered, laughing.

I laughed too. "I never met someone so mean!"

"Why did she take the violins out of the closet if she wasn't going to let us play them? Next-level mind games."

"Maybe next week?" I suggested.

James grimaced. "Hate to tell you, Violet, but there won't be a next week for me. I'm gonna get in my mom's car and kick and scream until she says I don't have to come back. If I wanted an old person to tell me I'm a hunchback with crooked knees, I'll go to my grandpa. At least he says it with love."

I sighed. The coolest girl I'd ever met, and she was fixing to walk out of my life forever.

"What's your phone number?" she asked, gripping her phone.

Or maybe not.

But I didn't have a phone, so she was about to discover that I was a baby, and she would pat me on the head and skip away.

"I'm not allowed to have one yet," I admitted. Only four kids in my class had cell phones. None of their parents were serious people.

"*Oh.*" She nodded knowingly. "You have a *responsible* mom. I'm sorry. Do you have email?"

No.

"Obviously."

"Email me tonight. It's James Veronica Parker Rulezzz at gmail dot com. No spaces between the words, three z's in rulezzz."

"Got it!" I yelped, a little *too* excitedly.

"Cool." She looked around. My mom had parked by the curb, but hers hadn't gotten back from her coffee date yet. My mom waved. I raised a finger to signal I'd be there in a minute.

"I can wait until your mom gets back."

"Thanks." She fidgeted with her jacket. "Where do you go to school?" she asked.

"Crockett," I said. "It's okay. My teacher cried a lot last year."

"I go to Bluebonnet. It's fun. We have chickens."

"I wish my school had chickens," I said, depressed because my school sucked more than I'd realized. Maybe that was why Mrs. Copeland was so sad.

"Too bad you can't go to Bluebonnet." She leaned to the side and looked past me. "There's my mom. Email me later. I promise I'll answer."

A white minivan with a *Don't Mess with Texas* bumper sticker squealed into the lot. James said goodbye and ran to the van, waving at me the whole time. I waved back until she slammed her door, then walked to my mom.

"Who was that girl?" She asked.

"James Parker," I said. "She was in my class. She isn't coming back next week."

"Oh, that's too bad. You looked like you'd been friends forever."
It felt like it too.

A tiny seed burrowed its way into my brain, fertilized by words I'd heard my mother say to my grandmother in passing.

"Did you have fun?" she asked, starting the car. "Besides James."

"Mrs. Benchley wouldn't let us touch the instruments. She made us stand the whole time, and she hit us with her cane."

My mom snorted. "I'm sure it wasn't that bad."

"She wouldn't let me play bass," I said. I pouted and crossed my arms over my chest. I didn't care about the bass anymore, but I could use my perceived sadness to cut a deal. "Only violin."

"Well, that's not what the website said! I'm so sorry Violet. I know you wanted to learn the *Jaws* theme." She thought for a moment. "But there's another old movie with a famous theme song, and I'm pretty sure the main instrument is a violin. We can watch it this weekend. It's not that scary. It's called *Psy*—"

I placed my fingers on her lips. "It's fine," I said dramatically, staring out the window. "I guess I'll come back next week, since you paid for the whole summer and all."

"You don't have to."

"No, no." I mustered a single tear. "I made a commitment."

She stared at me with her head cocked. "What do you want?" she asked.

"What do you mean?"

"When you're upset about something, you whine until I want to tear my hair out. You don't longingly stare out the window and cry. What's this about?"

I shot straight.

"I want to go to Bluebonnet. That's where James goes. They have chickens."

"Chickens?" She was so startled that she stopped the car. "Huh. That's kinda neat."

I fought back a smile. "You told Grandma you need to sign a new lease. We can move."

She groaned. "No, no, no. I don't want to manage a move right now. It's fun that you made a friend, but you have plenty of friends at Crockett. What if we call Claire or Gracie's moms for a playdate, and when you start sixth grade, we'll move close to whichever junior high you want, but for now, you're staying at Crockett."

I'd anticipated her hesitance and gave a counteroffer.

"If we move to a house where I can go to Bluebonnet, I will never ask to sleep in your bed again."

The next day, my mother rented a house across the street from Bluebonnet Elementary.

I emailed James from my shiny new email address (violinviolet1428@gmail.com) to tell her the news.

> Hey!
>
> This is Violet Warren.
>
> Guess what? I'm going to Bluebonnet next year!
>
> See you then,
>
> Violet

I read it three times for typos, hit send, and sat and stared at my inbox, waiting for a response until I got bored and wandered away. When James finally replied, it was with a GIF of a screaming rubber chicken.

I took this as a positive sign.

A week later, I was the only kid who showed up for Mrs. Benchley's class. She hobbled down the hall to find me waiting alone, pushed past me with a grunt, and opened the door.

"I figured it would just be you," she said. "Most people don't make it to the second week. That's why I don't bother with the instruments. You came back for week two. You deserve to move on."

"Does this mean I can learn bass after all?" I asked hopefully.

"No. I told you last week. You're too little. Now go get two violins from the closet.

"May I please have a chair too?" I asked.

She gave me a once-over. "Yes. But if you slouch once, you're never sitting in my class again. Understand?" She gripped her cane handle. The iron bird stared straight into my soul.

"Yes, ma'am."

Mrs. Benchley spent the rest of the summer giving me private lessons, and by August, she even let me hold a bow. After our last scheduled session, when my mother arrived to pick me up, Mrs. Benchley handed her a business card.

"This one has something special," she said. "Takes instruction well, doesn't ask too many stupid questions. I teach lessons at my house on Sundays. Ages eight to eleven, invitation only. Violet is welcome if she likes. My three p.m. slot is available."

My mother smiled her fake customer service smile, thanked Mrs. Benchley, and said she'd hear from us soon. On the way to the car, my mother shuddered.

"I can't believe that mean old lady thinks you'd want to go to her house for violin lessons."

"But I do."

"You do?"

"She taught me how to pluck 'Three Blind Mice' with my fingers. It's called pizzaotto."

She shook her head. "No, it's not."

"It is!" I insisted. "And she just let me touch a bow, and I got rosin on my fingers and it's sticky but also dry, and *I liked it*. I won't ask for anything else, ever."

"You said that when you asked me to move to Bluebonnet."

"This is *bigger* than Bluebonnet," I insisted.

My mother screwed her face up and did the mental math. "Sundays are my second-busiest day at work. You go home and call Grandma. If she can take you, I will call Mrs. Benchley. But if you miss one Sunday, you're done."

I never missed a single Sunday, out of sheer stubbornness. By the time my eleventh birthday rolled around, I hated Mrs. Benchley, the violin, my mother, and myself. I never wanted to touch any musical instrument again. I inexplicably started telling everyone who would listen that I wanted to be a court stenographer.

But laziness got the best of me, and when they forced me to pick an elective prior to sixth grade, I enrolled in the orchestra since it would be an easy credit.

Belldam Junior's orchestra director, Priscilla Gassman, was a stocky woman, thirty-five at most, and she was firmly stuck in another decade. She wore too-tight, flared jeans, and dingy white socks with clogs. Her oversized square glasses looked like they belonged to a woman three times her age, and she sweated more than anyone I'd ever known. Because of the unfortunate combination of her career—teaching middle school students—and her surname, she asked that we call her by her first name. Most kids just made fart noises at her instead, and she tried her best not to react. I always got the feeling she'd been teased mercilessly growing up, and she understood how to take idiot kids in stride.

As part of her welcome speech, Priscilla asked if any of us had musical experience. Two hands went up. One was mine, the other belonged to a gawky girl who whispered, "I took piano," so softly that only the boy next to her heard.

"She said she plays piano!" the boy yelled to Priscilla.

"Thank you, Alberto. Violet and Lolly, you both read music, yes?"

The girl and I nodded. Mrs. Benchley wouldn't let me have my own violin to practice ("You ain't gonna practice with it! You'll take it home, irritate your mother, and never touch it again!") but she would give me sheet music and force me to copy it onto blank paper until I had the songs memorized.

Lolly and I nodded.

Priscilla let everyone choose their instruments—and not just violins. She had those, plus violas, cellos, two stand-up basses, and a harp.

"The harp is for eighth graders," she told us. "You have to learn one of the other instruments first."

Lolly and I each selected a violin, and we sat side by side, right in front.

"How long have you been playing?" she asked me.

"Since before third grade," I said. I placed the violin under my chin and played a serviceable snippet of "Greensleeves" from memory.

Across the room, Priscilla's head snapped in my direction, but she said nothing to me until the end of class, when she asked me to hang back.

I glanced at the clock, then the door. "I have Geography."

"It'll only be a second."

I sat, unable to control my nervous energy. My trembling knee nearly knocked a music stand over. "Sorry," I told her as I steadied the stand. "Sorry, sorry, sorry."

"Who taught you to how play violin?" she asked. "Wait. Let me guess. Was it Ida Mae Benchley?"

I nodded. Lolly stood next to Priscilla's piano, gently brushing her fingers over the keys. She plinky-plinked, then jerked her hand back.

"I'm sorry," she said. "I got carried away. I wanted to talk to Ms. Gassman. It can wait."

In the hallway, Alberto and his friends blew raspberries on their arms.

"It's Priscilla, sweetie." Priscilla closed the orchestra room door. "I'll be with you in a sec." She turned back to me. "Mrs. Benchley taught me how to play too. She's been around a long, long, long time. Did you like her lessons?"

I didn't say a word.

"I figured."

"I wanted to play bass," I told her. "My mom traumatized me with *Jaws*, and I wanted to learn the theme song. Mrs. Benchley only teaches violin."

She smiled. "Fortunately, I'm not Mrs. Benchley. I'd offer you a bass, but Alberto and Sam already claimed them, and besides, you're the most talented violinist I've ever seen. I'd like to ask you to stick with it."

My heart swelled with pride. I knew I was good, but I didn't know I was *that* good. Mrs. Benchley never offered positive reinforcement. Sometimes, if I played particularly well, she would stop criticizing me for a few minutes.

It didn't happen often.

"Really?" I said, a smile plastered on my face." I'm the most talented violinist you've ever seen?"

Over at the piano, Lolly's head shot up to listen.

Priscilla continued. "Yes! Well, I may have oversold it a touch.

For a sixth-grade student who learned to play from a feeble croco-dile skeleton like Mrs. Benchley, you are *absolutely* the best I've ever heard. You have real potential."

I deflated. "*Oh.*"

"Sorry. I oversold it. Had to temper your expectations. But if it makes you feel better, if you can play one stringed instrument, you can play them all."

"You can?" Mrs. Benchley never said anything of the sort.

"Well, *I* can." She glanced over at the window, where Alberto was pressing his butt against the glass. She raised her eyebrows. "Not everyone can."

"Can I?" I asked.

She smiled. "If you like. You have to master the violin first."

Three loud booms rang out. Alberto was gone, and James was now in the window with her open mouth suckered to the glass.

Priscilla turned her back on James. "Please tell me that girl isn't in my next class."

I laughed and assured her she was safe. She told me she'd see me in class the next day, and I said goodbye.

In the hallway, James linked her arm with mine and pulled me toward our shared geography class, but I asked her to wait. I wanted to debrief with Lolly. When Lolly emerged, James stuck her hand in Lolly's face.

"James Parker," she said.

Lolly looked alarmed.

"James is normal," I assured Lolly as I forcibly lowered James's hand. "Well, not *normal*, but she's…harmless. Is everything okay?"

"Why wouldn't it be?" she asked.

"Priscilla said nice things to me, and you looked upset."

"Oh." She hemmed and hawed as she considered her words. "Listen. I want to be first chair. I don't care which instrument, I just want to be the best. If I'm competing against you, it's going to make both our lives a living hell, unless you intend to roll over and let me win. Do you?"

I didn't know much about Lolly, but any kid her age with such clear goals was not someone to be trifled with. I didn't have a competitive bone in my body, but I also would not roll over and play dead when we both knew I had a leg up.

"I do not intend to do that, no."

Lolly nodded. "I figured. Priscilla said I could switch to viola. I'm trying to maintain perfect grades and perfect attendance, and I can't waste time competing with you. You're too good. I'd have to work way too hard to eclipse you."

It was the greatest compliment anyone had ever given me in my life.

"So we can still be friends?" I asked.

James flung her arm around my shoulder and licked my cheek. It was gross, but Lolly deserved to know what she was getting herself into. Her eyes flicked back and forth between us before she finally sighed.

"Yeah. We can be friends." She held her hand out to James. "Lolly Bishop."

James recoiled. "What kinda sixth grader shakes hands?"

Lolly avoided James for a while after that.

Priscilla turned out to be the teacher I needed all along. She asked our class lots of questions about why we want to play music and what kind of music we liked. Lolly said she liked Elton John, and she knew I wanted to make music for movies, so we learned "The Circle of

Life." Alberto requested Christmas music in March, and Priscilla obliged. She even brought candy canes. Anything to keep us playing.

Best of all, she allowed me to take a violin home. Mrs. Benchley was right. It irritated my mother, but not because I was screwing around. I wasn't great at recovering from mistakes, so every time I made one, I restarted the song, whether I did it in the first bar or the last.

One afternoon, she burst into my room without warning.

"Finish a song!" she yelled. My mother didn't yell often. "Stop playing the same six notes over and over and over and over and over! I'm losing my mind!"

"But I'm trying to learn the *Jaws* theme," I said, grinning. "You were wrong. It's not just a bass. Mama! There are violins in the song too!"

She pursed her lips and left without saying a word.

That weekend, she built me a practice space in the attic, and glued cut-up egg-carton mattress pads to the walls to absorb sound.

"It's not soundproofed, but if I have two fans running in my room, I won't be able to hear you." She considered her words. "Not that I don't want to listen to you play. I do. I just don't want to suffer through the process. You can stay here as long as you want, but I don't want to hear a screech out of that thing until you can play a perfect rendition of the *Jaws* theme. Are we clear?" I hugged her so tight it hurt. She kissed me on top of my head. "You've got something here, baby. Keep going."

———

At 7:30 a.m., one final alarm rang. This one read "GET OUTTA THE ATTIC AND BE A HUMAN." I hit snooze and grumbled to myself.

"You wonder why Annie Wood doesn't give a shit about you? Mediocrity."

I accidentally bumped Katniss, the secondhand violin my mother got me when she finally believed I intended to keep playing, against my music stand, knocking it over. I gasped and examined her to make sure she was okay. When I didn't find any broken parts, I gave one of the pegs a turn, twisted a little too hard, and snapped the E string. It popped against my left index finger, slicing it open.

Blood dribbled from my finger onto the lining of Katniss's case. "Goddamn it," I mumbled.

I slipped Katniss back in her case and carried her downstairs, where I wrapped a Hello Kitty Band-Aid around my finger to stop the bleeding. It went numb, and the tip turned white.

My phone buzzed.

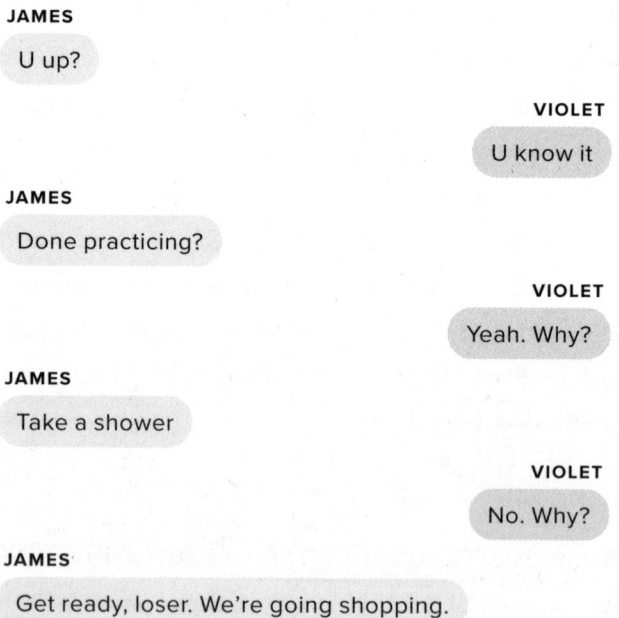

JAMES
U up?

VIOLET
U know it

JAMES
Done practicing?

VIOLET
Yeah. Why?

JAMES
Take a shower

VIOLET
No. Why?

JAMES
Get ready, loser. We're going shopping.

When I didn't automatically respond to her text, James called me.

"You are not going to sit around and wait for the mail all day today," she said. "My mom is dragging me to Austin to pick up some boxes from Grandpa Jimmy, and you're coming with us. When we get back, we're going to dinner with everybody. Pack whatever you need for today and tonight because you won't be back home until after breakfast on Sunday."

James sounded chipper as a chipmunk, which made me want to crawl back in bed and not get out again until school started. I'd promised my mom I would go to the Scavenge, but it still felt like a chore, and I knew if I didn't at least *try* to have fun, I'd ruin it for everybody else.

I still needed to wallow in bed for three or four hours first.

"I'm in for dinner, but I can't go to Austin."

"Uhh, Violet, don't do this. Don't let me down."

"I promised my mom I'd go through my old clothes to see if anything can be donated," I lied. "And I said I'd mow the backyard."

James laughed. "You don't give a shit about either of those things, and neither does your mom. Take a damn shower. We'll be there soon."

———

James and her mom Heather pulled into my driveway in their minivan just as I was tying my shoes. I checked to make sure my ID and debit card were in my phone case and shoved it in my pocket. I debated bringing a hoodie in case it got cold later, but decided against it. James would have her old green jacket—she'd grown into it and covered it with a million pins and patches—and I could steal it if I needed warmth.

James flung herself onto my porch and screamed.

"It's Senior Scavenge Day!"

She did fast feet, spun in a circle, and body-slammed me onto a hedge.

"Okay!" I yelled, holding my hands up in surrender. "It's Senior Scavenge Day! I'm excited!"

Honestly, seeing James in person did it for me. I *was* excited about the Scavenge, after days of wishing I could find a way to skip it.

"What did you do to your hand?" James asked, grabbing me by the thumb.

"Katniss bit me."

"That *bitch*!"

Heather leaned on her horn and waved us to the car.

"Y'all can scream at each other while we drive," she said when we climbed into the van.

"It's Senior Scavenge!" James screamed.

"Yaahh!" Heather growled, her fingers in a "rock on" gesture.

As a teenager, Heather had purple hair and a nose ring. She went to concerts of bands her parents hated, got drunk, and stumbled in at dawn. She staged an anti-meat protest at her school, complete with gallons of fake blood sprayed on the cafeteria walls. She dated a boy with a lime green Mohawk who gave himself a stick and poke tattoo of a flaming skull on his forearm.

All the adults told her she'd be dead by twenty if she didn't change her ways.

Now she was pure soccer mom, in pastel polos with a blunt bob. She married Mohawk Guy, who grew out his hair and spent big money getting his tattoo covered by a professional artist. Now when Mr. Parker rolls up his sleeve, he's got a bouquet of purple heliotrope on his arm. James picked it out for him. She chose it because it was the same color her mother's hair had been when her parents first met.

Though Heather fully embraced her new mom life, when we went on road trips, a little bit of her old self shone through. On the morning of the Scavenge, we drove to Austin while blasting music from back in Heather's glory days, screaming along with Marilyn Manson and Hole. She drove so fast the van shuddered, and when we were on the open road, she put it on cruise control and rested a bare foot on her window.

"Mama?" asked James, her voice quiet. "Is it safe to drive with your leg up?"

Heather sheepishly put her foot back on the floor, turned down the music a touch, and announced we were stopping at Torchy's for breakfast tacos.

James rolled her eyes in the rearview.

I sat back, smiling, and squeezed my injured finger.

———

James's grandfather was selling their old house so he could move to be closer to his daughter's family. The boxes were a mixture of Heather's old junk and her deceased grandmother's dishes, photo albums, and Christmas ornaments.

"Ninety percent is going in the garbage," James said under her breath as we stuffed everything in the back of the van.

"It's the ten percent that counts," I said.

James sneered. "Then you can come over and help her sort out that ten percent. Ooh. Here's a whole box of notes my mom and her best friend passed each other in high school."

James lifted the lid off a Doc Martens shoebox, and sure enough, a hundred little folded pieces of paper were stuffed inside. I pulled one out and read the first sentence aloud.

"We should go to Lone Star Mall next weekend, drive around the parking lot, and scream at the tiny stop signs." I frowned and folded the note into a triangle. "What the hell are tiny stop signs? Your mom was really weird."

"*Is* really weird," James corrected me. "Look at this one. It's written backward. I could only read this if I held it up to a mirror. My godmother seriously had way too much time on her hands."

"Do you ever wish you lived back in the nineties? Before phones and stuff?"

"Uh, no. I'd die if I didn't have my phone. We wouldn't have internet, and I'd probably die of boredom without a computer to screw around with. What if there was an emergency or something? Don't romanticize the good old days, especially when you never lived them."

"Fair."

Heather approached us, a plastic tub packed with photo albums under her arm. "We had computers and cell phones in the nineties. We even had the internet. Did I ever tell you girls about AOL?"

James's eyes bulged. "Run," she said and bolted for the garage with Heather's shoebox.

I followed.

"I did something weird," James said, grimacing.

I froze. "That's. Huh. Do you?" I composed my thoughts. "James, what's normal to you is out-of-this-world bugfuck crazy for the rest of us. I'm talking right out there orbiting Nepmoon. I'm scared to hear more."

"I texted Meg."

I chuckled. I'd had the same impulse, but I held back. Meg was rarely *openly* hostile to me, but if anything was going to bring the claws out, it would be me saying the wrong thing about her snub.

"What did she say?"

"She didn't respond. Why would she? I ghosted her in June."

"I did it in May," I said. "I couldn't listen to her any longer."

"Samesies. Blythe triggers my gag reflex the same way Meg does, but at least she's still fun sometimes. Meg is walking sad trombone sound, you know? *Womp-womp*." She pulled her lips down in an exaggerated frown. "And now it's a double *womp-womp*. *Womp-womp womp-womp*, if you will."

"You're enjoying making that sound, aren't you?"

"*Womp-womp.*"

There had been a dark little thought haunting my brain ever since the invitations arrived and I heard how everyone talked about Meg.

Were they thinking the same thing about me? And when it became official that I wasn't going to be spending Christmas with Annie Wood, would they joke about me the same way they did Meg?

"Do you think this whole Meg thing feels a little ominous?" I asked.

"How do you mean?" James asked. She found a pair of pink-lensed sunglasses buried inside Heather's shoebox and slid them on my face. I pushed them up on my head.

"It's dark that the girl whose only 'thing' is that she's 'that girl who obsesses over being invited to the Senior Scavenge' didn't get an invitation."

"I wouldn't say dark." She squinted in the sun. I offered her the glasses, but she threw them back in the box. "Where are you going with this, and how are you going to tie it back to you and the Annie Wood workshop?"

My jaw dropped. "Do you think I'm just like Meg?"

"Dude, your ability to make *everything* about you and DSU is astounding. You should be part of a study."

"Like Meg?" There was desperation in my voice. I heard it, hated it, but couldn't turn it off. "I'm just as bad as her, aren't I? You hate hearing me spin out. Now that Meg's whole thing is over, I'm next, and instead of being there to pick up the pieces, you'll be behind my back talking shit to Claire about how you knew all along that I sucked, and you were being nice to humor me."

"Finished?" she asked when I paused to catch my breath.

I nodded.

"First of all," she said. "I would never gossip about you with Claire. I would gossip about you with River. And you know if River's involved, she'll want Gracie's input too, *so*."

I didn't crack a smile.

"You aren't the same as Meg," she continued. "Do you remember freshman year how much we all used to worship the older girls, and they always made it seem like getting picked for the Scavenge was the highest honor and it meant you were as cool and awesome and pretty as they were?"

"Oh ew," I said, cringing uncontrollably at my past self.

"And then you got to know those girls, and got older, and realized that everyone is bullshit and the Scavenge is just a dumb game?"

"A fun one. Or it's supposed to be."

"Meg never grew out of that, and she spent years trying to achieve a frivolous short-term goal. That ain't you. You're freaked out about your future, not some fleeting high school thing. You're like that dude in *Whiplash* and Annie Wood is your J. Jonah Jameson. You wanna blow right past this and into her program. You're done. You've been extra whiny lately, but it's understandable. And I wouldn't be secretly happy if you didn't get into DSU. Only a sociopath would think that way."

She said so many lovely words, but I only heard the bit about me not getting into DSU.

"Oh God," I said. Panic ran through my veins. "You're prepping me for a soft landing. I'm kidding myself. I need to pick a backup school."

James dropped the shoebox on the ground, threw back her head, and screamed at the sun.

"Everything okay?" Heather yelled from the front window

"Yes!" James and I yelled in unison.

We waited a beat for her to go away, then continued.

"It's easy for you to act like I'm overreacting," I said. "Your aunt is an admissions counselor at A&M. You have been given the gift of nepotism."

James maintained perfect grades in all the classes she cared about, and got at least *B*s in everything else. She was president and founder of the Pritchett PeaCODES, an organization that taught elementary school kids how to code. She was an abysmal test taker, and spent more time doing test prep for the ACT test than anyone I knew, and A&M didn't even require it. It was an insult to imply that James hadn't worked hard, and we both knew it.

"I'm sorry," I said. "I'm just tired."

She relaxed her face. She wasn't mad. She was disappointed.

"Dude, I'm going to tell you the cold, hard truth, and you will know I'm serious because I am not going to make a single joke. You think you're a failure at life if you don't get into a violin workshop. Violet, it's not tied to your college acceptance. It's a fast pass, nothing more. Only ten percent of DSU's freshman class gets into Annie Wood's workshop. You told me that yourself. That means *ninety* percent of the freshman class will not get in. It's only the best of the best."

"Am I not the best of the best?"

She grunted in frustration. "Stop only hearing the bad parts!"

"If I'm not good enough to get into a workshop, how am I good enough to get into the school? What if I'm not even in the ninety percent?"

"I am positive that if you don't get into the workshop, you are part of the ninety percent. I may not commit to saying you're the best of the best out loud, but I have no problem admitting you're *at least* the best. Now can we please move on and enjoy the rest of our day without talking about Meg or how much you suck?"

I wanted nothing more. "Yes."

She turned to dramatically walk away, but stopped and turned on her heel. "But I really hope you get into the workshop, because I do *not* want to have to listen to you freak out about this until spring when college acceptances start rolling in. I can't, Violet, I won't."

But we both knew she would.

———

When we were done at Jimmy's, James noted that we still had tons of time, and Heather didn't want to return to suburban mom life yet, so we stopped at Waterloo Records to check out the vinyl. She bought James a Billy Joel album Jimmy had recommended, and even though I said no, she got me the *Beetlejuice* soundtrack.

"I saw that movie in theaters," she said.

"Jesus, Mom. How old *are* you?" James howled.

"Someday." Heather shook her head. "Someday you'll be my age and your daughter will ask you about being old. You'll see."

Heather flipped through a stack of used records and gasped.

"What?" I asked.

She pulled out an album and hugged it to her chest.

"Oh, *The Downward Spiral!* I loved this album in high school. I remember my senior year, I had it on cassette, and I listened to it on a loop when I drove to visit your dad at A&M. I had the biggest crush on Trent Reznor."

James tapped out something on her phone and laughed.

"He's a gross old man! He's like, Grandpa's age!"

Heather shook the album at her daughter. "Trent Reznor is *not* Grandpa's age," she said, disgusted at her child's taste in men. "And I had a crush on him when he was young and hot. He's *still* handsome if you ask me."

"I absolutely did not ask you if you thought some puffy old goth was hot," said James. "Violet, did you ask?"

I shielded myself with *Beetlejuice*. "Please exclude me from this narrative."

James whipped out her phone and waved it in my face. "I'm going to text your mom and ask her who she had a crush on and if she still thinks he's hot now," she threatened.

"She already told me," I said. "Bill Clinton."

Heather snorted so hard she choked.

5

Heather needed to pee, so we stopped at a Buc-ee's. She hit the bathroom while James and I got buckets of Dr Pepper Icees. James took a swig and squealed.

"Sugar high or brain freeze?" I asked.

"Por qué no los dos?" she replied.

We paced the aisles, spying on the other patrons.

A short, round, blond woman stood at the checkout with an extra-large gas station nacho plate in her hand and a baby balanced on her hip. The baby reached for the nachos and swiped a handful of electric orange cheese sauce. She shoved her entire hand into her mouth and sucked her fingers clean. The woman didn't flinch.

"Babies can have nacho cheese?" I asked James.

"Well, you see, Little Addison there has the same constitution as a frat boy." She spoke through her nose and used the generic first name she gave all obnoxious children. "Cheese goo, cold pizza, week-old Chinese. Trans fats give her power."

Little Addison gagged, and a cheese shower sprayed down her pink onesie.

"She really *is* a frat boy," I said.

James rolled her eyes and took another hit off her Icee.

"Do you feel weird?" she asked.

I lifted my drink. "I'm not drinking mine until it's paid for because I'm not a criminal."

"No, not the Icee. About tonight. And next week. And the entire year. We almost had a real fight back there, Violet. That never happens. This is the beginning of the end, isn't it? We're seniors, and before you know it we're married to men with beards, and we're wearing yellow polo shirts, peeing every five minutes because the bladder suspensions we got after our hysterectomies left us unable to hold it for more than fifteen minutes."

Her voice got faster and faster until she gasped for air. When she finished, she looked at me, her face blank.

"I thought I was the anxious one," I said, patting her on the back.

"It's the notes we found."

"Heather's? The ones in the shoebox?"

"Yeah. My godmother Leslie wrote them. They haven't seen each other in like eight years. My mom told me they don't talk much anymore either."

"Did they fight?"

"No. They used to talk daily, and then they texted, then they just...*stopped*. Isn't that strange?"

James frowned and cradled her cup like Little Addison's mother cradled her baby. It left a dark green wet spot on her jacket between a PRITCHETT PEACOCKS, CLASS OF 2021 patch and a heart-shaped enamel pin with the phrase DROP DEAD written in the center.

"It won't happen to us," I assured her.

"We say that," she said. "But… What if it does?"

James wanted me to give her a big speech like the one she'd given me, but I didn't have one. I felt as lost as she did. It sucked.

"It won't happen to us," I promised, making up my speech as I went along. "Heather can act sassy about having dial-up in the nineties all she wants, but we have *real* technology. We didn't see each other in person for all of June, but we spent twelve hours a day binge-watching *Gilmore Girls* via FaceTime."

"Those last couple seasons," she said, shaking her head, "wasted a lot of our time."

"Are you okay?" I asked.

"You got to have a dramatic freak-out. I wanted one too." She bit her bottom lip. "We should get beef jerky."

She took her human baby-sized Dr Pepper Icee and bolted for the jerky rack and pulled a few bags off with her free hand. She ripped a bag labeled "Sweet and Spicy" open with her teeth and shoved her face inside. She nipped at the dried meat, but couldn't grab any. I took the bag from her, pulled a strip out, and held it for her to bite. Her eyes were watery, and not from the spicy jerky.

"Please don't cry," I begged. "You cry, I'll cry."

"It's the last first day of school."

"Not today, it's not. Today is party time! We're breaking into a carnival with all our friends. Don't you wonder what it's like when it's dark and empty? What if maybe… *It's haunted?*"

"Everything in Belldam is," she said, jerky gluing her teeth together. "Gracie told me all about it."

"So expect evil clowns," I said.

"A psycho killer security guard," she said, grinning. "Or the Eaton family ghosts, pissed we're getting into the carnival for free."

"Lolly will probably chicken out," I said.

"We'll drag her ass in and feed her fried Coke."

"Do you think they have fried Coke just lying around, ready to eat?"

"We'll find the batter and fry it ourselves!"

"We don't know how to deep fry food!"

James held out the bag and offered me some jerky. I declined.

"I wouldn't call fried Coke food," I said. "I wouldn't call the jerky you're shoving into your gaping maw food either."

"Claire is going to dump Chelle," James said, changing the subject at lightning speed. "She's taking her to see a movie at the Brunson Theater, and then she's setting up a picnic at Roseland Park. She's going to give her the chop while they feed the ducks."

I gasped. Claire and Chelle had been together since homecoming our sophomore year. Our principal was an ass about two girls going to the dance together, so instead they ditched it and saw *Empire Records* at the Brunson and made out in the park after.

"Did she tell you that?" I asked.

"Mila did. Isn't it gross she's re-creating their first date?"

"I guess. Why is she doing it?"

"Claire wants to be single for senior year. All those away games."

I gasped and clutched imaginary pearls. "Such a slut."

An older woman with a stiff bouffant walked past, frowning at my language. I smiled sweetly and whispered to James: "We should watch *Hairspray* tomorrow."

"Oh man, we should do both *High School Musical* and *Hairspray*. Zefron double feature!"

I gasped. "*Hairspray*! I never told you! Remember how they forced Gracie to be Tracy Turnblad in the school musical because she was the only big girl who could sing?"

"Yeah."

"Did you know the play traumatized her so badly she went to fat camp the next summer?"

James laughed. "I did *not*. That's how she lost all the weight?"

"Mmmhmm. She told me on the trip to Corpus. You should've come."

"I'd sooner die than be so close to a major body of water. Besides, I had a lovely time in Michigan at my great-aunt's funeral that weekend instead."

Across the store, Heather emerged from the bathroom. She strained on her tiptoes, surveying the store for us. I hit James's shoulder and pointed at her mother.

"It's time, huh?" James asked. She turned to walk away.

I stopped her.

"This is going to be awesome!" I assured her. "Don't waste tonight worrying about tomorrow. Look, I'm smiling!" I stuck my fingers in my mouth and stretched the skin wide. "If Mail Girl can smile, so can you."

"You have gas station hands," she said, hitting me back.

"I'm building immunities," I said, shrugging.

James sucked on her Icee, loud and wet.

"Set our hearts in tune with thee, Violet," she said, speaking our school song's first line.

"Let wisdom be our light, James," I replied with the second line.

"Let my ass be our light, dude."

James lifted her leg and farted at me.

The stiff-haired old lady gasped in the next aisle.

I almost peed my pants laughing.

Heather paid for our snacks.

The van hit the road.

Back in Belldam, a man named Ted reported to work.

6

Ted told people he took his job at the Poison Apple Carnival to get health insurance. This was a lie. Though nerve damage kept him from feeling his left upper thigh, and some semi-regular chest pains scared him, he refused to see a doctor. If you never find out you're sick, you can't die... *right?*

In truth, he became a security guard for Eaton Industries because he was lazy. He worked for their resort hotel for years, then when he got too old to eject rowdy or nonpaying guests, they transferred him to the carnival. Eight hours a night, in a squishy office chair, a stack of true crime novels by his side. A dream job for a man with no interest in exerting any energy at work.

The dead girl on the candy apple statue ruined his night. Captain Bell came with an unmarked ambulance, and the driver hauled her off not too long after John discovered the body. Ted was mildly creeped out, but he was fine until he received a phone call from his boss's boss.

"I want you walking the grounds every half hour," Rynn told him. "I want every security camera checked to make sure they're functioning properly. I want you to work overtime, because I need a guard there round the clock."

Ted protested. If they wanted someone there twenty-four-seven, they could hire a third guard. Maybe even a fourth, in case someone got sick.

"We've never had an overnight guard, and we're closed for two more weeks for maintenance. The girl at your pool didn't hire anyone to set up the Halloween overlay, so John's been stringing up orange lights everywhere. She had *me* interview scare actors, and now you're asking me to work twelve-hour shifts? Did John agree to this?"

"John is taking a few days off. Personal reasons. I'm coordinating with the hotel's director of security. We'll have a replacement to relieve you in the morning."

"This is bullshit."

"It's that or lose your job," she said curtly. He violently waved his middle finger in the air. It made him feel better, even though she couldn't see it.

"Do they know who killed the girl?" Ted asked.

"Are you accepting the terms? You work twelve hours, time-and-a-half, and patrol the grounds instead of sitting on your butt in the security booth."

"Yes, ma'am." He intended to look for a new job the next day. He couldn't afford to quit without a backup.

"Captain Bell told me it was a car accident," she said. "The girl flew through her windshield and impaled herself on the apple."

"John said she had ride tickets stuffed in her mouth."

"Captain Bell's private doctor said John was in shock."

"But I saw the girl's car before they towed it. How did she go through the windshield if it was intact?"

Rynn cleared her throat. "Perhaps you were in shock as well. Captain Bell himself called me and told me the car was totaled. Do you believe what you saw when you were under a lot of stress, or is Captain Bell mistaken? Is he lying? We can call him right now. He has a right to face his accuser. What do you think he'll say?"

Ted had no desire to find out. People who had too many opinions about Belldam PD, and things never ended well for them. Ted just wanted peace, so he promised Rynn he would stay at the carnival until six a.m., when John's replacement would relieve him.

She thanked him and hung up.

He called her a four-letter word and went to patrol the carnival, wondering the whole time: If the girl died in a car accident, why were they beefing up security?

———

The late August heat made him lazier than usual.

Before the "car accident," they expected him to walk the perimeter twice a night, several miles on foot made difficult by his numb leg. No one ever supervised him, no one really cared. Some nights, when the air was so hot it was like inhaling fire, he didn't bother to leave his security booth at all.

He did his first lap, then went back to the booth to rest for round two.

Helen at the library suggested he read up on the Texas Killing Fields. Thirty young women murdered and left by I-45 down south. Ted didn't have a violent bone in his body. He would never understand how one person could snuff the light out of another person's eyes.

His ex-wife got him into true crime. She read the books because she wanted to be prepared in case someone tried to kill her; he read them to feel closer to her. It didn't make any difference: She left one day in 2002 and never looked back.

Half an hour into his shift, Ted got bored and put his book down. He ripped three pages off the True Crime daily trivia calendar John left on their desk.

He paused on Friday, August 28.

MATCH THE REAL-LIFE KILLER WITH
THE ACTORS WHO PLAYED THEM

1. Zac Efron   A. Aileen Wuornos
2. Jeremy Renner   B. Ted Bundy
3. Gary Oldman   C. Jeffrey Dahmer
4. Charlize Theron   D. Lee Harvey Oswald

He scratched lines pairing 1 with B, 2 with C, and so on. Though he'd finished the quiz, he didn't rip the page off to reveal that day's challenge. He left Friday's page up because he wanted John to know he had brains in his head, even if it was for useless murder trivia.

Ted returned to his book. When he got to the middle, he found ten glossy pages of crime scene photos, including gory, full-body shots of human remains. He flipped past those as quickly as possible.

When the door behind him opened, he was too engrossed in his book to notice the squeak. He didn't hear the soft footsteps or sense the figure creeping slowly behind him. It wasn't until he felt a tap on his shoulder that he realized he wasn't alone.

He gasped in surprise and twisted around in his chair.

A figure in a dark hoodie, with black gloves and big dark sunglasses over its eyes, stood behind him. The person smacked their lips and blew him a kiss. He took a deep breath to yell at them and inhaled a mouthful of bitter powder.

He was out cold, slumped over his desk before he even knew what hit him.

———

Ted awoke later, dizzy from the drugs. They were powerful enough to make Ted feel like he was in an ocean, caught in the tide, being pulled out to sea. He blinked and tried to shake it off. When the world didn't stop spinning, it was clear the motion was not caused by drugs in his head, but instead because his body was bound and tightly anchored into a seat on the Crazy Cauldrons.

A pair of taut wires crisscrossed the ride at exactly the height of Ted's Adam's apple. The cauldron whirled and flew toward the wire. Ted ducked just in time for the wire to slice off a quarter inch of his hair.

"Stop the ride!" he yelled, furious at someone for playing a prank they didn't understand was dangerous. "Y'all are gonna get me killed!"

The ride shifted. Ted's cauldron spun counterclockwise, jerked, and spun in the opposite direction. He immediately understood that the only way to avoid the wires was to shrug his shoulders and tilt his head, an act made almost impossible by the way his hands were tied behind his back. He could crouch for ten, maybe fifteen seconds before he got tired and had to stretch his neck.

A wire got dangerously close, but Ted hunched over at the last second.

Nearby, Ted's captor gently plucked a wire. It sliced through his glove, but didn't break the skin. He cranked the handle on the reel to tighten it just a hair more.

Ted flew under the wire again, dodged the wire, then flew around again and nicked his cheek. Blood dribbled into his eye, tickling his lashes. He shook his head and rubbed his shoulder against his eye, and in that split second, he passed under the wire and lost his left ear.

Ted screamed. Finally, he understood. His captor wasn't playing a prank that *might* end in death. He'd been tied to the cauldron because it *would*.

"You got away with it!" he yelled. The coffee in his stomach sloshed around. Acid burned his throat. "Cops said it was an accident. They might not do it a second time!"

Ted's captor turned the crank until it clacked and wouldn't rotate any further.

Ted heard the crank. He instinctively looked up to check the source at exactly the wrong second. The freshly tightened wire slipped through his neck, cleanly decapitating him.

His head fell back, bounced along the ride, and popped onto the sidewalk. His body remained in the cauldron, whirling and twirling, shooting blood through the air.

Ted's killer grabbed his head by the hair, then skipped through the spray like a child playing in a sprinkler on a hot summer day.

7

VIOLET

Where are we eating?

RIVER

I don't care as long as they have tasty desserts. I want to go into a sugar coma.

GRACIE

My mom has diabetes.

RIVER

Oh, whatever. Why can't we go to the Crave Inn? 25 kinds of pie...

BLYTHE

No. We're going there tomorrow. Variety is the spice.

"I seriously don't know why she's fighting this," James said, staring at her phone. "We always end up at the Crave Inn. Their menu is two miles long and it's cheap. Why can't Blythe stop acting like Belldam is some great culinary wonderland. There are like three good restaurants. Pick one!"

"Culinary wonderland," Heather said, nodding proudly. "Those ACT prep courses are paying off."

CLAIRE

If you want spice, the Kluckin Chicken has it.

JAMES

I nearly burned my face off at that place. It was awesome.

BLYTHE

Heartburn. Plus, they serve their food in Styrofoam containers. I'll get shit about climate change if I post from there.

GRACIE

Styrofoam is gross. They wouldn't be wrong...

RIVER

Aren't we the wet blanket today, Gracie.

GRACIE

STFU, River.

LOLLY

Indian food? There's a new place called Kurrypinch open over on Genesee.

MILA

Cute name!

JAMES

No way. First, let's ask ourselves if we think a place in Belldam will have good Indian. Second... does anyone really wanna smell Violet's ass all night?

VIOLET

I'm going to murder you, James.

JAMES

Not if I murder you first!

BLYTHE

I'm a no on Indian too. Idk if I can craft a post about Indian food without sounding racist.

CLAIRE

wtf

JAMES

Have you tried...not saying something racist?

BLYTHE

I'm not a racist! I just don't know if there are things out there that might be offensive to Indian people, and I don't wanna mess with it.

JAMES

Have you tried...not posting every meal on social media?

BLYTHE

It's easy content.

JAMES

Fine. What about burgers? Straight up, I'm okay with Whataburger.

BLYTHE

Nooooooooooooooo! It needs to be unique!

CLAIRE

Seafood?

BLYTHE

Posted the catfish dinner from the Monument Inn on Wednesday.

MILA

How about at Sweet Orange?

BLYTHE

I did a vegan challenge last month. Ate at Sweet Orange six times. Don't y'all watch my videos?

CLAIRE

No. Never watch your videos. How about Duvall's?

BLYTHE

Maybe...

JAMES

No! Everything there tastes like brown gravy, even the banana split.

CLAIRE

JFC James. We almost had her.

VIOLET

Blythe, what do you suggest?

BLYTHE

I'm open to anything.

James turned in her seat to face me and lowered her window. She mimed throwing her phone from the car. I laughed and kicked the back of her seat.

"I'm going to strangle Blythe," she said. "You're prepared, right?"

I sighed. "Yeah."

"Why?" Heather asked.

"Group text," James said. "We're all on it. Everyone except Blythe is making suggestions. Blythe is shooting them down."

"She didn't shoot down Duvall's," I said.

"I'm not wrong about the gravy thing. You said yourself that their chopped chicken salad smelled like pot roast!"

"Why don't you go to Clary?" Heather suggested. "Blythe loves it, and she hasn't gone in months."

"How do you know?" I asked.

"I follow her on social media."

"Of course you do," James said, shaking her head. "I hate Clary. I want cheesy potatoes!"

I fired off a text to the group.

VIOLET

> I want cheesy potatoes. Can we please go to the Crave Inn?

BLYTHE

> I LOVE their cheesy potatoes!

I kicked James's seat.

"See?" I said. "Problem solved."

———

Minutes after we got back to James's house, Blythe's white Tesla X silently pulled into her driveway. She leapt from the car and threw her arms around Heather.

"Mrs. Parker, I haven't seen you in *forever!*"

"Please God, call me Heather, sweetie. Mrs. Parker makes me feel older than my daughter's sick burns."

James screamed. "I'm going to go on a goddamn killing spree. I'm going to murder you and anyone else who heard you say that!"

Heather smirked.

"How have you been, Blythe?" she asked.

"Swamped. I have no idea how I'm going to keep up once school starts. I'm filming three times a week, and I already have a full schedule of meetings in LA and New York for fall break."

Heather gave a tight-lipped smile. "I'm sure you can handle it. You always do."

"I know, right?" Blythe said, beaming.

In private, Heather made it clear she didn't like Blythe's online fame. She didn't find it healthy for a kid to be a "brand."

Blythe once offered to help James make some coding tutorials to upload to YouTube. She even offered to appear in them and promote them. Heather flipped out.

"You're not going to put yourself out there in that way," she'd said. "You're a child. I don't want gross old men watching videos of you."

"They're tutorials for girls like me," said James. "Not old men."

"That's what you believe, and I'd love it to be true. It's not reality, though. You don't know who is watching you, or why. You want to do this after you move out, fine. You'll be an adult. Until then, only people you know in real life get to follow your social media, and I get to monitor it how I see fit."

James smacked their kitchen counter. "Just because you grew up scared to meet people online doesn't mean that's how life is now."

Heather sighed and shook her head. "You're a very, very smart girl, James, but you don't have any idea what the real world is like. Even if pervs aren't watching you, it's not healthy. That girl doesn't have a plan. She's lost."

James punched a couch cushion. "She bought a hundred-thousand-dollar car and a beach house in Hawaii!" she squealed.

"That beach house was a rental. Besides, it's not about money. I don't expect you to understand. My answer is no, discussion over."

Ever since then, when anyone mentioned Blythe, Heather looked sort of sad. Whether it was for Blythe or James, I couldn't tell.

Blythe hit a button, and her car's falcon-wing doors rose into the air. James slid into the second row. I sat shotgun. Heather waved and told us to be careful. James rolled down her window.

"In case I die, I love you, Mama! See you tomorrow morning!"

"Love you too, baby!" Heather yelled back. "See you if I don't die!"

Morbid goodbyes were a Parker family tradition. Their family always said they loved each other when they said goodbye in case something bad happened. Heather insisted. "You might not get another chance," she said.

James thought it was corny. I thought it was sweet.

———

More and more, we all questioned why we were still friends with Blythe.

We hadn't hung out in person in a while, not since the weekend after July 4th, when she had a pool party and invited about five million people. She asked Mila and me to come by early. James drove us.

Blythe had the full run of the second floor. She had three bedrooms, a bathroom, and a big living space where she set up a mini movie theater.

One of the bedrooms was, of course, where she slept. The second was a beauty room with overstuffed clothes racks and floor-to-ceiling built-in cabinets for her massive makeup collection. It was roughly half the size of a Sephora and overflowing with all the free junk beauty brands sent her.

The third bedroom was her filming room. Wallpaper from Anthropologie lined three walls—black and white doodled strawberries and peaches on soft mint green. The fourth wall was plain white and cluttered with industrial shelves and hooks to organize her filming equipment. Blythe hired a crew to set up a professional lighting rig in the center of the room, and several microphones hung from the ceiling, just out of frame from her camera.

A vintage cinema lightbox sat on a bookshelf next to the vanity. Blythe changed the message on the lightbox for each video, usually to some weird sentence or funny quote. Previous messages included: "How self-aware can a woman be with a parrot on her shoulder?" and "Lasagna: I'm only in it for the noodle."

When Mila, James, and I arrived for the pool party, Blythe's next door neighbor—who was only twenty-three, but insisted everyone refer to him as Mr. Corman—greeted us at the door and drunkenly ushered us upstairs, where we found Blythe beating her face in her beauty room.

"Ahh!" she screamed. "I need so much help! I don't know what to wear!"

She pointed to a pile of bikinis on the floor.

"Why do you own so many plain red bikinis?" Mila asked. "And why is this old man here?" She edged away from Mr. Corman, who apparently intended to stick around for the teenage bikini fashion show.

Blythe looked past Mila. "Thank you so much for fixing the garbage disposal Mr. Corman! Bye, bye!"

Mr. Corman sipped from the red cup in his hand. "Okay, but I'll be right across the street if you need me. I told Gwen I'd watch out for y'all while she's on her...*staycation*."

Blythe turned redder than the bikinis.

"You should staycation your ass outta here before I call my mom to give you a knuckle sandwich!" snapped James.

"James I don't need you to defend me." Blythe's words were fast, with zero inflection. "Von, get the fuck out of my house or I'm going to throw you down the stairs, drag you into the kitchen, and demonstrate to my friends how well you fixed the disposal. I'll even let you pick which hand I stick down the drain."

Mr. Corman mumbled, *crazy bitch*, under his breath and shuffled away.

Blythe sighed and looked at the bikinis. "They're all different. Why? Should I do another color? Maybe a pattern?"

James slid down the wall to play with her phone, while Mila dug through the pile and sorted the pieces into tops and bottoms. I opened a random drawer. Blythe's impeccably organized nail polish collection was inside. I reached for a white cap, and flipped the bottle over. "Rest in Peach," I read aloud.

Blythe clapped her hands. "That's a fun one! Gimme!" I tossed it to her. She caught it and painted her big toe. "Does peach go with red?" she asked, wiggling her foot.

Mila shrugged. "Does it matter? It's kids from school. Who is looking at your feet?"

"Yeah, but I need pictures. I'll probably throw up a couple video stories too."

James raised her head. "I'm sorry. Blythe, did you say you're posting feet pics online? Is that how you paid for the Tesla?"

Mila snorted. "Sorry to interrupt, but I'm done."

Blythe stared at the neat rows. "I hate all this red. I just got a new one that's blue, pink, and purple tie-dye. That will probably go better with the peach. Does that sound like it works?"

"Yes," James said. "Especially if you put it on your body right now, and we don't have to play dress-up anymore."

Blythe gave James a once-over. "Are you wearing a swimsuit under your stupid army jacket?"

James slipped off her jacket to show a simple black one-piece. Blythe picked up James's jacket and examined the pins and patches. My eyes watered when she breathed; the smell of vodka on her breath could've made her wallpaper peel.

"Oh my God!" Blythe screeched. "The 1970s Astros patch I got you for secret Santa!"

James nodded. "Yup. And the Game Boy Advance pin you got me for my birthday is next to it."

Blythe folded the jacket and placed it on a chair.

"I'm sorry I insulted your dad's jacket," Blythe said playfully. "I know how much it means to you."

"It's fine," said James.

Blythe dug into a drawer and threw even more red swimsuits over her shoulder, creating another Bikini Mountain while destroying Mila's hard work.

"Here it is!" Blythe ran behind a curtain, banged around, then flung the curtain back with her arms above her head. "Ta-da!"

Mila gasped. "Blythe, your body looks incredible!"

"Thank you! So many eggs, so much chicken, so much spinach, so many squats."

"Sounds like work," said James.

"Too much work," I said. "I'll stick to being skinny fat."

Blythe ignored us. She found a white kimono and put it on over the bikini, then she ran to her filming room, returning with a camera and some white poster board.

"Let's go out on the balcony and take some pics," she said, handing the camera to me and the poster board to James.

"What is this?" James asked.

"A fill card," said Blythe. "For lighting. We probably won't need it if the natural light is good. Better to bring it and not need it."

James made a stank face, which Blythe also ignored.

"Mila, Violet, do you want to be in the pictures?"

Mila said sure. I turned her down. I said it was because I'd already slathered myself in greasy sunscreen, but that lie was the latest entry on a long list of excuses I'd cooked up to minimize my appearances on social media, Blythe's in particular. My accounts were private, but that didn't keep her curious fans from trying. And then there were the Mr. Cormans of the world…

We followed Blythe onto her balcony, and I photographed Blythe and Mila while James stood off to the side. Blythe declared the natural lighting good and dismissed James, leaving her with no task.

"I'm not going to follow this bitch around all day playing camera crew," she whispered into my ear when we took a break so Blythe could fix her lipliner.

"No one asked us to," I said, rubbing my scalp. We'd been outside long enough for a fresh sunburn to sear my scalp.

"Not. Yet." Her words were short and sharp.

James lurched toward the door. We'd all been in this situation with Blythe before. I checked the time on my phone and decided we'd be leaving early. I'd rather hang out in a half-full kiddie pool in my backyard than babysit Blythe's drunk ass while listening to James bitch all day.

Luckily Nolan Flynn arrived, and suddenly James was on her best behavior. She had a painful crush on him. Everyone knew but Nolan. He zeroed in on me.

"Hey Violet," he said.

I smiled and waited for him to greet James as well, but she'd disappeared with no warning the second she'd seen him.

"I don't know where she went," I told him.

"Wha…uh…what do you m-mean?"

"James. Don't play dumb." I pulled a James Parker and walked away without saying goodbye.

After a few minutes of searching, I found her hiding in the kitchen behind a pantry door.

"I've never been so embarrassed in my life," she whispered.

"What did you do?" I asked.

"Nothing yet, I just don't want Nolan to be aware of my existence."

"Dude. He's an oily weirdo. No girl in her right mind would give him a second glance."

On cue, Blythe poured herself into the room with Nolan on her arm. She led him to us, her eyes locked on James.

"James built my website for me this summer," Blythe whispered to Nolan.

His face lit up. "You did?" he asked James.

James stared at him blankly, saying nothing. We all leaned in, waiting for her to answer.

Finally, she breathed a soft, "Yes."

"You founded PeaCODES, right?" Nolan asked.

James nodded.

"Can anyone join?" he asked.

James blinked.

I wanted to shove my arm up her butt, turn her into a puppet, and answer his incredibly basic questions for her. Blythe sensed my incoming intervention and pulled me away. James watched us leave, panic in her eyes.

"I invited him for her," she told me. "I saw her quietly freak out around him at Hannah Tyson's graduation party last May, and I knew. His dad owns the company that does our landscaping. Nolan works for him in the summer. He's mowed my lawn for months, and when I see him, I tell him about my amazing friend James."

"She's going to kill you," I said.

"She's going to make me a bridesmaid," Blythe slurred, eyes half open.

"How much have you had to drink?" I asked.

"Not enough," she laughed. She pulled me close and made me smile for a selfie. She examined the photo and tapped the screen. "Your scalp is bloodred. Let's go find you a cute hat before you burst into flames."

That day was a perfect illustration of who Blythe had become. Half the time, she was only concerned about her next post, but then the old Blythe would shine through—the one who forced us to wear sunscreen so we didn't get wrinkles, and who had no shame in serving up a guy on a platter for one of her less-experienced friends. Those glimpses of Old Blythe almost made up for her constant need to convert every moment of her life into content.

If you could get past the photo shoots, that is.

————

To my surprise, photo shoots weren't going to be an issue at the Senior Scavenge.

"I'm confiscating phones tonight," Blythe announced when we reached our table at the restaurant. The hostess placed lemon water next to our plates. Blythe took a dramatic sip. "I'll be locking them in my glove compartment."

"Including *your* phone?" asked Gracie.

Blythe nodded.

Mila pretended to fall off her chair. "I'm sorry, did Blythe Lennon, makeup guru, comedienne, influencer, internet-goddess-queen say she's leaving her phone in the car?"

Blythe dipped her fingers in her water and flicked them at Mila. "Bitch, don't. I'm capable of having fun without documenting it. I need to get a good chick pic first. I have a great joke about chicken breast I want to use for the caption."

"That's our girl!" laughed James.

River elbowed Claire. "Can you let me out? My sister's over there with Bamma and her parents. I wanna go ask her why she is wearing my third-favorite blue dress."

"Tell Riley hi," James said.

"Will do." River stomped off to lay down the law.

I didn't bother with a menu. I wanted cheese fries.

While the others decided their orders, I scanned the room. One of the waitresses seemed particularly stressed. Little identical twin boys crawled around under their table as she tried to take their order. They each had a red balloon and snarled like monsters.

"Please stop playing Pennywise and sit in your seats," begged their mother. Mom looked like she wanted to sink into the floor. Dad looked like he wanted to storm out and leave them. The waitress looked like she wanted to cry. She twisted her head to the side, rubbing her temples.

I gasped when I recognized her.

"Isn't that Emma Tucker?" I whispered to the group. "Y'all, do not turn around."

Blythe, unable to resist, turned her front-facing camera on and lifted it to sneak a covert peek.

"It totally is," she said.

Mila's eyes widened. "Didn't she go to Harvard last year?"

"Yeah," said James. "I got food poisoning at her going-away party. The chicken salad buffet was incredible, but I got so sick Violet had to drive me home."

"If it was bad enough to let Violet drive, you must've been *decimated*," Blythe said.

I kicked Blythe under the table. James grinned.

Then, as if she could sense us watching, Emma's head snapped in our direction. She closed her eyes for a second, took a breath, and walked over.

"Hey, guys! Long time no see!" she said, flashing a strained smile.

Mila jumped up and gave Emma a tight hug. "What are you doing in town?" she asked.

"Working to save money for when I go back to school," Emma said, her eyes fixed on the salt and pepper shakers.

"You're at Harvard, right?" asked James.

"Mmmhmm. It's great."

"When do you go back?" I asked. It surprised me to see her in Belldam so late in the summer. Most college kids were back in their dorms by the end of August.

"A week or so," Emma said. "Hey, I'm so sorry. We're super busy tonight. What can I get you guys?"

We sat in awkward silence while Emma stood frozen with her pad and paper. James shot me a look. Emma's story didn't add up, and we both knew it.

"I'll go first," said Mila. "Can I please have the chicken sandwich with waffle fries and instead of a side salad a fruit cup? And a lemonade, please."

"You got it," said Emma, scribbling on her pad.

Mila gave her a little salute and switched her attention to her phone.

"Cheese fries and a lemon bar please," I said.

"What's the tortilla thing with the Parmesan garlic crust?" asked James.

Emma craned her neck to check James's menu. She pointed her pen at an item. "Vampire quesadilla?"

James smiled. "I'd like the quesadilla and a Shirley Temple."

"Turkey chili and another water, please," said Claire.

"Chili in August?" River asked, gagging.

"Protein," said Claire.

River ordered for Gracie and herself. "Two grilled cheese sandwiches, and two Cokes, please."

"What kind of Coke?" Emma asked.

"Sprite for me. Gracie, you want root beer?"

Gracie nodded.

Lolly got a big salad and a Neapolitan milkshake.

All heads turned to Blythe.

"Okay, this might be strange, bear with me." We fought back groans as she tapped the menu. "I want the fried chicken breast, but I want the crunchiest, brownest, most unappetizing fried chicken you have. If you can, have the cook leave all the grease on it when it comes out of the fryer. I'd like french fries, but I'd like them mushy and covered in black pepper. I'd also like creamed corn. Is that okay? Oh, and a slice of zebra cheesecake. If possible, can it come out at the same time? Please?"

Emma blinked. "Um, I'll see what I can do. Does anyone want anything else?"

We told her we were good. Emma left to explain to the kitchen that she had a lunatic customer demanding placation.

"Are you for real?" asked James.

"What?" Blythe asked. "I'm going to claim it came from a snooty French bistro. It's *funny*." She shrugged and dug around in her bag. "I'm going to eat all the food, leave a huge tip, and I'm not saying the restaurant's real name."

I wondered whether or not a big tip made it worth the headache.

"What you got there, Blythe?" Claire asked.

"*Apple juice*. Want some?" Blythe held up a star shaped flask.

James pushed her glass toward Blythe. "If by 'apple juice' you mean 'liquor,' then I would like some please." Blythe poured Pine-Sol-scented alcohol into James's glass until the lemon water turned the faintest shade of brown.

Blythe wagged the flask at Claire. She gulped directly from the bottle.

"I want some when my Sprite comes," River said.

"Noted," Blythe said as Claire returned the flask. She held it out to me.

"It smells like floor cleaner." I only liked drinking fruity drinks, preferably frozen ones where you didn't know how much you'd drunk until it was too late.

"Bleh." Blythe shoved the flask back in her bag.

Mila slapped the table. "Y'all! Emma acted all weird, so I texted Jaden Peters."

James gulped some water. "Her ex who broke up with her for the middle-aged Forrest High tennis coach?" she asked. "He seems like a reliable narrator."

"Yeah. Anyway. He said Harvard kicked Emma out. She stopped going to classes after February."

"Why would you just stop going to class?" I asked, stunned. If I managed to get into DSU, I'd do anything I could to stay.

"She had a nervous breakdown or something. The stress got to her. She's taking a year off, and she's applying to local schools after."

Emma swung past the table, silently refilled our water glasses, and avoided all eye contact. I held my breath, praying she hadn't overheard us gossiping about her.

"That was *close*," Mila said.

"Too close," Claire agreed.

Lolly's phone chimed. Her mom's face filled the screen. She excused herself and climbed over River and Grace to run outside, and answer the call.

"Let's change the subject," I said.

"Should we talk about the elephant in the room now that Lolly's outside?" Mila asked.

"What elephant?" River asked.

"Meg," Blythe whispered.

River's jaw dropped. "It's not nice to call people fat, Blythe."

"I wasn't!" Blythe screeched.

"I will," said Claire. "She should've spent more time working on her high kicks and less time eating Taco Bell and being a general asshole."

"What do you think she's gonna do now that she's lost her favorite hobby?" Asked Mila.

"What hobby?" I asked.

"Shit talking us to make us look bad so she can score one of these." Mila pulled her postcard from her bag and slapped it on the table. "Do you know how happy I was to see Lolly tonight? We could've gotten stuck with a two-faced, lying sack of shit, but instead we got sweet Lil' Ol' Lolly… Lol. *She* never spread lies about me having a pregnancy scare."

"Meg told people I committed vehicular homicide after I hit the fence outside Budd's Barbecue," said Blythe. She'd twisted upper torso into her classic selfie pose: big smile, head tilted, neck straight, chin up, but also down. She took a photo, then slightly shifted her head to take another. "It was a speck of red paint, not blood! If I was gonna kill someone, I'd make a *way* bigger mess."

Claire flared her nostrils and demanded everyone scoot out of her way so she could go to the bathroom. She shot me a funny look that compelled me to follow her.

I found her behind the mint green bathroom door, gripping a sink.

"Are you okay?" I asked.

"I hoped we might go all night without mentioning Meg," she said, baring her teeth in the mirror. "You have no idea how happy

I am she's not here." Claire and Meg hadn't gotten along in awhile, but neither ever elaborated on why. I figured Meg ran her mouth and Claire shut it down, because I couldn't imagine what else would've happened.

"She threatened to tell Chelle that I cheated on her at the Pritchett/ Forrest girls' basketball game. I didn't—pinky swearsies—I just showed a Forrest girl the secret bathroom by the Peacockettes' dance hall. Meg followed us and freaked out. Took pictures and everything."

"Pictures?" I asked.

"We were washing our hands and sharing a sink. Meg acted like I had her bent over the paper towel dispenser. I yelled, and she filmed me. I snapped, and went into a rage state and came to as I was tearing the Peacockettes' handmade tradition quilt in half."

"With your bare hands?" I asked, marveling at her dexterity.

"I was *pissed.* That's not the worst thing I did. I shoved Meg in a locker. Her hair got stuck in the door and a whole handful got ripped out when she tried to free herself. It was all bloody. The roots were still attached."

Claire didn't have an ounce of remorse. She sounded *proud* about the roots.

"Why didn't Meg have you arrested?" I asked. Ripping out hand-fuls of bloody hair sounded like assault to me.

"I called Coach Walker while Meg was in the locker. She and Ms. Holden-Jones came and took care of it. They threatened to suspend her for filming in a bathroom, told her spreading rumors counted as bullying. Meg actually apologized to me. After that, she talked shit about everybody else, but not me. Never again."

Even though I knew better, I asked if Meg ever said anything about me.

Touch the hot stove, Violet.

"You wanna see? I kept receipts." She waggled her phone at me and showed me screenshots she'd taken years ago. "She called you the Makeout Queen of Pritchett High."

> **MEG**
>
> I'm at Kylie's. Violet and Blythe just stumbled off to the bathroom together. Think they're in the tub again?

My face burned. Fuck the Scavenge, I wanted to spend my night skinning Meg alive.

"The tub was dry and we were fully clothed!" I insisted. "Did she tell people I had sex with Blythe?"

"Keep reading," Claire said.

> **CLAIRE**
>
> Stop starting shit. Violet and Blythe are not fucking in Kylie's guest bath.

> **MEG**
>
> Duh. Violet is too lame to be a slut.

When I read that, Claire's blackout story became way more believable.

"If I wanted to be a slut," I told Claire. "I could be a slut! She has a huge crush on Evan Breck. Maybe I'll call Evan right now, invite him to the Scavenge, and be a slut all over him in the Mirror Maze so I can take pics from all angles and send them to her!"

I had no clue what I was talking about. Other people's genitals scared me. There were too many expectations. But Meg didn't know that, and I didn't think anything about her genitals one way or the other, so it was none of her business.

"If you wanna skip the Scavenge and drown Meg in a bathtub, I'll drive."

Okay.

"No," I said. "I don't want her dead. I want to think about how she has to sit at home knowing we'll be having a blast at the carnival tonight. Then while we're eating pecan pancakes in our I Survived The Senior Scavenge 2020 T-shirts, she'll be crying her eyes out. *Alone.*"

"Meg deserved everything she got, and then some. She almost cost me the love of my life! She had to pay!"

I smiled. "James told me you're dumping Chelle."

"Goddamn it."

"The speech was very impressive, right up until the love of your life stuff."

"I knew I was laying it on thick, but I hate gossipy bitches like her, and I know you hate it too." She poked me in the ribs. "Word of advice, if you don't want people to know you like to wander off and drunkenly kiss randoms, don't be so obvious about it. Blythe, Alberto, Declan, Gavin, Paisley…*James.*"

I nodded along with every name until the last one.

"How did you know about that?" I asked.

Claire cackled. "You just told me! I knew it! Y'all aren't even slick about it."

I didn't feel the need to explain myself. The awkward conversation James and I had where we agreed it should never happen again was bad enough.

"I don't like James," I said, *mostly* telling the truth. "James doesn't like girls. James likes Nolan Flynn. Nolan Flynn likes James. I'm not involved."

"Violet, do me a favor, okay?"

"*What?*"

"When you eventually head to therapy to unpack all this," she said, waving her hands in my direction. "Please call me. I hate gossip, but I love firsthand drama, and this shit is my favorite flavor."

Back at the table, our postcards were laid out in a neat row. James's dunk tank and my Ferris wheel lay side by side next to a creepy palm-reader-robot-puppet-thing and a plaster clown head with a gaping mouth.

"We're figuring out the riddles," Mila told us.

I picked up Mila's card—the clown—and flipped it over. Her poem read:

Here in Texas, we like guns
Shooting evil clowns is so much fun.
No bullets for this guy, only a squirt
Look under his chin, but above the dirt.

"What's under the clown's chin?" I asked.

Mila took her card from me and put it back in her purse. "You squirt water into his mouth, and it fills a balloon stuck under his chin. I think I need to get a balloon."

"Makes sense," said James.

"I have to get one of those generic palm reading cards from the mannequin," said Blythe, clearing her throat. "Madame Lavona can't turn her head, she's got those blank eyes, like the walking dead. She might be creepy, held together with twine. Still, she can answer, how long's your lifeline?"

"Kinda dark," said James. "*Awesome.*"

"Delilah has a dark sense of humor," Blythe said, shivering. "I hate Madame Lavona. The song and the way her whole body judders back and forth, then her eyes roll back in her head while the card prints. Then it's like, 'Here's your fortune: Beware of women dressed in red!' What I really need is for a psychic to tell me why my latest video is getting half my usual view count. *Ugh.*"

"Perhaps no one wanted to watch you walk around on your knees for half an hour?" James suggested.

"I wanted to see the world through the eyes of a child! I'm aware it wasn't the best concept. I half-assed that video because I'm burnt out, and it was quick to film." Her voice was shaky, and I didn't want James to make her cry.

"Maybe take a week off?" I suggested.

"If I take a week off, the algorithm shifts, and my views drop! Then I have to work twice as hard to catch up, so that's twice as much time spent brainstorming content! I can only do so many 'Eat my makeup' videos before people unfollow me! Sometimes I'd rather be dead than have to worry about thumbnail A/B testing! Just slit my throat and put me out of my misery already!"

"You've heard of first world problems? You've got *digital* world problems," James said, patting Blythe's hand. "No one is forcing you to live your whole life online."

River raised her hand. "James is right. And you of all people should be more selective about what you post, especially after Nemo-gate."

I had no idea what Nemo-gate was. I prayed no one would ask, because it sounded like a long and irritating story.

"Once something's on the internet, it's there forever," Gracie sang.

"Forever ever?" James asked. "And ever ever?"

"Forever. Even after you're dead," said Gracie.

Mila gasped. "Oh my God, that's so true! That reminds me of this totally messed-up thing. My cousin got bit by a bug on a camping trip and died. Her old Facebook page is a memorial. My aunt posts on there all the time, talking directly to her. It's so sad, and unless Facebook deletes it, it'll be there until the end of time. The worst part is that her profile pic is terrible, but her mom won't change it. Forever and ever and ever and ever, there's Brandy, in her ugly hat with a terrible sunburn. It's the worst. Now I always make sure my picture is something I'd want people to see twenty years from now, just in case. You can't escape the internet. Not even in death."

"That's my worst nightmare," said Blythe.

"You could put the phone down," James suggested. "Pay attention in class, graduate, go to college. Nothing is holding you back."

"You don't get it. You make people's eyes light up when you tell them you started a club to teach blind toddlers how to use computers."

"They're not blind, and they're not toddlers. I don't know how many times I have to tell you that."

"My point is, people are proud of you, James. Someday you'll program a robot that helps Lolly end climate change, and I'll still be a loser photographing chicken."

James drummed on the table. She gnawed on her lower lip, a technique she employed to stop herself from running her mouth.

"*Says the girl who gets paid millions to photograph chicken,*" she said, unable to help herself.

"You don't understand." Blythe sighed.

"Yeah I do. It's easy work and you get a ton of attention. If you quit, you have to go be a generic blond sorority girl in Tampa."

"I live in *Florida* in this twisted fantasy?" Blythe wadded her napkin and chucked it in James's face. "Everything is perfectly planned for you. Your dad is gonna have his sister get you into your dream school. My dad only visits to yell at me about my engagement. Making videos was so fun when I first started, and I still had fresh ideas. Now I can't stop, or it's gone, and I won't be able to get it back once it slips away. So forever and ever, I'm trapped on the internet, screaming for a way to make myself heard."

"Sounds like hell," I said, praying James wouldn't chime in.

"*You* understand," Blythe told me, her eyes fixed on James.

Then dinner came, and Blythe spent twenty minutes photographing her food while the rest of us ate on our laps and glared at her. Her brief moment of self-awareness had passed, and now she was back to torturing herself and everyone around her with her poorly planned, unoriginal content creation.

Despite what she said, I didn't understand Blythe at all.

8

Blythe paid the check while I went to pee, and everyone else went outside. When I finished in the bathroom, I passed Emma cleaning our table. The other patrons had cleared out; she was alone in her section of the dining room. After a brief internal argument, I approached her.

"Hey, Emma," I said.

She placed her tray on the table. "Violet. Hey." Her voice was flat, her skin mottled gray, and half circles darkened under her eyes.

I immediately regretted saying hello. If I'd been smart, I'd have mumbled *goodbye* in the same sentence and hauled ass toward the exit.

Since I was a dumbass, I ripped out her throat and spewed word vomit into the wound.

"I heard you left Harvard," I said, my voice high and thin. I smiled, my worst nervous tic.

Emma's shoulders slumped. "Wow. Cool. A little girl who has never left her mommy is about to mock me. *Awesome.* I'll give you credit. At least you have the guts to do it to my face. Nobody can shut up behind my back."

A voice inside my head screamed, *Run!*

"Emma," I said. "Oh God, I didn't mean it that way. I meant it's awful. I've been going through something, and I thought you might understand, and maybe I understand you."

"I've got tables to clean before I can leave this hellhole, Violet. Can you please skip to the part where you explain what you're talking about?"

"I applied for this workshop at my dream school, taught by my idol. If you're invited to Annie's workshop, it's basically a guarantee that you get accepted to the school. But it looks like I'm not getting an acceptance letter, so I'm dealing with that while my friends have all this amazing stuff lining up for them after next year. I'm petrified."

Emma pressed her lips into a straight line. She picked up a fork and threw it on her tray. Then she slammed some glasses on the table. She grabbed a steak knife, got a glint in her eye, and stared right into my soul.

"I wanted to go to Harvard more than anything in my life," Emma said. She stepped forward and held the knife under my chin. "My mom didn't go to college, and she was always ashamed. I wanted to make her proud. I didn't want to go to just any college. I wanted to go to *the* college. I worked my ass off my entire life to get there. And unlike *you*, I did. Early admission even. No one had ever cried as hard as my mom did when I told her. Pure pride."

She gently pressed the knife into my jugular. Nervous laughter jittered inside my body, but I swallowed it before it could burst through.

"It's sharp," I whispered.

Emma ignored me and continued. "I walked around all cocky senior year bragging about Harvard to anyone who would listen. I even mentioned it in my graduation speech. Then I got to Harvard. All the students worked as hard as I did, many harder. Literal geniuses are around every corner. There were some dumb ones too, but they came from *major* money. Intimidation as far as the eye can see. I stopped sleeping to study, and I started having panic attacks. I couldn't handle leaving my bed to go to class. I was so freaked out I'd fail them. Turns out, if you don't go to class, you fail by default. I hid in my dorm room until someone from the school came and dragged me out."

"That's awful," I said. I took a step back.

Emma took a step forward. She kept the knife at my throat.

"My mom won't even look me in the eye now," she said. "I moved into the garage because I can't be around her, and I can't afford to leave. I get to sweat my ass off waiting on people who know about Harvard, and who say stupid, hurtful shit to me about it. Like you, a girl who is comparing my waking nightmare to her not getting into…a workshop? It's not a rejection from the school, right?"

"No," I whispered, hearing how stupid I sounded.

She narrowed her eyes and used the knife to scratch the soft flesh under my chin.

"I-I'm sorry," I stammered.

"You will be," she said, tossing the knife onto the tray. She snatched the bills Blythe left as a tip and counted them. "One day, you'll see. You'll be sorry. Tell Blythe thanks, but $100 isn't enough to deal with her bullshit."

Emma folded the cash and put it in her pocket.

I whispered another apology.

She'd already walked away.

———

River and Gracie got into Gracie's Honda and sped off.

I slid into the front seat of Blythe's Tesla. The others debated who would ride in which car.

"All y'all can fit in the X," Blythe insisted.

"I don't want to leave my car here overnight," Mila said.

"It's open twenty-four hours, and the lot is well lit," Blythe countered. "It's probably safer to leave it here than in the woods by the carnival."

Mila stood firm. "I saw you drinking. I don't want to die tonight."

"I didn't have any myself! Claire, James, and River aren't driving, so I let them pregame. I'm waiting for the carnival."

"Lolly," Mila said, her eyes still on Blythe. "You wanna ride with me?"

"Oh, come on!" Blythe whimpered.

Lolly followed Mila to her car. Claire followed.

James walked behind them and brushed me with her shoulder. "Read your texts," she said as she passed, then followed Lolly and Mila.

I checked my phone.

JAMES

Hit my limit on Blythe. Don't wanna be trapped in an enclosed space with her. Luh u byeeeeeeeeeeeeeeeeeee!

"Seriously, y'all?" asked Blythe as they walked away. She fell to her knees and swayed with her arms over her head. "Fine. If people don't want to ride with me, I won't hold them hostage. Violet and I will go it alone!"

"No crawling on the ground tonight!" Claire yelled at Blythe. She hunched forward with her lower half sticking out of the back seat. She was stuck, and cried to Mila for help.

Blythe climbed into her driver's seat, slammed the door, and lowered her window. "I didn't want their raggedy asses messing up my seats, anyway. I needed some alone time with my buddy Violet, and now I have it."

She threw the car in reverse and shot out of her spot, nearly mowing Lolly down.

I twisted around in my seat to make sure she was okay.

"Geez dude, you didn't have to murder Lolly just because James wanted to ride with Mila."

"Is she mad at me?" Blythe asked.

"Who?" There were *several* people who had the right to be mad at Blythe.

"Who? James. Duh."

"No," I said. This was true. James wasn't mad at Blythe, she was *bored* with her. "She didn't say anything to me." *That* was a lie.

"She's pissed I took the photos at dinner."

I ignored her and ran my fingers along the white leather seat.

"How is this car not filthy?" I asked. "White seats, white steering wheel, white everything. If it were mine, it would be brown by now."

"I don't have a choice."

"Didn't you choose white? Isn't it custom?"

"Not the car. The photos. I don't have a choice. I have to take them. I do three posts a day to keep my engagement up. Meal pics are easy. They generate tons of likes. Selfies get the most, but I don't want my entire online presence to just be pretty photos of myself. With school starting, I can't leave Belldam as much, and I've exhausted all my options around here."

I had zero interest in talking to Blythe about the crushing pressure of internet fame. "You gotta do what you gotta do," I finally said.

"This is why I love you, Violet. You get it. Speaking of getting it, have you heard from DSU?"

"No," I groaned. "Annie Wood hates me, DSU doesn't want me, my life is over."

"You could always be my intern after graduation! We could go to Europe!"

I smiled. It was an offer most people couldn't refuse. To me, Blythe's offer to let me carry her bags sounded like my dreams being flushed down the toilet.

"While a trip to Europe would be awesome," I said. "I'm still *devastated*. I thought this was going to be easy. Play for Annie Wood, make her love me, skip all the will-I-won't-I stress of college admissions."

"Right, but imagine being devastated in *Paris*." She spoke in the same tone as a mother trying to convince her preschooler to eat her vegetables.

"I don't speak French."

She scrunched her nose, threw her head back to laugh, and almost swerved into an oncoming bus.

"Whoa!" I yelled. "No one is going to Paris if we're dead!"

Blythe turned her attention back to the road. "Yikes. Sorry, I almost killed us."

"Speaking of killing people," I said. "Emma tried to slit my throat."

"What?" Blythe laughed. "When?"

"On my way out. I stopped to say goodbye. I mentioned Harvard."

"Wow. You're an asshole!"

"I completely lost my mind!" I screeched. "I wanted to commiserate with her!"

"Yeah…"

"I almost wish she'd done it. I'd rather be dead than end up waiting tables at the Crave Inn next to her."

Blythe rolled to a stop at a red light. The street was empty, save for us, and a black cat strutting across the intersection.

"Well, I don't know about you," she said. "But I plan to live forever, even if I fall on hard times and have to become a waitress." She gasped. "Hey! Let's play the traffic light game!"

We created the traffic light game one night not long after Blythe got her license. Her mother banned her from leaving Belldam without an adult, and she made her boyfriend assign one of his hotel employees to watch Blythe's GPS like a hawk. When we got bored and had no place to go, we would drive around town aimlessly until the battery needed recharging.

One night, Blythe's phone buzzed in her purse. She asked me to check if the text was from her mom. It wasn't. It never was.

CLIFF H

When RU back in LA?

Blythe strained to see. "Is it Mama?"

"Who is Cliff H?" I asked.

She deflated. "Did he text?"

"Yeah."

Blythe sighed. "Cliff Horne."

I dropped the phone. "The guy from that dumb horror movie about the xylophone-bug-skeleton thing? An ad for it snuck into my algorithm. Haunted me for *months*."

"Yes. Same guy. Killed third in *Xylophone Man 2020*."

I waited for her to explain why Cliff would text her. Instead, she turned up the radio and sang along with Dua Lipa. I leaned forward to catch her eye. She ignored me, so I slapped the screen and turned off the radio.

"What?" she asked. "I was getting into the song!"

"Why is there a twenty-five-year-old actor texting you?"

"He's twenty-*seven*. When I was in LA doing press for my Alumma Seltzer sponsorship, my agent took me to dinner. Cliff was one of the other guests. We bonded over our love of the Muppets, and he bought me my first old-fashioned."

"He got you drunk?"

She snorted. "I was already drunk when he met me. I'd just never had an old-fashioned before."

I felt small, like a lost child with no mother in sight. Blythe liked to party at home with boys from Belldam, but I didn't know she went to bars with grown men.

"Does he know how old you are?" I asked.

"I don't care."

"Does your mom know?"

"She doesn't care. Aleister made her a standing reservation at the hotel so she can be available whenever he wants her. It's not even a suite, it's a standard room with two double beds. She has no self-respect. I haven't seen her in a month."

My mother wouldn't leave me alone at night for more than a few hours. She irritated me, but a helicopter mom was better than a neglectful one.

Blythe turned the music back on and shimmied in her seat.

"Are you going to text him back?" I asked.

"Let's find out. If the next light is green, I tell Cliff we can hook up when I'm back in LA. If it's red, I say no."

When we got to the light, it was red.

"Go ahead," she said. "Shoot Cliffy Boy down."

"What do I say?"

"Whatever your sweet lil' heart desires."

I bit my lip and tried to think like Blythe.

> **BLYTHE**
> I'm seventeen.

> **CLIFF**
> So?

> **BLYTHE**
> Aren't I a little mature for you?

I showed the text to Blythe. She approved. Seconds later, Cliff said he was joking anyway, she was too fat for him, and her accent made her sound like a hick. I'd have been devastated if someone said those things to me, but Blythe laughed.

Less than a week later, the cops arrested Cliff for having an intoxicated fourteen-year-old girl in his car. Blythe dodged one *big* bullet thanks to the traffic-light game.

Ever since that night, when we had a dilemma, we asked the traffic lights for an answer.

"Should Violet come to Europe with me after graduation?" she asked the next light. It flipped from green to yellow as we reached the intersection. "Damn. We'll see what the next one says."

She continued driving. As we approached the next light, Blythe asked, "Can I con Violet into coming with me to Europe?"

The second light also turned yellow.

"One more time," she said, accelerating the car. "Violet, you do the honors."

I laughed. "Will me and Blythe go to Europe after graduation?"

She turned left onto Cedar Bayou Road. Ahead, all the shops were closed, all the porch lights were out, all the street lights were dark, and all the traffic lights for miles flashed red.

Blythe pressed the brake, and we sat frozen in the street, staring out at the sea of lights screaming *No!*

"What the hell does this mean?" I asked.

A chilly breeze blew through the cabin. Blythe raised her window. She gripped the wheel, her breathing slow and dry.

"Maybe it means no one is going to Europe," she whispered. "The lights never lie."

9

We didn't want anyone to see our cars in the lot, so we parked in the woods.

Claire, ever the team captain, appointed herself our leader.

"We should break into pairs," she said. "I've got a map on my phone. We'll split up based on which landmarks are in closest proximity."

"*Boo*," said Mila. "I want to get this done so we can get out of here. Let's go alone and meet at the entrance after."

"No," said James. "We need to get it done so we can explore the creepy abandoned carnival."

"What a stupid idea," said Lolly. "We could get caught. We could get arrested. I want to go to college next year, not prison."

"Speaking of prison," Blythe said, her eyes sliding in River's direction. "Whatcha got in your pocket, Miss Ellis?"

River grinned, showing the slight gap between her front teeth. She'd had braces in middle school, then refused to wear her retainer, so they shifted apart. Her parents were pissed. I thought it gave her character.

She reached into her leather crossbody bag and produced a Ziploc filled with squishy orange circus peanut candy.

"Why would we go to prison for those?" asked Claire. "Are we locking people up for sugar abuse now?"

"My cousin from Denver gave these to me when he visited in June. These low-dose babies each have five milligrams of THC in them. I figured they'd make tonight a little more fun."

We looked around to gauge each other's reactions.

Finally, Lolly asked, "Is five milligrams a lot?"

"*Low dose*," River repeated. "For normal people it's fine. For you… Well, I guess they're easy to tear in half."

"No effing way," said Lolly. "Never mind getting caught. Who is driving us home?"

"My brother said he would," River said. "He's got his pickup. We can ride in the back."

I'd been in the back of Reed Ellis's truck before. A girl he graduated with was in a band. They had a show in Austin, and River invited a few people. I went and found myself lying in the back, one hand grasping a spare tire, the other gripping James's leg, as the old Chevy barreled down the highway at 110 miles per hour.

Plus, the band sucked.

I pictured the eight of us, high off our asses, riding in the back of Reed's truck through the streets of Belldam. It was easy to imagine a situation where someone—*probably Blythe*—jumped and tried to fly. I pictured the ugly tree statue "growing" on Belldam Boulevard, and Blythe's body hurtling through the air, impaling herself on its iron branches.

I'd feel safer letting a rabid monkey drive us home.

"Lolly has a point," I said. "Do y'all really want to leave your cars here in the woods?"

"Thank you, Violet," Lolly said. I nodded in solidarity.

Lolly was the ultimate Goody Two-shoes. Awake at six, in bed by ten. She'd had perfect attendance since kindergarten and was the only teenager I'd ever met who watched their fiber intake. Once she got a 94 on an algebra quiz and ugly cried. Despite her "terrible" grades—insert James-style eye roll here—there was no question she would be our valedictorian.

She didn't hang out with us often, but when she did, she served as the voice of reason in precarious situations. Who else would keep James from hacking into a teacher's emails? Or tell Blythe it was a bad idea to post pictures of herself drinking a margarita online? Lolly was the best type of mom friend, always saving us from ourselves.

"*Lame,*" River whined.

James raised her hand. "I'll do it. Gimme." She held out a hand. River beamed and pressed a peanut into her palm. As she opened her mouth to warn James to take it slow, James shoved the whole thing into her mouth.

"Mmmm," said James. "It doesn't have a weedy flavor, but it sure does taste like food dye!"

"I will not be the one cradling you, telling you that you're fine," Lolly warned James. "If you flip out and demand to go to the ER, I won't be the one to talk you down."

James grinned. "Yes, you will, because you love me."

Lolly scowled to hide her smile. "Yeah, yeah."

Gracie took two, ate one and a half, and put the rest in her pocket. Mila told her she would get lint all over it. Gracie pointed out that by the time she was ready to eat it, she'd be so stoned she wouldn't care about lint.

Claire insisted her metabolism was too fast, so she needed five peanuts. Lolly asked what would happen if her coach drug tested her.

"Weirdly she doesn't drug test. The district doesn't require it, and secretly she's scared to find out someone's on steroids."

River held out a peanut for Mila. "Mila wants one, but she's not going to ask."

Mila took the candy and nibbled it daintily. "A lady doesn't ask for illegal substances," she said. "A lady waits to be invited."

"I'll take three," Blythe said, ignoring us. She nodded at River. "The gummies you gave me last time didn't do a thing."

River did a quick headcount. "Violet and Lolly, you're the holdouts."

Lolly grabbed my arm, squeezing the skin until I yelped.

"I need to talk to you alone," she said.

She led me around behind the cars, away from the other girls.

"What's wrong?" I asked.

"Are you gonna do it?" she asked.

Lolly needed a buddy so she could have someone to share the shame when the others made fun of her for not eating the candy.

"I don't have to," I told her, even though I *wanted* to. Anything for Lolly.

Her bottom lip quivered. "I've never done drugs."

This news wasn't a surprise.

"Yes, you have," I said. "When you got your wisdom teeth out. You took Vicodin and sang Selena Gomez to me for an hour. Off-key, I might add."

"That's different."

"I know. It was a joke. Look, you don't have to if you don't want to."

"The last time I took communion, I drank the little wine thimble, tripped on the stairs going back to my pew, and cried because the organ was out of tune and God deserved better."

"I don't know if it's fair to attribute that behavior to a dribble of wine."

"I can't have fun. Ever."

"I don't know if it's fair to call communion 'fun.'"

"It was a metaphor!" she screeched.

"Was it?" I asked, doing my best impression of James.

"Everyone sees me as the mom friend!" she hissed. "That's my point. One slurp of wine and I think I'm going to hell! We're fixing to be seniors. I'm sick of taking care of everybody. My number is under 'Uber' in River's contacts because she knows I'll pick her up anytime, anyplace. I sprained my wrist when I fell at church, and still held Gracie's hair back after she had too many Jell-O shots at Maddy's graduation party. Speaking of parties, I've faked slumber parties so Mila could spend the night with Tyler. And I've spent hours counseling my crazy friend Violet when she has anxiety attacks over DSU and Annie Wood."

"You're comparing my freak-outs to Mila banging her boyfriend in his basement?"

"Answer my question. Are you going to eat a peanut?"

I took her hand. "If you want me to stay sober with you, I will."

She recoiled. "*That's* what you think I want?"

"Yes…"

Lolly clung to a tree and watched our friends. Mila sat on Claire's shoulders. Claire growled and stomped, while Mila screeched and snapped at the others with her finger-claws. The other girls ran screaming as though they were fleeing Godzilla. River crashed into Claire, and Mila went flying but landed on her feet.

I snorted.

"They look so stupid," Lolly said. "I wanna be stupid too. I came to you because you're their *other* mom friend."

She wasn't wrong. River had me saved as "Lyft," for when Lolly was unavailable.

"So you want me to stay sober and babysit you? I can do that, no problem."

Lolly winced. She was going to make me work for it.

"I don't want that. I don't want to ruin your fun. We can act like the Scavenge is no big deal, but come on. We made it, and let's be honest. We're the nerdiest ones. We need to stick together."

Suddenly, I didn't want to help her as much.

"I'm not a nerd," I said. "I'm quiet, and it's mostly because James can't shut the hell up."

"It was a *compliment*. Is being a nerd is inherently bad?"

No matter which path I took to answer that question, the road would still lead to certain death. I chose to turn back.

"I will do whatever you want me to do," I told her. "Eat a peanut, leave a peanut, give a peanut, take a peanut."

"Share one with me. Eating a full dose—even a small one—scares me. We split it in half, and you check in on me tonight and save me if I freak out."

On one hand, Stoner Lolly could've been a ton of fun. On the other, she might freak out and cry because God deserves a better carnival.

"Question," I said. "What's your item for the hunt?"

"A stuffed muscleman prize from the test-your-strength game. Why?"

"If we move fast, you can get the toy before the peanut kicks in. You run for the toy, I'll haul ass for the Ferris wheel, and we can meet at the carousel and wait for everyone else."

Her eyes lit up. "You're gonna do it?"

"Sure," I said, patting her hand. "When we're done, we'll go over to Blythe's house, lie by the pool. There are so many stars out tonight."

Above us, through the trees, tiny twinkling lights dotted the sky. We stood in silence, gazing, while Lolly took a minute to digest her decision.

She exhaled and nodded. "Please don't tell anyone I needed you to talk me into this. They'll make fun of me twice as hard."

"Pinky-swearsies," I said, holding out my finger.

She looped hers around mine. "What?" she laughed.

"I dunno. I stole it from Blythe."

I put my arm around her shoulder and pulled her back to the others.

"River," I said. "Give me a peanut."

River held out the bag. I took one, ate half, and handed the rest to Lolly, who threw it back and swallowed it without chewing.

Everyone else froze for a second, processed what they'd witnessed, and broke out into applause. Lolly's face turned pink.

A crash deep in the woods cut our celebration short.

"What the hell?" whispered Blythe.

"Probably a deer," said Claire.

Blythe motioned toward the sound. "Claire, go check it out."

"Why me?"

"Because you can deadlift an SUV."

"I can't deadlift an SUV!" Claire said. "But thank you so much for thinking I could! I saw Brie Larson push a Jeep online, and I want to do it so bad!"

Blythe gasped. She'd been lifting weights since February as part of an online fitness challenge. Claire was her coach; they got together four days a week to work out.

"You and me pushing Jeeps by Thanksgiving?" Blythe stuck out a hand to seal the deal.

Before Claire could respond, the bushes shook. A man's shadowy figure burst from the leaves.

"What are you girls doing?" he yelled. "You shouldn't be out this late!"

The bushes rustled again, and a huge black dog bolted toward the man. As he stepped into the light, I recognized the shadowy figure was Mr. Moerkerke, a ninth-grade English teacher at Pritchett.

River cocked her head. "Mr. Moerkerke?"

"River?" he asked. He took a headcount. "Mila? *Lolly?*"

My skin crawled. Mr. Moerkerke was a creep. He liked to rub girl's shoulders during class and often offered to tutor the prettiest girls at his house.

"Hello, sir," Lolly said. She stepped forward to create a barrier between us and Mr. Moerkerke. "How are you?"

"Fine," he said. "Walking my dog, Bubbles. Little surprised to see you ladies out here."

"Well, we're doing the Senior Scavenge," Lolly said in the syrupy voice she always used with authority figures. "Incoming senior girls do every year."

"Isn't the scavenger hunt supposed to be at the school?" he asked.

"This year, it's at the carnival," Lolly replied.

Mr. Moerkerke stroked Bubbles's head. Bubbles growled low and long. The ground vibrated beneath my feet.

"You get permission?" he asked.

Lolly smiled. "Of course. The girls who arranged it talked to security. We promised not to damage anything, and we aren't taking anything valuable. As long as we're out before sunrise, we're fine."

It was stunning. Lolly lied so smoothly it sounded like *she* believed it.

But Bubbles didn't buy it. She barked and gnashed her teeth at Lolly.

Mr. Moerkerke grabbed Bubbles by the collar. Bubbles growled. Mr. Moerkerke yanked her back, choking her and making her yelp in pain. James stepped forward, ready to fight Mr. Moerkerke to death for hurting an animal, but Bubbles didn't want her help. She snapped at James, missing her fingers by inches.

"Don't mess with my dog!" Mr. Moerkerke yelled. "She's attack-trained!" He hunched over and put his face a little too close to Lolly's. My muscles tightened; I prepared to intervene. He raised a finger at me.

"There are wicked people in this town," he said. "People who like to hurt little girls. You should've kept this at the school. It's safer there."

Lolly didn't flinch. "It's safe here too. There's a guard on duty. We'll be less than an hour."

"A guard, eh?" Mr. Moerkerke chuckled. "Funny thing. I like to walk Bubbles around the parking lot. The night guard Ted and I are friendly. I stopped by the guard stand earlier to say hello. He wasn't there. When we finished our walk, I swung by again. No Ted. His car is missing. I don't think he's working tonight."

"I'm sure that's not true," said Lolly. "Maybe he ran to get dinner. He's letting us in at midnight. It's only 11:50 now. He'll probably drive up as we reach the gate."

Mr. Moerkerke considered her words. Bubbles pulled at the collar and snapped at James again. Foamy spit formed at the corners of her mouth and flew through the air.

"You should worry less about our scavenger hunt and more about your dog's rabies," James said.

"My dog ain't got rabies. She's anxious because she wants you away from her territory."

"*Ain't got rabies*," Lolly chuckled. "Impressive language for an English teacher."

Mr. Moerkerke turned red. He sputtered a nonsensical reply and poked her in the chest with his index finger. I took her by the shoulders and moved her away.

"You just put your hands on a teenage girl," I said. I stared into his eyes, refusing to blink. "Didn't you get in trouble for that a few years ago? Didn't you tell a freshman she needed to button her top button and then try to do it for her?"

His hand twitched. I prepared for him to release his hound.

"What is your point, Miss Warren?" he asked.

"We have permission to go to the carnival," I said. "You don't have permission to touch us. If you think we won't tell the entire town you're a perv, you're sadly mistaken. What will everyone say when they find out you touched sweet little Lolly Bishop's chest?"

"I barely touched her!" he yelped.

"Doesn't matter," I said. "Do you see who's standing before you? Concertmaster of the orchestra? Head cheerleader? The athletic department's sweetheart? A legit celebrity? We're at the top of the Pritchett High food chain. You're a gross old man with years of nasty rumors following you around. Are they going to believe your scummy ass, or eight sweet little girls?"

Someone behind me gasped. I couldn't tell who.

Mr. Moerkerke's face was purple and sweaty. "Fine," he said. "Have it your way. If you want to wander off to your deaths, be my guest."

"Is that a threat?" I asked.

"*Psh.* As if I'd waste my time threatening you little bitches."

He yanked Bubbles again, this time back toward the bushes.

When he was out of sight, we all started talking at once.

"Did he call us bitches?" I asked.

"Did you two seriously talk to him like that?" asked Mila.

"What if he calls the cops?" asked Blythe. "If we're arrested, my dad can talk to the cops. *If* he answers my call."

"Is there actually a guard?" asked Gracie.

"Is anyone else high?" asked Lolly.

———

Blythe held out a zippered leather clutch with HELLO embossed on the front and GOODBYE on the back. She demanded our phones. There were grumbles, but she insisted.

"If I'm leaving my phone in the car, y'all are too," she told us.

"Let me text my mom first!" Lolly yelled.

James scrambled to get a "before" photo of the carnival as Blythe wagged the bag in her face.

"I'm texting my mom too," I said.

VIOLET

At the carnival. Leaving phone in the car, I'll text
before we leave!

MOM

K. Love you!

"Blythe, give me a second," Gracie said, pushing her away. "I'm checking my messages. I'll give it to you as soon as I'm done!"

I held my phone up. Blythe shuffled toward me. "Thank you, Violet!"

"Thank you, Blythe!" I laughed.

One by one, the phones dropped into the bag. Blythe kept hers in her hand. When the bag was full, she put it on the ground and told us to squeeze together for one last picture. We huddled, arms across shoulders, short girls in the front, tall girls crouching behind us to rest their chins on our shoulders. Mila wrapped her fingers around mine and gave me a squeeze; then she grabbed Claire in a headlock. James tried to keep some personal space, but Blythe wrapped her arm around James's hip and jerked her into the frame.

"Okay everybody!" Blythe yelled. "You know the drill! Head tilted, neck straight, chin up, but also down. I don't want any three-chinned gremlins ruining our pic!"

She raised the phone, snapped the selfie, and examined the photo with a smile. "I don't know what kind of witchcraft this is," she said. "But we got the perfect pic on the first try!"

She locked her phone and dropped it in the bag.

"You aren't going to post the pic?" asked James.

"Nah," Blythe said. "It's for us. The internet doesn't have to see *everything.*"

River snorted. "Since when?"

"Since right now," said Blythe. She opened the Tesla's passenger door and disappeared into the car to hide her HELLO bag under the seat. Her legs flailed in the air. Her stacked heel came within inches of shredding the white leather on the open door. Blythe's commitment to fashion amazed me, but she'd be begging Claire to carry her around the carnival piggyback within the hour.

Knowing Claire, she'd probably do it too.

Blythe popped out of the car with her familiar star-shaped flask in hand. She chugged the contents and tossed it over her shoulder into the car.

"What was that?" asked Lolly.

"Apple juice," said Blythe, rolling her eyes. "What else would it be? Now come on, ladies, let's boogie!"

———

We crossed the dark parking lot and stopped at the front gate, where a golden candy apple stood outside the entrance. A giant had taken a big bite from the top, and a skull smiled back from the peeling skin. A plaque on the apple's concrete platform read:

POISON APPLE CARNIVAL

EST. JULY 24TH, 1973

James, River, and Gracie sat on the platform while Claire loudly debated strategy with herself.

"It makes the most sense to pair off based on location," she said. "The circus peanuts complicate things. Lolly and Violet can't go off by themselves. They're lightweights. They'll wind up dead." She turned to River. "We should've waited on the edibles until after."

"Spilled milk, toots," said River.

Claire stuck her hand in River's face. "Don't interrupt me. Cards! Give me your cards!"

River took a step back and said, "Whatever you say, Cap'n!"

We surrendered our postcards to Claire. She shuffled through the stack and laid them in a grid on the ground.

"Are you sure we shouldn't all go our separate ways and meet at the carousel in twenty?" asked Gracie.

"No!" Claire yelled. "The carnival spans like *miles*. There's no way some of you are going to collect your items and be back in twenty minutes, and I don't want anyone alone when the weed kicks in. Give me a second."

Claire nibbled her lip. My eyes went from her face to the cards, to her squintier face, then back to the cards. Blythe stood next to her, doing the same thing as me. A moment passed. Blythe got testy.

"This shouldn't be so hard!" she said, stumbling forward.

She placed a toe on my card and wavered slightly. I gasped and leaned in to grab her, but she caught herself. I offered my shoulder for support while she used her foot to push the cards around. "River and Gracie, you're together, obviously. The House of Mirrors and Axe Throw are super close. James, you take Lolly over to the dunk tank, then head over to the test-your-strength game."

Lolly would panic if I wasn't with her, and she would lose her ever-loving mind if she were stuck alone and high with James.

I patted Blythe on her back. "I need to be part of that group."

"*Guhh.* That doesn't fit my plan!" She tapped her foot near the cards. "James and Lolly are both at the front of the carnival. Ferris wheel is in the back. Plus, if you go with them, I won't have anyone, because no one else is going in my direction."

I glanced at Lolly. She silently repeated, *Please, please, please*, while wiggling her pinky.

"I want to be with James!" I blurted. It came out way more desperate than I intended.

"This is why people think we're hooking up," James mumbled.

"No! I don't want to be alone…" she trailed off. "Violet," she whispered. "I wanted to hang out with you tonight. I know you're cosmically bound to James, but you're *my* favorite person here."

I sighed. Lolly gasped.

"What's wrong, Lolly?" Mila asked.

Lolly told her nothing, because if she protested, she'd give herself away.

"Let's recap the plan!" Claire said. "Lolly and James, Blythe and Violet, River and Gracie, Mila and me. Sound good?"

"Yup!" James clapped. "Sounds good Claire. Love your plan." She winked at Blythe, who was stewing. "Hey Lolly, babe, you don't have to raise your hand! This isn't school. Why don't you tell us what's up?"

"How are we getting through the gate, jackass?"

"Excellent question," said Claire. "Check the note at the bottom of my invite." She handed it to Lolly.

"The lock on the employee entrance gate is faulty, opens from the inside without a key. Voilà!" Lolly read.

"The employee entrance is over there," Claire said, pointing at a narrow door fifty feet away, near the guard stand. "Mila, I'll give you a boost, then you go open the door and let us in."

Claire knelt and held her hands out for Mila's foot. Gracie stopped them before Claire could launch Mila into the air.

"Uh, have y'all taken a good look at the gate?" she asked, pointing at the bars. "Those points at the top are like tiny swords."

"So, knives?" James asked.

Gracie glared at James, but James wasn't wrong. Each iron bar was topped with an apple-shaped finial, and each apple had a serrated arrowhead for a stem. The bars were only four or five inches apart, and they were slick with dew.

Mila placed one foot on the lowest rung of the gate and gave it a shake. Water droplets rained down.

"It'll be fine," she said. "I can avoid the spikes. Claire, let's do this."

Claire nodded. She grunted and flexed her muscles to lift Mila, who jumped high enough to grab the top bar. She did a pull-up and swung herself onto the top of the gate.

"Ah!" she yelped.

"You okay?" I asked.

"These things are like razors!" she said. "I cut the rubber on my sneaker!"

"Jump down before you cut more than your shoe!" River yelled.

Mila kicked her legs, swung through the air, and stuck the landing.

"If I tried to do that, I'd break my neck," James said in my ear.

"*Me too-oo*," I sang.

Mila tiptoed past the guard stand and gave the door a push. It opened with no resistance.

"No security guard and a broken door," River said. "It's like they're asking people to break in."

"Where *is* the guard?" asked Lolly. Her eyes shifted from left to right. She hadn't forgotten about her potential arrest.

James closed the door behind us. "He's probably jerking off in the House of Horrors or something. Stay in the shadows, and you won't get caught."

"What about security cameras?" I asked.

Every head turned to James. She sighed.

"Let me check," she said.

We found the door to the guard stand unlocked. James and I went inside. There were two flatscreen monitors, each divided into a grid displaying multiple shots from cameras all over the carnival. James sat in a rolling chair, spun around, and attacked the keyboard.

"I'm shutting them off," she said.

"Is there footage of us breaking in?" I asked.

"Probably. It can be erased. There isn't a ton of space on the hard drive. I doubt they save the footage. They won't miss it."

She clacked away, swiveling and fidgeting the whole time.

"Are you okay?" I asked.

"The peanut is hitting me," she said. "Harder than I expected. My skin is all fuzzy inside."

"Isn't it a bit soon? I don't feel anything."

"Maybe my metabolism is faster than yours."

I laughed. "Are you calling me fat?"

"Yes, I am. But for real, I ate a higher dose than you. That's probably why."

"Are you going to be okay?" I asked. I could've pointed out that she'd also been drinking *apple juice* at dinner, but I let her off the hook.

"I have to be. Poor Lolly is going to lose her mind."

"Be nice to her," I begged.

"Don't worry. I'll watch her, we'll be fine, blah blah blah. Anyway, check this out."

She pointed at one of the screens. A hundred buttons blinked at us.

"The whole carnival is online," she said. "You can control the rides and lights and stuff from here. It's a pretty sophisticated system."

"Did you know before?" I asked. "Is this a problem?"

"No. I didn't know. Doesn't matter. I can turn the switches off too. If the guard comes back, he'll spend his time getting the system back online instead of hunting us."

She clacked on the keyboard. Both monitors went dark. James gave the chair a few final spins and jumped to her feet. "All good," she said.

"Okay," I said. I peered through the window. Lolly swayed with her arms folded across her chest. River and Gracie played hopscotch on the blank pavement. Blythe flipped her hair to the wrong side and fluffed it. Claire stretched, prepping like she was about to run a marathon.

"We'll meet at the carousel, yes?" I asked.

"Yes, ma'am," James said. "Forty-five minutes from now, an hour tops."

She raised her hand to give me a high five. I slapped it too hard. She screeched and wrung her wrist.

"Save your energy for the hunt," she said.

10

Blythe grabbed me and held me in place. She smelled like she'd dabbed on Jack Daniel's as perfume.

"Let them go," she slurred. "I don't want Claire to see us."

"See us what?" I asked.

"I'm not following the gate and sneaking in shadows. We're going to go straight through the carnival."

I breathed a sigh of relief. We had to walk farther than the others, easily a mile. If we went around, we'd add a mile to our hike. The carnival was dark enough that I wasn't worried about the lone security guard tracking us, if he ever showed up. We stepped into the moonlight and headed for the carousel. Blythe tripped over her own feet, but I caught her before she hit the ground.

"You sure you're okay?" I asked.

"I'm fine," she said. "Look."

Blythe stood straight and touched the tip of her nose with each index finger, and walked a straight line, heel to toe. She swayed a bit, but she stayed upright for about six feet. She asked if I wanted her to say the alphabet backward.

"Can you say the alphabet backward while sober?" I asked.

Blythe narrowed her eyes. She didn't answer right away. I leaned in, waiting, watching her eyes slide in slightly different directions.

"No," she said. She opened her mouth to say more. No words came out.

"I can't believe we're here," I said, changing the subject. "Remember freshman year? We talked about being chosen for the Scavenge. It's so surreal." I started walking again. Fortunately, she followed.

"You excited for school to start?" she asked.

"Honestly? No. Maybe if I knew about DSU. It's like I'm walking a tightrope without a net."

"I feel you." Blythe held her arms out as though she were keeping her balance while walking on a wire.

"You have a net, though, right?" I asked. "When school is over, you get to focus on your career."

Blythe snorted. "My *career*. I pretend to be a perfect goofball for the internet and get paid for it. I'm not a doctor or lawyer or anything. I'm not even a professional comedian. When I make something funny, it's by accident."

Her voice was flat, almost sad.

Maybe she wasn't just pretending to be perfect on the internet. Perhaps she was faking her way through real life too.

"A million years ago, back in elementary, we had to do drawings of our future selves," I told her. "Doctors, lawyers, teachers, you know the drill. I already knew I wanted to play music. Professional musician wasn't a proper job in my mind, so I drew myself in a Belldam Tower uniform. Our teacher walked around, and when she saw mine, she asked me to tell her about it. I said I wanted to work at my mom's hotel. She said I seemed upset about it. I told her yes, I was, because I didn't want to work in a hotel and wear a uniform. I wanted to be a musician, but everyone else drew *real* jobs. Then she said something that always stuck with me. 'Violet, someone has to play music. Why not you? Besides, most of your friends won't be doctors and lawyers. Your minds will change as you grow older. I bet a lot of you will do jobs that don't even exist yet. The world moves fast. There's always something new.'"

"We had the same lesson in my class," Blythe mumbled. "My picture was a puppy. That's what I wanted to be. A dog." She paused, stretched, and cracked her neck. "Maybe I still have time."

I laughed. "My point is, what you do now didn't exist when we were little. You're one of the kids she was talking about. You say it's not a real job. What does your bank account say?"

"Ugh. I don't want to talk about this anymore."

"Fair enough. Conversation dead and buried. Back to the task at hand: Do you want to go left past the House of Horrors or right past the House of Mirrors?"

"Right. There's a bathroom if we go that way, and I have to pee so bad I think I might burst." She did a little pee dance to show the direness of her situation.

"Too much apple juice?" I asked slyly.

She snorted. "Too much whiskey."

I extended a hand and allowed Blythe to lead the way. The moon made us a dimly lit, gray path, barely putting off enough light to cast our shadows on the ground. She stomped her long legs like a model on a runway. I shuffled at her heels.

We ducked into the dark bathroom. I ran my hand along the wall until I found the switch. The lights sizzled, blinking on, bathing the room in too-bright blue-white light.

"I'm good," I said. "I'll keep watch outside."

"You should at least try to pee," she said. "It's my mom's number two rule, because you never know if you'll get stuck without a bathroom when you need it. Her number one rule is 'If you're going to cheat on your husband, do it with a dude with more money.'"

"Life Lessons with Gwen Lennon," I joked.

Blythe paused. "Do you think I could turn that into a series for my channel? *No.* That wouldn't work. She'd have to come home so I could interview her, and that never happens."

I went into the accessible stall and pulled down my pants. Sure enough, I needed to go. I was mildly embarrassed for Blythe to hear me, so I held it in and waited for her to finish. Despite her overflowing bladder, Blythe was completely silent. She flushed, then turned on the sink to wash her hands.

As soon as she turned on the water, I relaxed and peed as quickly and quietly as possible.

When I stepped out of the stall, the faucet was running, but Blythe was gone. I bent over to check for her feet under the stall doors. She wasn't there.

"Blythe?" I called out. "You still here?"

She didn't respond. I half-heartedly ran my hands under the water. The paper towel dispenser was empty, so I rubbed them dry on my jeans. My fingers found the light switch, but I left it on. Even if I wasn't staying in the bathroom, the little bright spot in the dark carnival comforted me. The blackness creeped me out more than I wanted to admit.

I turned the knob and pushed on the bathroom door with my shoulder. It didn't budge.

"What the hell?" I said aloud.

I twisted the knob harder. This time, it turned, but the door didn't budge. I slammed my body into it a couple of times until it finally cracked open. I could see an inch of night. The door refused to open any farther.

"Blythe?" I whispered through the crack. "Are you out there?"

She didn't answer. I let the door go, allowing it to close.

I paced. My head spun. I wasn't usually claustrophobic, but edible-induced paranoia hit me, and the ceiling lowered as the walls closed in. I hit the door with a fist and screamed for help. When I didn't get an immediate answer, I flipped out, slapping the door and grunting unintelligibly. I stuck my hand in the opening, my fingers disappearing into the darkness, and slammed my hip into the door until I pried it open wide enough to jam my foot in the space. Then slowly, a millimeter at a time, I jimmied the door back and forth until I twisted around and sucked my stomach in enough to slip out of the bathroom. The door scraped shut behind me.

"Ungh," I groaned. My muscles throbbed from squeezing through the tight space.

With the door closed, the light disappeared. I squatted to examine the ground to investigate how I'd gotten locked in. My fingers fumbled along the concrete until they found the culprit. I yanked it free and brought it into the moonlight.

It was a wet, rolled-up, folded copy of our local paper, *The*

Belldam Bell. It was jammed under the door, holding it shut. I threw it into a nearby trash can. It left my hand caked in mud, and moisture crept under my Hello Kitty Band-Aid. I peeled it off and threw it away as well. My cut still stung a little, but the bleeding had stopped hours earlier.

Blythe was nowhere to be found. I searched the immediate area, hoping to find her sprawled on the ground waiting for me or wandering in the open space by the carousel.

But she wasn't there. She wasn't anywhere.

"Blythe?" I whisper-yelled. I didn't dare raise my voice too loud, for fear I might freak out the others. When she didn't answer, a tiny jolt of panic made the hair on my arms stand on end. I walked toward the House of Mirrors, still softly calling her name.

My head felt light. My brain threatened to inflate until it cracked my skull. The circus peanut had begun to take effect, no question. Panic set in. I wouldn't be able to navigate to the Ferris wheel in the dark if I got too high.

Then, as if on cue, a loud crack echoed through the carnival and the lights switched on. A deep, demonic laugh boomed from the House of Horrors, drowning out the cheerful song from the carousel. Bright bulbs lit the arcade, and strobes flashed in the distance. A prerecorded voice boomed, "Step right up! Test your strength! Only musclemen need apply!"

Somewhere, far across the carnival, a shrill scream rang out. I didn't recognize the voice, but it was female, and most likely, one of my friends.

Suddenly, the light wasn't so comforting anymore.

11

"Gotta move," Blythe mumbled to herself. "If I stop, it's over. I'm dead."

Greasy vomit rose in her throat. She regretted eating the nasty fried chicken at dinner and cursed herself for not being able to eat one stupid meal without posting it online.

She walked along the gate slowly; then when the power turned on, she picked up the pace. Her head felt light. Pure adrenaline powered her body. The carnival rotated around her. The lights spun faster and faster until they were as bright as the sun.

Someone screamed. Blythe stopped cold. Whoever it was, they were far away. Based on the direction of the scream, it was probably Mila, maybe River or Gracie.

Violet was still back at the bathroom. Blythe thought she heard her calling out. They'd run into each other again soon. Right now, she needed to be alone.

Ahead of her, tiny explosions inside a Paulie's Pop-a-Corn cart filled the air with a salty, buttery aroma. It surprised her. It made sense for the rides to power on, but not the popcorn machines. The salty scent of rich popcorn butter made her stomach turn. It would be a miracle if she kept the fried chicken down.

"God, I really don't want to be here," she said aloud. "The fucking carousel music. It's gonna be stuck in my head for days."

Once upon a time, she loved the carnival. Before the divorce, she would come every December with her dad when they did a Winter Wonderland overlay on the carnival. It was the only place in Belldam where you could see snow. There was a vast swath of land in the back corner where the staff loaded in piles and piles of the fake stuff for guests to build snowmen and have epic snowball fights. She and her dad would get sugared up on hot chocolate–flavored cotton candy and fall in the faux snow to make angels.

Nowadays, she barely got a phone call on Christmas. There were always plenty of gifts to open, but there hadn't been snow angels in years.

Thoughts of her father made her chest hurt. This wasn't the time to cry. This was the night she'd waited for. Blythe pictured a lit candle, focused on the flame. Her therapist taught her that trick. She forgot about her dad, about the chicken, about the carousel music. When her mind was clear, she blew out the candle and opened her eyes.

She needed a place to regroup, somewhere along the midway. Lolly and James would be there. She desperately needed to find them.

Her shoes crunched in the gravel. Her head felt unbearably hot, and the humid air made it almost impossible to breathe without choking. She should've worn shorts. She wished she could text her friends. It would be so much easier to find them.

"This isn't nearly as fun as I imagined it would be," she said to herself. "This night needs to end. In an hour, the hunt will be over. One hour and I'll be done. Sixty little minutes. That's it."

Someone else's shoes crunched in the gravel. Lightning shot up her spine, shocking her out of her skin. She leapt out of sight and pressed her body against the cold gate.

As the dark figure approached, Blythe pulled herself together. It was a friend. It had to be. She just couldn't tell which one.

She gulped for air, then stepped directly into the path of the oncoming person.

Her head spun again, and as the person's face came into focus, Blythe's vision blurred until the whole world went black.

12

We learned about the fight-or-flight response in science. Our lessons left out the third option: freeze.

I read about it in an article on women's self-defense. I asked my mom why no one ever mentioned freezing. She told me to google it; she was busy with a project for work. Instead, I asked James what she thought.

"Probably because people like to think they can survive a dangerous situation. It's a control thing. Like, any choice they might make would lead to the defeat of their attacker," she said. "Plus, it gives dickheads a reason to judge victims."

"What do you mean?" I asked.

She put on a condescending voice. "Jane Doe deserved what she got. A maniac with a chainsaw ran at her, and just she stood there. I'd never do that. I'd run and never look back."

I agreed with her, but when the carnival sprang to life and a scream ripped through the night, I froze. My mind raced as I calculated my next move.

Something is not right here.

Where is Blythe?

Who turned on the lights?

Who screamed?

Was it James?

Where is James?

Does the popcorn machine really start when the power goes on? Why is that necessary?

I should find Blythe. She can't have gotten far.

Has the security guard found us?

What if he called the cops?

Where is everyone else?

I should call out. Someone will answer.

Why isn't anyone else calling out?

What if everyone is dead?

Why do I automatically assume people are dead?

We're more likely to be arrested than murdered.

I should walk toward the scream.

I should run away from the scream.

I should hide and try to ride this out.

My gut pulled me toward Blythe. My feet pulled me to hide. My brain told them both to shut up as it drew me to the center of the carnival. The others would be there or close by. We could find Blythe together. It was stupid to split up in the first place, and I wouldn't be making that mistake again.

I snuck along the alley behind the arcade, my body pressed

against the plywood exterior. I did my best to run between the shadows, ducking and pausing after each step. When I turned the corner, I found Lolly, still as a statue next to the Black Kitten Coaster, as frozen as I'd been moments before.

"Lolly." I called softly. "*Lolly.*"

She stared at the Black Kitten Coaster's worm buggies. Her hand drifted to the little gate like she might push it open to hide inside.

Emboldened by the knowledge that I wasn't alone, I sprinted toward her. I said her name again, this time at full volume. Her head shot up, and she flashed a smile.

She never saw him coming.

A black fabric swirl appeared behind Lolly, as though the monster manifested from thin air. It wrapped one gloved hand around her throat, holding her tight in a headlock. Lolly—her brilliant mind melted by the edible—was too stunned to fight back.

I screamed, and the monster looked at me.

I recognized him immediately.

———

Each October, the carnival had a massive Halloween celebration.

Somehow, the staff made the already spooky carnival into an over-the-top, almost gratuitous celebration of the macabre.

They covered everything in spiderwebs, including the poor ticket takers. Thousands of pumpkins got hauled in to be carved by world-famous carving artists. The deep-fry carts, which already sold death-defying treats as a matter of course, sold even weirder stuff like fake fried blood and very realistic fried rats.

Special events call for seasonal employees, and it felt like management intentionally chose the creepiest applicants to help set the mood: close-talkers, touchy-feely men, ride operators who asked too many personal questions. Sorry, Mr. Mirror Maze Man, it's none of your business what my first crush's lips tasted like.

Yuck.

Worst of all were the scare actors, not because they were creepy, but because they seemed dangerous.

From September to mid-November, a portion of the carnival turned into a free-range haunt. People in costumes followed and harassed you, jumped in your face to yell. That kind of thing. They had ultrarealistic weapons, and their masks emboldened them to swing their chainless chainsaws a little too close to carnival guests.

On nights when the actors were energized and well-behaved, it was fun to walk around feeling free to scream as loud as you wanted when a zombie or haunted doll lumbered after you. It was a safe release, and for a few hours, I could turn my brain off and live a little. A thirst for those nights kept me coming back year after year.

The previous October, James, Blythe, River, Gracie, Mila, Meg, and Everly Putnam, River's art geek friend, piled into Heather's van and headed to the outskirts of town.

As soon as we entered the carnival, two scarecrows with machetes chased us toward the midway. We screeched and ran, bursting into laughter next to the ring toss. James took my hand, I took Everly's, then River joined the chain, then Gracie, then Meg, then Mila, with Blythe bringing up the rear.

We locked into our daisy chain any time we walked through the designated areas where scare actors patrolled, looking for guests to chase. Mostly, they swarmed the merry-go-round, and anything past the House of Horrors was out of bounds.

We unlinked at the food court. River had the munchies and

wanted a hot dog. Meg wanted some slime lime cotton candy. James needed to pee.

Blythe and I stood next to the spinning Crazy Cauldrons, bitching about the cold. We noticed a scare actor staring at us from a distance but didn't react. We were well beyond his boundaries.

He edged forward a bit, stomping a wide stride, his gloved hand gripping a realistic-looking axe.

"Is he coming over here?" I asked.

Blythe looped her arm in mine. "Maybe we know him," she said. "Most of the actors go to Pritchett. I bet it's River's ex, Brogan Whatshisname."

"Ooh, I bet. He's basically stalking her. He sent her flowers. She sent them back. He put them through a wood chipper and sent her the mulch with a 'this is what you did to my heart' letter."

"Well, I welcome him to try that shit around me," Blythe yelled. "I'll kick his fucking ass!"

The actor heard her and sped faster until he flew toward us in a full-tilt run. He passed a clump of people, shoving a girl in a pink cowboy hat into the mud. Blythe squeezed my arm.

As he moved closer, I got a better look at his costume. His rubber mask was one of the more grotesque ones I'd seen on a scare actor. It was a coal black demon face, with elongated bloodshot eyes and a shiny finish that made the skin appear to ooze.

The demon's tongue was the worst part. Pale gray-pink, hanging limply down his chest. When he shook his head, the tongue flopped side to side, making him look like he was salivating to slurp us right up.

I braced for impact. He stopped short of crashing into us, pushed me to the side, and pressed his chest against Blythe. He was a couple inches taller, but not big enough to intimidate her. When she tried to brush him off, he shoved her into the concrete barrier surrounding the Crazy Cauldrons.

"What is wrong with you?" Blythe asked, pushing him away.

"Pretty," he whispered. "Pretty pretty."

"Get off her!" I yelled. Faces turned in our direction, curious people wondering if they were witnessing a show.

The actor turned toward me and slammed the axe into the ground at my feet. The blade stuck into the ground and stood at attention.

Scare actors weren't supposed to have real, sharp weapons.

Cold sweat rolled down my face.

"So pretty," he said. He cradled Blythe's chin and rested his forehead against hers. The tongue threatened to dip into her shirt, right between her boobs.

"Get off me, or I'm going to scream, you asshole," Blythe said through gritted teeth. "And I mean a losing-my-shit scream, full-on bloody murder. My friend will too."

The actor slammed his fist into the wall, only an inch or two away from Blythe's head. She winced. My fingers curled into claws. I was ready to rip the mask off and shove it down his throat.

With little fanfare, he backed off, pulled his axe from the dirt, and wandered back into the designated scare actor zone.

"What the hell was that?" I asked.

"No idea," she said. She pulled on her shirt where the tongue had been, making sure she wasn't exposed. "He might be a fan. Or maybe he hate-watches my videos. Or—most likely—he's a jerk who gets off on harassing cute girls. I don't think it was Brogan. He's been terrified of me ever since he hit on me, and I told him to die in a pile of fire ants. No way that pussy is the Licker."

"The Licker?" I laughed. "That's the name you're going with?"

"What else you gonna call something with that tongue?"

———

Past Blythe whispered in my ear as the masked man threw Lolly around like a rag doll.

"The Licker," she hissed. "What else?"

Lolly's face turned purple. She made a fist and repeatedly punched his neck, but he didn't flinch.

I screamed, losing my shit, full-on bloody murder. The Licker dragged Lolly backward, almost out of sight. This time my brain let my body take charge, and my body wanted to fight.

The Licker was ready when I slammed into him. He didn't miss a beat; he had me on the ground before I even threw a punch. I searched for a weapon but didn't see any nearby. The Licker didn't like how mobile I was, so he kicked his black sneaker into my chest twice. It knocked the wind out of me. I panicked when I couldn't catch my breath.

Lolly went limp. He dropped her and dragged her across the gravel. At first, I thought he was taking her into the arcade so they would be alone, and he could do whatever he wanted in private. But he kept going and dragged her to the test-your-strength booth.

The giant measuring stick at the back of the booth stood ten feet in the air. A bell hung at the top, a puck sat at the bottom, a metal plate laid in front. The player would slam a mallet into the plate, and the puck would shoot up to ring the bell.

The Licker threw Lolly on the ground. She rolled away, far enough to piss him off, not far enough to escape. He caught her locket—the one she inexplicably filled with a picture of Seth Rogen—tightened it, and used it to drag her back.

She screamed my name.

"I'm coming!" I groaned through gasps.

He grabbed her shoulders and pounded her back into the ground. Lolly fought as best she could, spitting, clawing, even biting his hand, but he was too strong. He head-butted her so hard that I heard the *clonk* of their skulls banging together, and then he gently lowered her head onto the plate.

"Hey!" The Licker yelled at me. A screechy electronic device disguised his voice. "You like lollipops?" One summer when I was little, my family stayed at the beach for a week in a massive hotel in Corpus Christi. My cousins Cory and Brett had their own room on the fourth floor, overlooking the pool. The boys snuck into the pastry kitchen and stole some watermelons. Strangely, not a single staff member questioned the sight of two massively pregnant teenage boys roaming the hotel halls.

My cousins sent me to the ground floor to be the lookout. Though they were dumb enough to toss watermelons four stories onto the pavement, they had enough brains in their heads to understand someone walking under them could get hurt.

I was excited to be included.

Brett, my oldest cousin, had the bigger watermelon. He raised it over his head and—with as much force as his twig arms would allow—threw it to the ground below. I'd expected it to crack like in half like an egg. Instead, it exploded. Juice and pink goo flew through the air hard enough to make me flinch when it hit me in the face. The rind broke apart into a dozen big chunks. The largest piece caved in on itself, vomiting up more of the pink meat inside.

When the Licker slammed the weighted mallet on Lolly's head, I saw the watermelon. Her skin was the rind, her bones the thick white lining, her brains and blood the sweet pink meat. Some teeth landed at the Licker's feet.

"They're the seeds," I whispered.

My face was warm and wet. Lolly's beautiful brain sprayed across my shirt in a lovely abstract pattern. Her body lay limp, nearly within my reach.

The Licker left the mallet on her face. He walked toward me, close enough to see the slight shimmer in his cheap Party City cloak. I closed my eyes. Lolly was dead; it was my turn now.

He dropped onto one knee in front of me. He leaned forward and pressed his tongue to my cheek. My mind flashed back to October, to Blythe and the rubber tongue on her chest.

He breathed a muffled wheeze inside the mask. Hot air blew through the mesh guard over his mouth.

"How ya like lollipops now?" He asked, giggling to himself. His laugh was like a fork stuck in a garbage disposal mixed with digital static. He gave me a little wave. "Hey Violet. Remember me?"

I pulled away, squeezing my eyes shut until fireworks appeared on the inside of my lids. He leaned closer. I braced for his touch.

Without warning, he stood. I opened my eyes. The Licker turned and skipped away, kicking up a cloud of dust behind him. "Lolly popped! Lolly popped!" He sang in tune with the old timey song. "Oh Violet, Lolly popped!"

I looked over at Lolly's dead body. It jumped, one last twitch from her muscles before she never moved again.

13

When I caught my breath, I sprinted for the entrance. I figured anyone who heard my screams would've decided to get the hell out of the carnival.

My assumptions were incorrect. Claire stood paralyzed in front of the photo printing shop, out in the open, fixated on the pretty lights on the Whirling Witch Coaster.

"It's like a postcard," she said. "They made it look so real." She turned to face me. Her pupils were the size of saucers.

My edible hadn't affected me as much as hers had...or so I thought. I'd been too preoccupied running for my life to realize the world seemed a little hazy. But now, next to Claire, I felt myself slipping away.

I grabbed Claire and gave her a good shake.

"Lolly is dead!" I cried. "There is someone in a black hooded cloak and demon mask. It's a scare actor costume from Halloween. Blythe named him the Licker. We have to get outta here."

Claire tilted her head. "What's on your shirt?" she asked, pulling at the hem.

"Lolly," I told her. "Lolly is on my shirt. Now come on, we have to go!"

I grabbed her hand and pulled her toward the exit. She stood firm. Claire was 140 pounds of solid muscle. I, on the other hand, could barely help our orchestra director move a cello.

"We. Can't. Leave. Them," she said dreamily.

"Yes, we can! We'll get out and go to Blythe's car and get our phones and call nine-one-one. We won't be able to help the others if we're dead."

"What about James?" she asked.

"I'm not worried about her right now," I lied. "The best way to protect her and the others is to get help. We gotta run."

"No. No, that won't do at all. Did you ever read the one book we were supposed to read in English? Something something no man left behind."

"I have no idea what you're talking about. Claire, we gotta go."

"No, listen to me. Listen." She paused and stared back up at the Whirling Witch Coaster. "They might not even know they're in danger. Mila screamed earlier when the lights came on. No one noticed."

"I noticed. That's why I made the stupid decision to find you guys. It didn't work out, now Lolly is freaking dead, and if we don't leave this carnival, so are we."

"Lolly is dead?" Claire asked, suddenly alert.

"I hope so, or it's going to take a lot of surgery to reconstruct her head."

Claire pushed me away. "If you want to leave, go. I'll get you outside the gate, and then you can run to Blythe's car. If the doors don't open, keep running to the subdivision behind the woods. Scream your head off once you're in the clear. I'm going to try to find the others."

"Claire," I said flatly. "You're too high to function. You can't go looking for them alone."

"I'm not so high that I can't outrun this guy, maybe even take him down. My last training session, I deadlifted two hundred and thirty pounds."

"Is two-thirty a lot?"

Claire gave me a side-eye. "Yes, bitch. It's a lot."

———

Claire wasn't always an athlete.

One night, at a sleepover, she and I were the only two girls still awake. We went outside and lay in the driveway, staring at the starless sky. We talked about everything from my missing dad to her desire to adopt and train a Rottweiler. I'd brought cookie dough bites with me and offered her one. She declined and told me a story.

For a long time, Claire was so skinny every bone in her body poked through her skin. People would stare at her when her parents took her out, whispering that Mr. and Mrs. Smithson must be abusing their daughter. They took her to the doctor, who declared Claire was a perfectly healthy girl who just needed to eat more.

"Put sweetened condensed milk in her oatmeal," the doctor said. "She will get nice and chubby."

Claire's parents were at the end of their rope, so they bought sweetened condensed milk and gave Claire three bowls of oatmeal a day in addition to her regular meals. The excess sugar made Claire's eyes bulge, made her throat burn, and kept her on the edge of nausea all day long, but she kept quiet and did her best not to puke because she didn't want to upset her parents.

She suffered through the oatmeal until one Mother's Day when her Grandma Stephanie came to visit. When Stephanie saw her son prepare sweetened-condensed-milk-spiked oatmeal for her sweet granddaughter Claire, she flipped out.

"What are you feeding my baby?" Stephanie asked.

Claire's mom ran into the room and came out swinging. "She's not your baby, she's my baby! You don't know what we went through! She looked so sickly. Her pediatrician said this would make her gain weight."

"It's also going to give her diabetes! She's as skinny as ever, and she's shaky and sweaty! You need to take her to another doctor, Jason, and you need to do it today."

After a brief fight—he told his mother he knew how to raise his own kid; she said it was crazy to feed sugar syrup to a nine-year-old—her dad tried to prove her wrong by asking Claire how she felt about the oatmeal. Claire threw up on his shirt. Her dad agreed to take her to a new doctor, and her mom agreed not to poison her mother-in-law.

It turned out Claire didn't need to eat more. She needed medicine because her thyroid was out of whack. The doctor wrote a prescription and gave a stern order to stop feeding Claire sugary food to fatten her up.

Six months later, medicine combined with a healthy diet changed

Claire's body for the better. She finally had enough energy to play with other kids, and she begged her dad to enroll her in swimming lessons.

"The first time I hit the pool, I almost drowned," she told me. "I sank. I wasn't scared, though. My swim teacher fished me out, handed me a kickboard, and I fluttered around in the water like a fish until I was a raisin. If I could live in the water, I would."

"Like me and the violin," I said. I took another brownie from my bag and ate half. "Is that why you don't eat sugar? A training diet for swimming?"

"Hell no," she laughed. "I'll pig out on anything salty, spicy, or sour. It's just after the oatmeal… I'd rather die than eat anything sweet."

———

I squeezed Claire's fingers, and we prepared to make our run for the little door in the gate. We hadn't even taken a step when the lights around us cut off.

My eyes couldn't adjust to the dark. Everything was black, so black that I couldn't make out the shapes around us. My body felt light like I might float away. I was a balloon, barely tethered to the earth by Claire's sweaty hand.

A scratchy electronic screech ripped through the night. Claire wrapped her arms around our heads to block the sound.

"Lolly popped, oh Lolly-Lolly popped!" sang a demonic voice. "Hey, Violet, wanna gimme some sugar?"

I slid from Claire's arms and crawled under her legs.

"Why is he taunting me?" I whispered. "Where is he?"

"I don't—will you please get off the ground? No crawling on the ground tonight. Stop dragging me down with you."

Across the carnival, near the House of Horrors, lights flashed on and off.

"Look!" I gasped.

"Is that where the killer is?" Claire asked.

Killer. There was a killer on the loose, and James was out there alone.

"Not necessarily. James told me that computers control the power. If anything, the killer's in the security office." Saying her name made my heart race. Did she make it to the dunk tank? Did she even know we were in danger? "Didn't Mr. Moerkerke say something about a guard?"

Claire nodded. "I'll bet you a shiny nickel Ned ain't guarding anything tonight."

"I thought his name was Fred? Or was it Frank?"

"I don't know, Violet. It's not like I'm friends with the dude. Ugh. I'm dizzy." Claire squeezed the bridge of her nose. "Wait. His name was definitely Floyd. Or maybe Ralph."

"Do you think the Licker got Ralph?" I asked, pulling at her legs.

She lifted me to my feet and coaxed me behind a recycling bin. We crouched in the dirt to debate.

"We can't go back to the entrance," she said. "If *the Licker* is running the lights from the security office, we'd have to walk right past him."

"I like how you say 'the Licker' like it's a ridiculous name. He's got a ten-inch-long rubber tongue he likes to rub on people."

"Gross."

"Exactly."

"Okay," she said, her tone harsh. "We're going the long way around to the House of Horrors. We'll stay close to the structures and avoid the lights if they come on again."

I sighed, slightly relieved.

"Are we going to make it out alive?" I asked.

"Sure," Claire said. She dropped her voice to a whisper. "Or die trying."

14

When the power came back on, Mila was unprepared. She stood out in the open, feeling naked. Something wasn't right. The screams that rang out across the carnival weren't from surprise. They were from terror.

She kicked herself for losing Claire. If anyone could keep them safe, it would be her. But when the carnival lit up, and the screaming started, she ran, and Claire didn't follow. By the time Mila realized they'd been separated, there was no way to find her.

Mila ducked into the midway. The ring toss had a prize wall displaying stuffed animals, a perfect hiding place. She climbed into the booth and made a fort out of teddy bears. They brushed softly against her skin. Thanks to the circus peanuts, the sensation mesmerized her, and she couldn't help but stroke their silky fur with her cheek.

Footsteps crunched in the dirt. Mila froze. She didn't breathe, didn't even blink. She peeped through the toys. If it were one of the other girls, she would crawl out and grab her friend and never let go.

It wasn't a friend.

A tall figure dressed in all black walked past the ring toss booth. Or rather, he *stalked* past with his shoulders hunched, his pace slow. He barely picked up his feet at all. He stopped at a Paulie's Pop-A-Corn cart across from her and knocked a stack of red-and-white-striped popcorn boxes on the ground. Mila gasped.

The figure whipped around. His comically long rubber tongue flopped back and forth.

Mila had a nasty habit of breaking out in nervous laughter at the worst possible times, like at her beloved grandfather's funeral. She was heartbroken, but when a group of tiny old veterans stood to honor her grandfather, she burst into thunderous laughter. "They're the Munchkin gang!" she told her brother Mikey. He was not amused. She bit her cheek and pinched her wrist, and the giggles subsided.

In the midway, she chomped onto her tongue so hard it bled, dug four nails into her wrist, and scratched up her arm.

The Licker's feet scraped the dirt as he walked to the ring toss booth. She squinted, opening her eyes just enough to see him hover over the counter. When she saw his demonic mask, she didn't need to hold back laughter. Instead, she held back a scream.

He stayed at the counter for about thirty seconds, but with her brain on stoner time and her inability to breathe without being heard, it felt like hours. Finally, he straightened his back, turned toward the heart of the midway, and walked away.

The stuffed animals didn't provide enough cover. Several body parts threatened to pop out and expose her. A shift in the wind would reveal her hiding spot. A little wooden shelf inside the counter hung a few feet away; it was her best shot at a hiding spot. Her body would barely fit, but as long as he didn't step inside the ring toss booth to look around, she'd be safe there.

She made herself as small as possible and slid out onto the dry dirt. She lowered herself onto her belly and slithered like a snake toward the shelf. Her palms and forearms scraped the dirt, stinging as the skin split.

She wondered if her injuries would affect cheer practice.

When her hand touched the wood, she flipped her body around and folded herself in half. She scooted sideways onto the shelf.

I'm safe, she thought.

She was wrong.

Black gloved fingers wrapped around the counter, mere inches from her head.

"Did you think I wouldn't see you?" He asked. His voice sounded garbled, like a robot shoved underwater.

He pulled on the counter with one hand. It shook a little but didn't fall. He grabbed it with both hands and yanked hard. This time, the whole counter moved. Cheap plywood cracked as the nails let go. The Licker summoned all his strength. The counter finally gave and tipped over on top of him.

This was Mila's last chance. A broken shard of wood stuck up from the remnants of her shelf. She cracked it off and ran. It wasn't a *great* weapon, but it was *something*.

The midway was the first structure built on the carnival grounds. It started out as six simple booths, and morphed into a sprawling, filthy labyrinth that truly was the perfect setting for a stalker to confuse his prey.

At first there were six games, each one involved throwing various balls against targets. Then an apple-bobbing booth and a game where players shot little racing horses with a popgun. The apple booth's owner didn't like guns, so they insisted the racing horse game be moved. More booths were added, and the layout became convoluted, with many more recent additions having the same games with similar-sounding names. Turn a corner and you could either find six ring tosses, or a dark corridor leading to a dead end. It was a coin-flip.

Mila knew better than to head deeper into the midway. The lights might go out again at any moment, and she'd be screwed. She took a left and ran toward the House of Horrors. Unfortunately, the Licker beat her to the punch.

He caught her by her ponytail and gave it a hard yank. She refused to go down without a fight. Her legs were strong enough to hold her on another girl's shoulders before doing a back somersault to land on a football field, a big bright smile never leaving her face. She kicked him in the chest, then in the crotch. She stabbed at him wildly with her stick. It slid into his skin; with all the wrestling, she couldn't tell what body part she'd penetrated. An electronic screech howled as he screamed in pain.

She hadn't done enough to stop him, only to anger him. He was done with their little scuffle. He threw her on the ground so hard her shoulder snapped, then he crawled on top of her, straddling her stomach.

"Get off me!" Mila yelled.

"Is this yours?" He took Mila's stick and scratched it across her neck. If he wanted to, he could've ended it all right there. A stake through the neck, not quite a vampiric death, but pretty damn close.

That wasn't what the Licker wanted. He'd spent months making plans. Good plans he didn't want to abandon. Shocking deaths for the best and brightest.

It's what they deserved.

Still, he needed her incapacitated. She would fight until her dying breath. The wood pierced her shoulder with ease. He felt it tear through the muscle. It might've even scraped bone. The pain overwhelmed Mila, sending her into shock.

The Licker threw her over his shoulder and walked her to a booth. Through bleary eyes, she saw six plaster clown heads, their mouths gaping, ready to be filled. The closest clown had fat orange lips and a black star over its left eye. Mila remembered him from her Scavenge invitation.

The Licker laid her on the counter. She rolled toward him, landing inside the booth. He glanced at her and decided she was too weak to escape. She watched as he pulled back a curtain to reveal a hidden toolbox. Mila wanted to run, stand, or even pull herself into a sitting position, but the blood loss and clanging in her head kept her under his control.

The Licker reached into the box and produced two long nails and a hammer. He held them high for Mila to see. She moaned, blubbered, gasped for air. If she kept panicking, she'd do his job for him.

He put the hammer and nails on the little stool where the carnie sat when carnival traffic was slow. Then he propped Mila against the back wall between two weathered ceramic clown heads. He put her right hand above her head and placed a nail in her palm. Mila squirmed and begged for him to stop.

The Licker didn't listen.

The first time he struck the nail, it didn't go all the way through. He hung his head in shame as Mila howled in pain.

"Please! It hurts, it hurts, it's enough!"

The Licker shook his head and wagged a *no, no* finger at her. He raised the hammer and struck the nail.

Mila counted each thud.

One.

Two.

Three.

After three, her hand went numb. She wouldn't have known it was still attached if he hadn't given her a high five. He clapped his palm against hers, then had the audacity to pretend that the protruding nail hurt *him*.

To punish the nail for its insolence, he resumed hammering.

Four.

Lightning zapped her forearm, traveling down her bicep, until she could feel the aftershocks in her rib.

Five.

Six.

Mila forced herself to look at her hand. The nail couldn't hold her weight, and her skin was splitting vertically toward her knuckles.

"It's gonna rip open!" she screamed. "I'll fall!"

The Licker produced a second nail. Mila never thought she'd be grateful for someone to hammer a nail into her flesh, but he put the second nail through her hand in only three strikes. Her weight was redistributed, taking pressure off her right hand, providing her slight relief. She flexed her fingers as best she could. He'd done too good a job for her to move them much.

At seventeen, Mila had never worried much about her last

moments. Her best guess was she'd die at ninety, surrounded by her great-grandchildren in a sunny hospital room. If she had fantasized about dying young, she would've guessed her final thoughts would've been of her parents or her brother, maybe her boyfriend or her friends. Certainly she would've thought about cheerleading, the sport she'd loved since she took her first tumbling class.

It turned out all she could think about was when—as a toddler— she stole some scissors and used them to cut quarter-inch baby bangs. It was her earliest memory. She didn't know why she'd done it, but she vividly remembered the snipping sound the blades made as they sliced through the hair, and the satisfying sprinkle of hair falling on the *Blue's Clues* coloring book in her lap. Mila was so lost in her memory that she didn't notice the Licker pick up the water gun.

Mila screamed when he pressed it against her lips and shoved it past her teeth. He wasn't worried her friends would hear; the barrel of the gun muzzled her nicely. He pressed harder until it slid down her throat. She screamed louder, which pissed him off. He pulled the gun out and shoved it back into her throat, cracking several bottom teeth as he did it.

Mila shut her eyes and focused on her breathing. Her tongue blocked her throat, triggering her gag reflex. If she took short, quick breaths through her nose, she would stay alive longer, but she wouldn't be able to hold out until sunup when the security guard came.

But that wasn't his plan.

The Licker fondled the rubber hose that connected the gun to a massive water tank under the counter. He turned the rusty knob— the squeaky creak startled Mila—until the hose kicked back and water flowed toward the gun.

Mila pictured the coloring book. Yellow scribbles across Blue's face. She always had so much trouble staying inside the lines.

The Licker leaned in close. A familiar scent clung to his clothes. Girly. Gourmand. She couldn't quite place it.

The gun clicked when he pulled the trigger. Water burst into her throat. A nodule swelled under her chin.

"Bullfrog neck," the Licker growled into his voice changer.

He poked at it, flicked it, and giggled as it bounced around like a water balloon.

Mila shuddered as the water filled her lungs. She went limp, but the Licker didn't release the trigger. Mila appeared dead, but he wasn't about to make assumptions.

Her lungs overflowed, and with nowhere else to go, the water rushed up her throat and into her mouth. It spewed all over her white T-shirt, revealing a baby blue bralette.

The Licker released the gun, but left it stuck in her throat. He removed a glove and pressed his fingers to her neck. No pulse.

Before he put his glove back on, he checked the time on his phone.

Two o'clock, two down, too many to go.

15

When we heard heavy footsteps running toward us, Claire snatched my wrist and dragged me behind a trash can. She peeked around the side and watched the Licker sprint past.

"He went around the corner," she whispered. "Toward the Mirror Maze."

"River and Gracie," I said. "That's where they were supposed to be."

"I know."

In the distance, the lights on the Whirling Witch Coaster turned off. Behind us, the entrance lights blinked on and off for a moment until they lit up permanently. I shivered. There were eyes on me, a stranger close enough I could feel his breath on my neck. I whipped around, expecting to find myself nose to nose with his hideous mask.

No one was there.

"What if it's more than one person?" I asked. "One guy running around killing people and another controlling the lights."

"Plausible," Claire said. "This is good, though. He's running away from us, and the lights are on out front. He's probably turning on the lights for himself. It's a lot harder to chase girls when we're under cover of darkness. We can split up now."

My hand twitched, and before I could stop myself, I slapped her cheek for her stupidity. "*No. Fucking. Way.*"

I stared into her eyes, daring her to challenge me. She picked at the hem of her shorts.

"All right. We stay together and go in the opposite direction," she said. "Do you have a watch?"

"No. I have a phone," I said, rolling my eyes. "It has a clock."

"Do you have your phone with you?"

"Well. *No.*"

"Then don't be a smart-ass. I don't have one either. See the moon?" She pointed at the sky.

"Does the moon have a watch?" I asked. The idea of the moon unfolding his arms to check the time cracked me up.

"You're out here accusing me of being to high to function? What about you, jackass?"

I shook my head. "I'm fine. No more stupid questions."

"Good. The moon will be straight above us soon. When it moves west above the woods, we're leaving whether we've found the other girls or not. Okay?"

"Mmmhmm." My body was so loose I couldn't even form words.

Claire led me toward the House of Horrors. It struck me as ironic we were planning to save ourselves from a killer by hiding in a haunted house. I tried to point this out to Claire. Instead, I told a rambling, incoherent story about a movie I'd watched the night before.

"They're trapped in this castle, and they can't leave," I said. It felt like I was using too many words, but I couldn't stop myself. "There's a monster. Then this girl comes. She hid in plain sight. He saw her. He didn't kill her. They danced a lot."

"You're describing *Beauty and the Beast*," Claire said. "That has nothing to do with right now."

"Do you think James is okay?" I asked.

"For better or worse, James Parker is indestructible. She'll be around acting a fool for decades to come."

"Okay," I said. I didn't believe her, but I wanted to.

We were past the midway, almost to the carnival entrance when she held out an arm to stop me.

"Do you hear that?" she asked.

A tiny sound, like a mewling kitten, came from behind the fried Coke stand. Claire gave me some random hand signals I didn't understand and chose to ignore. She sighed and laced her fingers through mine. Her usually perfect manicure was marred; the peacock blue polish had half peeled off her stubby nails.

She gently pushed me to the left; she snuck around the right. We circled the stand, ready to pounce. Claire jumped into place, eyes wild.

"Please don't hurt me!" Gracie yelped. She lay in a ball on her side, with her eyes smushed shut and her fingers in her ears. Her Edna Mode glasses had disappeared.

I breathed a sigh of relief and tapped her with my toe. "It's us."

Gracie relaxed and rolled onto her back. Claire pulled her to her feet.

"Have you seen him?" Gracie asked.

"Oh, we saw him," said Claire, nodding violently with her entire body. "Violet *especially* saw him."

I nodded. "He talked to me."

"Whoa, whoa, whoa," said Claire. "That is some vital information you neglected to share. What did he say?"

"My name."

"You know him?" asked Gracie. "From where?

"Here, maybe. At least I know the mask. Last October, when we came here with James and Blythe and River and everybody, there was a scare actor who cornered Blythe and acted gross."

"Oh my God," said Claire. "She said the guy's mask had a big floppy tongue. That's what the killer is wearing!"

"Yeah," I said. "Something struck me as odd that night. He had a real axe. No one else carried real weapons. He left the scare zone too. Went out of bounds."

"You think it's the same guy? Like he stalked her before, and now he's after all of us?" Claire asked.

"No," Gracie said. "Later Blythe found out the creepy guy did it on a dare. There were a few assholes who broke the rules and egged each other on to do stuff like bring real weapons and grope girls. One of the idiots stabbed himself with a real chef's knife. He ratted the others out to keep his job. They fired him anyway."

I vaguely recalled Blythe telling me that story.

"What if this is those guys out for revenge?" Claire asked.

"Maybe," Gracie said. "Or maybe it's someone else. Who would want to kill us? What did we do?"

I flashed back to Emma at the Crave Inn, knife in hand, snarl on her lips.

"Is getting kicked out of college the kinda thing that would make someone break from reality?" I asked.

"Are you talking about Emma?" Gracie asked.

"I opened my big mouth and tried to commiserate with her. She did *not* want to hear it."

Claire shook her head. "No. No way. This was pre-planned."

"It's not like the Scavenge was a secret," I said. "She's friends with Kylie and Delilah and some of the other grads. Maybe—"

"No!" Claire snapped. "It's not Emma!"

We froze.

Claire had yelled loud enough to alert the Licker. Gracie gripped my hand so tightly that I shrieked in pain and yanked it away before she ground my bones to dust. Claire glared at me, flared her nostrils and took fast, shallow breaths.

"You're gonna get us caught!" she growled.

Her harsh tone stung—especially since she'd been the one to yell first—but I didn't have time to pout like a kicked puppy. I made a mental note to tell James that Claire was a drunken, drugged-out mess while I saved the day and solved the mystery.

Gracie patted my back. "Maybe Mr. Moerkerke is pissed we threatened him, or it's a crazy Blythe fan who snapped. Maybe the security guard is a sadist, and we walked into his playground. It could be anyone."

Claire rubbed her temples. "I'm less concerned with who he is and more concerned with getting out alive. We can let the cops play derective."

"Derective?" I asked.

"I said *detective*." Claire swayed a little, and her eyes went crossed.

"Between one to ten, how high is everyone right now?" I asked. "Don't lie."

"I'm fully at a six," said Gracie. "It's weird, because I only ate about seven milligrams. Usually it takes twice that for me to feel anything. I'll be okay as long as I don't hit an eight. On the plus side, being at a six is enough to keep me from peeing my pants with fear, so that's good."

"Nine over here, bitches!" Claire laughed. She held her arms above her head in triumph.

"Jesus, it's not a contest. I'm probably a three," I lied. In truth, I was closer to a five. Any more than that and I'd be toast. Lolly saved me when she asked me to split the candy. Still, I was shocked how high I was from such a tiny dose.

A lump formed in my throat as I thought about her sweet apprehension at the weed.

Claire pushed me and brought me back to reality. "Where are the others?" she asked. "Violet, where's Blythe?"

"We went to the bathroom, and she wandered off. She was wasted. Best-case scenario, she passed out in a dumpster somewhere."

"I lost River when the lights came on." Gracie pointed toward the Mirror Maze. "We were over there. What about James? And Lolly?"

James is fine. She has to be.

Claire and I glanced at each other. A tear rolled down Gracie's cheek.

"Lolly is dead," I said. "The Licker killed her."

"How?" Gracie asked.

"Not important."

"How?"

I swallowed. "He smashed her head with the mallet at the test-your-strength booth," I said.

Gracie turned away and vomited her grilled cheese sandwich on her shoes. I patted her on the back as she continued to heave. Her eyes rolled up at me. She gave a grateful half smile.

Then she noticed my shirt.

"Violet, what's all over you?" Gracie asked, knowing.

I paused. I told myself I wanted to save Gracie from the gory details. This was only half true. I also wanted to spare myself the trauma of reliving it. Even our conversation made me replay it in my head over and over. If I said the words, it made Lolly's death real, and the mental movie would never end. Any time I heard her name from then on, I would picture watermelon.

Gracie pressed, and Claire nodded.

"I was next to her when she died," I said. "Her blood got all over me."

"There's spatters on your face."

"Yes."

Gracie scanned my front, pulling my shirt close to her weak eyes so she could get a clear view.

"Why is this blood chunky?"

I begged Claire for guidance with my eyes. She shrugged.

"Gracie," I said softly. "He hit her head pretty hard. Have you ever seen a watermelon explode?"

Gracie jumped back and wailed. "Are those Lolly's brains? Is this really happening? Is this really fucking happening? Where is she? I can't look at a dead body. Tell me this is a joke. I won't be mad. I swear. Tell me it's a joke by the old seniors. I don't care. Please. Please. *Please*."

Claire bent down and covered Gracie's mouth.

"She's still where he left her," Claire said through gritted teeth. "We aren't going over there. You're not going to see it. We're going to hide, and if he finds us, we're going to kill him."

"Kill him?" I asked, stunned.

Claire let Gracie go. "You think Lolly is his only target? This is us against him, and if I have to fight him, I'm playing for keeps."

My chest twitched, followed by the corners of my mouth. I couldn't help but laugh. Gracie giggled too. Claire stared at us like we were nuts.

"You sound like the hero in an action movie." I said, laughing. "No one talks like that."

Claire sucked her cheeks in. Her fingers curled into a fist, and I took a step back.

Claire took a step forward, erasing the space I'd added between us.

She stabbed my chest with her index finger. "Everyone needs to get the hell up right now, or I will throw you to the Licker so I can run away and save myself."

By the tone in her voice, I could tell she meant it.

16

For the first time, maybe *ever*, River admitted to herself that she'd had too much weed.

She'd lied about the dosage of the circus peanuts to everyone else as a joke. The candy was harmless, and it should've been hilarious to watch the girls wander around, stoned beyond their wildest dreams, but she'd played herself.

Once everyone else took theirs, River still had a ton of peanuts left in the bag. Despite knowing they were *twenty* milligrams and not five like she'd told the others, River snacked while they waited for James to kill the cameras.

A peanut from the bag nibbled in six bites.

A second in four bigger bites.

Three more ripped in half, each half-eaten one after the other.

By the time she got to the last few candies, she stopped pretending that she wasn't going to eat them all. She threw her head back and swallowed the last few whole.

The bag was empty before Mila even let them into the park.

The bright lights paired with the prerecorded carnival barker's cheers made life unbearable. River, already far too high to handle so much stimulation, ditched Gracie to hide behind a *Ms. Pac-Man* cabinet in the arcade after the first screams rocked the carnival.

River had zero qualms about hiding behind the cabinet for a while. She was a stoner, not a fighter, and she knew Claire would lead the charge against their attacker. River would just get in the way.

Despite the slaughter outside, River kept nodding off. She often joked about using edibles to sleep, but in truth, they never actually sedated her. Now she'd discovered the proper dose to knock her out, and it was probably too late.

Darkness cradled her. Heavy, warm air filled her lungs. Her head rolled onto her shoulder, lolled forward, snapped off her neck, and fell into her lap.

River shot up, gasped for air, and grabbing her cheeks to make sure her head was still attached. Her heart hammered in her chest.

I'm too high for this, River thought. *If I fall asleep again, I might wake up dead.*

Her chest tightened. Her lungs wouldn't fully inflate. Fearing a heart attack, she took short, sharp breaths.

As she panicked, player number two entered the game.

Something crashed near the entrance. River clamped a hand over her mouth and peeked around *Ms. Pac-Man*. She spotted the rubber demon mask and slid farther behind the machine.

"Is that wet sand?" the Licker asked. He laughed. Shrill metallic feedback shrieked. "Smells kinda fishy in here. Like salmon. Salmon swim in rivers. Fishy River. River. Do you get it? I'm saying your vagina stinks! No? I guess it didn't really land. But I can do better. How about this?"

He walked toward the air hockey tables and the Skee-Ball games. He paused next to an air hockey table, raised his baseball bat in the air, and pounded it into the thick plastic. It clanged and bounced, but didn't break. The Licker hit the table again and again, desperate to destroy it. Each smack of the bat made River flinch; he'd demolish her if he caught her. Still, she couldn't look away.

"They build these things to last, huh Rivvy Kitty Kitty? Why don't you come out and play?" He paused as if he actually wanted a response.

River bit her palm to keep from screaming.

The Licker purred into his voice changer. "Fine. Don't play along. But guess what?" He paused for about thirty seconds, listening intently for any sign of his prey.

Tears welled in River's eyes.

"There's more than one way to skin a cat!"

The Licker swung the bat into the digital scoreboard mounted above the table. Glass sprayed across the room. He crushed it under his feet as he stalked the arcade. It was a satisfying crunch for him, and a devastating threat to River.

Energized by his destruction, the Licker jumped the ticket exchange counter to destroy the prize wall. Hats, T-shirts, and other souvenirs got ripped apart with his bare hands. He growled as he beheaded stuffed witches and mummies and drop-kicked plastic pumpkins filled with candy corn.

One pumpkin landed dangerously close to *Ms. Pac-Man*. The

Licker followed the bucket, and River choked back a scream as he paused a few feet away.

One more step and I'm pushing this over on him, River thought.

She breathed a sigh of relief. Now she had a plan.

But she didn't need it.

The Licker, bored with wrecking the place, tossed the bat over his shoulder and slunk out the back.

———

If you stay here, River told herself. *You're gonna suffocate. Your tongue is going to swell three times its size and you're going to choke.*

River stuck her tongue out and gently held it between her teeth. The physical pressure made her feel secure.

She had the urge to run. Negative thoughts crept in. Her skin heated the metal cabinet, and her hiding spot became an oven.

He was outside, ready to beat the brats with a baseball bat, and River wanted to join him.

A voice in the back of her head—it sounded suspiciously like her mother—ordered her to stay put, but it was too late. River pulled herself to her feet, stretched, and stepped away from *Ms. Pac-Man*.

Since the Licker had gone out the back, River snuck out the front.

A black and blue swirly sign reading MIRROR MAZE hung crookedly above a building forty feet from the arcade.

River cracked her back, bent at the waist, and sprinted for the double door entrance. When she was halfway there, the Licker cut the lights, drowning her in darkness. Her eyes struggled to adjust. She roughly rubbed them with her index fingers until she saw stars.

"Bathroom," she whispered. "Easy hiding spot."

River bolted for the girls' room. When she opened the door,

ice-cold air stung her lungs. Despite evidence to the contrary—
toilets, stalls, and sinks—River couldn't shake the feeling that she
was inside a giant refrigerator.

Which made her think of drinks.

Which reminded her of how thirsty she was.

The faucets were short, which made it hard for River to stick
her head in the sink for a drink. Almost none made it into her
mouth, but her hair got soaked. She searched the room for a cup,
a bottle, anything she could use to scoop up water and pour it into
her mouth.

She never once thought to cup her hands.

Instead, she stepped out into the night and tried to retrace her
steps back to the Ghostly Blue Cotton Candy stand she'd seen earlier,
because they always had water, juice, and soda.

The stand's siren song led her away from the bathroom and into
an open space with nowhere to hide. Time had become an illusion,
and while River believed she was sprinting toward the stand, in reality, she meandered from side to side, dragging her feet, and barely
staying vertical.

The Licker, who saw her from across the clearing, couldn't
believe the luck. He walked straight toward her, but she slipped
past, too focused on her thirst to notice him lurking in the nearby
shadows.

A little fridge tucked behind the stand held the beverages. She slid
the door open and was disappointed to find they were warm. Water
seemed like the best option, but the lemonade made her mouth
water. Unable to decide, she swiped both.

The Licker didn't even bother hiding. River stood right there in
the open, bent over to one side, swaying as she ambled toward the

Mirror Maze. It would've been funny if River hadn't been so high she could barely walk.

Or maybe that made it funnier.

River chugged half the water. It hit her stomach hard, causing an immediate wave of nausea. Her chest seized to keep the water down. *Success.*

There was no way River could carry both beverages into the Mirror Maze. The glass lemonade bottle—which now weighed fifty pounds—had become an anchor tethering her to the ground, so the water had to go. She took a few more careful sips and placed it gently at her feet before entering the Mirror Maze.

The Licker entered behind her, keeping a safe distance.

Arrows painted on the floor pointed River toward a black wall. The walls closed in, narrowing until she had to turn her body slightly sideways.

"Thanks for the broad shoulders, Dad!" River yelled.

The Licker held back laughter.

River pushed the black wall. It swung open, revealing the silvery labyrinth. The mirrors chilled her skin as she grazed the glass, but she needed them to lead her toward the center. She closed her eyes and implored the maze to protect her.

Behind her, the Licker had trouble keeping it together. River didn't realize it, but as she maneuvered along the walls, she hummed the *Winnie the Pooh* theme song. It started as a slow dirge, then sped faster until she sounded like a cartoon character riding on a spinning top. When lips could no longer keep up, she emitted a shrill screech.

Something inside the Licker snapped. River had to die, if only to get her to shut the hell up.

River rounded a corner and opened her eyes. A dim lamp softly glowed in front of her, with brighter strobes flashing at the sides. She followed the shapes across the reflective surface and landed on a dark shape.

"I'm going to keep walking this way," she told the figure. "If I don't pay attention to you, it takes away your power, and you can't hurt me."

The Licker snorted. "Whatever you say."

Ice shot through her veins at the sound of his demonic voice.

River picked up speed.

The Licker wildly swung the flashlight above his head.

Light reflected off every surface. A swarm of glowing bugs threatened to engulf River. She ducked and ran.

The Licker kept up.

He turned the flashlight off. Lucky for him, River wasn't as smart as the others. She didn't think to conceal her deep, fast breaths. No matter which way she turned, her piglike grunting made her easy to track.

Ahead, River thudded into a wall. The Licker tiptoed behind her as she regrouped, getting closer and closer until his mask brushed her neck.

River felt the gentle weight of the tongue drop onto her shoulder. She froze.

Use the bottle as a weapon, she thought, making her first smart decision of the night.

The Licker balanced something on her other shoulder. A button by her ear clicked, and the mirror in front of her exploded in blue-white LED light.

As her vision adjusted, the Licker's coal-black rubber eyes came into view.

River elbowed him in the gut. It wasn't much, but it was enough for her to dodge him and break into a sprint. She ping-ponged off the walls, sometimes slamming into dead ends, sometimes making real headway.

The Licker stayed on her heels the whole time. He repeatedly flicked the flashlight off and on, which disoriented River. She was never particularly competitive, but River understood she was losing the game. If she didn't fight back, he'd easily overtake her.

"Now's as good a time as any," she said aloud.

River twirled around and went on the offensive. If she put her strength into it, she could crack the creep's skull with her lemonade bottle and seriously injure him. She flapped her arm around until she had a vague idea of where his head was, then took a hard swing.

The bottle crashed into a mirror, shattering it.

The Licker cackled.

"Don't laugh!" River yelled, with genuine fury in her voice. "If it can break a mirror, it can break you!"

"Try me," he growled.

River swung the bottle again. It thumped against his torso. He grunted in amusement. She flailed in front of him, swiping at him a second time with the bottle.

"Enough!" he yelled after she whacked his rib cage. "You've had your fun. Let me show you how a professional does it."

The Licker shoved her square in the chest. He turned the flashlight on and dropped it to the ground. A thousand Lickers loomed over a thousand Rivers. Their gray shadows stood in perfect rows over the dim light. River turned her head; her doppelgängers turned theirs. She raised and lowered her chin. The other girls did the same. She didn't know where she began and where the reflections ended.

Every version of herself gripped the lemonade bottle. Though it wasn't the best weapon in the world, it would do.

He wrapped his fingers around her neck. His touch triggered one last rush of energy. River sprang to life, and with all her strength, slammed the bottle into the mirror next to her. The glass exploded, revealing a concrete wall. She threw the bottle into the wall. Sharp, glittering glass and sticky, sweet smelling liquid flew through the air. The bottle slipped. River tightened her fingers and kept her grip on the neck.

She thrust the last shards of the lemonade bottle at the Licker, aiming for his face, but missing. Her next swipe made contact. The jagged shards sunk into the Licker's side. He groaned in pain, reached out, and twisted her wrist until the bottle fell to the floor.

He pushed River back, slamming her head into the exposed concrete. Slivers of glass dug into her bare thighs, like ten thousand needles pricking her skin. When she rocked and swayed to stand, the finely ground pieces pierced her and opened holes in her thighs, hands, and knees.

The Licker stood over her, bottle in hand. River raised an arm across her face. Dim rays from the flashlight bounced off the mirrors, doubling and tripling in brightness, offering her the once-in-a-lifetime opportunity to watch herself be mutilated from every angle.

He brought the broken bottle down on her head. Bombs burst in her brain. Crunchy, wet squishes echoed in her ears. The Licker breathed loud and hard, muffled by the mask. Her tongue rolled around in her mouth. She bit it weakly, still afraid she might choke.

In the end, he stabbed her twelve times. Three times in the skull, twice in the face, four times in the upper back, once in the lower back, once in the thigh. The last blow went straight into her gut.

As River bled out, the Licker picked up the flashlight.

He knelt over her and wrapped his gloved fingers around the tongue. To her surprise, he slid the mask off and held the flashlight under his chin.

No.

Under *her* chin.

He was a *she*.

A familiar smile spread across the girl's face, devastating River.

"Why?" she gasped, her last breath imminent.

The Licker laughed. Her authentic voice was clear and bright without the voice changer. "Does it even matter?" she asked.

"Yes," cried River.

She died before the Licker gave her an answer.

17

When Claire suggested we hide in the House of Horrors, I laughed so hard Gracie punched me in the arm to shut me up.

"There's a psycho in a cloak and mask chasing us around, and you want to run into a haunted house," I said. "Neither of you can guess the five thousand ways that could go wrong?"

"It's enclosed, and there are plenty hiding places," Claire said. "But that's not why I want to go in. Last summer, I took my little cousin on the ride. It broke. A glow-in-the-dark skeleton dancer guy pulled back a curtain and called someone on a red phone. The ride started again in like thirty seconds."

"Can you make calls outside the park?" I asked.

Claire shrugged. "There's a chance. The phone was in the

graveyard. We should get in there before the lights go out again."
She paused. All the color drained from her face.

"My immortal soul drifted up," she said. "Just now. It bloomed."

"Oh shit," I mumbled. "Did you get higher?"

"Parts are. My feet are locked. Once again, I find myself tarred
and feathered."

Gracie turned to me, mouth open. "We're going to die, aren't
we?" she asked.

The facade of Wickett's Despicable House of Horrors was a giant
skull with red eyes bulging from the sockets. Lights inside the eyes
pulsed as steam blew from the nose. Jaws stretched wide. Three-foot-
high teeth threatened us as we walked toward the entrance, into the
cavernous mouth.

An icy wind accompanied by prerecorded ghostly moans greeted
us as we stepped inside. Gracie whimpered.

During an ordinary trip through the House, you ride through an
old abandoned Victorian, from the swampy front yard to the attic,
then your coffin-car falls, and you end up in a graveyard. We stood
in front of the swamp. Gracie refused to move.

"I'm not going in there," she said.

Claire, whose bones threatened to go full noodle, slung an arm
around Gracie's shoulder.

"My four year old cousin giggled her way through this when it
was packed with people jumping out to scare us. It's just Halloween
decorations, flashing lights, and prerecorded sounds."

"Smells too," I added. "They pipe in stinky stuff to make it
scarier."

We all inhaled.

Fresh dirt. Moldy wood. Sour, acidic vomit.

I gagged.

"Puking is bad," said Claire. "No!" She swatted at my face, missed, and patted me on the head.

"Are you aware I'm not a dog?" I asked.

Gracie ignored me and twisted toward Claire. "Did you put your arm around me to guide me into the building, or did you do it so I could hold you?"

"Yes," said Claire. She blinked. Her eyes reopened at different speeds. "Maybe I ate too much weed."

"Trust me," I said. "You did."

She booped my nose.

"We have to go," I said as calmly as possible. "Let's follow the tracks. Move as fast as you can while we still have light."

I ducked under Claire's arm to help Gracie carry her. Her skin was damp; her hair smelled like coconut. Heat radiated from her core. Her chin fell to her chest; her head rolled toward me.

"I love you, Violet," she said. "Mean it. Do you love me?"

"Yes," I said, my dry lips sticking together as I spoke.

"If we don't die, you wanna get married?"

I sighed. We didn't have time for a drugged-out lovefest. My high—which the Licker decimated when he smashed Lolly—had worn off and had been replaced by sweaty drowsiness.

"Sure," I said to quiet her.

"I love you too, Gracie."

"Yeah, Claire, everybody loves everyone," grunted Gracie. She pointed to a dark corner. "Can we cut through those curtains over there to get to the graveyard?"

We dragged Claire through the fake swamp. A cigarette butt and Starburst wrapper floated in the green-tinged water. Plastic reeds slapped our calves. Claire stepped a little too hard and splashed herself in the face.

Gracie gave me full control of Claire while she peeked through a curtain.

"This is the haunted dining room," she said. "If we go in here, we can turn right and go through the attic. Graveyard is right after."

"You sure?" I asked. I didn't have the energy to drag Claire around for much longer.

"Seventy-five percent," Gracie said.

"I'll take it."

We pulled Claire through the curtain. She immediately broke free to sit on a creaky wooden dining chair. I held my breath, preparing for it to disintegrate under her weight. It swayed a little but remained intact.

"Whoever decorated this place did a great job," Claire said. She rubbed her finger in a circle on the table and drew a *Ghostbusters* slash across the center.

She wasn't wrong.

From the bloodstained damask rug on the floor to the water stains on the walls, to the too-realistic roasted pig on the table, the details were impeccable.

I leaned in to check out poor Porky. Fake flies dotted the rotten apple in his mouth. Claire booped the pig's nose and pulled out a chair to join him for dinner.

"No time to sit," I said. "We're super close."

"Leave me," said Claire. "Slowin' ya down."

Something inside me snapped.

"Can I ask what part of 'no one is splitting up' did y'all not understand?" I yelled. "Claire, snap out of it. When you slept over after Avery Eaton dumped you, I watched you make a grilled cheese sandwich with no less than *eight tablespoons* of River's super-potent homemade THC butter, and eat it in three bites. Even *River* was scared you'd gone too far. Four hours later, you helped my mom mount our new kitchen cabinets. Tonight you had a fraction of that amount of weed. You can walk. Now take a big breath, stand straight, and walk behind me. Gracie, you take the rear."

Claire shivered, gripping the table. She did a full body roll with her eyes closed. Gracie's brow furrowed.

"Claire," she began.

"Wait," I mouthed to her, holding up a hand.

Claire shook, tapped her fingers on the table, and hummed "The Yellow Rose of Texas" at half speed. I'd seen her do this before hitting the pool at a meet. Her coach taught it to the swim team as a grounding exercise. I didn't understand it, but they were the number one team in their division, so it must have had some value. After the first chorus, Claire stopped and sat manne-quin-still, then did another body roll out of the chair, kicking it over behind her.

"Violet, ho!" she cheered, clapping a hand on my right shoulder. Gracie placed a shaky hand on Claire's shoulder. We were a real human centipede.

The attic was built on an incline that slightly tilted to the right. Strobe lights beat faster and faster, causing my pulse to race. Stacks of old televisions —the boxy kind my Grandma had in her guest room—flashed static as crunching white noise played from the cheap, tinny speakers. Hands hit the windows, and hungry zombies climbed the house trying to break in. A prerecorded orchestra played a mediocre version of "Don't Fear the Reaper."

When the ride is active, zombies break through and lurch toward your car. They get as close to your coffin as the rules allowed, clawing at the air, miming your dismemberment.

That night only the strobes, televisions, and orchestra greeted us. Even without the zombies, the room gave me the creeps.

"The exit is through the bookcase," I said. "It splits in the middle."

We pushed the doors open and stared into a black hallway.

"There's a drop, right?" asked Claire.

"Yeah," I said. "I wonder if there are stairs hidden somewhere."

"We can climb in," said Gracie.

I shook my head. "It's too dark. Anything could be hiding in there."

Claire squatted, turned, and lowered a leg into the darkness. Her foot softly thudded against the ground.

"It's not steep," she said. "It's not flat either. We have to crawl. Once you're in here, there's gray light at the end. Those strobes are giving me a headache, and I might lose my shit again. If you want me to stay coherent, y'all gotta hustle."

Without fanfare, Claire climbed into the opening and parkoured her way down the drop.

"Who wants to go first?" I asked Gracie.

She squinted into the darkness. "It's wide enough for us to go side by side."

We crawled backward on our knees. Damp concrete scuffed my hands while the cold metal track pressed against my belly. I breathed a sigh of relief when the ground leveled enough for us to walk.

Fog floated to our knees, intensified by pale, static blue light.

Tall, fake headstones in crooked rows with names like "Anita Moore-Tishan" and "Rustin Peece" made good hiding places for actors dressed as ghosts. They'd jump out and scream, inches from your face. Though I knew the room was empty, I braced myself for a jump scare.

Claire and Gracie walked the rows while I climbed over a dead tree to reach the phone.

My hand gripped the thin curtain. I said a quick prayer and pulled it to reveal the red phone.

"Found it!" I called out.

I swallowed a cry and lifted the receiver. There were no buttons on the phone. It must've rung directly to another line. I pressed the phone to my ear, praying it might somehow dial 911.

A tone chirped in my ear, followed by a bubbly ring.

Ring ring.

Ring ring.

Ring ring.

"Hello?" a robotic voice growled. "You've reached customer service."

I slammed the phone back on the receiver.

"What's going on?" asked Gracie.

"He answered," I said.

"Who?"

"Who? Who else! *Him.*"

Grace placed a hand on her throat. "Does that mean he's in here with us?"

Somewhere in the background, Claire quietly called out to us. "Y'all?"

"I don't know," I said, ignoring Claire. "The line could connect to the security office or a control room or some random phone across the park or pretty much anywhere."

"What do we do?" asked Gracie.

"Y'all?" Claire repeated.

Gracie panicked, pacing and wringing her hands. I ignored her.

"What, Claire?" I asked.

"Can you come here? I'm so high I'm hallucinating. Or I hope I am."

Claire stood over four gravestones. Someone had turned them around and carved new names on the reverse side.

LOLLY BISHOP

MILA KELLEY

RIVER ELLIS

MEG MCCLENDON

THEODORE GORDON

"What are these names?" I asked.

I didn't say it out loud, but I was relieved James didn't have a headstone. I didn't know what they meant, but it's never a good thing to find someone's name on a grave.

"What names?" asked Gracie.

"The names on the gravestones," I said.

Claire squatted and traced the Y in Lolly's name with her finger.

"If Lolly is dead," Claire whispered. "Are Mila and River too? And why is fucking Meg's name here? I want her to suffer, but I don't literally want her dead!" Her chest twitched, she gasped for air. I knelt next to her. She groaned into my shoulder as I wrapped her in a hug. Tears and snot soaked my shirt.

"Something might have happened to the others," I said. "Or maybe not. Maybe this is the Licker's wish list and he hasn't gotten to some of them yet."

Gracie walked behind me. She read the gravestones, silently mouthing each name. She stopped at River.

"River's dead," she said, a whisper of a whisper.

"Don't say that," I said, reaching out to her. She slid away.

"River's dead," Gracie repeated, louder and faster, her words filled with alarm. "This is a setup. We're about to be sex-trafficked. Last week I found a hair tie looped around my car's antenna. That's how they tag you for containment!"

"Gracie," I said firmly. "He could be in here listening to us. Do not freak out. You're jumping to conclusions, and you're being loud."

"Why's her name on a gravestone, Violet? Why her and Lolly and Mila and not us?"

Claire pulled away from me. She sniffed. "Maybe ours are over there," she said.

"No," Gracie said. "River is dead. What. What do I do? I can't be a person without her. We're supposed to be writing a book. We were going to do a tour next year. We were going to rent a house in Austin and get nerdy boyfriends and a cat. We were going to name it Raccoon."

I flashed back to the day a literary agent sent a direct message to the Instagram account where River and Gracie posted their daily comics. They started the comic as a way to spend more time together, they never expected it would turn into anything more. River cried, and Gracie skipped through the halls at school singing, uncharacteristic behaviors for each of them.

"Gracie," I said. "This doesn't mean River is dead."

Gracie stood and kicked River's gravestone over. She fell to her knees and beat it with both fists until her hands bled. Claire bent over to restrain her.

"Don't you fucking talk to me!" she screamed. "What if it was James?"

My heart stopped. *If it was James…*

"We don't know what the names mean," I said.

"Yes," said Gracie. "We do."

"If they're dead, where the fuck are the bodies?" asked Claire.

Gracie wailed.

I knelt next to Gracie. "If something happened to River or James, there's nothing we can do right now." I told her. Big talk from someone whose best friend didn't have a headstone. "We need to keep moving, and we need to have a plan. Now let's think. Who is Theodore Gordon?" I asked. "Is he from Pritchett?"

"I have a neighbor named Mr. Gordon," said Claire. "I can't remember his first name. He works at night. I don't see him much."

I slowly turned my head toward her. "Works at night where?"

Claire swallowed.

Tiny words were written on the grave, both above and below his name. I leaned in to read them. Above Theodore, it read, *Here Lies.* Below his name, they'd scratched the words, *His Head.*

My foot brushed against something in the fog. Soft. Firm. *Heavy.* I gently kicked it.

"I really hope this is a soccer ball," I said.

I fanned at the fog. Blue light reflected off something at my feet. Glasses.

On a head.

On a *severed* head.

I screamed and ran. Red, orange, and yellow plastic strips flew in the air around the exit. The words WELCOME TO HELL screamed from above a bleeding arch. I ran through and burst free from the House of Horrors.

My body hit another, knocking us both to the ground. I crawled away, flopping back and forth like a fish.

"Wait!" a little voice cried. "I found you! I found you!"

Blythe sat sprawled on the ground with blood smeared on her clothes. She smiled. Her teeth were streaked with red.

"I found you," she said again. "We are found."

18

Claire and Gracie appeared behind Blythe.

"What happened to you?" Gracie gasped.

Blythe laid on the ground and made a low bun out of her hair so she could use it as a pillow.

"I have to sleep," she said. "I'm so sleepy."

"She's more baked than me," Claire said, laughing.

"She's not even a person anymore," I said.

Gracie hovered over Blythe. "Where is the blood coming from?"

Blythe didn't react when I lifted her leg to examine the deep cut on her calf, or when I lifted her shirt to check for bruises on her stomach. Her fingers were rubbed raw. More bruises encircled a small, bloody gash on her forehead.

I gently slapped her cheek.

"Blythe, what happened?"

Blythe took the end of my ponytail and twirled it around her fingers.

"You make mousy brown work for you," she said.

Claire snorted.

"No paper towels in the bathroom," Blythe said. "Couldn't dry my hands. I thought there might be some at a drink cart outside. I lost you. Stuff happened. A hurricane went through the midway. I got scared and hid. I heard him hurt Mila. She made the worst sounds. Screaming, then gurgling, then nothing. Then he found me. The gross tongue mask from before."

"You saw him?" I asked.

"Telling you duh, bitch," Blythe said. She pushed herself up on her elbows. "He had, um, something heavy. He dropped it and chased me. Dragged me through the Black Kitten Coaster by my leg on my face. Couldn't feel anything. Numb. Something happened, and he left me. I think he thought I was dead. He went away. I stayed a long time. I left. Hid behind a trash can and a picnic table. Saw a huge blood trail outside the Mirror Maze—"

I interrupted her. "Blood outside the Mirror Maze?"

She nodded. "Mmmhmmm. Tongues coming back to the Black Kitten Coaster for me. Ran. Fell a couple of times. Found you." She wrapped my hair around my neck like a noose and pulled me close, choking me. "When you see blood, you know blood, you feel blood."

"So… Blythe's no longer with us!" Claire cackled.

I freed my hair from Blythe's grip and sat back. She fell to her hands and knees.

"I'm dizzy," she slurred.

"No, no, no," Claire said, lifting her. "No crawling on the ground tonight!"

Blythe was way too out of it to walk around, and Claire wasn't much better off. It would be impossible to wrangle them both. A thousand scenarios ran through my head.

Hide. Then what? The new security guard wouldn't be here until morning. That's plenty of time for the Licker to find us.

Security booth. What if the Licker was holed up there? That could've been where he picked up the phone.

Climb the gate. Those spikes at the top were too sharp. Mila cut her shoe. I'd probably cut my throat, if I could even climb it.

Return to the door where we broke in. Possibly the best option, but again, we couldn't carry Blythe and stay hidden.

"Blythe!" I snapped my fingers. "If we hide you, will you stay put?"

"No promises," she said, a sly grin on her face.

I shoved her. "I'm serious. This is life or death. All you have to do is curl up like a kitty and fall asleep. We will get help and come find you."

"I'm *so* sleepy," Blythe reminded us.

"Where do you want to put her?" Gracie asked me.

"The last coffin car on the House of Horrors train," I told her. "There's a hidden latch on the lid so someone can pop out for a scare when you're in the graveyard. We'll stick her in there."

"We're putting people in coffins?" Gracie asked. "Is this really happening? Like, for real?"

"You're coffining me?" Blythe asked, pouting.

I rubbed my temples. "It's not like we're burying you. Pretend it's a tanning bed. You like those."

Ever the drama queen, Blythe flopped back on the ground and went limp.

Claire threw Blythe over her shoulder and carried her around the House, and back into the entrance. She laid her neatly in the coffin and sealed the lid.

Blythe cried out when it clicked shut.

"You're fine," I said. "Safer than the rest of us."

"Meow," she said, her voice muffled. "Purr, purr, meow. Night!"

"What the hell?" I asked.

"You told her to act like a kitty and fall asleep," Gracie told me. "It's your fault."

Claire, Gracie, and I waited. After a few minutes of silence from Blythe, Claire left us to dig around in the employee stand at the House entrance for weapons, and I led Gracie away to explain my plan.

"We have to help Blythe and anyone else who might still be alive," I told her. "We're going to head to the front of the park. If the security office is empty, we're calling 911, and we're escaping through the gate and running until we either get help or die of natural causes. Got it?"

"What if we stayed in the office and locked ourselves in?" Gracie asked.

"Don't you think he might break through the windows?"

"I don't know," she said. "I'm not a fast runner. I've got asthma."

"Asthma, or death by carousel?" I asked. "Which is scarier?"

"How do you kill someone with a carousel?"

I held my index fingers up by my temples to mimic horns. "The devils have horns," I said. "Impale someone through the heart."

Gracie raised her eyebrows and gave me a once-over.

"Violet," she said, leaning in close. "You can tell me. Are you the killer?"

I paused. "Yes. I'm the killer, and I'm going to murder you at the fortune teller booth when I shove her crystal ball down your throat."

"Graphic."

"It's been one helluva night," I said.

Claire came to us, bearing gifts. A hammer for me, a matte black metal flashlight for Gracie.

"There aren't any batteries in the flashlight," Claire said. "But it's heavy enough to hurt someone if you swing it real hard. Hammer is self-explanatory. I have this."

She lifted a power drill and pulled the trigger twice. It buzzed with promise. Claire wiggled her eyebrows in excitement.

"Maybe Claire's the killer," Gracie said under her breath.

"Gals? What's the plan?" Claire asked.

I laid it out for her. She agreed we should head for the security office. "Violet, I swear those windows aren't glass," she promised. "They're some kind of plastic. But this guy practically teleports, and if you and Gracie can't run fast enough…"

"I can run fast," I protested.

"You joined the marching band to get a PE credit because you didn't want to run the mile. You don't even play a band instrument. No one marches with a violin!"

"I carried the Texas flag!" I yelled.

"They bought a lighter flag because you couldn't lift the original pole!"

"Fair point!"

A crack echoed through the carnival as the lights cut out. The rides droned as they wound down, then went silent.

Gracie instinctively tried to turn on the flashlight.

"I told you. No batteries," Claire whispered.

Gracie shook the flashlight aggressively. "Just checking."

The quieter I tried to make my steps, the louder they became, so I gave up and walked like a normal person. Claire and Gracie were close behind me, and I was only mildly worried Claire might slip and accidentally drill into one of us.

When we made it to the midway, something swished past us. I caught a glimpse of the Licker's flowing cloak. He didn't pursue us, but he was too close for comfort.

Claire, ever the hero, corralled us into the midway. Gracie and I hid in the kissing booth while Claire kept watch. Footsteps pounded the ground, louder and louder, then stopped abruptly before moving in the opposite direction.

Claire knelt. "He ran toward the carousel," she said.

"See. Carousel as murder weapon," I told Gracie. I turned to Claire. "This means if we go to the security booth, he'll see us."

"Not necessarily," Gracie said. "He could be doing a sweep. The carousel is past security. If we cut around to the left, we can cling to the gate and go around that way. It's longer, we'll be out of his reach. For a minute, anyway."

"Or," said Claire, standing tall and brandishing her drill. "We know where he's going, so we follow him and end this." She revved the drill.

"Do you have a death wish?" I asked. "Because I sure don't."

"Us three can overpower him," she said. "Blythe survived."

"Because she is so high, he thought she was dead!" I yelled.

Gracie leaned close to me. "Wait. Her plan might work. Claire can kick a grown man's ass. She can pin him while we bash his brains in. The hard part is doing it in the dark."

"Without lights, what's your suggestion?" I asked.

"Gate. Security. Hide."

Claire protested until she realized she'd been overruled.

I led them down the alley behind the midway, past the bathrooms, behind a trio of yellow leaved trees. As we rounded the corner, the lights came back on.

The Licker stood twelve feet away, staring directly at the trees.

"Aren't you dumbasses supposed to be hiding from me?" he asked.

"Run!" yelled Gracie.

"Yeah!" Claire said. She grabbed Gracie, spun her around, and shoved her toward the Licker. "Run that way!"

Gracie did a U-turn and ran the opposite direction.

Claire pressed on, bursting through the trees with the drill high over her head. The Licker reached into a deep pocket and pulled out a hunting knife as long as my arm. He stomped toward Claire, ready to slice and dice.

"Come on," I told Gracie as she ran past, holding out my hand. To my surprise, she took it instead of bolting away.

Claire and the Licker collided in front of us. Claire smashed him with her shoulder and elbowed him in the stomach, dropping him to the ground with a thud. She pinned him and tried to pry the knife from his hand. He held on for dear life. He shook his head back and forth violently, slapping her in the face with his stupid tongue. Claire bit his shoulder. Her teeth left two holes in his cloak. The Licker let out a robotic yelp, which scared Claire enough that he wriggled from her grasp.

"Hit me!" he cheered, laughing gleefully.

I jumped in before I could second-guess myself. I don't remember exactly what I did, what Claire did, or even what the Licker did. Bodies rolled in the dirt; weapons flew. A fist hit his face. The flashlight slammed into the ground. My hammer crushed the Licker's empty hand.

I clawed at the mask. He gripped the tongue with one hand and pressed the opposite forearm into my chest to keep me at arm's length. Claire stood above us, flexed her bicep, and dropped her body—elbow first—onto the Licker's chest.

She missed by about four inches, and slammed ass-first into the concrete.

While Claire recovered, I dug my fingers under his rubber neck. He wrapped his gloved fingers around my hand and squeezed until something under my skin popped. I yelped and twisted my wrist to freedom.

I shook it off. Gracie pinned his arm to the ground and motioned for me to take the other. I fumbled for his hand, and we held him while the drill purred. Claire leaned in, ready to jam the bit straight into his chest.

Unfortunately, her aim was off, and she slid it across my arm instead. I yelped, falling backward. The Licker pushed Gracie aside and scrambled away. Claire dropped the drill and checked my arm.

"Grazed the skin. Didn't go through. You're fine, you're fine. Keep moving."

Gracie shrieked. The Licker was on his feet.

Claire's drill was in his hand.

He revved it while pulling his tongue taut with his other hand. He held the bit to the back of his tongue and drilled up through the rubber. He laughed into his voice changer.

"Thanks for the gift," he said.

I bolted, with Claire slightly ahead and Gracie close behind, gasping for air.

I screamed for Claire to turn around and run for the security booth. She either didn't hear me or didn't want to listen, because she ran into the midway. Gracie crashed against my back.

"Listen," she gasped. "The hissing. It's his breathing!"

A rhythmic, whistling wheeze approached.

"Why aren't we moving?" I asked.

She waved me on. "Go, go, go! Follow Claire!"

I stood frozen in confusion, so Gracie dug her fingers into my side and—before I could protest—pulled me into the midway.

19

The midway was my third-least-favorite part of the carnival, behind the Whirling Witch Coaster and the Ferris wheel. I hated the rides because I thought I might end up dead if I rode them. I hated the midway because it was *filthy*.

Whoever cleaned the carnival skipped the narrow, sharp rows. Shredded napkins and wrappers littered the ground. Years-old water stains crept up the fabric dividers between booths. Dusty plywood walls with sharp splinters stood ready to rip your clothes. The men and women running the booths weren't required to be friendly like the ride operators and ticket takers. Instead of neatly branded Poison Apple Carnival uniforms, they wore sweat-stained T-shirts and ugly baseball caps with crooked, peeling carnival midway logos emblazoned on the front. You'd give them a token, and you'd get a chance to toss a beanbag or fire an ancient popgun. If you lost their game, they'd grunt and demand a token to pay for another round. If you won, they'd chuck a cheap prize at your chest.

The worst ones were dirty old men who asked our ages and grumbled slurs under their breath when we said seventeen.

"He likes them *young*," River once told me after the man at the ring toss booth called us ugly sluts. "A few years ago, I told him I was fourteen, and he tried to give me a stuffed heart. I guess since I got my license I'm not the freshest produce anymore."

I pictured River's House of Horrors headstone. The memory was a knife in my ribs.

"I'm gonna hurl," Gracie groaned. "It stinks like cheese, rotten lemons, and wet metal in here."

I nodded. A stink tornado from a dozen Paulie's Pop-A-Corn carts popping a dozen different flavors choked us. I loved their salted birthday cake flavor, but I didn't love it mixed with the pickle relish flavor, and I despised it mixed with the scent of blood.

I wrapped an arm around her and pulled her behind a face-painting booth. We waited for the Licker to pop up and attack us. When he didn't, I fell to the ground and crawled under a stool. Gracie joined me.

"My eyes hurt," I told her. "There's sweat in them."

She offered me a white cocktail napkin emblazoned with the Crave Inn's logo. I mopped my brow and asked if she wanted it back.

"Gross," she said. "Keep it. Keep this too." She handed me a hammer.

"Where did you find this?" I asked.

"I picked it up when we ran. Did we learn our lesson about dropping our weapons in front of a murderer?"

"Yes," I said. "We did."

"Good. Now what?"

I surveyed the area. We were near a little booth where you could throw Ping-Pong balls into goldfish bowls to win a live goldfish. Rusted shelves displaying glass spheres lined the walls. Black and orange fish delicately swam inside their tiny, solitary prisons, except for one who floated limply at the top of his bowl.

I tapped the glass, and the water rippled. The dead fish's eye squished against the bowl. I leaned in for a better look, and movement in the reflection made me spin around, my hands squeezed into fists, ready to fight.

No one was there.

"I'm so tired," I told Gracie. I relaxed my hands. The adrenaline fueling my survival instinct had drained. "I'm lightheaded. I can't do this much longer."

"We'll do it as long as we have to," she said. "He's in here somewhere. We have to keep running, or we have to find a better hiding place. We also have to be prepared to fight." She sneered, cracked her neck, and spit on the ground.

Gracie was possibly the calmest, most even-keeled person I'd ever met. When in a group of over three people, she rarely spoke at all. She would sit in the corner and let everyone chatter like chickens while she doodled little pictures in her pink-and-white checkered sketchbook. Most of the time I'd forget she was even there until I checked *Graceful River*'s social media and saw our conversations reenacted by Gracie's squatty-faced, bug-eyed characters.

"Since when did you become a badass?" I asked, nodding at the spit puddle on the ground.

"He killed my best friend. If I get my chance, I'm going to make him pay."

The phrase "best friend" made my heart skip. James disappeared into the carnival earlier that evening, and she could've been anywhere. I reminded myself that her name hadn't been on a tombstone, as though that guaranteed her safety.

"He's going to pay," I assured her. "For River and whoever else he hurts. He's going to rot in jail."

"I don't want him to go to jail. I want him dead. If I see him again, I'm going to take your hammer and bash his brains in. I wish I'd drilled a hole in his face when I had the chance. You said he crushed Lolly's head? I want to crush all the bones in his body. I want to taste his blood."

My eyes bulged. "Let's not get too upset yet," I told her. "Emotions breed mistakes."

In the distance, a siren blared, followed by childish giggles. A Choo Choo Train whistle tooted. Someone had turned on the Black Kitten Coaster.

"There are eyes on us," said Gracie. "It's like I have a million spiders running down my neck. When I turn my head, I expect his nasty-ass tongue to flop in my face."

The same paranoia plagued me. The whole situation felt like a setup, like my friends and I were pawns in a gory chess game. He messed with the rides and lights to disorient us, kept us apart to torture us. He probably wanted us in the midway, trapped in our own little fishbowl, lying in wait until he won the game and could claim us as his prize.

"Are you still high?" I asked.

"I can function, but I'm so overstimulated when the lights are on. They're *so* bright. Then when it's dark, everything is extra black. And if the stupid coaster doesn't stop laughing, I will tear my hair out and shove it in my ears."

"I'm worried about Claire," I said. "She couldn't even speak proper English."

"Blythe was worse. Bitch couldn't stay on her feet."

"She's safe in her coffin, though. Claire's out in the wild."

I picked at the rubber rim on my shoe until a strip peeled off like a banana skin. I stretched it between my fingers until it snapped.

"Should we try to find her?" I asked.

"We should think. Use our brains. Let's make a list."

Gracie retrieved her sketchbook and a ballpoint pen from her crossbody bag. Blocky letters on the pen spelled out: I STOLE THIS.

She made two columns, one a list of our names, the other a list of locations.

LOLLY	–	*TEST YOUR STRENGTH*
RIVER	–	*?*
MILA	–	*?*
CLAIRE	–	*MIDWAY*
BLYTHE	–	*HOH*
VIOLET	–	*MIDWAY*
JAMES	–	*?*
GRACIE	–	*MIDWAY*

"What are you trying to figure out?" I asked.

"Lolly is dead. It's likely Mila and River are too. We need to rule them out. Blythe is hidden. I have faith she will stay put."

"I don't."

She sighed. "Neither do I. I lied. But I have to hope. Claire is somewhere near us. I can sense her out there, alive. You and I are okay. James is the only one left."

Gracie added a few more question marks next to James's name.

"What if Lolly wasn't the first victim?" I asked. "What if he got James before her?"

"No. Stop imagining the worst, and think critically. When would he have had time to kill James? Didn't he move straight for Lolly after the lights came on?"

"What if he snatched James in the dark?"

"There is no way someone put their hands on James Parker without her screaming bloody murder."

"What if he surprised her?"

Gracie drew a circle, then two more, to make eyes on a face. She drew little X's for pupils. The mouth was a straight line with a little half-moon tongue hanging limply from one side.

She sighed. "I'd believe James was the psycho in the costume before I'd believe the Licker killed her without an earthshaking fight." She drew a second face, this one with sharp fangs and cat eyes.

I ripped the pen from her hand.

"Don't joke about James hurting people. She would never."

"I was being flippant. I'm sorry. James is fine. There's a nonzero chance she escaped to get help. The police might roll in here any minute with James perched on the hood of a cop car, pointing the way like George Washington crossing the Delaware."

We sat in silence. Gracie traced a blank page with a finger. I returned her pen.

"What do we do with your list?" I asked.

"I don't know," she said. "I thought if I wrote a list on paper, I'd magically have a plan, but I don't. I can write names all day long, and it won't change anything. James and Claire are missing. Blythe is barely human. Everyone else is dead. We're on our own."

"Do you want to find Claire?"

Gracie's face cracked. "Am I a horrible person if I say no? I'm scared, Violet. This doesn't feel like reality. Is it? Is this really happening?"

My head throbbed. I needed her to get a grip, because if I had to hear her ask, "Is this really happening?" one more time, I was going to sacrifice her to the Licker.

"It's happening," I said softly.

"I love Claire. I love all our friends. But I don't want to die here. I want to save myself."

"Then that's what we'll do," I said, gripping my hammer. "If we go straight and kinda follow the turns without changing direction, we can go behind the face-painting stations and turn right at the end by Madame Lavona. From there, it's a straight shot down balloon game alley, and we exit at the dunk tank. Once we escape, we'll call for help to save the others."

"Is this really happening?" she repeated for the umpteenth time.

"Yeah. It is."

"And Claire?"

I swallowed. "It's like you said. We have to save ourselves. We aren't acting selfish. Claire's stronger than us. She's fine."

C laire wasn't fine.

Though she'd successfully escaped the Licker upon entering the midway, she'd hit her head during their earlier scuffle. He also crushed her arm under his foot and wrenched her wrist, twisting it behind her back. Fortunately, she scrambled away, but he'd left her in such excruciating pain that without River's edibles, she would've gone into shock.

Her right temple throbbed. One of her back molars wiggled when she poked it with her tongue. Her left arm was at least sprained, probably broken. The fingers on her right hand were *definitely* broken. Tears welled in her eyes when she pictured Hattie Bakely pitching softball in her place.

She doubled back to the entrance and stepped into the open area by the carousel. In the distance, the fat pumpkin on the Ferris Wheel grinned at her, flashing his broken teeth as a sign of solidarity.

"I'm smashed up too," he said. "Won't be stopping me."

Claire's skin crawled. Overwhelmed by the pumpkin's gaze, she stumbled away and hid in the shadowy space between the midway and the gate. Dumpsters lined the row. Claire thought it must be awful to be an employee who had to walk the alley in the summer, inhaling the stink of lawn trimmings and wet cardboard boxes. She sniffed her armpits. It stank like she'd used a raw onion as deodorant. The dumpsters had nothing on her.

For a while, she could still hear Violet and Gracie. Hard breathing, squeals, shushes. They were on the move. Their voices grew faint as they headed deeper into the midway. Claire strained to listen.

If Claire didn't move, she would lose track of her friends, but an abundance of choice paralyzed her. Run into the midway and risk getting lost? Find a hiding spot? Search for a hole in the gate?

Her inability to form a plan left her locked in place.

Move one toe, she told herself. She suffered from sleep paralysis off and on for years. She would wake in the darkness, her mind firing on all cylinders, her body refusing to cooperate. Over time, she learned that if she could move one pinky, one toe, or even wiggle her nose, energy would rush over her body and jolt her back to life.

Move! she told her feet. *He knows where you are, and that you're alone. Your feet are fine. You can run. One in front of the other.* She pushed her foot a little farther, then farther still, until her legs slid in opposite directions. She fell, but caught herself before hitting the ground.

It would be impossible to scale the gate with her injured hand.

Her only option was the employee entrance. Get to the door and walk out.

No. *Run* out.

Stay in the dark, she told herself. *Get to the phone. Call someone. Save the other girls. Get home alive. Stay in the dark. Get to a phone. Get across the parking lot. Get to a car. Get to a neighborhood. No one can outrun you. You're the fastest girl in school.*

Claire jogged along the pavement, but the speed and heat and bright lights messed with her head, sickening her. She doubled over, took a few deep breaths, and switched to power walking. Even at a slower speed, Claire was still faster than most. She pictured spectators in the stands at a swim meet, all chanting her name. She got carried away and chanted it herself.

"Go Claire, go!" she cheered. She might as well have blown an air horn to give away her location.

The cheers in her head faded into laughter as she sensed someone looming behind her.

She stopped.

"Whatcha doing, Claire?" asked an amused evil robot.

The Licker knew her name.

He gripped the drill in his gloved hand, pressing the trigger to show it still held a charge. Her heart hummed in time with the sound.

"No," Claire said. "This isn't happening."

"Rah-rah, go, Claire, go!" he teased. "Oh. Speaking of 'rah-rah,' you shouldn't expect Mila to pop out with her pom-poms. It's hard to cheer with a water gun jammed down your throat."

"What did you do to her?"

"I had to crack her jaw in half to jam it in. All that money her parents spent on veneers, wasted."

His words took Claire's breath away.

Little Mila, with her powerful voice and dimpled cheeks, was gone forever. Her parents adored her. They went to every single game and cheer competition to cheer their cheerleader. For events, cheer parents wore T-shirts with their child's face hand-painted on the front and their graduation year and squad position on the back. Claire was at Mila's house when her mom's shirt for senior year came in the mail. She actually squealed when she unfolded it. Mila's cartoony face on one side, MY DAUGHTER IS THE CAPTAIN on the other. She put it on over her clothes and wore it out to dinner. Mila begged her not to, but her daughter had worked her ass off for almost a decade, and Mrs. Kelly intended to milk it for all it was worth.

Claire pictured Mila's mother standing over a casket wearing the shirt.

Her body tensed as she prepared to run, dizziness be damned.

"If you run, I'll catch you," he told her. "Don't run. I'm not moving, don't you move either. Turn around and look at me. Everything's all muffled inside this mask."

"Maybe you should take it off," Claire yelled over her shoulder.

"Or maybe I should take your fucking head off with this drill," he countered.

Terrified, Claire gave in and turned around. The Licker kept his promise; he didn't move.

"I'm curious, Claire. Have you wondered why I'm doing this? What's my motivation? If I were in your shoes, I'd have so many questions."

"There's never a good reason to murder people. You're crazy."

"False," he said. "Tell me, Claire. What are your plans for tomorrow?"

"What?"

"What are you going to do tomorrow?" he repeated. He buzzed the drill to hint that Claire needed to take him seriously.

She pictured her pool. Her parents built for her to practice at home, her cool blue haven. She could stick her earbuds in and crank her music, dive in, and glide through the water for hours. Sometimes she only stopped when the music died.

"I'm going swimming," she said. "Actually, I'm going to breakfast with the girls at the Crave Inn. I'll shower and nap when I get home, *then* I'll swim."

"You swim every day?"

"Yes."

"To keep in shape for racing?"

"No," she said, shaking her head. "I swim because I love swimming."

"See," he said. He tucked the drill under his arm and clapped his hands. "Right there. I don't love anything. I don't even *like* anything."

"Do you especially not like us? Me and my friends? What did we do to make you hate us?"

The Licker took a step forward. He pointed the business end of the drill directly at her face and pressed the trigger. Claire braced herself, clenching her jaw until her gums bled. Electricity shot through her back teeth. Her mouth tasted like pennies. She snorted and spat in his direction.

"It's not that I *hate* you," he said, dodging the flying spit. "I hate what you represent. As people, you're fine. *Ish*. Except James. I can take or leave her." He cackled. "Maybe I'll take her and leave her in chunks." He leaned close to her and growled. "Maybe I already have."

She ignored his comments about James. She couldn't handle more than one dead friend at a time.

"So we know you?" she asked.

"As much as anyone can know anyone else."

Claire put her hands in the air in surrender.

"Take off your mask," she said. "If you're going to kill me anyway, you might as well show me who you are. It's only fair."

"Do you think I'm stupid?"

"Kinda," Claire said, smirking.

The drill stopped.

"You have some nerve," he said.

"You don't. If you did, you wouldn't be hiding behind some nasty mask."

He took another step toward her.

"I'm not taking off the mask. I might take yours off, though."

He crashed into her and wrapped his biceps around her waist, pinning her injured arm behind her back. Her screams overpowered the evil canned laughter at the House of Horrors. He pressed the drill bit into her cheek and hit the trigger.

The drill cut into her cheek at an angle, ripping the flesh apart and cracking her bottom teeth into dust. Blood filled her mouth and rushed down her throat, choking her. The pain burned white-hot until she felt nothing at all. He chucked the drill, stuck a leather-clad finger into the hole in her face, and then tore off her entire cheek.

He sniffed the skin, winced, and tossed it over his shoulder.

"Trust me," he hissed. "Smelled infected."

She cried, begging with words neither he nor she could understand. Without her teeth and cheek, her tongue flopped out of her mouth, mirroring the Licker's mask.

Claire fought weakly as he dragged her into the alley behind the midway. When her blood made her arms too slick to grip, he reached under his cloak and pulled out a belt.

He kneed her in the chest and dropped her at his feet. She tried to crawl away. He tsk-tsked her, looped the belt around her neck, and used it as a leash to drag her to her feet and lead her to the food court.

Claire clawed at the belt with her mangled fingers, desperate to release tension so she could breathe. Air finally came in shallow, short bursts.

Claire held this position until her fingers brushed against the exposed bones in her jaw. Her jagged teeth shocked her, but the texture of her tongue through the hole in her cheek *repulsed* her. Without thinking, she jerked her hands from the belt. The Licker tightened the strap. Her vision blurred. Dim yellow lamps above them dotted the sky like jaundiced fireflies until they entered the food court. Claire whimpered as bright white fluorescent lights stung her eyes.

"I can't see!" she cried.

"Too bad." He dumped her on the ground like a sack of potatoes and walked past the tables. He lifted a plastic café chair and threw it in her direction, not close enough to hit her but close enough to make her think it might.

Claire cried.

"What are you doing?" she begged.

He ignored her. He hurled two more chairs over Claire's head. Again, she begged for his plan. He flipped a table.

"What monster wants to hurt little girls?" Claire asked, her words mushy. Blood sprayed across the concrete as she spoke.

The Licker froze with another chair over his head. He brought it over to Claire and slammed it down in front of her. He sat, crossing his legs daintily. He paused for a beat, then slid from the chair onto the ground next to her, smushing his rubber tongue against her forehead.

"You aren't little girls," he said.

"What?"

"You called yourself a little girl. You're practically grown."

"We're seventeen! Lolly is still sixteen!"

"You mean, Lolly *was* sixteen."

Claire moaned. The Licker pushed himself onto his elbows and stroked her hair.

"One more year to be kids, then you're off to school, right? Y'all will be adults in college. What were you going to be when you grew up, Claire? An Olympian?"

"I don't know," Claire sobbed. "I don't know."

"Won't be able to compete again, since you can't hold your breath underwater anymore. Unless… Do they allow cheek transplants? I know a couple of dead girls who don't need theirs anymore."

He pulled Claire onto the chair and used the belt to secure her upright. As he dragged her—chair and all—to the row of food carts, he rambled.

"Not everyone has choices, Claire. Not everyone has a bright future on the horizon ahead. The clock is running out for some people. It's running out for me. Maybe it ran out a long time ago."

"What do you mean?"

The Licker punched her torn cheek. Red and purple fireworks exploded in her vision. "Don't interrupt me," he snarled.

"I'm sorry!" she sobbed. "I'm so sorry."

He patted her on the head. "There's no happy ending for me. I threw it all away."

"Why is that my fault?"

The Licker stopped next to a pink-and-blue cotton candy machine and stuck his face in hers. Dark, shiny orbs darted back and forth beneath the webbing over his eyes, revealing a bit of the human behind the mask to Claire.

"It's not your fault," he said. "I'm pissed off, and what you're witnessing is me doing my best to feel better."

He walked around the cart, rubbing his fingers around the rim of the large silver bowl. He knelt and dug through the shelves below. "Here we go," he said, holding up a white carton. A cartoon clown on the box smiled at Claire. The design looked dated, like something from the 1950s.

A red switch blinked on the side of the machine. The Licker smacked it with his palm, and its motor hummed like the engine on Claire's grandmother's classic Mustang. He shook the carton at Claire and made a big show of pouring the fine pastel pink powder into the bowl. He raised the box high to extend the sugar stream and cranked a knob on the front of the machine all the way to the right. A meter twitched as it preheated.

"It has to be hot enough to melt the sugar," he said. "Are you a baker? Nah, probably not. You look like you've never so much as *sniffed* a cupcake. You'd have to live off chicken breast and spinach for a body like yours, right? So much muscle for a girl."

The cotton candy machine growled. The meter twitched back and forth, slowly edging to the right. Claire realized she was reading a thermometer. It bobbed between 200 and 225 degrees, inching toward 300. The scent of toasted vanilla wafted in the air.

The Licker waved his hand over the bowl like a witch with a cauldron. "Boiling water is hot," he said. "But melted sugar is molten.

A sugar burn is excruciating, and it's syrupy, so it sticks to the skin. Uh oh. Here we go."

He dipped a gloved hand into the bowl and pulled out a light strand.

"Want some fresh cotton candy?" he asked.

"No!" screamed Claire. She struggled against the belt as she tried to rock the chair.

"*Open your mouth*," he sang.

When she refused, he took his index and middle fingers and jammed them into the gash in her cheek. The flavors of blood and sweet flossy sugar mixed and made her gag.

"Please," she begged. All the vowels came out as squishy hisses.

He replied with a fist to her face. Her nose broke with an audible crack.

Claire was too stunned to move. Her brain spun inside her skull like one of the Crazy Cauldrons. The Licker lifted her from the chair, pressed on her back, and wrapped his fingers around her throat. The motor in the center of the bowl squealed as it spun as fast as her brain, maybe faster.

The heat hit her skin before the sugar did. Melted candy strands licked her face, leaving red zebra stripes. He'd been right; it stuck to her skin, layering upon itself, growing fuzzier and thicker as he rubbed her face clockwise around the bowl.

Her vision went first; the cocoon he'd spun around her head was the last thing she saw. Her hearing went next; the machine's echo stopped whirring in her ears. Sugar burned against her skin until her pain receptors short-circuited, and she went numb.

Her nose went last. When everything went silent, black, and

cold, the scent of sticky, sweet, burnt sugar still lingered in her final thoughts.

The Licker marveled at his fluffy pink treat, but he didn't trust it. He dropped Claire on the ground, wrapped the belt around her throat, and squeezed until he was positive she was dead. Then he stared at her body a few minutes more, just to be sure.

When Claire lay limp long enough, the Licker raised his mask, peeled a wad of cotton candy off the corpse's head, and ate it.

It was *viciously* sweet.

21

Violet, did you hear the sound that time?" Gracie asked. We were still fumbling around inside the midway, listening as someone howled in pain.

"Yeah," I said. "You're right. That's Claire."

Gracie and I stood in the mini bowling booth, huddled together, shaking.

"Are we going to die?" she asked.

"No," I lied.

"Yes, we are. If this guy can overpower Claire, who is solid muscle and is training to drag a fucking Hummer, you and I don't have a shot in hell."

"It's not about physical strength," I lied again. "We're smarter than him."

"Lolly was smarter than both of us put together."

I hesitated. "The Licker surprised her. If she'd had a minute to think, things would've been different."

"Bullshit."

It was bullshit. Every positive word I'd spoken since we entered the carnival was bullshit. I didn't even believe *myself* when I said we'd be okay, how could I convince someone else?

"I'm scared," I said.

"I want my mom," said Gracie.

I wanted my mom too. She would've been at home, asleep. Usually, she expected me to text her hourly if I was out past ten, but she'd made a special exception for the Scavenge. She didn't want to ruin my fun. She asked me to send her pictures from breakfast and bring home two sides of crispy bacon and a lemon crepe when I returned home. My lower lip trembled.

"Are we done?" I asked. "Should we hide the best we can and wait?"

"He'll find us. He's had no trouble so far. It's like he can teleport."

"Maybe it's two people."

"Multiple killers?" she cried, her voice cracking. "Jesus Christ, I couldn't wrap my head around one person wanting us dead. What could we have done to two?"

"Nothing. No one deserves this."

A crash silenced her for a moment. Two more crashes followed, farther in the distance.

"He moves fast," said Gracie. "It sounded a mile away."

"No," I said. "The first crash echoed. He hasn't gotten far."

We leaned forward a bit as we waited for more screams. When it seemed like they had stopped, we relaxed, until Claire's wails filled the night as she begged for mercy through the speakers surrounding us.

"It's coming through the sound system!" I gasped.

The Licker's robotic screech buzzed around us. "I've been futzing with the audio setup all night," he told Claire…and *us*. "Thought it was too late, but I got it fixed, just in time for the big show!"

"He's killing her," Gracie said, eyes wide. "And he wants us to hear it."

I pressed my hand against my lips. "I know," I said. "And we're next."

———

We decided that Claire was most likely in the food court at the back of the carnival. Whatever technology the Licker used to amplify Claire's torture kept cutting in and out. It would be silent for a minute, then we'd hear Claire begging for her life, then the sound would drop long enough for us to think it was over before it started back up.

"What is he doing to her?" Gracie asked.

I couldn't imagine. I didn't want to.

"We're safe as long as Claire keeps screaming," I told Gracie, trying to change the subject. I felt dirty thinking such a thing, much less saying it aloud.

She sobbed and gripped my hand so tightly my fingers went numb. I led her like a little child.

We took three rights around an apple bobbing booth.

"This is a full circle," I said. "It's pointless."

"There's a Cajun-spice Pop-A-Corn stand if we go forward from here," Gracie said, pointing.

"Didn't we pass a Cajun stand before?"

"No. Peanut butter flavor."

"Are you sure?"

"Nope."

I pulled her toward the popcorn cart anyway because I had no other idea what to do.

We had two options at the cart: run along another short row, or look behind curtain number one because the wall next to us was nothing but black plastic shower curtains hanging from a wire.

"Crawling through curtains worked in the House of Horrors," Gracie said. "Could work here too."

"I have the layout of the House memorized. This place is more confusing than the Mirror Maze. Anything could be behind that plastic. We could end up twice as turned around."

"I'm willing to take a chance," said Gracie. She pulled the curtains apart, took my hand, and we stepped through into an empty booth.

A red-and-white dartboard surrounded by yellow light bulbs blinked across the way. Gracie smiled.

"Come on," she said. "Jesse Chandler's dad owns the dart game. River was in love with him."

She said was. Past tense.

"Jesse's dad?" I asked, joking to lighten the mood. Mr. Chandler could've been Shrek's human twin.

"No," she said, disgusted. Apparently I hadn't inherited James's comedic timing. "*Jesse.* Come on. Anyway, she made me come here a whole bunch last spring. Let me think." She paused and waved her hands like a flight attendant as she mentally explored the midway. "There's a pretzel cart to the left, then we turn right, then right again, then we'll exit by the dunk tank. We'll head for the guard stand and go out the employee entrance gate where we came in."

Back at the food court, Claire's sounds were thicker, wetter, fewer, and far between.

Gracie led the way, breaking into a run and whipping around the corner, almost taking out the kissing booth.

We stepped out into the open. Ahead, bright lights lit up the giant candy apple at the entrance to the carnival. We saw it, squeezed our hands tight, and ran toward the guard stand.

Gracie tried to jerk away first. She saw the windows before I did. I panicked and pulled her back, thinking the Licker had somehow caught her and was dragging her to her death. She grunted, yanked my arm, and stopped dead in her tracks.

"What?" I asked. Then I saw it.

Blood was smeared all over the windows, from the inside. Random streaks, like a knockoff Jackson Pollock done in only red paint.

"It's blood right? I'm practically blind, but that's blood. I can't." She tried to fall on the ground, but I held her up.

"No, no, no," I said. "There's no crawling on the ground tonight, remember?"

Claire coughed through the speakers. It sounded wet.

Gracie needed tough love to keep going. I grabbed her by her collar.

"We are safe right now because the psycho killer is murdering Claire."

Gracie cried harder. I wanted to choke her, escape, and blame it on the Licker.

"Listen to me!" I hissed. "We know where he is right now. We know that we are sitting ducks out here in the open. We know there is a potential exit. What the fuck are you doing?"

She swallowed a breath, sniffed, and allowed me to drag her to the guard stand. As we got closer, I could see that the blood wasn't just on the walls; there was also a trail of it on the ground, leading from the door, around the little building, toward the gate.

I pulled Gracie toward the gate, keeping as much space between us and the guard stand as possible. Then the gate came into view. There was something hanging on it.

A navy sack, like a laundry bag, was tied to the bars over the employee entrance. When we got closer, I saw a leather belt wrapped tight around the middle. My eyes drifted down, *I realized the bag had feet,* and my own feet stopped moving.

Gracie paused to check me. "Violet, like you said, we gotta keep going." She pinched my tricep and attempted to drag me away. I stood firm.

"We can't go out the door," I said.

"Why not?"

"How much can you see without your glasses?"

"Basically nothing unless it's right in my face."

"Okay," I said. "I have perfect vision, and Ted, minus his head, is hanging on the gate, right over the door."

Gracie whipped her head toward Ted. "What?" she asked.

Goose bumps speckled the back of my neck. I shivered despite the humidity.

He knew the easiest escape route and guaranteed we couldn't use it.

I forced myself to move. Gracie followed.

"I can't touch a dead body," I whispered.

"What if your life depends on it?"

"Can you move him?"

"No."

"Why not?"

"Because I can't touch a dead body either," Gracie said. "Is there a way to go around him?"

"Might as well check."

When we got close enough, Gracie's vision came to focus, and she gasped. "Why is his neck stump so shiny?" She winced, looked away, and got an eyeful of the guard stand. "Oh my God, it's like someone took a paintbrush to the windows! Violet! What if someone is in there?"

I ignored her. "His hands are behind his back," I said. I leaned in as close as I could manage without gagging and examined him. "The Licker tied him around the bars. We will have to cut him free if we want to get through."

"Maybe we should try it. There could be scissors or a utility knife or something in the guard stand."

"We'd need bolt cutters," I said. "He's bound with chains, not rope."

"Shit. Fine. We can't be out in the open like this."

Claire howled like an animal, then grunt-screamed three times.

I had a suggestion, but she wasn't going to like it. "We can check the guard stand. If it's just blood, we can hide inside."

"If it's *just* blood? Is that not enough for you?"

"As opposed to blood and a second secret killer waiting to pop out? Or blood and someone's intestines inside the filing cabinet? Both of those things are a possibility, and both are way worse than *just* blood!"

"What if the blood is the point?" she asked, pausing to listen to Claire's wet whistles. "What if this is a satanic ritual to steal the blood of virgins?"

"That's four out of eight. Seems like there could be a more efficient way, like maybe attacking the Purity Club on their bimonthly camping trip out in the Barkuloo Woods. Have you never heard of Occam's razor? What's more likely? Bloodthirsty satanic witches, or a lone wolf psycho with a grudge against us? All signs point to lone wolf, dude."

She deflated. There's nothing conspiracy nuts hate more than when someone pokes a commonsense hole in their theory.

"Let's check the stand, and if it's empty, we'll lock ourselves in," Gracie said.

She turned away. I edged closer to Ted for a better look. His name badge had come unpinned and hung loosely in place, threatening to fall into his breast pocket. A roll of orange fabric tucked into the pocket popped out enough to prop up the badge and keep it from falling.

"There's something in here," I said, reaching for the fabric. Ted's name badge fell into my hand. I put it in my pocket, took the orange roll from his, and stretched the material taut.

Gracie peered into the windows of the guard stand on her tiptoes to survey the area.

"What do you have? She asked.

"This," I said, handing it to her, my hands shaking.

"Screwed Tour 2017," she read. "Ted is a punk fan?"

"No. James is," my voice was low and frantic. "We go to Screwed every summer. This is a patch from her jacket from the first year we went. Why is this here, Gracie? What happened to James?"

It was the first physical manifestation of James in hours, and it burned my hand like fire. I flung it at Gracie, who caught it, crumpled it in her hand and pressed it to her heart. "Are you okay?" she asked.

"No," I said.

"Goddamn it," she said, shaking the doorknob. "This thing is locked. Why wouldn't it be?"

"Have you heard Claire lately?" I asked, looking around.

On cue, heavy machinery whirred, and Claire gurgled.

Gracie, stunned with fresh panic, slammed her body into the door several times.

"Let's hit it together," I said.

We took a step back and counted to three. On three, we struck it at full force.

It didn't budge.

"Can you pick a lock?" I asked.

"No. I have a bobby pin, though. Maybe it's like the movies? A little wiggle?" Gracie reached behind her ear and produced the promised pin.

I asked if she had a credit card.

"Yes!" she gasped and tossed the bobby pin on the ground. "A card is probably easier."

She pulled a slim wallet out of her crossbody bag. Hello Kitty peeked at me from an apple embossed on the red patent leather. Gracie dug through her wallet and produced a library card. She handed it to me.

"You want me to try?" I asked.

"Mmmhmm." Gracie nodded.

I knelt on the ground and peered into the crack between the

door and the frame. The pieces of the lock were visible, but I didn't understand the mechanics.

"I'm supposed to use the card to press against the curved part, right? Like, push it in?"

"Do whatever your little heart tells you," she said. "Please hurry."

I slid the card in and wriggled it back and forth. It clicked and squeaked against the mechanism.

"Speaker system is pretty quiet," I said without looking up.

"Yeah."

"Do you think Blythe is okay?" I asked, since I knew Claire wasn't.

Gracie didn't answer.

"I don't think she's okay either," I said. My chest felt hollow. "Or James. She'd die before she'd let anyone rip her jacket apart."

"What if we're the only ones left?" Gracie asked.

"We'll be testifying at this asshole's trial."

The library card slipped into place. I lifted it, and the door opened.

"You got it?" Gracie asked.

"I got it! I got it!" I said a little too loudly.

We slipped inside the office and locked the door behind us.

Two things hit me hard at the same time. One, the room stank so bad my eyes watered. Two, the room was more red than not. Fresh, shiny blood—mostly in the shape of streaky handprints—coated every surface, from the desk to the papers littering the floor, to Ted's red baseball hat.

I nodded at it. "Guess he won't be needing a hat anymore." I clamped my hands over my face. "It stinks like someone sprayed simple syrup on iron and it rusted!"

Gracie lurched and puked next to the bloody trash can.

I yelped and jumped back. "Jesus, you've been throwing up all night! How do you have any more food in you?"

Gracie—who had repositioned and now had the trashcan properly in place—heaved, then turned her head and dryly whispered, "Oh God."

I followed her eyes.

It's not just random streaks.

A thick, drippy circle was painted on the wall. All the way up near the wood ceiling, starting at twelve o'clock on the cheap wood laminate above the window, down onto the glass, curving around the white brick, and back up onto the glass to complete the loop. Inside was a poorly drawn cartoon peacock. He lay on his back, feet straight up in the air. His head rested near his legs, his little tongue drooped from his beak, and he had X's for eyes.

Written around the circle, in carefully painted letters, were the words:

NO ONE SURVIVES THE SENIOR SCAVENGE

For the first time that night, I was 100 percent convinced that I was going to die.

But I didn't want Gracie to see it.

"Watch the window," I said. "Scream if you see anyone coming."

Gracie did as she was told and watched the window while I scrambled for the phone. I lifted the receiver.

Silence.

"He cut the phone," I said.

Gracie glanced over her shoulder. "Of course he did," she said flatly. "Why wouldn't he?"

I dug through the creaky metal desk drawers. Loose ADMIT ONE tickets stuck to the blood on my skin. I tried to shake them off, but ended up attracting even more. I peeled them off one by one and flicked them on the ground.

"Poor old Ted must've had a cell phone somewhere, but it's not in this desk." I shook the mouse to wake Ted's computer. "No internet connection," I told Gracie.

She stared out the window, silent, shaking.

A loud click was followed by silence, and everything went dark.

"Why does he have to keep fucking with the lights?" Gracie asked.

"To fuck with us," I replied. "Same reason he just forced us to listen to Claire. It's working. Step away from the window."

I sat on the floor under the desk and held out a hand for Gracie. She took it and crawled in with me. We sat in the blue shadows, listening to each other breathe.

She dug through the papers littering the floor and found a business card. It was crisp white until she touched it with her dirty hands.

"Maurice Cotton, Haus of Flowers." Her eyes bulged. "Haus of Flowers! Haus of Flowers!"

Gracie had a long-standing suspicion that there were a series of murders connected to a cheap flower shop on Belldam Boulevard. Her evidence was shaky and was mostly tied to a sign outside that offered free roses.

"Just because the sign said Zarrah could get a free rose it doesn't mean that it was the same Zarrah you saw in the obituaries. You don't even know if any Zarrahs collected their flowers."

"My mom's hairdresser Laurynn's name was on the board and then she died in a boating accident."

"I'm more willing to believe that ghosts are real and Pritchett High is haunted than believe that a cursed flower shop is killing people. The world is chaos. Correlation doesn't equal causation." I paused. "That applies to this situation, right? I'm not sure I fully understand the phrase."

"I get what you're saying. But don't you ever feel it in the air? There's a hierarchy around us all these ultrarich people with the power to do anything they want to anyone they want, and there's no one to stop them."

I rolled my eyes. "We have a police department. Murder is still illegal."

"River's little sister Riley's best friend Bamma is Lieutenant Hanson's kid."

"Yes, I am aware of that branch of the Pritchett family tree. What's your point?"

"I've spent a lot of time with Bamma, and her mom. Amelia is so nice, but… She's a fairly mediocre cop, and she's probably the best on the force. Bamma told Riley they take bribes, and Captain Bell does a lot of favors for his friends. You've met Abigail Eaton, right?"

I'd seen Abigail at the annual Belldam Tower staff Christmas party, but we'd never spoken. Her face had a turtle-like beak and she had a small hump that James called her shell. She wore stiff, designer dresses with long sleeves and pearls and never looked the underlings directly in the eye. No one knew how old she was—she had to have been in her eighties at least—but she had the skin of a well maintained sixty-five-year-old.

"Okay," I relented. "Abigail Eaton absolutely hunts humans for sport."

"And no one could stop her. Her fingers are in everything around us, and no one is going to tell a billionaire 'no.' Dark power always attaches itself to people like her, and it puts a cloud over the whole town. People who can buy their way into the sunshine do just fine, but the rest of us? Normal people? It's all around us, in our lungs. Breathe enough in, and you'll wake up and start seeing all the bad shit around us like I did. I'm not imagining things, Violet. Read the bloody writing on the walls. Deep in the heart of Texas, Belldam is *fucked*."

The most disturbing thing about Gracie's story was how deeply she believed it. If my nerves weren't already fried from all the murder, she'd have convinced me too. But fortunately I had a real rubber-masked killer stalking me, so I didn't need to wander around hunting ghosts.

I didn't know what else to say, so I mocked her.

"So is it Abigail herself behind the mask?"

"No." She shook her head, eyes wide. "It's Meg."

I laughed, caught myself, and waited in panic for the Licker to appear. When he didn't I chuckled under my breath.

"What an intriguing hypothesis," I said.

Meg made a lot of sense. More sense than anyone other than bitter-ass Emma, who was still my prime suspect. Unfortunately, both guesses were duds because no woman had the physical strength take down Claire "She-Hulk" Smithson.

"At first glance it's a stretch," Gracie said. "I might not have proof about Casa de Flores, the ghosts of Pritchett High, or the satanic billionaires. Just because you don't see it, doesn't mean it's not true. But I know for a fact that the cops are pulling some shit right now with Meg. I just don't know why."

Gracie's idea of facts and my idea of facts didn't align, but I asked her to explain anyway.

"I got a text message from Meg's mom in the car before I handed my phone over to Blythe."

"*You what?*" I yelped.

"Just wait. She said Meg's been missing for a week. Belldam PD blew her off and said since Meg is already eighteen there's nothing they can do."

Thanks to movies and TV, I had been under the mistaken belief that an adult had to be missing for twenty-four hours before the police would investigate. James and River went on a true crime bender and set me straight. If there was a reason to expect foul play—like say, a teenager randomly disappearing with no warning—they'll start a search immediately.

"Why didn't they contact us sooner?" I asked. "We're her friends."

"I'm not her friend."

"Yeah, I'm not either, but in the grand scheme of things, we're her closest acquaintances. Why didn't her mom call us?"

"I don't know. My mom makes me share my location. If I go missing for more than an hour she hunts my ass down and takes my car keys. But the cops said they'd follow up with us. She waited for days, then called the station and they sent her to a voicemail. She panicked, and since she didn't have Meg's contacts, she found my family's landline in the phone book—"

I was horrified. "Your phone number is just in there? In a public book?"

"I guess! She talked to my mom, and my mom gave her my number. I shut my phone off after I read it."

"Why didn't you say anything sooner?" I gasped, holding back the urge to wrap my fingers around her throat and squeeze until her eyes popped. "None of us ever would've gone into the scary murder carnival if you told us!"

"I thought Meg ran away because she was pissy about the Scavenge! I wanted to have fun tonight, not let Meg make me feel like shit because no one invited her to the party. I couldn't predict the fucking horror show waiting behind that dumb gate. Why would I put those two things together?"

That was fair.

But if Meg was missing, and someone was out to kill us, didn't that put The Girl Who Was Snubbed at number one on the suspect list?

"I don't think Meg could wrestle Claire and win," I said.

"Maybe she could if Claire were heavily intoxicated." Gracie paused and scanned my face so intensely it felt like she could read my mind. "It's her, isn't it? It dawned on me that it might be her when we were in the House of Horrors, but that painting on the wall..." She pointed to the beheaded peacock. "I think it's safe to say that's a confession. What do you think?"

I rolled my shoulders to stretch. "Remember what I said about Occam's razor? After she's done with us, she's probably gonna go house to house and pick off all the graduates who planned this."

"Or she already did."

Outside, something hit the side of the guard stand. A flat smack hit the exterior wall, followed by a scraping drag on the brick. Footsteps pounded on the ground as the culprit ran away.

Gracie gasped for air. I shook my head to tell her no, it was not time to panic. I wriggled farther under the desk, folded myself in half, and told Gracie to do the same.

Her face was inches from mine. I could smell her salty sweat, could feel the grit on her skin between my fingers without even touching her. We stared into each other's eyes until she broke away and scooted sideways, away from our hiding spot. She rose up on her knees, keeping her head low, to scan the room.

"What about that?" she asked, pointing.

A small radio connected to a microphone sat next to the computer tower.

A CB radio.

I got up to examine it. I'd never used one before. I didn't even know if I could turn it to a channel people could hear outside the carnival. Still, we should take a shot, so I flipped buttons until a red light came on and it buzzed.

A round dial with notches labeled 1-10 was next to the red light.

I clicked it to the first notch and pushed the button on the microphone.

"Hello?" I said, picturing my words floating into the ether. "Hello? We're at the Poison Apple Carnival. There's a killer. Please call the police. We need help."

I turned the dial to two and repeated myself. Gracie stood and paced the small room as I pled for help on all ten channels over and over.

"You're shouting into the void," she said.

"Someone might hear us. We don't know for sure."

"We do know the Licker is out there, and he's coming for us."

I scanned the room, praying that a phone had somehow materialized in the five minutes since my last search. I pulled the desk drawers out and dumped their contents on the ground. Gracie kicked through the dried-out highlighters, old wadded-up pages from a daily calendar, and loose almonds.

"What are you looking for?" she asked.

"Cell phone."

"You're probably not going to find one."

"No," I said. I opened another drawer. "Here are fifty goddamn cell phone chargers, though."

"We're going to have to run," she said.

I slammed the drawer shut. "Why?" I shrieked. "Why would we do that?"

"Violet. Chill."

"No," I said. I cracked an almond under my heel and ground it into pink mush against the bloodstained carpet. "We're safe right now. We're waiting here until morning when Ted's replacement comes."

"Really?" Gracie asked. She knocked on the window. "Claire said this was shatterproof glass, right? To my ear, it sounds like normal glass, and it sounds pretty thin. He's going to bust in with a chainsaw or something any second."

We looked out the window, barely able to see anything. In the distance, the lights in the back of the carnival flicked on. Then a chunk of lights next to those closer to us lit up. Section after section turned on like a wave rolling in until it crashed into the guard stand.

We stood in a spotlight with the Licker somewhere out there watching us, waiting for us to perform.

"Gracie, please," I begged.

"I'm sorry, Violet. I can't die in a room that smells like feet and old coffee. Maybe there's a spot out back by the Whirling Witch where we can slip through the gate. I swear the bars are wider apart over there."

"No," I begged. "No, no, no. Don't leave me."

"Yes, yes, yes. Please come. We're safer together, we're safer on the move."

Gracie didn't wait for me to reply. She put her hand on the knob, gave me a nod, and opened the door. The fear of being alone outweighed the fear of being out in the open, so without thinking, I ran past her, and immediately stepped into a hole. My ankle twisted, and I slammed into the ground.

"Shit," I said through gritted teeth.

"Check yourself," she whispered. "Check yourself and make sure you're okay."

Gracie pulled me to my feet. I wiggled my extremities, anticipating pain. My ankle stung, but my head, neck, arms, and legs were fine.

In my peripheral vision, the Licker stomped toward us.

"Gracie," I said, choking back tears. "He's behind us. Gracie."

"Keep moving," she told me. "Don't turn around."

But she ignored her own advice, and she did exactly that.

Gracie glanced over her shoulder. The sight of him shook her. She stumbled, missed a step, and fell at my feet. She landed on the ankle I'd twisted. I howled.

The Licker laughed as I lost my balance and landed on Gracie. We were a tangle of limbs and hair, tearing each other back down each time we scrambled to stand. She finally made it to her feet, steadied herself, and tried to lift me one last time. I was halfway up when an axe flew past my right ear and hit her squarely in the chest.

Blood exploded from her mouth and dripped onto my face.

I hugged her again, this time to slow her fall.

"I want my mom," she whispered. "I want my mommy."

The light in Gracie's eyes went out, the quick flip of a switch. No struggle, no drawn-out suffering, no screaming through the speakers.

I didn't want to leave her there, but I had no choice.

As I ran away, the Licker yelled at my back.

"Don't run, Violet!" he said in his demonic voice. "I promise I won't hurt you. Pinky swearsies!"

22

When a murderer in a rubber mask tells you not to run, even if he "pinky swearsies," you should move like your ass is on fire.

Fortunately, that's what I did.

I headed straight for the carousel, intending to hide until I could swing back to the entrance and get the hell out of the carnival. I wanted to be worried about my friends, *especially* James, since she'd been MIA since we first split up.

But the time had passed for saving everyone else.

Air whipped my face as I ran, giving me a chill. The August heat mixed with sweat caused by visceral panic left me soaked. My shirt clung to my skin, a fine mist of sweat covered my face. A shiver nauseated me. I couldn't breathe.

"You can't outrun me, Violet," the Licker said. "You're too out of shape, my skinny fat queen!"

I grunted in response. His remark would've pissed me off if I'd had the energy to be offended.

Robotic static rang through the carnival as the Licker laughed.

I guesstimated he was about three car lengths behind me. If I wanted to lose him, I would need to go somewhere packed with hiding places. Ideally, the midway would've been an option, but I wouldn't risk getting lost again.

The arcade was the next best choice.

A Choo Choo Train whistle cheerfully signaled the Black Kitten Coaster to run as I sprinted past the ride. A chain of rotten zombie worms gently rolled over tiny hills at a moderate pace, their grimacing faces faded from the sun. It was the only roller coaster I'd ever ridden, and I'd only ridden it once. At the end, there was a small rise and fall. It was less scary than riding in a car with Blythe behind the wheel, but it still almost made me pee my pants.

"If you're going to hide in the arcade, don't bother," the Licker yelled.

Playing the "opposite game" with him had benefited me so far. Fire filled my lungs as my feet pounded against the concrete, propelling me faster than I'd ever moved in my life, straight into the arcade.

A hurricane had blown through the room. Broken glass glittered on the ground. Games knocked on their sides. Teddy bears ripped in half; their skins rested on piles of cloudlike stuffing.

I fell to the ground and crawled behind the ticket counter. My fingers twitched; I had to lock my hands as if in prayer to stop them.

"I already played hide-and-seek in here with River," he said. "I'm bored with that game."

My skin crawled at the realization River's body might be nearby. I couldn't take seeing another corpse.

The Licker kicked the mess on the floor as he stalked the arcade. Every few steps, he would stop. When he stopped, I held my breath. A broken game vomited a pile of wires and circuitry onto the tile. I listened as he shuffled through it. He stopped at the counter.

I felt him lean over to peek at me in my hiding spot.

"Look up," he said.

My eyes drifted to the ceiling.

To the mirrored ceiling.

The Licker's reflection gave me a little wave.

"Shit!" I shouted, because it didn't matter if he heard me.

"*Shit* is right," he said. "I told you not to come in here. Word to the wise, when you start running again, avoid the mirror maze. Too dark. Don't hide in the souvenir shops either. Or in the House of Horrors. In fact, don't hide at all. I'm not going to hurt you."

"Why?" I asked.

"You remind me of me."

Wondering what part of my personality screamed "spree killer" broke my brain.

I pulled myself together enough to take my shot.

"If you're not going to hurt me, can I leave?" I asked.

The Licker didn't respond right away. He rapped his knuckles on the glass, causing the whole counter to shake. He breathed into his voice changer, a perfect imitation of Darth Vader.

"No," he finally said. "You can't. You'll tell."

"I don't know who you are. You're wearing a mask."

"You'll tell people what happened. You saw everything."

"If you're not going to kill me, and you won't me go, what then?"

"You can come with me when I'm done."

I considered the words. If he wasn't finished, someone else was still alive.

"You want me to go to a second location with you and your nasty ten-inch tongue?"

"Some girls are into that."

"Gross."

Silence.

I shifted my body.

The Licker stood straight.

I squatted and prepared to run.

A near-toxic cocktail of adrenaline, fear, and stupidity helped me leapfrog over the counter. I laughed when I landed safely. He tilted his head, surprised by my move.

I ran from the arcade, past the Kiddie Coaster worms. I wished for the days when a drop on a coaster made for toddlers was still my biggest fear.

Until then, I hadn't even thought of hiding in the souvenir shops. I headed straight for the photo store, the little hut where happy carnival-goers could purchase pictures snapped during their visit.

As soon as the door closed behind me, it hit me.

He'd told me exactly where he wanted me to go.

"I'm so stupid. I deserve to die," I whispered.

I pressed against the wall, ready for him to walk through the door. But he didn't.

I waited.

He still didn't appear and didn't make a sound outside.

It was time for the big jump scare. I'd relax, and he'd burst through wielding a chainsaw.

Minutes passed.

The door remained shut.

I scanned the room for another way out. There was no other exit or even a back office where I could hide.

I slid along the wall toward the print station. A collection of photos dangled from the ceiling like Christmas ornaments. I'd seen them a thousand times before, happy couples on the Ferris wheel, little kids hollering as they ran from the House of Horrors, a baby grimacing while eating a sour pickle the size of his head.

Or that's what the pictures *should've* been.

Instead, I saw my face.

I sat at the edge of a chair, violin under my chin, eyes sharp as my bow danced across the strings. My orchestra director's husband took it at a rehearsal for the spring musical. Next to me, a photo of River and Gracie floated back and forth. Bright smiles lit their faces as they held the contract they'd signed with their publisher.

We were all there.

Claire kissing a gold medal.

James posing with her laptop on her head, eyes crossed.

Blythe squinting in a sunny selfie, her hot pink bikini glowing even hotter against her tan skin.

Mila flying through the air in a split.

Lolly giving a speech about climate change to elementary school students.

"He set us up on purpose," I whispered.

I knew he'd targeted us, but I hadn't realized it was so personal.

I plucked Mila's picture from its string and examined it. A stamp on the back told me it had been printed at the carnival in late June. The Licker had planned this night for *months*.

I jumped when someone knocked on the door. The photo fell from my hand and landed on the ground. Mila smiled at me, arms over her head in triumph.

The person on the other side of the door knocked again, then scratched at the door like a dog.

What kind of killer knocks before entering? I wondered.

The scratching stopped. The person on the other side slapped the door and screamed my name.

Knowing full well it could be a trap, I opened the door.

Long arms reached for me. I stepped back.

Blythe fell to the ground, laughing.

"Why didn't you save me?" she asked. "I would've saved you."

23

Violet?" Blythe whined. "You let me fall. Why am I down here?"

I could tell she thought she was whispering.

"God," I said. "You're in worse shape than before."

"This is all a dream," she said. "It's so weird."

"It's not a dream."

I tried in vain to get her on her feet. When I pulled her arms, she jerked them away and rolled into a ball.

"No, it's a dream," she insisted. "I fell asleep in that box. Where is everyone?"

I didn't want to freak her out, so I told her they were hiding.

"Someone is trying to hurt us. You have to be quiet."

I placed a finger on her lips to shush her. She yelped in pain.

"No!" she squealed. "I can't. I'm so dizzy, and my leg hurts. Oh! We can run away! Carry me piggyback!"

Blythe was 5'10". I was 5'4". Imagining her on my back with her toes dragging the ground made me chuckle.

"I can't carry you. You'll have to stay here."

I searched the room for something to barricade the door. The best thing I could find was a tall metal stool. I tried to jam it under the doorknob. It was about an inch too short.

"Remember the night we drove and saw the bats?" Blythe asked.

"The bats?" I asked in a bitchy tone. I understood what she meant, but I had no desire to reminisce.

"The Austin bats."

"Oh. Yeah."

A bat colony roosted under a famous bridge in Austin. Every evening, over a million little monsters would wake up and fly into the sky to spend their night snacking on bugs while dangerously blocking the views of people driving in the area.

One night after Blythe got her Tesla, she and I drove to the city to watch them take flight. I invited Lolly, who loved creepy animals and was thrilled to see the bats up close.

We stood on the bridge, Lolly in the middle, and watched batty black dots fly against the orange sherbet sky.

"This is the largest colony in the world," Lolly told us. "Most are female."

"Can you enjoy a moment without researching it?" asked Blythe.

Lolly tilted her head. "Learning is half the fun."

Blythe rolled her eyes. She got her phone out and snapped a few dozen photos. At one point, she turned the phone over to me to get some shots of her against the setting sun. I'd become quite the photographer thanks to Blythe.

"Can you come over next to me and get a profile shot?" she asked.

"You call me out for research," said Lolly. "What about you? Can you enjoy the moment without documenting it?"

Blythe blushed and extended a hand. I passed her phone back.

"The bats are so pretty, I want to share them," she whispered in my ear.

My chest tightened. Sometimes Blythe's mask would slip, and the "real" girl behind the fame would shine through.

Now, in the photo booth, I could see her authentic self again. Not a sweet girl wanting to share beauty, but a wasted mess who couldn't comprehend the seriousness of the situation.

"I remember the bats," I told her. "Why?"

Blythe pressed her back against the door and slid to the floor. She looped an arm through the stool's legs.

"I felt like such shit that night when Lolly called me out. She wasn't wrong. It was the top, you know?"

"The top of the bridge?" I asked.

"The top of *my life*. People loved me. I made a video where I compared fifteen different clear lip glosses, and *it got a million views*. I posted a photo you took on the bridge, and it got so many likes and comments. There were so many I couldn't reply to them all."

This was not the time for a pity party, nor was it time to reminisce about social media popularity.

"Blythe," I said calmly. "We have to leave this carnival. Someone is out there. He is going to kill us if he finds us. He already attacked you, that's why you're all beat up."

She stretched her legs out and examined the cuts and bruises.

"Oh yeah. Hey, where are the other girls?"

I knelt in front of her.

"I'm pretty sure they're all dead."

"Pretend dead?" she asked, her voice childlike.

"No," I said firmly.

"Weird."

"Very."

"Why kill us?"

I pointed to the photos. "Someone is obsessed with us."

She pushed me away and got up. She ripped a picture of herself off its string, tearing off the top in the process.

"You're all doing stuff in yours," she said frowning. "Playing your cello, Mila dancing, James being a geek. I'm in a bikini."

"It's a violin," I corrected her. She was right, though. Ours were all action shots, while hers was some lame thirst trap. "Didn't you once tell me you get weirdos online? Do you think some creepy guy might be stalking you?"

She ignored me and traced her photo with a finger.

I repeated my question.

"Some," she sighed. "It's mostly losers with nothing better to do. I report it to Belldam PD. They never care. No one ever does anything in this fucking town. The cops are useless."

I wanted to ask her if anyone threatened her more than once. I thought of the Licker at the carnival, of Heather's warning about creeps online.

"Blythe—"

A series of bloodcurdling screams cut me short. Blythe whipped around, eyes wide.

"What the hell?" she asked.

My hands shook. Sweat trickled down my spine.

"James," I said. I couldn't say anything else. "James," I repeated. "It's James."

Blythe mumbled to herself as she ran her hands through her still perfectly beachy waves. Her knuckles were purple and swollen.

"Get in the corner and don't move," I instructed.

"Why?" Blythe asked. The word came out low, her accent thicker than usual.

"Because I have to go save James."

24

My lungs burned.

My legs shook.

My brain pounded inside my skull.

I wasn't afraid. Not now. James was alive. I would save her, we would save Blythe, and we would be okay.

James's pleas for help echoed through the whole carnival. She was somewhere past the carousel, near the midway.

I'd never run so fast in my life. Every few steps, I glanced over my shoulder, expecting to be face-to-face with the Licker's horrible rubber mask. I tripped twice but didn't fall. A thousand unseen eyes fixed their gaze on me. Voices whispered in my ear.

"We should break into pairs," said Claire.

"We could get caught," Lolly said. *"We could get arrested."*

"These low-dose babies each have five milligrams of THC in them," River said.

Though it had been hours since I ate my circus peanut, the sticky melted marshmallow still coated my esophagus. I retched. Bile shot up my throat, flooding my nose, and sending me into a coughing fit.

"Who's there?" James yelled. "Help! Please, God, help me!"

"It's me!" I yelled back.

"Violet?"

"Where are you?"

She didn't need to answer. As soon as I passed the carousel, there she was.

She sat on a small board above the dunk tank, arms tied behind her back. Her legs dangled in the air.

Blood poured from a gash on her forehead. A shiny red and purple splotch highlighted her right cheekbone.

"Violet!" she sobbed. "Please get me down! Please! If I fall, I'll drown!"

The dunk tank was a twelve-foot-tall glass box filled with gray-tinged water. The little stairs that led from the ground to the podium were missing. A big blue sign hung behind James: LET'S GET WET AND WILD!!!

I almost ran straight into the glass. I stopped short and hit it with my fist.

"Where are the stairs?" I asked. "Where have you been?"

"Stairs are gone. Never saw them. I woke up thirty seconds ago. My mind's blank. No memories from after we entered the carnival. Now that I've shared my entire life story, will you please help me?"

"Dude, I can't climb glass! I need the stairs."

"Is there anything else you can use?" Her voice shook. James rarely cried. My heart stopped in fear as I watched her tears flow. "Why would someone do this to us?"

"It's Meg McClendon," I said. "She didn't get invited to the Scavenge, so she's getting her revenge."

James screwed her face up. "What?"

"That doesn't track for you?"

"Meg is mean enough, vindictive enough, and single-minded enough, but is she physically and mentally capable? She's book smart, but also kinda...*dumb*. My grandpa calls people like her 'educated dumbasses.'"

She had a point. But it didn't matter. We needed to escape.

"I can't find anything around here," I said. "Maybe in the midway. I'll check. Can you untie yourself?"

"Trust me, bitch. I'm trying. The knots are supertight. My wrists are shredded."

I scrambled to find something I could use as a step stool. I entered the midway, far enough to eyeball a few booths, but not far enough to risk getting lost.

A waist-high folding table was tucked behind the counter at the basketball toss. I ripped it from the booth and dragged it back to the dunk tank.

The table swayed under me when I climbed onto the slick laminate top.

"God, don't fall," said James.

"I'm doing my best."

My best wasn't good enough. Even standing on the table, I couldn't reach the top edge.

"On a scale of one to ten, how screwed are we?" she asked.

"Thirteen," I said.

"Shit."

I got on my hands and knees and climbed off the table. Without the stairs, I couldn't save her.

"I have to find help," I said.

"You can't leave me here!"

"I don't have a choice."

James's lips quivered. All the color drained from her face.

"Please don't leave me," she begged.

I punched the tank again, this time so hard I nearly broke my fingers.

"Listen to me," I said. "I've seen this asshole in action. If he wanted you dead, you would be. But you're not. He tied you up for a reason. I'm going to go to the employee entrance, rip a dead body off the gate, go back to the Tesla, and find my phone so I can call nine-one-one. I will be right back, and I will have cops with me."

"Violet," she said. She pressed her cheek against her shoulder to wipe away her tears. "Promise me I'm not going to drown. Promise me pl—"

She never finished her sentence.

She screamed, not like her cries for help before. Ear-shattering, ground-shaking, desperation.

Not the screams of someone who thinks she might die.

The screams of someone who knows she will.

I squeezed my eyes shut until I saw stars.

I took a deep breath, turned around, and opened my eyes.

The Licker had stolen James's army jacket, and he'd put it on over his cloak.

He had a screwdriver in one hand and an axe in the other.

He bolted toward us, waving the weapons above his head.

There was nowhere to run. I swallowed and prepared to meet my fate.

Then a funny thing happened.

The Licker stopped, dropped both weapons, and removed the mask. It flopped to the ground, tongue first.

James stopped screaming.

I gasped. "What the—"

"—fuck?" finished James.

Blythe laughed as she slipped off James's jacket. She wadded it into a ball, threw it aside, and removed her cloak.

"Why are you two all worked up?" she asked, smirking. "Did I miss something?"

25

An invisible fist slammed into my solar plexus, making it impossible to fill my lungs.

I channeled Gracie. This wasn't real, couldn't be real. High-ass Blythe found the costume and put it on, obviously.

Maybe I was hallucinating.

Or maybe the whole thing was a prank. My friends joined together to scare the hell out of me as an early, early birthday present. I scanned the distance, hoping the other girls would pop out from behind the rides. They'd laugh, maybe film my reaction. We'd get pancakes, and they'd tell me how they hatched their plan.

But no one came.

"Violet, honey," said Blythe. She gave me a little wave and snapped her fingers. "Did I lose you for a second?"

"I thought it was Meg," I told her.

Blythe grimaced. "You thought Meg could pull this off? That's offensive."

"My first guess was Emma Tucker. She's smart. She got into Harvard."

"She got kicked out of Harvard."

"Sorry."

"Violet!" James yelled. "Don't apologize!"

"Yeah, Violet. Allow me to feel my feelings. *Anyway.* I killed that bitch Meg last week. Gutted her. She was always on my kill list. I figured her Scavenge invite was a done deal with her being colonel, then fucking Julia borked my plan by ditching her for Lolly. But I recalculated and made it work."

"You have a kill list?" James asked.

"Yes. You were at the top. Lolly wasn't on it."

My stomach flipped. Blythe didn't like to compete for attention, so I could picture James in her top three, but I would've guessed she hated Mila the most, because Mila was prettier and Blythe was shallow.

"James was number one?" I asked. "Why?"

Blythe shrugged.

"Why wasn't Lolly on the list?" James asked.

"Why should she be? What did Lolly ever do to anybody?" Blythe asked sincerely. "She wouldn't hurt a fly."

"You smashed her head with a mallet!" I yanked at my shirt to show her the stains.

"Yeah, well. Wrong place, right time. And trust me, I could've done *a lot worse* than crush her head. But… I guess she's also guilty of the same infraction as the rest of them. Maybe more so. *Maybe Lolly deserved it most of all.*"

Blythe was getting a little too worked up. Before the Scavenge, I would've shrugged it off as petty drama, but clearly we needed to take Blythe's irrational mood swings more seriously.

"If you killed Meg, where's her body?" James asked.

Gracie's spooky satanist story from earlier reared it's ugly head. Blythe had made a lot of money as an influencer, definitely enough to buy a crooked cop or two.

"Did you pay the police to cover up her murder?" I asked.

Blythe clapped her hands and grinned. "Excellent question. I'm pretty proud of myself. Gracie's conspiracies always made a lot of sense to me. I didn't pay anybody off, but I gambled they'd hush it up on their own. It's not good for business if there's a hollowed-out corpse impaled on the candy apple statue. They hauled the body off and put her…*somewhere*. Don't know, don't care. If Gracie's hypotheses were correct, someone will find her trapped in a car at the bottom of Sheldon Lake in a week. It'll be ruled accidental, and that will be that."

Blythe spoke in a calm, rational tone that, when juxtaposed with her batshit crazy behavior, almost made me pee my pants in fear.

"What's happening?" My voice cracked. I backed away from her until my back pressed into the dunk tank's cool glass wall.

Above me, James repeated Blythe's name over and over again.

"Blythe?" she squealed. "Blythe? Blythe?"

Blythe laughed. "Blythe, Blythe, Blythe, Blythe. You've said it so many times it's lost meaning."

"What's happening?" I repeated.

"What's happening?" Blythe asked, mocking me. She unclipped the chest strap on the gray backpack she'd been wearing under her cloak and dropped it on the ground. "You have no idea how hot that mask is." She let down her hair, fluffed it, and tamed it with her fingers. "Look here! My sweat made beachy waves. *Nice.*"

Blythe unzipped the backpack and pulled out a bandana to wipe her face. She threw the bandana onto James's jacket and rummaged around in the backpack to find water. She was remarkably coordinated for someone who'd double fisted edibles and whiskey earlier that night.

"You're not high," I said. "Or drunk."

"Nope. Didn't have a drop, nor did I eat a circus peanut. Oh! Bee-tee-dubs, those peanuts y'all ate were *twenty* milligrams each, not five. I convinced River it would be hilarious to see you baked out of your minds. At first she was all, 'No, I don't lie to people about weed, it's mean,' but then I told her it would be great material for her comic, and she was all in. Y'all were so gone, it was easy for me to fake being fucked up too. I didn't fake these babies, though." Blythe twisted her arm to examine a gash on her bicep. "Those bitches totally put up a fight."

"You killed them," James growled. She'd stopped crying.

"Sure did. Fairly easily, too. Once the adrenaline kicks in, that's *power.*"

Maybe this wasn't really Blythe. Maybe it was one of Gracie's satanic billionaire demons wearing Blythe's face.

"How did you do it?" I asked.

"Hammers and glass and dunk tanks, darling," she said.

"Dunk tanks?" yelled James.

Blythe chuckled. "You ain't up there for the pretty view."

"You moved their bodies," I said. "You crushed Lolly's head. How could you physically do that?"

"I put on a shitload of muscle when I did my Better Booty

Challenge series for YouTube. I can deadlift as much as Claire! You assholes didn't say a word. I walked around half-naked all the time, even to the fucking doctor's office. I wanted to see if any of you noticed my ass."

"I did," I told her. This was true. One night we hung out at Claire's, and Blythe wore high waisted denim shorts so short her butt cheeks were on full display. I couldn't even look her in the eye that day.

"You didn't say anything," Blythe said.

"Was I supposed to?" I whispered. "We've never spent much time praising each other's asses."

"Eh," she shrugged. "No. I'm messing with you. You'd have to be crazy to kill someone because they didn't compliment your butt."

"Technically, you have to be crazy to kill someone in general," I said.

Blythe chuckled. "Man, Violet, when did you become funny?"

"Wasn't joking."

Her face fell. "You need to get out of my way, babe. James and I have unfinished business."

She reached into her backpack and dug around, her eyes never leaving mine. She expected me to fight or to run. I was too stunned to do either.

Blythe pulled a dusty softball from the bag. She tossed it in the air and caught it, then held it out to me.

"You want to do the honors?" she asked.

"What?"

"You have as much of a reason to be mad at these bitches as I do."

"Stop calling them bitches. And stop saying that about me. I don't want to kill anyone!"

Blythe rolled her eyes. "Fine."

"You can't kill me without telling me what I did!" James yelled.

"What did you do?" Blythe cackled. She made a strange gravelly noise and spun around in circles. "What did you do? Let's see. Claire has so many college scouts coming after her she could do a whole reality show to choose the winner. Gracie and River have a fucking book deal. James, you're gonna nepo your way into A&M. Scholarships, awards. Moving away, big things in bright cities."

I couldn't quite process her words.

"You're mad because they're gonna go to college?" I asked.

"Ding, ding, ding! But it's after college too." Blythe waved the softball in James's direction. "That one is probably going to found the next Google. Claire would've won an Olympic medal. Bronze at best, but still. Violet, I thought for sure you were off to join the New York Philharmonic. Unless you got your acceptance letter from Annie Wood at DSU and didn't tell me, I guess you're not talented enough."

Those words hit as hard as Blythe's big reveal. I'd had the same thought a million times over the summer. Hearing it spoken out loud by someone else made it more real.

But James was still suspended above eight feet of water, so I'd worry about that later.

My mother told me there was a famous quote. "You cannot reason someone out of a position they did not reason themselves into." She was 100 percent correct, but there was nothing left to do but try.

"You *are* talented," I said. "More than most people."

"At what?" she asked, tossing the softball from one hand to another.

"What you do. You're one of the most popular social media gurus on the planet."

"Well thanks for calling me popular, but no. I'm not. At my height, I was C-list at best, and social media influencers aren't exactly top-tier celebrities, so…"

"You have so many followers," I said. "You have brand endorsements. Jesus, you had an offer for your own talk show."

"Twenty other girls got invited to meet for the talk show gig. I was their fourth choice. Guess what. Fourth place doesn't get a show. As for my endorsements, I'm not getting the good ones anymore. A company that makes cleansing oak milk sponsored my last video."

"Oat milk?" asked James.

"*Oak*. Like the tree. They squeeze it from the bark or something. I don't know. I drank it for a week, and my stomach hurt more than the time I ate an entire family-sized bag of hot Cheetos. I used to book high-end handbags, expensive skincare. Not anymore. New people are climbing the ladder daily, people with *actual* talent. I have no skills. I'm not a makeup artist, I can't do interior design, and I can't bake. I make an ass outta myself for some laughs, nothing more." Blythe wiped her nose with her hand. "I hate myself," she mumbled.

"Apparently," I said soothingly. "What about all your money, though? You'd have no problem paying college tuition. You still have almost a whole year to apply."

"Ha. Funny thing. We all know my GPA is garbage. I didn't take the SATs. Never studied, probably couldn't pass it. I have no extracurriculars."

"You run a business!" I screeched. "That's an extracurricular!"

"*No*. I buy followers. Always have. I'm a fraud. I only get a fraction of the views I used to get, and no one is engaging with my content. Last month some assholes 'canceled' me and most of my remaining followers abandoned ship. My views tanked, which in turn wrecked my income. I had to stoop to calling my dad. He said he hired some professionals to fix everything. That turned out to be bullshit."

"Why?"

"Apparently dear old Daddy doesn't pay his taxes, and neither did I. He's been selling assets left and right. He's going to prison, and maybe I am too. Can you arrest a seventeen-year-old for tax fraud?" Her face fell, went completely blank. Her pretty features were mottled gray.

"I'm not sure," I said.

"Are we all getting the picture now?" Blythe asked. Her desperate tone rose to a squeal at the end. She was on the verge of spinning out.

To be honest, I did understand her point of view.

With the exceptions of Meg and Blythe, all the other kids in school were obsessed with starting senior year so they could finish school and move on. None of them knew how much it hurt me when River and Gracie spent hours on an app hunting for their future apartment, when James spoke of plans to turn Pritchett PeaCODES into a nationwide program, or when Lolly had a panic attack because she was worried she wouldn't be the smartest student at her university. It twisted me in knots I couldn't untangle, and the longer I went without a letter from Annie Wood, the more I felt soul-crushing jealousy.

Never enough to crush someone's head, though.

"You're right," I said. "I get it. I'm terrified about the future, and I'm such a loser compared to everyone else. I'm not getting into the workshop, I probably won't get into school, and I'll be stuck at Belldam Community with the corpse of Ida Benchley.

"Isn't Mrs. Benchley still alive?" James asked.

"*Yes*," I replied.

"The worst part is, no one notices," Blythe said, frowning.

"Yeah," James said. "Like they didn't notice your ass."

Blythe's left eye twitched. "Say one more fucking word, and you're dead, James!" She shrieked, waving the softball. James leaned back on the platform, lost her balance, and came dangerously close to falling.

"Please calm down," I begged.

Blythe took a breath and lowered her arm. "I don't have anyone to talk to," she said.

"You could've talked to me."

"It's embarrassing," she said, her voice shaky. "And I'm only your second-best friend. You care more about James."

"You said we're the same," I said, ignoring the comment about James. "If that's true, what do you have to be embarrassed about?"

Blythe's mouth twitched at the corners, and her features softened. She shook her head and returned to the task at hand.

"We're different enough," she said. "You might not go to DSU, but you'll go somewhere. You'll keep playing your violin until your fingers fall off. In the end, you'll get where you want to go in life, even if you have to take the scenic route. No. Violet, you'll be fine. James, on the other hand…"

Blythe reared back and hurled the softball at the tiny red target connected to the dunk tank. James's deafening screams made tears well in my eyes.

The softball missed the target by about two inches.

"Please don't," begged James. "I can't swim! I can't swim!"

"And water scares you shitless," Blythe said, laughing. "It's fun to watch you squirm. You should beg me."

"Beg you?" Asked James.

"Yeah. For your life. It's funny."

"Let me go, and I swear to God I will grovel at your feet," James said sharply.

"No one has to know it was you," I told Blythe. "There aren't any cameras, no witnesses. There's no way anyone will believe a girl committed these murders."

Blythe pulled her phone from her back pocket. She tapped the screen and turned it around to reveal a 3x3 grid of video feeds.

"There actually are cameras. James turned them off. I turned them back on, and I've been controlling them via my phone. "

"How did you learn to do that?" Asked James.

"From you," said Blythe.

James blinked. "I never gave you a lesson."

"You're always so excited to show off your mediocre hacking skills," Blythe said. "I paid attention and learned all the basics from you. Watched a few YouTube videos, took a few notes. It was fun. Did you think I was too stupid to work a computer?"

"You're not stupid," James said.

Blythe smirked. "I'm sure I look like a fucking genius from where you sit right now, huh?"

She slid her phone back in her pocket and walked toward the tank. She held out a finger and smiled at James. She got closer and closer to the red target. James's lower lip trembled. Blythe brushed the target with a finger. We all held our breath to see if James's seat would drop. When it didn't, Blythe waved her hand in front of the target, laughing.

"We'll lie for you!" I promised. "We'll burn the mask and say we chased the killer off."

Blythe stopped waving and crossed her arms over her chest.

"Interesting proposition," she said.

"Please," said James. "We'll say we never saw the killer without his mask."

"You two would seriously do that? Let me ride off into the sunrise after I killed six people?"

"Yes," I said. I meant it too. I'd have done anything to walk out of there alive, done anything to keep James safe. "We can't bring them back."

"You're not a teeny bit concerned I might try to finish the job later? Like maybe I'll sneak into your house and hide in your closet with a knife? Poison could be fun too. I researched 'how to poison someone' at the library in Austin for hours awhile back. At the time, I decided it wasn't for me. I wanted to play a more *active* role, not sit back and let rat poison do it for me."

"What if you agree to see someone?" I asked. "If you go to a therapist and maybe get on some meds, it'll be fine."

Blythe walked toward me. Each foot hit the ground with an earthshaking thud. She took my hand and intertwined our fingers. My intestines nearly slid out of my body.

"I love you, Violet. You'd do anything for a friend, wouldn't you?" She nodded in James's direction.

"Friends," I said. "Plural. I'll do anything for you too."

She squeezed my hand, three quick pulses, each one progressively harder. She twisted my wrist until it popped and pinned my arm against my back. I doubled over in pain.

"We were never that close," she said, her jaw locked. "You'd sell me out in a heartbeat. You'd probably do it the second the cops got here."

"You said yourself that the Eatons don't want the bad press! Maybe they'll let it slide!"

"Belldam PD might cover up one *insignificant* murder, but this shitshow? No way. People are *never* going to forget what I did here. I killed so many people I forgot the exact number, and I'm not done yet."

She let me go and pushed me to the ground.

Above me, James hyperventilated. I wanted to hug her.

"Please don't hurt me," she pleaded.

Blythe paced. She rolled her head from side to side and flapped her hands.

My eyes drifted to the screwdriver Blythe had tossed aside. One stab through an eye, through a temple, or straight through the heart would take her out.

"What are you doing?" Blythe asked me.

"Nothing."

"You looking at the screwdriver? Go for it," she said. "I dare you. I love a little drama."

"No," I stammered. "I wasn't. I won't."

She snatched the screwdriver and threw it into the dark carnival.

"You're such a little fighter, trying to find a weapon. I respect that. Maybe we *could* strike a deal."

A heavy weight lifted off my shoulders. Light glowed at the end of the tunnel.

"Yes," I said. "Anything. Anything."

"I'm going to ask you a question. Something you should be able to answer if you've ever paid attention to what I say. If you get it right, I won't drown James."

"Okay!" I exclaimed. "I listen to you. I really do."

Blythe pulled a second softball out of her backpack.

"If you get it wrong…" She waved the ball under my nose.

"I won't," I promised.

"Hmm," she said. "What do I even ask? This wasn't part of my plan."

"Something about your videos?" I suggested.

Blythe smiled. "You watch them?"

"Yes," I lied. Her videos had gotten far too repetitive, and I didn't bother wasting my time. "All your videos."

"I never knew," she said. "The other girls don't watch my stuff."

"I do," said James.

"I don't believe you for one second," Blythe snapped. "And, once again, shut the fuck up. This game is for Violet, not you." She frowned, her brow furrowed. She stopped pacing. She stared at the Whirling Witch Coaster. At some point, she'd turned the lights off. She pulled her phone back out. "You would not believe how easy it was to figure out the lights. A college student does maintenance on the carnival's electricity. A little attention, a little cleavage, and she told me everything. I didn't even have to sleep with her."

"Would you have?" I asked.

"Probably. But I only needed a password. She gave it up faster than Mila at a football game after-party."

My face burned. "Don't talk about Mila that way."

"Right, right. Shouldn't talk shit about the dead. My bad."

My stomach dropped.

Now it was confirmed, Mila was gone. Claire, Gracie, River, Lolly, all dead because Blythe lost some followers online.

"They really are gone," I whispered.

"Yup. All the girls who came with us, plus Ted the security guard.

And Meg. Why are you having such trouble with this? Honestly Violet, I'm a little concerned for your mental health."

I wasn't interested in her mind games. "Fuck you."

"What's that?" Blythe asked. She stuck her hand behind her ear in a "can you speak up" gesture. Her palm was stained red.

Blythe dropped her hand, and tapped on her phone. Lights on the Whirling Witch Coaster blinked to life. Another tap and music played through the speakers hidden around the carnival. The weird clown song from the carousel, canned cheers from the midway, and the funeral dirge from the House of Horrors mixed into a brain splitting cacophony. I pressed my hands over my ears.

Blythe beamed, her face lit from within like a child.

"I've got it," she said. "Violet, what horrible crime did I supposedly commit that led to my cancellation?"

"What?" I had no idea what she meant.

"If you follow me online you'd know. It was a huge thing, and I had to make an hour-long video groveling to twelve-year-olds. I wrote a little apology song and played it on this kid's DJ turntable, just to be funny, but people were not amused. All for some total bullshit completely fabricated by assholes who have nothing better to do than rip other people—*people who do actual work*—apart."

I tilted my head. "You said you don't work."

Blythe took five big steps and threw herself at me.

"I never said I don't work. I work. I wrote a marketing plan, I shoot and edit my own videos, and I'm constantly promoting myself. You wouldn't believe how many asses I have to kiss. Views increase when influencers appear in each other's videos. Turns out, I hate other influencers. I have to play nice and fake it to get included. That's work. I never said I don't work. I said what I do *doesn't have value.*"

"Those are all valuable skills. Why can't you edit someone else's videos or do someone else's social media?"

Blythe blinked. "Do you hate me?"

I paused to think. "Well, yeah, kinda! You just murdered all of our friends!"

Above us, James groaned. "Violet, please don't provoke the loony bitch."

"Uh uh uh," Blythe scolded her. "I wouldn't call me names if I were you."

Blythe shifting her focus to James scared the shit out of me. I needed to get her back.

"Why not work for someone else?" I asked. "What's wrong with that?"

"Because I don't want to. I don't want to answer to someone else. If people found out I'd stooped to editing one of these new girls' videos… There's an eighth grader in Idaho who exclusively does daily planner supply review videos. Notebooks, stickers, and shit. Her videos average seventy-five thousand views. I'm supposed to bend the knee for a bitch like that?"

"It would be better than murdering your friends in cold blood."

She turned back to me. Her eyes bulged, sweat glistened on her skin. Grease made her messy bun stringy. Runny eyeliner settled in dark circles under her eyes. Blood smears stained her cheek.

I wondered if it was her blood or someone else's.

"Tick tock, Violet. Why did I get canceled?"

———

I hadn't seen Blythe much that summer. While she spent the summer plotting mass murder, I spent it practicing violin and developing an ulcer over DSU. I'd barely been online. I uploaded some photos of my neighbor's Pomeranian to social media, googled random stuff, and made music playlists.

I definitely hadn't been watching Blythe's videos.

One of the few times we hung out was on a long drive to take pictures in a bluebonnet field. The ones near Belldam weren't good enough. Blythe needed the best, and she read that the best were near Brenham.

"We can stop at the Blue Bell creamery and go on the tour," she teased. "You get free ice cream at the end."

"I mean, I can't say no to ice cream," I replied.

She invited some other girls; only James wanted to go.

We piled into the Tesla. James cracked some jokes, and I played along for a little bit until I realized Blythe seemed more quiet than usual. I asked her what was wrong. She flatly said, "Nothing."

But throughout the day, she dropped hints.

In the bluebonnets, we found a squirrel family in a little nest.

"They're so cute I could steal them and take them home," James said.

Blythe snorted. "Better leave them alone. They might not be internet-approved pets."

"Internet-approved pets?" I asked.

"Never mind." she mumbled.

Later, on the way to Blue Bell, James suggested that we take a weekend trip to South Padre. She said she could get Heather to chaperone.

"Ugh, no," Blythe said. Her voice wavered a little. "I can't handle any more fish."

"Did you get drunk and puke up some fish or something?" James asked, laughing.

Blythe didn't laugh back, or even smile. She scowled. At the time, I wrote it off as her being irritated with James. Her sour demeanor hung around her like a dust cloud for the rest of the day.

That night, after flowers and ice cream and weird burgers at a tiny barbecue joint in the backwoods, we dropped James off at her house. Blythe drove the car down the street, pulled over, and slammed her head into the steering wheel.

"What the hell?" I gasped.

"Everything is too much. Right? You get it?"

I had no clue what she meant, so I gave a generic response.

"Life is pretty overwhelming lately," I told her. Nothing I said would matter. She needed to vent.

"You get it. You always get it. James doesn't. She's off in la-la land with her computers. Have you ever felt like the entire world is turning against you?"

"Sure. The other day my mom was super pissed at me, James and I got into a fight, and no one else would answer my texts. There's the whole DSU thing too. I'm pretty sure they hate me. Or worse, they're indifferent."

She hit her head on the steering wheel again, then grunted like a wounded animal. I looked around nervously, worried someone might be watching.

In hindsight, I should've anticipated her break with reality.

———

"Hey!" Present-day Blythe snapped her fingers in my face. "Where did you go?"

"Summer," I said. "The bluebonnets."

Blythe grinned. Blood rimmed her gums.

"Oh my God," she said.

"The world turned against you," I said. "Bigger-than-normal problems. Overwhelming."

"When you get canceled, that's generally what happens. You have no idea. I got death threats."

I had no memory of Blythe receiving death threats, but I couldn't say as much out loud. She might've addressed them in the apology video I didn't watch.

"I can't believe someone would threaten you for something so small," I said sympathetically.

"Right? Maybe a tweet or two to teach me, but not death threats."

"So stupid," James said.

Blythe took a breath, held it, and let it go. Her body relaxed. She dropped her head to her chest. "I'm not an idiot Violet," she said.

"What do you mean?"

"You're being vague. Why did I get canceled?"

I went blank. James's feet were dangerously close to the water. She couldn't swim, couldn't float, couldn't tread. Her hands were still bound. If she fell in, she'd drown. I placed a hand on the tank.

Then it hit me.

"You got a fish!" I yelled triumphantly. "You put it in the wrong tank, and people went crazy!"

Blythe slapped her hands together, a single crack that almost made me jump out of my skin.

"Damn fish," she said. "I won it here, over in the midway. Those assholes had a field day with it."

"You bought it a big tank," I said. I remembered the story, not because I followed her online, but because she told me in a series of voice texts after our trip to Brenham. In the first message, her voice was calm. By the ninth, she was howling, and I could hear her ripping her room to pieces in the background.

"I saved it from its claustrophobic little bowl, and I listened to the asshole at the pet store. That's what you're supposed to do, right?" Blythe sounded flustered. Her hands flew through the air, fists pointed in my direction. I braced for a crash, but she stopped short, leaned in, and stuck a finger in my face.

"What am I supposed to do?" She asked. "Get a PhD in *fish?*"

"You'd have to get your Master's first," I said sarcastically. I immediately winced, anticipating a slap.

Blythe ignored me and continued her rant.

"People never give each other the benefit of the doubt. God, it's not like I dropped the n-word or something. I'm not Sadie Fucking Cotton! And—by the way—I took heat for her bullshit too! But this was a fucking fish. A fish. They die if you look at them funny. My life is worth the same as a fish's to some people. *It's stunning.*"

I held back a snort. My freshly minted multiple murderer friend Blythe stood before me, pondering the value of human life.

"Did the fish thing make you do this?" I asked quietly.

Blythe laughed, manic and angry.

"I decided to do this almost a year ago, long before ol' Goldie showed up. It's the fish, it's the failure, it's all the fresh new fourteen-year-olds who grew up watching my videos and are now replacing me. It's my friends, who barely tolerate me. It's my father, who screwed me. It's my fear that I've lost at the game of life, and I haven't even graduated high school. I'm effed six ways from Sunday, and I'm so, so alone. *I'm over it.*"

Blythe leaned against the tank. The red target to trigger James's seat hung above her head. She saw my eyes flick up, then scowled.

"I'm sorry," I said.

She sighed. "I get it. Poor James is still in peril. You answered the question, though, so I'm keeping my word. I won't drown James."

I exhaled. James sobbed and thanked Blythe over and over.

"Where are the stairs?" I asked.

"We won't tell anyone, Blythe," James said. "Give us a story, and we'll stick to it."

Blythe smiled at her.

James peered at me from high above, hope in her eyes.

I took a step back and searched the area for the stairs.

Blythe's smile fell. Her cheeks were sunken, her eyelids heavy. Shadows slashed across her face, making her appear demonic. Her nostrils flared, her fingers twitched.

The relief faded from James's face.

Blythe leapt toward the target. I reached out to grab her.

I missed.

She laughed.

Her hand hit the target, a little slap barely strong enough to trigger the seat. It dropped out from under James, who gasped as she plopped into the water.

The water fizzed and hissed like Alka-Seltzer as red clouds bloomed around James, her mouth opened in a silent scream.

"No!" I gasped, running for the tank. Blythe grabbed me and spun me around, laughing with her head thrown back, her hair way too coiffed for someone who'd been inside a rubber mask all night long.

The lights were bright, bright enough to burn my eyes and make me squint.

This isn't happening.

Blythe gently let me go. I couldn't fill my lungs all the way. I panicked, gasping for air. Blythe messed with her phone and woke the carnival. A nightmarish cacophany of rides, games, and horrible fucking carousel music crushed down on me. I clamped my hands over my ears and tried not to puke. Blythe shoved her phone in my face, recording my reaction.

"Don't worry," she assured me. the Licker mask was tucked under her arm. She reached inside and pulled out her voice changer. "We're not live yet," she said in the Licker's voice.

James's lips stretched wide until her cheeks split, and her lower jaw separated from her face and floated away. Her eyes, wide open in shock, melted. The skin peeled off her skull and dissipated, leaving only bone behind.

Blythe had gum clamped between her back teeth. When she laughed I could see that it was pale pink bubblegum. It had gone grayish and stringy, like she'd had it in her mouth for awhile. The whole time she was murdering my friends—*the whole time*—she'd been chewing worn-out bubblegum like cud.

I shoved her away and clawed at the tank, ripping off two nails and twisting my ankle when I slid down the dew-covered glass.

"Violet, get the fuck back!" She gently wrapped her hands around my shoulders, pulled me away from the glass, and clasped her hands with mine. I fought her grasp, but she was too strong. She twirled me with enough force to lift me off the ground, then released me like it was nothing at all. I stumbled over my own feet. Everything in my field of vision tilted, and I fell onto my side.

"What" I yelled, stopping myself because if I said one more

word, I was going to vomit with such force it would knock me unconscious.

Digital static screeched. "She's splashing around in there!" the Licker said. "Please don't tap the glass, lest you end up in the splash zone!"

I crawled toward the tank, sobbing.

"No, no, no," Blythe sang.

The Licker cackled. "We aren't getting on the ground tonight!"

Blythe ran at me, scooped me up, and flung me at the tank. My hands slapped against the glass. She pressed her hand against the back of my head and snarled. "You watch."

James jerked wildly and slammed against the glass. I prayed it was involuntary, the last firings of her nervous system as her body tore to pieces. The meat in her chest dissolved, her ribs appeared. Her heart, tucked between the bones, became visible for a moment before breaking into bits.

I screamed, but it mutated into breathless sobs. Blythe released me and patted me on the shoulder as if to say, *There, there. There, there.*

I shoved her aside and scrambled around on the pavement, looking for anything to throw at the tank. My brain seized and I threw handful after handful of pebbles while James's legs kicked, continuing to tread water unsuccessfully.

One split off from her torso, followed by the other. Her clothes were gone, but her shoes were inexplicably still tied to her feet. All the things stitching her body together unraveled, and the remaining chunks drifted apart.

Somewhere behind me—might've been six inches, might've been sixty feet—Blythe posed like a cheerleader. A grin spread across her face as she raised her voice changer to her lips.

"James Parker's dead!" she chanted a perfect imitation of Mila with a robotic demon twist. "James Parker's dead! James Parker's dead!"

In the tank, bloody red remnants got smaller and smaller, until they turned pink, then disappeared altogether.

Only her disassembled skeleton remained. It started to dissolve too, more slowly than her flesh.

I fell to the ground screaming.

"James Parker's dead!" Blythe had dropped the voice changer and taunted me in her own voice. "Eww. It looks like someone spilled a smoothie in there."

I'd never felt so cold in my life.

"Why?" I begged. "You said you wouldn't kill her!"

Blythe shrugged, a bemused expression on her face.

"I said I wouldn't drown her. I didn't say a word about dropping her in acid."

26

Sixth grade.

We met in art class.

I couldn't draw. Blythe could.

Artists made me so jealous. There was always one kid in class who, without training, could produce a photorealistic flower bouquet or self-portrait. I'd been gifted with a musician's ears, but not with an artist's eye.

Our teacher, Ms. Daley, assigned seats. Blythe and I shared a table made for two. I wrote with my right hand; she wrote with her left. Our assigned seats made us bump elbows, so Ms. Daley permitted us to switch.

Blythe was prettier than all the other girls except Mila, even before her eventual internet celebrity makeover. She hadn't discovered bleach yet, so she still had dark hair, and she wore braces. Her body was a jumble of sticks she hadn't yet learned to maneuver.

Her desire to be friends stunned me. I wasn't a total loser, but she was much more mature. At first, I didn't particularly enjoy hanging out with her because it triggered an (unfounded) fear she would force me to steal a car or drink or hook up with guys. I befriended her anyway. Who doesn't want to be tight with the cool girl? Blythe was an outfit to try on, a costume to wear to impress the other kids.

One day, our teacher brought a huge canvas to class. She'd painted heaven as she saw it: serene blues, dogs with angel wings, cotton candy clouds with rainbow sprinkles.

"When I die, this is where I want to be. Puppies and candy, there's nothing better. I want you each to draw the place where you want to spend your afterlife. Is your heaven like mine? I want to be on a sunny beach with my fiancée and dozens of dogs. Perhaps you would prefer a garden, maybe a mansion? Who is in your heaven with you? What items are there?"

A girl raised her hand.

Our teacher called on her. "Eris? Do you have a question?"

"Does it have to be the same scope as yours? What if my heaven is smaller? What if it's one particular puppy instead of a puppy-filled beach?"

"Excellent question. If your idea of heaven is gazing into the face of a loved one, draw the person. A word to the wise, please take this seriously. As always, we'll be doing a critique at the end, so if you draw a bowl of fruit, you need to explain why you want to spend eternity with apples and bananas."

She asked if anyone else had questions. No one did, so she walked the room as everyone started their sketches.

My abilities were mediocre. I drew simple, cartoony pictures, not so awful you couldn't tell what I'd drawn, but bad enough you forgot about them as soon as you moved on to the next drawing.

Music was the foundation for my heaven, so I drew musical notes to represent stars in the sky and swirls I would later fill with a colorful rainbow to represent sound.

"Oh, yours is going to be pretty," Blythe said.

I smiled. "Thanks. What are you doing?"

She showed me her sketch paper. She'd drawn an ornate frame around the edge of the paper but had left the center blank.

"I'm lost. What should I put in the frame?"

"What do you love most?"

"Strawberry cheesecake," she joked.

I laughed. "Draw that."

"Cheesecake is what a wine mom would say. It's a cop-out." Blythe frowned at her drawing. "I accidentally drew the mirror above our dining room table."

"Does this mean your idea of heaven is staring at yourself in the mirror?"

"Who wouldn't want to stare into these Bette Davis eyes for eternity?"

I wanted to make a joke, raise my hand, and say, *Me, me!* but I couldn't risk her taking it the wrong way and thinking I didn't like her. I went with a deep interpretation.

As deep as a thirteen-year-old can go, anyway.

"Maybe it's not your reflection. Maybe you drew a mirror because your idea of heaven is looking into the mirror and being happy with what you see?"

Blythe leaned over and drew a tiny clef mark on my paper.

"You're a good egg, Violet. You get it."

She beamed. We'd had a moment, and now we were allies. My comment meant something to her; she'd finally been heard.

In reality, it wasn't some deep connection. My words stroked her ego. Our moment was one-sided.

But I took it.

Who wouldn't want to be friends with a girl like Blythe?

A week later, we reported to class with our finished assignments.

In mine, streaky rainbows and uneven music notes burst from a lumpy violin's belly. Nothing fancy, easy to describe to the class, and it wouldn't draw too much attention to my lack of talent.

Blythe arrived with her painting tucked under her arm. She held it up for me to see.

She'd drawn a girl lounging in a frilly purple bedroom inside the frame. Chestnut hair framing a heart-shaped face, chin resting on long, manicured fingers. The girl had no features, blank white space instead of eyes, a nose, and a mouth.

"You didn't finish it," I said. Something about the realistic body with the missing face unsettled me. My skin crawled as I felt her watching me, despite the lack of eyes.

"It's called *An Unfinished Portrait of Blythe*. She's not supposed to have a face."

"Why not?"

"You said it yourself. My heaven can be self-acceptance. I don't accept myself yet, though, so I don't know what that's supposed to look like."

Her explanation sounded surprisingly profound for someone our age. She made me feel like a child standing next to a woman.

"Is that really what it means?" I asked.

Blythe held her face still for a moment, and then her lips cracked into a smile.

"Uh, no. I got distracted and forgot the damn thing. I didn't have time to finish the face, so I pulled the meaning out of my ass. It's good, right? My masterpiece!"

"It's fantastic," I said, shaken by how easily she'd fooled me. "Even without being done. Your story sells it."

"Right? It's a trick I learned. This painting is a jumping-off point. I kept it basic so I could go over the top with the fake story. Art is subjective, so people will believe what you tell them. You need confidence."

She'd missed the entire point of the assignment unless her idea of heaven was a nap on a cloud of lies.

"What's your story going to be?" she asked.

"It's pretty music and rainbows," I said. "I don't think there is a story."

"Bor-ing! It's fine, though. The whole assignment is kinda boring. It would've been way more interesting if Ms. Daley had us draw our idea of hell."

"Can teachers say the word 'hell' in class?" I asked.

She shrugged. "This is Texas. Could go either way."

"What would you have painted?"

"Hmm. This same thing probably. I'd say, 'My idea of hell is a loss of identity.' Make shit up, say it like you believe it, make everyone else believe it too. What would you paint?"

Beyond fire and brimstone, I knew nothing about hell. I mumbled something about painting a broken violin. Blythe rolled her eyes and told me I wasn't any fun.

"Listen," I said. "My mom makes me go to church and all, but hell always seemed so far-fetched. How is it right for me to rot in hell next to Hitler if shoplifting a Snickers is the worst thing I ever do? I'm not sure hell exists. How can you draw something you don't believe in?"

"There's a famous quote," she said. "Hell is other people."

"In that case..." I took some scratch paper and sketched a terrible likeness of Blythe. I wrote her name in bubble letters and drew an arrow from the letters to the doodle.

"Oh, I'm not hell, baby!" she laughed. "I'm heaven all the way!"

"Hey!" I said, grinning. "Even Lucifer was an angel."

27

o you think she felt it?" Blythe asked, tapping on the glass.

I barely heard the words. The bright carnival lights twinkled around me. My screams grew louder and louder, drowning out the cheerful music from the carousel.

Blythe kicked me.

"Stop crying!" she yelled.

"Why?" I asked. "We had a deal. Why did you kill her?"

"Because her death was part of my plan. Get up."

"I can't."

She pulled me to my feet and slammed me into the dunk tank. Remnants of James's skull floated past in my peripheral vision.

I couldn't breathe. My vision blurred. As I gasped for air, I choked, coughed, and vomited on Blythe's feet.

"Oh gross," she said, kicking the chunks off her shoes. She'd traded her heels for sensible black sneakers. "Listen to me, Violet." She took my chin and turned my face. "Do not fall down. All right? Stay standing."

"Why did you do this?" I asked. "Don't give me some bullshit about internet views or colleges or the future."

"I'm *miserable*," she said, simply. "I thought it would make me feel better."

"Are you going to kill me too?"

She sighed. "At first, I planned to kill you. You're terrified of the Ferris wheel, right?"

I snorted. "I'm not giving you any ideas."

She rolled her eyes. "I figured we'd ride to the top, and I'd throw you off. I didn't want to mangle you or make you suffer. You were collateral damage, not a direct target. Then I second-guessed myself. It's been painful to watch you these past few months. How can a person be mopey and anxious at the same time? I'm shocked your hair isn't falling out. Like, how do I kill such a weak girl? You must be in as much pain as I am. Right?"

I nodded and blubbered.

"I'll take that as a yes. So I'm pathetic, you're pathetic, we're kindred spirits. A week ago, when I hacked Meg up, I realized I had no choice. Murder really gives you clarity. I can't be the sole survivor if you're around, and if you're around, you'll tell. Pathetic people always tell."

Blythe smoothed my hair and tucked it behind my ear. She smiled, light in her eyes, her blond hair glowing like a halo around her head. Still angelic, even covered in blood.

"Even Lucifer was an angel," I mumbled to myself.

Blythe tilted her head. "I, uh. Good? Does that mean something? Are you finding Jesus in this carnival right now?" She waited for me to answer. I didn't. She shook it off. "Anyway. Last week, I was going to kill you. Tonight at dinner, I saw your dopey sad eyes, and I changed my mind again. I'm never this indecisive. We might not be BFFs like you and what's left of James, but I always liked you better than those other bitches. Girls. *Sorry*. You don't like me calling them bitches."

"I don't care anymore. Just end it."

Blythe pulled her phone out.

"Who are you calling?" I asked.

"It's the only fair way to decide. Heads you win, tails you lose," she said. "Siri, flip a coin."

Of all the insane things I'd seen that night, Blythe telling the virtual assistant on her phone to flip a coin and seal my fate took the cake.

I held my breath.

"It's heads this time," the robotic voice announced.

"Listen to that! You win!" She reached into her pocket and pulled out a washcloth. "You win this!"

She shoved the washcloth into my face.

Everything went black.

28

regained consciousness but didn't open my eyes. I was weightless, cold. A hard metal seat was beneath me, a breeze blew my hair.

Blythe spoke at a frantic pace at full volume. We were in the middle of a conversation, and it didn't matter to her if I was awake or not.

"…put up a fight, though, more than I expected," she said, apparently mid-sentence. "The candy helped so much to make you weak. I put myself through training, all the weight lifting. I told everyone it was a fitness challenge. I gained weight, but it's all muscle, so I'm skinnier than before!"

Three hard smacks made me jump. Blythe's palm slapped someone's skin.

Not mine.

I cracked my eyes a little.

I didn't want her to know I'd come around.

But when I saw the corpses sitting on the seats around me, I screamed. Blythe grabbed my face and forced her fingers past my lips, teeth, and tongue to muzzle me. I gagged until she slid her fingers out of my mouth. She wiped them on her shirt.

"You and me were having a chat, Violet. Calm down and participate." She put an arm around my shoulder and nodded at the bodies. "Claire, can you believe this girl? We gotta get her to chill."

Claire's skin was blue. Her clothes were filthy, covered in dirt and grass, with gravel ground into her hands. Her letterman's jacket, which she wore whether it was forty degrees or one hundred, was folded in her lap.

Cotton candy completely enrobed her head: pink, fluffy, *bloody* cotton candy.

Lolly sat on the seat next to her. Or rather, Lolly's decapitated body. Her head was long gone. Maybe the leftover goo was back at the test-your-strength booth, or perhaps Blythe had hidden it for a satanic ritual later. Who knew what she was capable of at that point?

River was jammed between Lolly and the wall. Jagged circles marred her entire body, face to feet. Her eyes were open. Though her face hung slack, it retained a mask of horror. I didn't know what Blythe had done to her, but I could tell it hadn't been a pretty end.

Blythe tightened her grip on my shoulder and gave me a squeeze. I jumped at her touch.

"You make me so proud, Violet." She said.

"You butchered them. How are you not drenched in blood?"

She shrugged. "I brought extra clothes."

"Of course you did. Why wouldn't you?"

Skin peeped through a hole in her black jeans, on the knee. They were probably expensive and probably came pre-shredded. Rich girls will pay extra to look sloppy. I poked her bare skin. She giggled.

Then her words registered.

"What do you mean you're proud?" I asked.

"Uh, look down."

A metal grate surrounded us. We were in an iron box, swinging in the air. Maybe we were fifty feet high, maybe five hundred. I'd always been terrible with measurements. I gripped the grate to steady myself. We were locked in a gondola, rotating backward, on the Ferris wheel.

At least I *hoped* we were locked in.

"Why are we up here?" My voice trembled, but I refused to let her see me cry.

"One last ride. Check out the stars! Look at the pretty lights! Over there, on the Whirling Witch! I turned it all on, just for us."

Beneath us, the carnival was a wasteland. The empty cars on the Whirling Witch Coaster chugged uphill, then fell fast before flipping over in a loop. My eyes followed it as it dropped low and sped past the operator stand, where blood pooled on the ground, leading to the Ferris wheel. Smoke poured from the House of Horrors. Robotic demonic laughter mixed with the cheerful calliope, and the bleeps and sirens at the arcade. The Black Kitten Coaster went around and around on its track. The Crazy Cauldrons danced.

I pressed myself against Blythe, as though a ruthless killer might hold me tight and keep me from falling. She hugged me and smoothed my hair.

"I'm so, so sorry to do this to you, sweetie. Watching you suffer tonight was like a knife in my kidneys. But you don't have to worry, because I promise, it's gonna hurt you *way more* than it hurts me."

I squinted and scanned the earth below. "Where are the other two girls?" I asked, expecting to see them laid out on the ground.

"Right over there," Blythe said. She twisted in her seat and pointed to the gondola closest to ours.

Two bodies slouched over inside. Mila's bouncy curls were now flat, stringy, and sticky with blood. Gracie's head flopped forward, and her chin dipped into her gaping chest wound.

"What did you do?" I asked.

"Only one missing is James," she said, ignoring me. "There wasn't much of her left, and I'm not about to go fishing in acid for a gooey jawbone."

"How did you even get ahold of acid?" I asked.

"*Nolan Flynn*. Dude would do *anything* to impress James, so I told him she loves pranks. He is so head over heels for her, he volunteered to help before I even asked. I said I was going to scare everyone tonight and I wanted to drop a fake body into the dunk tank and dissolve it. Dumbass is a chemistry whiz. Did you know?"

Nolan and I had a couple of classes together, but I'd never given him much thought. He was blunt to the point of rudeness, and I was glad he'd never been able to pull himself together enough to con James into dating him.

"I was not aware of his prowess," I said, mimicking Nolan's cynical tone.

"Ha!" Blythe clapped and rocked the gondola. I instinctively gripped Claire's knee, then jerked my hand away when I felt how cold she was. "Oh. Sorry. Didn't mean to rock the boat. Anyway. Yeah. He told me some boring story about playing with his dad's lawn care chemical shit when he was little, then he graduated to crazy recipes for bombs and drugs online, and now I guess it's a whole thing for him. Anyway, he drove in and filled the dunk tank while we were at the diner."

"What kind of acid melts a human?" I asked.

"No clue. Didn't ask. All I cared was that it worked, insignificant details didn't matter. I threw a Costco rotisserie chicken in to test it, and it broke apart in the tank like cheap toilet paper, so I'm pretty pleased with his work."

"Did you just compare my best friend to a chicken?"

"Mmmhmm. And toilet paper. Like the thin, stiff stuff they have at Target." She gnawed on her nail. "I suck."

She bit off a hang nail and spit it out of the gondola. I pressed my cheek against the grate, straining to watch her skin fleck fly away toward the dazzling carnival. Lights from the midway lit the dunk tank from behind, making the acid appear neon red.

"Is that a problem?" She ran a finger across my cheek.

I recoiled. "Are you letting me live longer because we made out?"

She snorted. "Sorry. We think highly of ourselves, don't we?"

"It happened twice…"

"I made out with Claire three times." She poked Claire's chest with her finger. The cotton candy flopped forward. "Didn't win her any immunity."

"But you like me more than you like Claire."

"I like you more than any of them, but babe, *I don't like you that much.*"

"*You don't say.*"

Blythe cackled. She unceremoniously pulled River from her seat and tossed her in the corner, then shoved Lolly into the wall so she could sit next to Claire. She jammed her elbow into Claire's ribs and hooked a thumb at me.

"This bitch," she said to Claire, shaking her head as she slid her arm around Claire's shoulder.

"Please stop touching her," I begged, more exhausted by her schtick than upset or grossed out. Blythe had *decimated* our friend group, and she'd erased James. I didn't have any more fight left. "You won. You beat us. Go ahead and keep ranting, 'cause you seem super chatty, but please stop manhandling the bodies, and please *please* start blinking again, because all I can think about is how dry your eyes must be."

Blythe slowly narrowed her eyes until the lids barely touched, and snapped them back open.

"*Listen, Claire*," she said, ignoring me while making eye contact with two wet spots in the cotton candy where Claire's eyes oozed through. "Violet asked why James was number one on my list. Should we tell her?" Blythe pressed her ear close to the cotton candy and pretended to listen to Claire's response.

Or at least I hoped she was pretending. It wouldn't have been a shock to find out Blythe had been hearing voices.

Blythe sat up straight, her arm still tight around Claire's corpse. "The truth is," she said. "I *hated* James Parker! I hated her unfunny jokes! What the fuck is with the handshake thing? And the jacket? Why put twenty pounds of flair on it? I wish I'd left it on her in the drunk tank, but I figured *every serial killer needs a souvenir.* Still, I look better in teal than olive. " She pried Claire's jacket from her stiff fingers. She slid into it. "I hated her judgy mom who was so obsessive about James and social media. She acted like I was some monster trying to ruin her daughter. Mrs. Parker—I am *not* calling that bitch *Heather*—was always so *concerned*, you know? She was more worried about me than my own mom, and it's like back off! Pay attention to your own loser daughter! Heather is in for a real surprise now!" I kicked at her legs, but she dodged me. She hugged Claire close. "I hated *Violet* because she was like a little fun sidekick, and I'm like, 'Why does James get a sidekick and I don't?' Fucking *River* got a sidekick. Then it turned out I actually liked Violet, or at least I liked how she looked at me and put me on a pedestal, which made me hate James *even more*."

She paused and clawed at her eyes.

The bitch was *crying*.

"But most of all," she sniffed, "I hated her because I stole her stupid personality for my YouTube channel, and more people loved me when I was cosplaying James than when I was being myself! I didn't do it on purpose—not at first—then one day I moved my mouth in that overexaggerated, cartoony way she always does, and I felt myself becoming her! She crawled around under my skin, her voice came from my mouth! She infected me, and people wanted more, more, more until I didn't have any more to give, because I don't understand! Why do people like her so much? I don't see it!"

Blythe ceased her rant to gasp for air. Her eyes slid to meet mine. My face was stoic. Her performance was nothing more than a that of a spoiled brat breaking down, grasping at straws because her bad behavior was catching up to her, and she knew she was screwed.

It's hard to be scared of someone so pathetic.

"James's death was the first one I had planned." Blythe pushed Claire aside and addressed me directly. "James Parker, *plop, plop, fizz, fizz*, nothing left behind except some stringy bits. I wanted her *gone*, Violet. *Vaporized.* I never wanted to see her stupid face again, and

I wanted to make sure no one else did either, even if they wanted to. Think about it." She took Lolly's hand and laced their fingers together. "How much more fucked up would it be if this was James? How much more would you be freaking out right now? Maybe you'd even be crying or giving me some kind of reaction other than stone face! But the juice wasn't worth the squeeze. Not when I had the opportunity to turn James into *literal* juice."

"That's clever," I said, flatly.

"Ugh!" She screamed and threw Lolly's arm. "Why do people like her so much? I don't see it!"

I wished I could've given an impassioned eulogy for James, debunking Blythe's grievances in the heartwarming, funny way my best friend deserved. But my brain was fried, and I was ready for Blythe to get on with it already, so I repeated the words Gracie said to me right before Blythe put an axe in her chest. *Just because you don't see it doesn't mean it's not true.*

Blythe clucked her tongue. "Whatever."

"For what it's worth, news of your supposed Jamesification surprises me. I had no clue you were imitating her. She's energetic and clever. You're an attention whore who wasted thousands of dollars of makeup while making dick jokes."

"Au contraire!" Blythe beamed. "I'm a true artiste. This is my pièce de résistance!" She mispronounced almost every word, including half of the English ones.

"And you said you didn't have any talent."

"It's beautiful, isn't it?" She gazed at the crime scene below.

"I meant your half-assed French. Duolingo is really working for you."

"*Oh*. Ha. Ha. Ha." She punctuated each fake laugh with a clap.

"All this work, and I don't get to share it. Except with you." She gagged. "I can't exactly put this all online." She reached into her pocket and winked. "Or can I?"

She handed me her phone. I examined the pink opal case. She'd pasted a neon-green llama sticker under the camera lens. River always used to tap his sunglasses and say, "He's a cool llama friend," when she saw it. She'd draw out the "o" farther and farther each time until she broke out into uncontrollable laughter. No one else ever found it funny, but it entertained me when River tickled herself with a dumb joke.

And now she's a corpse covered in gashes.

Blythe grabbed my wrist and twisted it around so she could use facial recognition to unlock her phone.

A photo grid filled the screen. She'd posted a collage from the night to social media, dozens and dozens of photos. I scrolled through and tapped one.

Toward the end of dinner, Blythe had given her phone to a busboy so she could take a group photo. Claire crossed her eyes and stuck out her tongue, River sat beside her with her head on Gracie's shoulder, James and I sat front and center, her fingers wrapped in mine, raised above our heads in triumph. Each girl so happy, cheesing it up.

Except for Blythe.

She stared straight into the camera, one eyebrow raised, her canine clamped on her lip. While the rest of us clumped together into a lovely mess of limbs, she stood behind us, off to the side. Danger loomed behind us, ready to grind us into mulch, and we had no idea.

The next photo was the group shot we took in the woods. Again, while the rest of us smiled, Blythe sneered.

A third photo was Mila, James, and River from behind, walking to the dark carnival, followed by a pic that looked like she'd taken it from her pocket: Gracie in profile, half obscured by black fabric.

I gasped out loud as I scrolled, freezing on Blythe, alone in a mirror selfie in the girls' bathroom. In this picture, she pulled her classic pose: big smile, head tilted, neck straight, chin up, but also down. She flashed a peace sign. My feet were visible under a stall door in the background. Another photo in the same setup followed, but in the second one, she'd put on the Licker's mask. Instead of the peace sign, she gave the finger. *Edgy.*

"Did you document the whole thing?" I asked.

"*Duh.* It's what I do. Keep going."

I pulled up the next photo, gasped, and chucked the phone at Blythe.

She'd taken a close, artsy shot of Lolly's obliterated head, and *she'd posted it online.*

"What is wrong with you?" I asked.

"*So. Much.* There's video too. Check this out."

Blythe picked the phone up, offered it to me, then laughed and snatched it back before I could touch it. She stuck the phone in my face, close enough for the screen to kiss my nose. I leaned back enough to watch.

While I'd been unconscious, she'd recorded a video. In it, Blythe held the camera at a downward angle and positioned herself so the corpses and I were also in the shot. My body was limp, my head rolled back, resting on the metal seat. I appeared to be as dead as the others.

"You put this online?" I asked, stunned.

She paused the video. "I haven't uploaded it yet. I figured artsy photos were safe, but as soon as I post a video with dead bodies in it, someone's gonna call the cops."

"Oh," I said as sarcastically as I could muster. "*Smart.*"

She tapped the screen and the video started again. "Hey guys!" Video Blythe said cheerfully. "Welcome back! I told y'all earlier I'd be offline tonight, but I have a special surprise!"

Video Blythe flipped the camera around so the viewer could get a nice, long look at River, Claire, and Lolly. She held it on River's blank eyes for a second, before turning it back to herself.

"So in case you didn't know, at my school, we have this tradition. Every year, a group incoming senior girls has a midnight scavenger hunt. All my friends and I got invited! Like Violet here." She lifted her hand and patted me on the cheek. "Don't worry about her. She's having a little nap, but she's fine. The rest of them though... *Yikes Krispies.*"

Video Blythe turned the camera on the girls, zoomed in so the viewer could get a good look, then turned the camera on herself.

"I'd like to apologize to my friends, their families, my family, my hometown, and my viewers. I made a huge mess. I made mistakes. But if you knew what I was going through, you'd understand. You see—"

I ripped the phone from her hand, stuck it in my back pocket, and shoved her away.

"How long did you drone on for?" I asked.

"The video is fourteen minutes and twenty-eight seconds long. I had to explain myself."

I rolled my eyes. "My name is Blythe," I said, mocking her Kardashi-Spearsian vocal fry. "I'm a lunatic. Here are the bodies. Pay attention to me."

Blythe slapped me across the face, shoved me aside, and flung the gondola door open. She threw me to the floor and kicked me. My head and left arm flew out of the gondola. I closed my eyes and braced for a fall. Blythe seized a handful of my hair and yanked me back in, locking the gondola door behind me.

"Are you really in a position to make fun of me?" She asked.

"Oh what are you going to do?" I asked. "Kill me?"

She shrugged. "I *still* haven't decided."

"Please," I said. "You decided. You decided before we even got here. You just lied to yourself and said you'd spare me so you'd feel like less of a villain. How altruistic, to save the poor girl whose future sucks maybe more than yours. Well, guess what? That's not true. As always, James was right. Maybe I won't get into the DSU workshop. But even though I've been a little overdramatic about it, it's not the end of the world. I can still apply to the school, I just lose my leg up. I can apply to other schools too. There are other orchestras, other ways to get where I want to go. I'm not like you. I hit a bump in the road. I'll recover. You're just a useless asshole."

Blythe's eyes bulged. Her mouth twisted into a smile, and she clapped.

"I'd give you a standing ovation, but it would rock the gondola. I know how heights make you lose your shit."

"I'm less and less scared the longer we're up here."

"Finally! We always said you needed to jump in and go for a ride, and you'd see it wasn't bad!" Blythe gripped Claire's limp hand and used it to give herself a high five.

I scoffed. "Oh my God, why are you acting like this is a party?"

"Because as soon as I upload my confession, I'm gonna go viral. Give me my phone back." She roughly turned me around and stole it from my pocket. "Did you really think I was gonna let you take this? Anyway. Millions of people are gonna see it. Look. Look at the comments. People are sitting around waiting to see what I'll do next."

She scrolled through the comments on the photo of Lolly's smushed head, her face glowing. "'Dude, awesome effects!'" She read aloud, then turned to me. "They think it's fake! Should I be offended or flattered? Check this one, 'Always knew you were crazy, bitch! This is your best yet! Can't wait for more!'"

Other comments weren't quite as positive.

I pointed at the screen. "'You're a real sick piece of shit.'" I read aloud.

"Where's the lie? Maybe we should go live! I'm sure people want to know how it all ends!"

While Blythe squealed about internet clout, text message after text message poured into her phone.

"People are texting you," I said.

"Ooh, let's see." She checked her messages.

AMETHYST EATON

Are you okay?

BRIAN J - MANAGER

Is this a joke? Where are you? What did you do?

MOM

Call me. Now.

JACK BELL

I can help you. Please call me, Blythe.

RILEY ELLIS

River isn't answering her phone. I need to talk to her right now. This isn't funny. Have her call me.

"Dude, that last one," Blythe said. "Riley is in for a surprise."

"You murdered her big sister."

"Eh. She attacked me with a bottle."

"Because you put on a freaky costume and stalked her."

"Whatever."

Blythe quietly read the comments, a serene smile on her face. I watched her switch back and forth between six or seven apps, examining what she'd posted on each one.

I cleared my throat.

"What?" she asked.

"What now?"

She pointed the camera at me. "Any last words? I'm fixing to go live."

I stared at the lens.

"Someone will see this and call the cops. They're coming for you."

"Maybe. But they ain't gonna catch me." She tapped on her phone, held her breath, and uploaded her confession. "Now everyone knows. I wonder what happens next?"

"You confessed to everything. There's enough evidence on your phone to convict you ten times over. This is *Texas*. You're going to fry."

"No I'm not," she said. She pushed past me, opened the door again, and gracefully waved her arms above her head like a bird soaring on the wind. "I'm going to *fly*."

Blythe kicked one foot into the open air, giggling like a child. The gondola swung against her weight. Claire's body threatened to slide away.

"Suicide?" I screeched. I didn't want her to get off that easy. She deserved everything coming to her, and more. "Why didn't you just take yourself out first and save everyone the grief?"

"What's the fun in that? It's better to go out with a bang, right?"

I couldn't listen to her anymore. A hot, orange sun peeked over the horizon. No cops had arrived to rescue me. If I intended to walk out alive, it was now or never.

I straightened in my seat. "You ready?" I asked, cracking my knuckles.

"Oh, is this it?" she asked.

I nodded. "Guess so."

I dove for her and grabbed her upper arms. Blythe was much stronger than I expected. Her muscles felt hard and tight; she brushed me off and pinned me to my seat without breaking a sweat.

"You really have been working out," I said.

She lifted my shoulders and smacked me backward, banging my head against the grate. I saw stars. I wrapped my fingers around her forearms and pinched the skin.

"Whoa, your fingers are rough!" she said, her jaw locked.

She wasn't wrong. Years of playing the violin had left me with sandpaper fingertips.

I let go of her arm and jammed my thumb in her eye. She screeched.

"Too rough for you?" I asked.

"Little bitch," she grunted. She pulled my index finger back to pry my hand from her face. The joint cracked. Her eyes bulged. "I'm so sorry, Violet. I can't help myself."

Blythe crushed my hand against the doorframe. It hurt, but no worse than stubbing a toe or hitting my funny bone. She grunted and kept a tight grip on my wrist, refusing to let me pull away.

A demented smile stretched across her face as she closed my hand in the door.

My heart shattered into a million pieces. I screamed in pain and terror, begging her to stop.

Blythe cackled as she opened the door, then banged it shut a second time. Inhuman sounds came from my mouth as I tried to wiggle my fingers. I managed to fold my middle, ring, and pinky back, but I couldn't bend my index finger. I couldn't even *feel* my index finger.

I gulped for air. "*Stop.*"

"I decided, Violet. I'm not going to do it. I'm not going to kill you."

"Please stop," I begged.

Her eyes went from my hand to the gondola door. She wasn't going for my jugular, she was going for something *much* worse.

"I'm not going to kill you. *I'm just going to end your life.*"

Blythe screwed her face up, opened the door wide, and slammed it on my index finger with every ounce of strength she possessed. As I lay on the floor, thrashing and panicking, Blythe kicked my arm back into the gondola and dropped it onto my chest.

Blood gushed everywhere; it poured on my face, my torso, and River's shoes. One remaining sliver of skin held the finger on my hand.

My index finger was almost completely severed.

I couldn't watch when Blythe pinched it between her fingers, and plucked it like a flower petal. She loved me not, so she pitched it over her shoulder. It flew through the grate, landing God knows where.

"I can't have you bleed to death," she said. Lolly's T-shirt was shredded, so Blythe ripped off a few pieces of fabric and used them to bandage my hand. She could do as she pleased. I went numb, unable to process what she'd done. Satisfied with her work, she sat next to me and pulled her knees to her chest.

"Nobody ever becomes a professional musician anyway. Now you can let it go, and become an accountant or something." She paused, leaning forward, waiting for me to reply.

But there were no words.

My heartbeat hummed in my ears. Cold blue static clouded my vision. My breath quickened, coming in random bursts. Blue static became hot, white light. Rage simmered in my chest.

Fuck. This. Whore.

I lifted my feet, and kicked her pretty face, breaking her nose. She flailed wildly, and landed on River. She grasped for me, but instead pulled Claire's body onto her own, and became the meat in a dead girl sandwich. She sucked in a breath and cotton candy shot up her nostrils. She frantically spat it out.

"It's like licking copper pipes covered in sand," she yelled, clawing at her tongue. "Ugh! This bitch is crushing me! Get her off!"

Blythe squirmed away from Claire and grabbed a rail on the ceiling to pull herself to her feet. As she stood, the gondola swung.

I should've panicked. My body trembled; I'd lost too much blood.

We reached the top of the world. The Ferris wheel jolted as it locked into place for a few minutes so we could enjoy the view.

Though my legs shook and my blood-drenched hands slipped on the wall around me, I dragged myself to my feet and reached for a rail above.

"What are you gonna do?" she asked.

"This."

I gripped the rail and threw my back into the wall, knocking the gondola so hard that the horizon tilted. My sneakers slid in Claire's blood, but I didn't fall. I stomped and jumped and used the momentum to swing backward. We rattled from side to side.

"Stop it!" Blythe screamed. "You're going to kill us both!"

"So are you!"

"Yeah! But I earned it!"

"Crazy bitch," I mumbled as I hit the wall.

Blythe dove for me—one claw ready to sink into my neck, the other gripping her phone—but before she could catch me, she tripped over Claire's body.

She flopped face-first at my feet, and strained to raise her head. Blood gushed from her nose. One front tooth held on by a thread.

"Your fans would *die* if they could see you now."

"*You* could die," she said sarcastically.

"Not today."

Blythe coughed, choking on blood. She felt around for her phone. I saw it before she did, and snapped it up. She didn't fight me. The adrenaline had begun to wear off, and the injuries she'd sustained while playing psycho killer had caught up to her. She lifted her head high and smiled.

Her tooth fell out. She didn't even flinch.

"I was never going to walk away from this," she said.

"I know," I whispered. "Please don't make me do it."

"Yeah," she nodded in agreement. "You don't need that. I've already given you enough therapy material for the next thirty years."

"Forty."

"Glad I made an impression. One final request?"

"What's that?"

"Can I have my phone?"

Butter yellow light shone through the grate, casting square shadows on her face. Tiny cotton candy strands clung to her chin. My blood coated her hands. Her clothes were ribbons, and she smelled like a Whataburger, the burger, not the restaurant itself.

Unable to deny her last request, I handed her the phone. She took a deep breath.

"You can blame the traffic lights, if you like," she said. "On the way here, while you were asking about Europe, I was silently asking if I should go through with this. The lights never lie. Those miles and miles of flashing red traffic lights, they told me I should follow through. Ya gotta listen to the lights."

Blythe glanced over her shoulder, her chest heaving as the gravity of the situation sank in. She tapped her phone, raised it above her head, and gave me a little wave.

I waved back with my mutilated hand.

"Hey guys," she said, her voice shaky. "It's Blythe. I thought I'd go live one last time. I hoped you enjoyed following me along in my journey, and I hope it's been a trip you'll never forget. I should probably say something else, but I'm not deep enough to put my feelings into words. I just… I have no idea what I'm doing."

Blythe timidly lined her heels up with the open edge, then scooted back, one millimeter at a time, with her hand high above her head. She adjusted her hair in the camera, and smiled, showing off her bloody teeth.

The glowing screen reflected on her face. Pink and red lights dotted her cheeks like freckles as her followers tapped the "like" button and sent her love via little animated hearts.

Blythe was poised to elegantly fall backward, drifting into the air, eyes fixed on her social media, wrapped in adoration from her followers. She leaned back and let gravity take control.

As she fell, she maintained her signature pose: big smile, head tilted, neck straight, chin up, but also down. The phone remained glued to her hand until her body crunched against the metal gears at the bottom of the ride.

I closed the gondola door, stared at the ceiling, and the Ferris wheel clicked back to life. When the gondola got low enough, I leapt to the ground. I landed on my side, ribs bruised but unbroken.

Blythe's body was sprawled out, butter-side-up. I tried not to look; I was *mostly* successful, but it's pretty hard not to stare when a human body is leaking its guts all over the place. Her head hung to the side, her face still perfectly pretty, maybe even prettier since she was no longer a threat.

Her phone lay in the grass a few feet away. I expected it to be shattered, but not only was it fully intact without a scratch, it was also still streaming. I squatted next to it and glared down into the camera. I was a gremlin with three chins who had been caught in a rainstorm of blood. The messages and hearts poured in so fast I couldn't read anything on the screen, but the icon in the corner told me that a hundred thousand people were watching.

"What the fuck is wrong with y'all?" I asked her viewers, and turned the phone off.

A pile of junk lay at the Ferris wheel ticket stand. She'd left her backpack, the Licker's mask and cloak, a hunting knife, and her serial killer souvenir—James's jacket—behind. I slipped my arms into the jacket and dug through the backpack to find Blythe's fob. I stuck it in my pocket and stumbled away.

I took six steps, paused, and went back to the stand, where I snatched a paper fast-pass, then dragged myself to the exit.

———

"Who buys a white car with a white interior?" I asked out loud as I fumbled around with the seat placement. Trails of my bloody fingerprints spotted the car, from the door to the wheel. My remaining fingers adhered to the white leather. I squeezed the wheel and wiggled them until the stickiness wore off.

I'd had my license for nearly two years but rarely used it.

James always drove us everywhere.

My heart leapt into my throat. I swallowed hard, refusing to cry.

Police sirens wailed as they sped toward the carnival. I watched through the trees as ten or fifteen cop cars swarmed the parking lot, followed by a pair of fire trucks. They would bombard me with questions, and I needed to process the events before I could handle an inquisition. Plus, I had a pancake breakfast to attend, and I didn't want to keep the girls waiting.

I put the Tesla in reverse and drove away, unseen.

EPILOGUE

My brain recorded no memories during my drive. When it clicked back on, I found myself in the parking lot of the Crave Inn.

We always end up at the Crave Inn.

Only a handful of other cars were parked around me. A neon sign blinked in the window, promising pizza. I stretched against the wheel like a prairie dog to see a few familiar heads of hair inside the restaurant.

When I walked in, the hostess gasped. Every patron turned to stare. The cook burst from the kitchen with an oversized whisk in hand, his mouth a gaping O. Gloopy batter dripped off the whisk and onto a woman dining on a large Belgian waffle.

I caught a glimpse of myself in the glass door. My nude bra peeped out from a boob-sized hole in my shirt. I closed James's jacket and hugged myself. For a second, I was embarrassed I'd flashed the room, totally forgetting that I was also drenched in blood and covered in bruises. My shoe had come untied. I bent over to tie it and found a cotton candy fluff stuck to the toe. I rubbed it away, then clumsily looped my laces into loose bunny ears with my mangled hands. No matter how I twisted them, they simply would not tighten.

"Violet?" asked a familiar voice softly. "Are you okay?"

Maddy Bryant, my friend, the person whose innocent invitation doomed me to a night of terror, stood over me, shaking. She wore a faded teal T-shirt with a circular logo on the chest. The words I SURVIVED THE PRITCHETT HIGH SENIOR SCAVENGE 2019 wrapped around the logo. A goofy cartoon peacock shot finger guns at me from the center. Maddy had another shirt in her hand. She helped me remove the jacket and pulled the fresh shirt over my head.

I immediately put the jacket back on.

My shirt was a variant of Maddy's. It was black instead of teal, and instead of finger guns, my peacock wore a clown costume and brandished a cotton candy cone. Blocky letters under the bird screamed, I SURVIVED THE PRITCHETT HIGH SENIOR SCAVENGE 2020!

No one survives the Senior Scavenge.

More girls in 2019 T-shirts surrounded me, each one making the same slack-jawed face as the cook.

A chorus of voices assaulted me with questions.

"What happened to you?"

"Should we take you to the ER? Somebody call 911!"

"Where are the other girls?"

"Is this a joke? Please tell me this is a joke."

I reached under the hostess stand, snatched a menu, and flipped through the pages.

"Pecan pancakes might be tradition, but I think I'd prefer cranberry orange with a scoop of Blue Bell," I told no one in particular. "Homemade vanilla flavor for sure."

Maddy slid into the chair next to me. She placed a hand on my back and rubbed small circles.

"Violet, can you please acknowledge us?"

I put the menu on the table and stared deep into her eyes.

"I acknowledge you," I said. I turned to the other girls. "Seems like y'all haven't been online. Check Blythe's social media. Go fast before they delete it."

Everyone pulled out their phones. Within seconds, death screams poured from the speakers. Gasps from the girls around me overpowered them.

The waitress stopped by the table to refill the water glasses. She eyeballed me up and down, then turned on her heels to walk away. I stopped her and asked for chocolate milk. She nodded, eyes wild.

"This is real?" asked Maddy.

"Very," I said. I stole Delilah Cortez's water and chugged the entire glass. She owed me. She was the one who'd invited Blythe to the Scavenge.

"Everyone is dead?" Delilah asked.

"Even Lolly?" Julia Leigh asked.

"*Especially* Lolly. Turns out Blythe lost a bunch of followers and was a little uncertain about her future after high school, so she chose to channel her fear into an evening of mayhem and murder." I looked around me. Eight blank faces stared back. "Yes. Everyone is dead. Blythe was nuts. Have you guys ordered yet?"

Kylie Dunn stared out the window. Blue and red lights flashed on her face. "Police are here," she mumbled. "Ambulance, too."

I took another glass of water and gulped until it froze in my chest. "I guess that's my ride," I said.

I stood and squeezed past Maddy. Before I could leave, she grabbed my wrist.

"I'll call your mom, and we'll meet you at the hospital," she said. "But you should take this. It's yours."

Maddy handed me a weighty envelope. My name and address were scrawled on the outside in crisp calligraphy.

"Where did you get this?" I asked.

"Your mom called me last night. It came in the mail while you were in Austin with James. She didn't want to interrupt the Scavenge, so she had me pick it up. She wanted it to be a surprise."

I turned the envelope over. My bloody thumbprint stained the flap, right next to the official wax seal of Desert Springs University. I snapped the seal, opening it.

I read the words Annie Wood had written on the paper three or four times, absorbing next to nothing, but managing to get the gist.

"What does it say?" asked Maddy.

I looked up at her, wild-eyed, hands shaking, covered in flaky dried blood. I smiled, because James would've found the situation hilarious, and held out the letter for everyone to see.

"I got in."

HOW THE HELL DID WE GET HERE?

And now, a history lesson.

In December 2019, a novel virus emerged from China, and the whole world went crazy.

I, a mild-mannered horror fan, did what I always do to cope: I spent an ungodly amount of time binge-watching slasher movies from the eighties and nineties. Chucky, Jason, and the Driller Killer droned in the background until I realized my brain was rotting out of my head and I needed to read a book.

I was not a stranger to the whole "I want a book that feels like a movie" game. Growing up, I wasn't allowed to watch horror movies. Since I hate being told I can't do something, I became utterly obsessed with Freddy Krueger and spent many a trip to our local indie video store—Funtime Video—whining until my mom dragged me out. At the time, I was furious, but now I understand and agree with my mother. Three-year-olds should not be watching *A Nightmare on Elm Street*. To her credit, she never cared what I read, so I was always free to read horror, but as much as I loved

Mary Downing Hahn's *Wait Till Helen Comes*, I knew what I really wanted was *blood*.

I found it courtesy of R. L. Stine. On my eighth birthday, I had a party at the mall I would later write into my book *Maul Rats*. I'd asked for books but didn't specify what books I wanted, so my mom went to our local Walden Books and asked for something to scare a third grader. The clerk suggested Fear Street. Mama got me the entire series, which at the time was around ten books. I vividly remember running my hands over their creepy covers and landing on *The Sleepwalker*. Between the title and the cover—a girl in a nightgown zombie-walking through fog—I knew my mother had given me the greatest gift of all: a horror movie I could read. She had no clue what was between those pages, but I quickly found out that not only were they scary, they had *murder* in them. They were also fun, sprinkled with pop culture references, and a little girly. It was like getting my first taste of a drug I'd been craving since birth. I read all ten books, then added Christopher Pike into my rotation and kept up with both authors for years, even after I'd moved on to the King. In the end, it was the woman who tried to block me from my one true love (Freddy) who set me on the path to creating my own little slasherverse in Belldam. *And I ended up watching the movies anyway.*

In 2020, I was on the hunt for something that hit like those Fear Street books did in the nineties. Nostalgia was a booming business, and there were Fear Street movies being made for Netflix, so I figured someone must've capitalized on the idea to write Fear Street–esque books for adults. To my surprise, no one really had, or at least they weren't marketing them as such. But there were plenty of slashers and thrillers-in-slasher-clothing out there, so I forgot about Fear

Street and went looking for a book that blended old-school slasher movies with the snarky wit from my favorite dark comedies. I found books with such intense gore that they put Art the Clown to shame, but—this may surprise you—I don't want to read page after page of graphic descriptions of blood, guts, and torture. I'm glad those books exist for the gorehounds who love them, they're just not for me. Other books promised slasher-style stories but held back *too much* on the kills, or they had flat characters, or they were downright boring. Stephen Graham Jones was, of course, a bright spot. His slashers cross the line from bloody fun into *literature*. But while I read and enjoyed *The Last Final Girl*, let's be honest. Stephen Graham Jones is no R. L. Stine. (*That is a joke, fans of those men, please don't hate me…*)

Frustrated, I decided to do it myself. I had a handful of possibilities. A retro nineties mall slasher. A story about a deadly flower shop run by a mother/daughter serial killer duo. Massacres set on April Fools', Easter, and Valentine's. A supernatural slasher about a beach vacation gone horribly wrong.

One idea kept rising to the top. A carnival slasher with one of the girls as the killer. It was a simple concept: carnivals and theme parks abound in horror. I knew it would be easy to outline a paint-by-numbers slasher with a simple storyline that I could use as a skeleton for the difficult stuff, like creating characters the reader actually cares about before you dunk them in acid.

Final Girl Violet was easy. She's a standard-issue teenage girl, with a best friend she adores and a passion she intends to turn into a career. James had to be fun because I wanted it to *hurt* when she died. The other girls were conceived death first. Each had to have their own "thing," but I wanted them to all be strong, smart, successful girls who didn't compete with one another or worry too much about their love lives. How do you kill the smartest girl in school? Crush her head. How do you crush someone's head at a carnival? Test-your-strength booth. It was a fun puzzle to solve.

And then there's Blythe. You can't have a good slasher without a good villain.

In-between slasher binges, I watched way too much YouTube. Jenna Marbles was a staple, but around the time I began writing *Tastes Like Candy*, Jenna retired. I'd followed her for years and was saddened by her departure, but I completely understood why she did it. Years of grinding to make videos, years of inviting strangers into her home to watch her be a lovable goof, years of internet comments picking apart every word she said… It's enough to drive a girl crazy.

Fortunately, Jenna is an adult and knew when to say when, but that's not always the case. Teenage social media celebrities exist too, and many are not properly equipped to deal with internet fame, especially not long-term. If you put the pressures of online fame onto a neglected and exploited teenage girl, you might end up with someone like Blythe. A real-life girl might not go on a horror-movie-style killing spree, but it's not hard to imagine someone in that situation harming herself or someone else.

When I finished the book, I asked a friend, Paul Sucharski, to paint an old-school *Paperbacks from Hell* meets Lisa Frank cover. He used the poster for *Halloween II* as his inspiration to create the fluffy pink cotton candy skull we later named Igor. Despite the praise people have given the story, I remained convinced that Igor is the main reason people decided to buy the book. It makes sense. How could anyone say no to his sweet face?

I independently published *Tastes Like Candy* on October 20,

2020, under the pen name Ivy Tholen. Tholen is a family name, and Ivy was chosen at random. I used a pseudonym for two reasons. One, privacy. Two, if people thought the book sucked, I didn't want to "ruin" my real name. I imagined new acquaintances googling me and finding my flop self-published horror novel *or worse*, my friends and family, who didn't even know I'd written a book. It would've haunted me for the rest of my life and beyond, because as we all know: *Once something's on the internet, it's there forever.*

Tastes Like Candy sold one copy on release day and then nothing for months. I hadn't been expecting any sales, because the rule in indie publishing is, "No one writes one hit book and becomes successful. You need to have a backlist." I didn't even advertise the book. I'd written it to make myself happy, and I put it out there hoping it could make someone else happy too. I figured if it was good enough, it would find its audience, and if it wasn't, I'd try again.

I started work on my next slasher (*Maul Rats*) and stopped checking my Amazon reports. *Tastes Like Candy* eventually caught on, but sales remained in the triple digits for a couple of years until out of nowhere, people were buying the book. I scoured the internet but couldn't find a reason why, until I received a message from a reader telling me that Stephen Graham Jones had done an event for *My Heart Is a Chainsaw*, and when asked about recommendations for other slasher novels, one of the books he mentioned was *Tastes Like Candy*.

Getting the stamp of approval from *the* slasher guy himself had not been on my bingo card. I jumped on the opportunity and published two novels in 2024, a sequel to *Tastes Like Candy* called *Sugarless* and my mother/daughter slasher team-up *Mother Dear*. While writing *Sugarless*, I reread *Tastes Like Candy* for the first time in years, checked my Amazon reports to see how many copies I'd sold, and wanted to die. It wasn't bad, but it was *cringe*, and the words on the page didn't match the vision in my head. I could've updated it, but other people were happy with it, so I left well enough alone and focused on new work. I was all set to publish three more books in 2025, but a week before Thanksgiving 2024, I received a message on Instagram that set those plans on fire.

Meg Gibbons, an editor at Sourcebooks, read *Tastes Like Candy* and its sequel, *Sugarless*, and wanted to chat. This was late November. By New Year's, I had an agent and a deal with Sourcebooks. It all happened so fast that as I sit here in April 2025 writing this, it still doesn't feel real. They let me bring Paul along, too, and he gave Igor a facelift for the new cover.

Now we're here. *Tastes Like Candy* is as I always intended her to be. With an additional four years of practice and Meg's expert help, she's now the bloody, glittery, *nasty* little mess I always wanted her to be. I even put my real name on her, because while she might not be a Fear Street novel, she absolutely feels like someone put *Heathers* and *Scream* in a blender and poured them onto the pages of a book. Whether or not that's a good thing is for you to decide. Even if it wasn't Fear Street or Freddy, I hope you had fun, and I hope you'll visit Belldam again soon. Ivy Tholen's *Sugarless*, *Maul Rats*, and *Mother Dear* are no longer available, but if you want to read them, they'll be back soon.

On to the thank yous…

To the people who read my books when I pretended my name was Ivy Tholen: Thank you so much for sharing them, posting them, reviewing them, and helping me spread my glitter-gel-pen horror to the world. The book in your hands exists because of you. Extra big thanks to Kelsi (@SlimeandSlashers on YouTube), the guys at *The Average* podcast (@theaveragereviews on YouTube), and *The Horror Vision* (@thehorrorvision1437 on YouTube) for y'all's constant support over the years.

To Meg Gibbons, my editor: Thank you for lighting the match, burning down my 2025, and saving me from myself. Now please go watch *The Substance. Please.*

Eddie Schneider, my agent. I have no idea what I'm doing. Thank God you do.

To Paul Sucharski, my cover artist and my partner on these books from the beginning: I quite literally couldn't have done this without you, and I can't believe someone wants us to keep going. Also, you were probably right about skulls with eyeballs, but this is the only time I'll admit it.

To the staff at Sourcebooks Fire: I've only spoken to a handful of you, but I've seen your names on emails, so I know there are people working behind the scenes to get my story out there. Thank you so, so much for your work. Special shout-outs to Taylor Geldermann, Harper Stewart, Shannon Thompson (the editorial team), Thea Voutiritsas and Jessica Thelander (the production team), Erin Fitzsimmons, Nicole Hower, and Stephanie Rocha (cover design team), Tara Jaggers (internal book design), Erin LaPointe (manufacturing), and Karen Masnica (marketing).

To the staff at JABberwocky: samesies. Thank you for your work as well. Shout-outs to my fellow Texan Susan Velazquez (subsidiary rights director), Valentina Sainato (my agent Eddie's assistant), and Christina Zobel (foreign and subsidiary rights).

To Wes Craven and R. L. Stine: the men who made me love horror and taught me how to make it fun.

To Stephen Graham Jones, who kindly praised the original *Tastes Like Candy* multiple times while promoting his classic slasher *My Heart Is a Chainsaw*: Your endorsement not only convinced people to read my book, it convinced me that I might be half decent at this because, well, you would know.

To the friends I've made via Ivy: I'm grateful to have people in my life who care about my opinion of the third act of *A Nightmare on Elm Street Part 3: Dream Warriors*. Big thanks to Missi Schmid (wolfpack!), Tim Umpleby (the guy who yanked me out of my shell without even knowing it), Shawn Baker (one of the most decent dudes I know), and Trent Donaho (my Gen-Z envoy).

To the friends I've known so long you've become family: The Bohuslavs, The Chapas, Danielle, Dina, Jeremy "Josh Wyatt" Anthony, Mattmanandann, mLe & Bobby, Shannon G., and Shannon N. I love you all. I know none of you are horror fans on my level, but I'm going to keep forcing you to read about bitchy teenage girls getting their heads bashed in. I'm sorry, but it won't stop. It will *never* stop.

To my family: Mama, Otto, Dolly, Paul, Ethan, Grandma, and Grandpa, I love y'all to death.

ABOUT THE AUTHOR

 Jessica Lacy is an author of young adult horror novels, including *Tastes Like Candy*. Her stories are slasher comedies, inspired by old-school horror movies, R. L. Stine's Fear Street, and various YouTube beauty tutorials. Jessica is the proud vice president of the Slumber Party Massacre II fan club, an organization where she is the only member. She prefers blue cotton candy.

Jessica can be found on Instagram at @bloodandlacy or at her website, bloodandlacy.com.

Jessica previously wrote under the pseudonym Ivy Tholen.